OUTSTANDING PRAISE FOR THE NOVELS OF LISA JACKSON

SHIVER

"Fans of Jackson should be pleased."
—*Publishers Weekly*

LOST SOULS

"Jackson creates relentless suspense . . . builds the tension to an unbearable and satisfying pitch."
—*Booklist*

LIAR, LIAR

"The author's managing of the past and present separately is an effective method of clue dangling to keep readers in the dark until the huge OMG reveal. Fans of Lisa Gardner, Paula Hawkins, and J. T. Ellison will devour this one-sitting nail-biter."
—*Library Journal* (starred review)

YOU WILL PAY

"This suspenseful thriller is packed with jaw-dropping twists."
—*InTouch Weekly*

NEVER DIE ALONE

"Jackson definitely knows how to keep readers riveted."
—*Mystery Scene*

TELL ME

"Absolutely tension filled . . . Jackson is on top of her game."
—*Suspense Magazine*

Books by Lisa Jackson

Stand-Alones
SEE HOW SHE DIES
FINAL SCREAM
RUNNING SCARED
WHISPERS
TWICE KISSED
UNSPOKEN
DEEP FREEZE
FATAL BURN
MOST LIKELY TO DIE
WICKED GAME
WICKED LIES
SOMETHING WICKED
WICKED WAYS
WICKED DREAMS
SINISTER
WITHOUT MERCY
YOU DON'T WANT TO
KNOW
CLOSE TO HOME
AFTER SHE'S GONE
REVENGE
YOU WILL PAY
OMINOUS
BACKLASH
RUTHLESS
ONE LAST BREATH
LIAR, LIAR
PARANOID
ENVIOUS
LAST GIRL STANDING
DISTRUST
ALL I WANT FROM SANTA
AFRAID
THE GIRL WHO SURVIVED
GETTING EVEN

Cahill Family Novels
IF SHE ONLY KNEW
ALMOST DEAD
YOU BETRAYED ME

**Rick Bentz/
Reuben Montoya Novels**
HOT BLOODED
COLD BLOODED
SHIVER
ABSOLUTE FEAR
LOST SOULS
MALICE
DEVIOUS
NEVER DIE ALONE
THE LAST SINNER

**Pierce Reed/
Nikki Gillette Novels**
THE NIGHT BEFORE
THE MORNING AFTER
TELL ME
THE THIRD GRAVE

**Selena Alvarez/
Regan Pescoli Novels**
LEFT TO DIE
CHOSEN TO DIE
BORN TO DIE
AFRAID TO DIE
READY TO DIE
DESERVES TO DIE
EXPECTING TO DIE
WILLING TO DIE

Published by Kensington Publishing Corp.

YOU DON'T WANT TO KNOW

LISA JACKSON

KENSINGTON
PUBLISHING CORP.

www.kensingtonbooks.com

KENSINGTON BOOKS are published by

Kensington Publishing Corp.
119 West 40th Street
New York, NY 10018

Copyright © 2012 by Lisa Jackson LLC

This book is a work of fiction. Names, characters, businesses, organizations, places, events, and incidents either are the product of the author's imagination or are used fictitiously. Any resemblance to actual persons, living or dead, events, or locales is entirely coincidental.

To the extent that the image or images on the cover of this book depict a person or persons, such person or persons are merely models, and are not intended to portray any character or characters featured in the book.

All rights reserved. No part of this book may be reproduced in any form or by any means without the prior written consent of the Publisher, excepting brief quotes used in reviews.

All Kensington titles, imprints, and distributed lines are available at special quantity discounts for bulk purchases for sales promotion, premiums, fund-raising, educational, or institutional use.

Special book excerpts or customized printings can also be created to fit specific needs. For details, write or phone the office of the Kensington Sales Manager: Attn.: Sales Department. Kensington Publishing Corp., 119 West 40th Street, New York, NY 10018. Phone: 1-800-221-2647.

The K with book logo Reg US Pat. & TM Off.

First Kensington Hardcover Edition: August 2012

ISBN: 978-1-4201-3093-5 (ebook)

ISBN: 978-1-4967-4305-3

First Kensington Trade Paperback Edition: January 2024

10 9 8 7 6 5 4 3 2 1

Printed in the United States of America

Prologue

Again, the dream creeps in.

It's a foggy, gray day and I'm in the kitchen, on the phone, talking to someone . . . but that part changes. Sometimes it's my husband, Wyatt; other times it's Tanya, and sometimes it's my mother, though I know she's been dead a long, long time. But that's how it is. . . .

From the family area, the room right next to the kitchen, here in this house, I hear the television, soft cartoon voices speaking, and I know that Noah's playing with his toys on the rug in front of the flat screen.

I've baked some bread—the kitchen is still warm from the oven—and I'm thinking about Thanksgiving. As I glance out the window, I notice that it's nearly dark outside, dusk at hand. It must be cold, too, as the trees shiver in the wind, a few stubborn leaves hanging on to thin, skeletal branches. Across the bay, the town of Anchorville is invisible, shrouded by fog.

But inside this old mansion, the one my great-great-grandfather built, it's cozy.

Safe.

Smelling of cinnamon and nutmeg.

And then, from the corner of my eye, I see movement outside. It's Milo, our cat, I think, but I remember that Milo, a prince of a tabby, is dead. Has been for years.

I squint, suddenly fearful. It's hard to see through the fog rolling in from the sea, but I *know* something's out there, in the yard, behind the hedgerow of roses where the scraggly bushes are thin and bedraggled, a few shriveled petals visible in the dead blooms and thorns.

Creeeaaaak!

My skin crawls as a shadow passes near the porch.

For the briefest of seconds, I fear there's something evil lurking just beyond the arrow-shaped spikes of the surrounding wrought-iron fence.

Creeeaaaak! Bang! The gate's open, swinging in the buffeting wind.

That's when I catch a glimpse of Noah, my son, in his little hooded sweatshirt and rolled-up jeans. He's gotten out of the house somehow and wandered through the open gate. Now, in the twilight, he's running joyfully, as if he's chasing something, down the path to the dock.

"NO!"

I drop the phone.

It knocks over my water glass in slow motion.

I spin around and think I'm mistaken, that surely he's in front of the couch by the TV, that . . . I see the room is empty, some Disney thing—*Aladdin*?—still playing. "Noah!" I scream at the top of my lungs, and take off at a dead run.

I'm in my pajamas and my feet feel as if they're in quicksand; I can't get through this damned house fast enough, but as I race past each of the windows looking out at the bay, I see him running through the descending darkness, getting closer and closer to the water.

I pound on an old pane with a fist.

The window shatters.

Glass sprays.

Blood spurts.

Still he doesn't hear me. I try to open the windows to the veranda overlooking the bay. They don't move. It's as if they're painted shut. Blood drizzles down the panes.

I slog forward. Screaming at my son, and for Wyatt, I run in slow motion to the doors. They're unlocked, one swinging open and moaning loudly as I push myself onto the porch. "Noah!"

I'm crying now. Sobbing. Panic burns through me as I nearly trip on the steps, then run past the dripping rhododendrons and windswept pines of this godforsaken island, the place I've known as home for most of my life. "Noah!" I scream again, but my voice is lost in the roar of the sea, and I can't see my boy—he's disappeared beyond the dead roses in the garden, no sight of him in the low-hanging mist.

Oh, please, God, no . . . let him be all right!

The chill of the Pacific sweeps over me, but it's nothing compared to the coldness in my heart. I dash down the path strewn with oyster and clam shells, sharp enough to pierce my skin, and onto the slick planks of the listing dock. Over the weathered boards to the end where the wharf juts into the mist as if suspended in air. "Noah!" *Oh, for God's sake!* "NOAH!!!"

No one's there.

The pier is empty.

He's gone.

Vanished in the mist.

"Noah! Noah!" I stand on the dock and scream his name. Tears run down my face; blood trickles down my cut palm to splash in the brackish water. "NOAH!"

The surf tumbles beyond the point, crashing and roaring as it pummels the shore.

My boy is missing.

Swallowed up by the sea or into thin air, I don't know which.

"No, no . . . *no*." I'm wretched and bereft, my grief intolerable as I sink onto the dock and stare into the water, thoughts of jumping into the dark, icy depths and ending it all filling my mind. "Noah . . . please. God, keep him safe . . ."

My prayer is lost in the wind . . .

Then I wake up.

I find myself in my bed in the room I've occupied for years.

For the briefest of instants, it's a relief. A dream . . . only a dream. A horrible nightmare.

Then my hopes sink as I realize my mistake.

My heart is suddenly heavy again.

Tears burn my eyes.

Because I know.

My son really is gone. Missing. It's been two years since I last saw him.

On the dock?

In his crib?

Playing outside under the fir trees?

Oh, dear God, I think, shattered, heart aching . . .

I can't remember.

Chapter 1

"I'm serious, you can't tell a soul," a breathy voice whispered. "I could lose my job."

Ava Garrison opened a bleary eye. From her bed, she heard the sound of voices beyond the big wooden door that stood slightly ajar.

"She doesn't even know what's going on," another woman agreed. Her voice was deeper and gruffer than the first, and Ava thought she recognized it, a headache pounding behind her eyes as the nightmare retreated into her subconscious. The pain would recede, it always did, but for the first minutes after waking, she felt as if steel-shod horses were galloping through her brain.

Inhaling a deep breath, she blinked. The room was dark, the curtains pulled, the rumble of the ancient furnace forcing air through the registers, muting the conversation beyond the heavy oak door.

"Shhh . . . she should be awake soon . . ." Breathy Voice again. Ava tried to place it and thought it might belong to Demetria, Jewel-Anne's dour nursemaid. For a woman not yet thirty, tall, slim Demetria always wore a severe expression that matched her harsh hairstyle, dyed black and pulled back, restrained by a heavy clip at her nape. Her only concession to whimsy, it seemed, was the hint of a tattoo, an inky tendril that curled from beneath the clip to tease the back of her ear. The tattoo reminded Ava of a shy octopus, extending one questioning tentacle from beneath its hiding spot of thick dark hair and tortoiseshell clip.

"So what is it? What's going on with *her*?" the second voice demanded.

Oh, Lord, did it belong to Khloe? Ava felt a jab of betrayal; she knew they were talking about her, and Khloe had been her best friend while growing up here on this remote island. But that had been years ago, long before fresh-faced and happy-go-lucky Khloe had turned into the unhappy soul who couldn't for the life of her let go of a love that had died so swiftly.

More whispering . . .

Of course. It was almost as if they wanted to have her overhear them, as if they were taunting her.

Ava caught only phrases that were as crippling as they were true.

". . . slowly going out of her mind . . ." *Khloe again?*

"Has been for years. Poor Mr. Garrison." Breathy Voice.

Poor Mr. Garrison? Seriously?

Khloe, if it were she, agreed. "How he's suffered."

Wyatt? Suffered? Really? The man who seemed intent on being absent, always away? The man she'd contemplated divorcing on more than one occasion? Ava doubted her husband had suffered one day of his life. She could barely restrain herself from shouting, but she wanted to hear what they were saying, what the gossip was that ran rampant through the wainscoted hallways of Neptune's Gate, this hundred-year-old house built and named by her great-great-grandfather.

"Well something should be done; they're richer than God!"

one of them muttered, her words thin and reedy as she walked away.

"For God's sake, keep your voice down. Anyway, the family's making sure that she gets the best care that money can buy . . ."

The family?

Ava's head was throbbing as she threw off the thick duvet and her bare feet hit the plush carpet that had been cast over hardwood. Fir . . . it was fir planks . . . she remembered, planed by the sawmill that once was the heart of Church Island, named without a drop of modesty by that same great-great-grandfather who had built this house. One step, two . . . She started to lose her balance and grasped the tall bedpost.

"Everyone in the family . . . they need answers . . ."

"Don't we all?" A sly little snigger.

Please, God, that it wasn't Khloe.

"But we don't own any part of this damned island."

"Wouldn't that be something . . . if we did, I mean." The voice sounded wistful as it retreated.

Ava took a step and a wave of nausea washed up her throat. She thought she might throw up as bile teased her tongue, but she bit down hard, took a deep breath, and fought the urge to vomit.

"She's crazy as a loon. But he won't leave her," one of them, she couldn't tell which, said, and the words were as crippling as they were true. She silently cursed her cloudy memory, her fractured brain.

Once, she'd been brilliant, at the top of her class, not only a stellar student but also a businesswoman with the acumen of . . . of . . . *what?*

Gritting her teeth, she forced herself to the doorway and peeked out. Sure enough, two women were stepping down the stairs, their bodies slowly disappearing. But neither one was Khloe, as Ava's mind had suggested. They were Virginia Zanders, Khloe's mother—a woman twice the size of her daughter and the cook for Neptune's Gate—and Graciela, a part-time maid, who, as if sensing Ava in the doorway, glanced over her shoulder and offered a smile as saccharine as the iced tea that Virginia poured on hot summer days. Half the size of her companion, Graciela was petite, with lustrous black hair knotted at the base of her skull. If she wanted to, Graciela could turn on a brilliant smile that could charm the coating off an M&M. Today, her smile was more like that of a Cheshire cat, as if she knew some deep, dark, and oh-so-private secret.

About her employer.

The hairs on the backs of Ava's arms lifted. Like a snake slithering along her vertebrae, cold seeped down her spine. Graciela's dark eyes seemed to glint with a secret knowledge before both she and Virginia were out of sight, their footsteps fading.

With a quick push, Ava slammed the door shut, then tried to lock it, but the dead bolt was missing, replaced by a matching faceplate to cover the hole left in the door. "God help me," she whispered, and drew in a long, calming breath as she leaned against the door.

Don't give in. Don't let them make you the victim. Fight back!

"Against what?" she asked the dark room; then angry with her plight and her attitude, she stalked to the windows. When had she become such a wimp? *When?* Hadn't she always been strong? Independent? A girl who raced her mare along the ridge over the sea, who climbed to the topmost spire of the mountain on this island, who swam naked in the icy, foaming waters of the Pacific where it poured and swirled into the bay? She'd surfed and rock climbed and . . . and it all seemed like a thousand—no, make that a million—years ago!

Now she was trapped here, in this room, while all those faceless people were speaking in hushed tones and assuming she couldn't hear them, but she could; of course she could.

Sometimes she wondered if they knew she was awake, if they were taunting her on purpose. Perhaps their soft, condoling tones were all part of a great façade, a horrible, painful labyrinth from which there was no escape.

She trusted no one and then reminded herself that it was all part of her paranoia. Her sickness.

With pain shooting behind her eyes, she stumbled to the bed and fell onto the pillow-top mattress with its expensive sheets, waiting for the pain to abate. She tried to raise her head, but a headache with the power to make her tremble stopped her, and she had to bite down so that she didn't cry out.

No one should suffer like this. Weren't there painkillers for this sort of thing? Prescriptions to stave off migraines? Then again, she took a lot of pills and couldn't help but wonder if the pain slicing through her brain was because of the medication rather than in spite of it.

She didn't understand why they were all out to torment her, to make her feel as if she were crazy, but she was pretty damned sure they intended just that. All of them: the nurses, the doctors, the maid, the lawyers, and her husband—most certainly Wyatt.

Oh, God . . . she did sound paranoid.

Maybe she was.

With extreme effort, she gathered her strength and eased off the bed again. She knew that eventually the stab in her brain would slowly dissipate. It always did. But when she first woke up, it was always a bitch.

With a hand on the bed to steady herself, she walked carefully to the window, pushed back the curtains, and opened the blinds.

The day was gray and grim, as it was on that day . . . that horrid day when Noah . . .

Don't go there!

It serves no purpose to relive the worst moments of your life.

Blinking, she forced her mind back to the present and stared through the watery, leaded-glass panes that looked out from the second floor of this once-elegant mansion. Autumn was seeping toward winter, she thought as she squinted, looking toward the dock where twilight was descending, fingers of fog sliding over the blackened pier.

It wasn't morning but nearing evening, she realized, though that seemed wrong. She'd been asleep for hours . . . days?

Don't think about it; you're awake now.

Placing a hand against the cool panes, she took in more of her surroundings. At the water's edge, the boathouse had grayed over the years, the dock next to it listing toward the wind-ruffled waters of the bay. The tide was in, foamy waves splashing against the shore.

So like that day . . .

Oh, sweet Jesus.

A chill, as cold as the depths of the sea, washed over her, a chill that was born from within.

Her heart clutched.

Her breath fogged on the window as she leaned close to the glass.

The back of her neck tightened in a familiar way; she knew what was coming.

"Please . . ."

Squinting, she stared at the end of the dock.

And there he was, her tiny son, teetering near the edge, a ghostly image in the fog.

"Noah," she whispered, suddenly terrified, her fingers sliding down the pane as panic surged within. "Oh, God, Noah!"

He's not there. It's your fractured mind playing tricks on you.

But she couldn't take the chance. What if this time, this one time, it really was her boy? He stood with his back to her, his little red hooded sweatshirt damp in the misting fog. Her heart squeezed. "Noah!" she screamed, beating on the glass. "Noah! Come back!"

Frantically she tried to open the window, but it seemed nailed shut. "Come on, come on!" she cried, trying to force open the sash, breaking her nails in the process. The damned window wouldn't budge. "Oh, God . . ."

Propelled by fear, she yanked open the door and raced barefoot out of her room and down the hall to the back stairs, her feet slapping against the smooth wood of the steps. Down, down, down she ran, breathless, one hand on the rail. *Noah, oh sweet, sweet baby. Noah!*

She burst from the stairway into the kitchen, then through the back door off the kitchen, across the screened porch, and out to the sweeping grounds of the house and beyond.

Now she could run. Fast. Even though night was falling swiftly.

"Noah!" she yelled as she sped along the weed-choked pathways, past the deadened rosebushes and through the dripping ferns to the dock where darkness and fog had disguised the end of the pier. She was breathing hard, screaming her son's name, desperate to see him, to witness his little face turn around and look up at her, his wide, expectant eyes trusting . . .

The dock was empty. Fog playing in the shadows of the water, seagulls crying hollowly in the distance.

"Noah!" she screamed, running over the slick boards. "Noah!"

She'd seen him! She had!

Oh, honey . . . "Noah, where are you?" she said over a sob and the rush of the wind as she reached the end, the last board cutting into her feet. "Baby, it's Mama . . ."

One last, wild search of the dock and boathouse told her he was gone. She didn't hesitate but jumped into the icy water, feeling the rush of frigid cold, tasting salt water as she splashed and flailed, frantically searching for her son in the dark depths. "Noah!" she yelled, coughing and sputtering as she surfaced. She dived back down into the black water again and again, searching the murky depths, desperately hoping for some glimpse of her son.

Please, God, let me find him. Help me save him! Do not let him die! He's an innocent. It's I who am the sinner. Oh, dear Jesus, please . . .

Again and again, she dove, five times, six, seven, her night-gown billowing around her, her hair loosened from its rubber band, exhaustion overtaking her as she drifted farther and farther from the dock. As she surfaced slowly one more time, she was vaguely aware of a voice.

"Hey!" a man yelled. "Hey!"

She dove down again, her hair floating around her, her eyes open and burning in the salty water, her lungs so stretched she thought they might burst. *Where is he? Noah, oh, God, baby . . .* She couldn't breathe, but she couldn't stop searching. Had to find her son. The world grew darker and colder, and Noah grew ever more distant.

Someone dived in next to her.

She felt strong arms surround her rib cage in a death grip. She was weak, about to pass out, when she was jerked upward, roughly dragged toward the surface, a ripple of air escaping her lungs.

As they broke through the water, she gasped, coughing and spewing as she found herself staring into the stern, uncompromising gaze of a total stranger.

"Are you out of your mind?" he demanded, slinging the water from his hair with a muscular twist. But before she could answer, he snarled, "Oh, hell!" and starting kicking hard, holding her tightly, dragging her to the shore. She'd drifted away from the dock, but his strokes, strong and sure, cut through the water and pulled them both to the sandy beach, where he deposited her in the waist-high water. "Come on!" he snapped. His arm steadied her as they slogged through the lapping water and up the sandy shoreline. Her teeth were chattering, and she was shivering head to toe, but she barely felt anything other than a deep-seated and painful grief. Swallowing against the pain, she tasted salt and finally roused herself enough to look at this man she'd never met before.

Or had she? There was something remotely familiar about him. Over six feet tall, in a wet, long-sleeved shirt and soaked jeans, he was rugged-looking, as if he'd spent most of his thirty-odd years outdoors.

"What the hell were you thinking?" he demanded, shaking the hair out of his eyes. "You could have drowned!" And then, as an afterthought, "Are you okay?"

Of course she was not okay. She was damned certain she would never be even remotely okay again.

"Let's get you inside." He was still holding on to her, and he helped her past a pair of boots thrown haphazardly on the grass, then up the overgrown sandy path toward the house.

"Who *are* you?" she asked.

He eyed her up and down. "Austin Dern." When she didn't respond, he said, "And you're Ava Garrison? You own this place?"

"Part of it." She tried to wring the cold salt water from her hair, but it was impossible.

"*Most* of it." His eyes narrowed on her as she shivered. "And you don't know who I am?"

"Not a clue." Even in her state of shock, the man irritated her.

He muttered something under his breath, then said, "Well, now, isn't that something? You hired me. Just last week." He was pushing her toward the house.

"Me?" Oh, God, how bad was her memory? Sometimes it seemed as thin and fragile as a cheesecloth. But not about this. Shaking her head, feeling the cold water drip down her back, she said, "I don't think so." She would have remembered him. She was sure of it.

"Actually it was your husband."

Oh. Wyatt. "I guess he forgot to tell me."

"Yeah?" His gaze skated over her bedraggled, freezing form, and for a second, she wondered just how sheer her sodden nightgown was.

"By the way, you're welcome." He didn't so much as crack a smile. Though darkness was settling over the island, she saw his features, set and grim. Deep-set eyes, their color undetermined in the coming night; square, beard-shadowed jaw; blade-thin lips; and a nose that wasn't quite straight. His hair was as dark as the night, somewhere between a deep brown and black. They trudged together toward the behemoth three-storied manor.

On the back porch, the screen door flew open, then banged shut behind a woman running from the house. "Ava? Oh, God, what happened?" Khloe demanded, her face a mask of concern as it caught in the porch light. She sprinted past the garden and jumped over a small hedge of boxwoods to grab Ava as the stranger released his grip on her body. "Oh my God, you're soaking wet!" Khloe was shaking her head, and her expression was caught somewhere between pity and fear. "What the hell were you doing . . . oh, don't even say it. I know." She held Ava close and didn't seem to care that her jeans and sweater were soaking up the water from her friend's nightgown. "You have to stop this, Ava. You have to." Glancing up at the stranger, she added to Ava, "Come on, let's get you into the house." Then to Dern, "You too. Dear God, you're both soaked to the bone!"

Khloe and Dern both tried to help her up the path, but she shook them both off, startling Virginia's black cat, Mr. T, who had been hiding behind a withering rhododendron. With a hiss, the cat slid into a crawl space under the porch just as Ava's cousin, Jacob, came running from his burrow of an apartment in the basement of the old house.

Some of her old pluck began returning. She was tired of playing the victim, bored with the pitying stares and the know-

ing glances shared between others as if to say, *Poor, poor thing.*
So they thought she was crazy.

Big deal.

It wasn't as if she hadn't questioned her sanity herself, just
minutes ago, and yet everyone's concern was really beginning
to get under her skin.

"What happened?" Jacob demanded. His glasses were off-
kilter and his reddish hair mussed, as if he'd been asleep.

Ignoring him and everyone else, Ava clambered up the stairs,
dripping, her nightgown sucked tight to her body. She didn't
give a damn what they thought. She *knew* she'd seen Noah, and
no matter what Khloe or her cowboyesque savior or even the
damned shrink Ms. Evelyn McPherson thought, she wasn't insane. Had never been. Wasn't ready for the loony bin.

"Let me help you," Khloe said, but Ava was having none of it.

"I'm fine."

"You just jumped into the ocean, Ava! You are definitely
not anywhere close to *fine.*"

"Just leave me alone, Khloe."

Khloe glanced at Dern, then backed up, lifting her hands,
palms out. "Ooookay."

"No need to be melodramatic," Ava muttered.

"Oh, yeah. *I'm* the drama queen!" Khloe sighed heavily.
"Just for the record, who was it who flung herself into the bay
a few minutes ago?"

"Okay, okay." Ava was up the stairs and opening the screen
door. "I get it." Once inside, where the heat hit her like a wall
and the tangy scent of tomatoes and clams swept through the
hallways, she hurried past the wall of windows that overlooked
the yard, taking another quick glance. Now, aside from a few
security lights, the grounds were dark, the fog too dense to see
the end of the pier. Her heart ached at the thought of her son,
but she pushed her grief aside.

At least her mind had cleared somewhat; her headache, if not completely gone, at least had receded to somewhere far away from her frontal lobes. She heard the screen door open and close behind her and knew that her confrontation with Khloe, and possibly the man who had leaped in after her, wasn't yet over.

Great. Just what she needed!

Teeth chattering so hard they rattled, she was heading toward the back stairs when she heard the clunk of the elevator from the shaft that ran along the east side of the stairs, then the whisper of the elevator doors slowly opening.

She prayed the occupant wasn't Jewel-Anne. But, of course, she wasn't so lucky, and within seconds her pudgy cousin emerged, her electric wheelchair carrying her into the hallway. Through thick glasses, she threw a look at Ava, taking in her soggy nightgown, plastered hair, and probably nearly blue skin.

"Swimming again?" she asked with that smug little smile Ava would have liked to wipe off her face. Jewel-Anne pulled out an earbud from her iPhone, and Ava heard the strains of Elvis's "Suspicious Minds" sounding tinny at the distance.

"*We're caught in a trap,*" he warbled, and Ava wondered why a woman who had been born long after the rock icon had died had become such a die-hard fan. Of course, she knew the pat answer, because she'd posed the question to Jewel-Anne just this past year. Over her oatmeal, with one earbud plugged in, Jewel-Anne had turned deadly serious. "We shared the same birthday, you know." She'd added a second scoop of brown sugar to her cereal.

Somehow, Ava had managed to keep her sarcastic tongue in check and said only, "You weren't even alive when—"

"He speaks to me, Ava!" Jewel-Anne's lips had compressed with certainty. "He was such a tragic figure." She paid attention to her breakfast, stirring her butter and brown sugar and swirling her hot cereal in her bowl. "Like me."

Then she'd looked up at Ava with innocent eyes, and Ava had felt the deep jab of guilt that only her paraplegic cousin could inspire.

You're not the only one he speaks to, she'd wanted to say. *There are hundreds of Elvis sightings every day. He's probably "speaking" to those lunatics, too.* Rather than escalate a fight with no end, she'd pushed out her chair, scooped out the remainder of her cereal into the sink, and dropped her bowl into the dishwasher just as Jacob, Jewel-Anne's only full brother, strolled into the kitchen without a word, found a toasted bagel, and walked out the back door, his backpack slung over one thick shoulder. Once an all-state wrestler, Jacob, with his curly red hair and acne-scarred fair skin, was a perpetual student who owned every electronic gadget imaginable. He was a full-blown computer geek and as strange as his sister.

Now Jewel-Anne, with her straight, waist-length hair and trusting, so-sincere blue eyes, didn't have to utter a word but Ava knew she still believed she had a special connection to the King of Rock and Roll. *Oh, sure, Elvis speaks to Jewel-Anne.* Even in nonliteral terms, Ava doubted they had even the most tenuous of connections and quickly took the stairs two at a time.

Why should she worry about her own sanity when she was living with a group of people who, at one time or another, could have been certifiably nuts?

Chapter 2

The lights flickered twice as Ava stood under the hot shower spray. Each time darkness flooded the bathroom, she tensed and placed a hand on the tiled shower wall, but fortunately the power didn't go out. Thank God. That was the problem with this island, which was set off the coast of Washington with no access to the mainland except by private boat or a ferry that ran twice a day to Anchorville, weather permitting.

It had been a haven for her great-great-grandparents, Ava knew, who had settled here, commanded the largest chunk of real estate, and somehow, through logging and sawmilling, had made a fortune. When other people had settled on the island, Stephen Monroe Church had offered them lumber and supplies and, more importantly, jobs.

Ava had always wondered about the population back then. Why leave the comfort of the mainland? What had the settlers been running to . . . or, more likely, from?

Whatever their reasons, they had helped Stephen and his wife, Molly, construct this grandiose home, complete with three sets of stairs, three floors above ground (not counting the attic), and a basement now used for storage and Wyatt's wine cellar and Jacob's apartment. Built in the Victorian style on one of the highest points on the island, Neptune's Gate had nearly a three-hundred-and-sixty-degree view from its westerly turret, which rose over a widow's walk. Hence it was a house of windows that winked and caught in the summer sunlight. This time of year, though, with the fog and rain, sleet and hail, the refracting rays were few and far between.

Scrubbing with lavender soap and some guaranteed-gentle shampoo, she washed the salt and grime from her skin and hair, letting the soothing water calm the fear that split her soul—fear and confusion about her son.

What had she been thinking earlier?

Noah hadn't been on the dock.

It was just her willing, weak mind playing tricks on her, vestiges from her dream remaining to confuse her.

Yet the image of him standing in the rising mist, teetering on the edge of the dock, eerily real, still stayed with her.

It's been two years . . . let him go.

She rinsed off, thinking that her son would be four years old now, had he survived.

Tears filled her eyes and her throat grew thick. She turned and faced the nozzle, letting warm water wash the damned tears away.

By the time she'd dressed and combed the tangles from her hair, she felt better. Rested. No longer balanced upon a mental precipice.

She was just walking out of the bathroom when she heard a tap on her bedroom door. "Ava?" her husband's voice called softly as the door opened.

"I thought you were in Seattle," she said.

"Portland." His smile was thin, his features marred with worry, his sandy-colored hair rumpled as if he'd been forcing stiff fingers through it.

"Oh. Right." She'd known he'd driven south. Wyatt's client was from Seattle but had real estate holdings in Oregon and had some kind of lawsuit leveled against him.

"Doesn't matter." Wyatt stepped closer to her, and she tensed but didn't back up, not even when he brushed an errant curl off her forehead, his fingertips warm and familiar as they grazed her skin. "Are you okay?" he asked, his hazel eyes dark with concern. That same old question that no matter how she answered, everyone had already come up with their own conclusions.

"I'd like to say fine, but . . ." She tipped her hand side to side. "Let's just say I'm better than I was an hour ago."

She remembered falling in love with him, or at least she thought she had. They'd met in college . . . yes, that was right. At a small private school near Spokane. That had been nearly fifteen years earlier. He'd been handsome and athletic and sexy, and those attributes hadn't changed over the years. Even now, with his light brown hair mussed from raking his fingers through it and a day's worth of whiskers darkening his chin, he was a good-looking man. Strapping. Bold. A take-no-prisoners attorney who now looked rumpled, his suit jacket wrinkled, his white shirt open at the throat, his tie loosened. Yes, indeed, Wyatt Garrison was still a sexy, attractive male.

And she didn't trust him as far as she could throw him.

"What happened?" Wyatt asked as he sat on the edge of the bed, on "his" side, the mattress sinking a bit under his weight. How many times had she lain in his arms in that very bed? How many nights had they made love . . . When had they stopped? "Ava?"

She snapped out of her reverie. "Oh. You know. The same thing." She glanced to the window where she'd been certain she'd seen her son. "I thought I saw Noah. On the dock."

"Oh, Ava." He shook his head slowly. Sadly. "You've got to stop torturing yourself. He's gone."

"But—"

"No 'buts.' " The mattress groaned as he climbed to his feet. "I thought you were getting better. When they released you from St. Brendan's, the doctors were convinced you were on the road to recovery."

"Maybe it's just a bumpy one."

"But it shouldn't have U-turns."

"I was getting better," she said, preferring not to think of the hospital from which she'd been recently released. "I mean I am!" She swallowed hard, didn't want to think about having to go back to the psych ward at the inland hospital. "It's just the nightmares."

"Have you seen Dr. McPherson lately?" Evelyn McPherson was the psychologist Wyatt had personally chosen upon Ava's release from St. Brendan's. He'd said it was because she practiced in Anchorville and was willing to visit Ava on the island, which made sense, but there was something about the woman that bothered Ava. It was as if she were listening too intently to her, was too damned concerned, as if Ava's problems were hers. It was all too personal.

"Of course I've seen her. Didn't she tell you?" When had it been? "Last week."

His dark eyebrows lifted as if he didn't believe her. "When last week?"

"Uh . . . Friday, I think. Yes, that was it." Why was he doubting her? And why did he care? Ever since Noah's disappearance, their marriage had been tenuous at best. Most of the time Wyatt was in Seattle on the mainland where he lived in a high-rise only a stone's throw from the office where he was a junior partner in a prominent law firm. He specialized in tax law and investments.

She'd suspected that his interest in her had waned, that she was an embarrassment, a "crazy" woman and a wife best left concealed on a small island off the Washington coast.

"I was afraid I'd lost you." He sounded sincere and her throat closed for a second.

"Sorry. Not this time."

He looked as if she'd slapped him.

"Bad joke."

"Very."

She needed to change the subject and fast. "So, Austin Dern," she said as she pulled the curtains shut. "You hired him?"

Wyatt nodded. "For the stock." He threw Ava a glance. "Let's face it. Ian's really not cut out to be a ranch foreman, isn't really a horseman and cattleman. I thought he could take over after Ned retired and moved to Arizona, but I was wrong."

"I took care of the horses."

"Once upon a time," he said with a faint smile. "And even then you weren't the best at keeping up the fence line or taking care of the brush or the barn roof or a frozen pump. Dern's a handyman. You know, a jack-of-all-trades."

"How did you find him?"

"He worked for a client of mine who sold his ranch." One side of his mouth lifted. "I thought I'd give Ian a break."

"He'll appreciate that," Ava said of her cousin, Jewel-Anne's half brother. Ian wasn't exactly a ball of fire. She walked to the end of the bed and held on to one of its tall posts. "You know, I'm surprised you're here."

His jaw tightened almost imperceptibly. Almost. "I was on my way back anyway. Jacob was waiting with the launch." Usually his sister's chauffeur, Jacob had also been the driver assigned to Ava when her license had been taken away.

Wyatt added, "Khloe called my cell. Luckily I was nearly to Anchorville anyway."

"Nice of her."

His mouth twisted downward as if in distaste. "Listen to you. Khloe used to be your best friend."

That much was true. "She's the one who pulled away."

"Did she?" He threw up his hands and shook his head. "Are you sure about that?" When she didn't answer, he added with a trace of sarcasm, "Whatever you say. But Dr. McPherson's on her way. You need to talk to her."

"Whatever you say," she mimicked, then hated the harsh sound of her words when she noticed a wounded light in his eyes.

"I give up." He was out the door in seconds, and once again, her throat tightened.

"Me too," she whispered. "Me too."

"You know that you didn't really see Noah." Dr. McPherson was kind, if slightly patronizing. A pretty, slim woman, she wore a skirt and boots, her streaked hair brushing her shoulders, her gaze filled with concern. She seemed sincere and caring at times, yet, true to her paranoia, Ava didn't trust her. Never had.

Now they were seated in the library, a room off the living area with floor-to-ceiling shelves filled with old volumes and a fire that was glowing softly in the grate. Propane hissed softly as the wood stacked on ancient andirons caught fire.

"I saw him," Ava insisted. She was seated on the worn couch, her hands fisted on her lap. "Whether he was there or not, I don't know, but I saw him."

"You know how that sounds." Wyatt was standing in a corner, his tie loosened further, his expression dark.

"I don't care how it sounds. That's the way it is." Ava met the concern in her husband's eyes with simmering mutiny. "I thought I was supposed to be honest."

"You are, you are," Dr. McPherson said with a quick nod. Perched on the edge of the recliner that was wedged between the hearth and the couch, the firelight caught in her pale hair. Though her office was on the mainland, she often came to the island, a deal she'd worked with Wyatt. "Of course."

Now Evelyn glanced over her shoulder at Wyatt, and for a split second Ava thought she saw a tenderness in her gaze, but it was quickly masked. Maybe she'd misread it.

"I think it might be best if we were alone," the doctor suggested to Wyatt.

"It's all right," Ava said. "I don't mind. Maybe we can turn this into a marriage counseling session instead of a determination to find out if I'm off the rails or not."

"No one said anything about that," Wyatt remarked. He walked to the fire and turned off the propane, and the flames withdrew, like frightened snails into their shells, leaving the mossy chunks of fir to glow a deep, pulsing red.

"Look, I know it sounds crazy. Nuts. Even to me, but I'm telling you, I saw my baby on the dock in the fog." She wanted to add that she thought the medication she'd been given might have been the cause, but that would have made the doctor defensive, as she was the one who had prescribed the antianxiety pills.

Wyatt walked behind the couch, reached over, and squeezed her shoulder. Fondly? Or out of frustration? She looked up at him and saw nothing but concern in his expression. "You have to let go of your fantasies, Ava. Noah's not coming back." With that he left the room, closing the door softly behind him.

The psychologist's gaze followed after him; then when the door was shut, it turned back to her patient. "What do you think is going on here, Ava?" she asked.

"I wish I knew." Ava glanced to the windows, dark with the night. "I wish to God I knew."

Before they could really get into it, there was a tap on the door and Wyatt opened it again. "Thought you should know. Sheriff Biggs is here."

"Why?" Ava asked.

"Khloe called him."

"Because I jumped into the bay?"

"Yeah. She thought you might be attempting suicide."

"I wasn't!"

"Humor her. Biggs is her uncle."

"Big deal." Ava was having none of it. "What is this?" She looked from her husband to the psychologist. "Are you trying to get me committed?"

"Of course not."

"Good, because just so you know, I don't need to be on any suicide watch!"

"No one said a thing about—"

"You didn't have to, Wyatt. Okay?" She was on her feet and out the door. "Where is he?"

"In the kitchen."

"Great."

She left him and the damned doctor to talk about her state of mind, or lack thereof, and walked through the formal dining room and butler's pantry to the kitchen, the big warm room painted in shades of yellow, with the scent of coffee and baked goods always lingering in the air. The black-and-white tile floor was worn at the door to the back hallway, and the white cabinets were desperately in need of a new coat of paint, but this was, without a doubt, the cheeriest room in the house. Off to one side was a family area, with a couple of worn sofas, a flat-screen television, and toy box stuffed into a corner. This evening the air was thick with the warm scent of baking bread and the tangy aroma of Virginia's clam chowder, Manhattan style.

Aptly named, Sheriff Biggs sat on one of the chairs tucked around a cracked marble-topped table. Spilling over the edges of the woven seat, he'd already accepted a cup of coffee from a grudging Virginia, who now was elbow-deep in dishwater and trying to appear as if she wasn't interested in eavesdropping on the conversation about to ensue between her employers and Biggs, who just happened to be her ex-brother-in-law and Khloe's uncle.

As ever, Virginia was wearing a plain housedress over her

heavy frame, and a wildly colored apron was tied across her rounded abdomen and heavy breasts. Scuffed tennis shoes and dark tights completed the outfit. Ava had rarely seen her in any other attire, even years ago, before she'd been hired here, when she was just Khloe's mother. How they'd all gotten entangled since those grade-school years . . .

"Hello, Ava." Biggs stood and extended a hand, which she shook with more than a hint of trepidation. They'd met a few times before and never had it been under anything but tense circumstances.

"Sheriff." She nodded and pulled her hand back. Hers was clammy; his was irritatingly cool.

"I heard you ended up in the drink," he said, reseating his bulky form and cradling his cup. His eyes narrowed suspiciously as he stared up at her. Then again, she and Biggs had never been friends. Especially not since her brother, Kelvin's, death nearly five years earlier. "Wanna tell me about it?"

"It's not a crime, is it?"

"To go for a swim?" he asked. "Naaah. 'Course not. But the folks here, they were concerned." His face was fleshy, his cheeks showing a few capillaries that had burst, his deep-set eyes intense but not unkind. He motioned to the other people in the room. "They seemed to think maybe you were having a spell of some kind, or sleepwalking."

"I called Joe," Khloe piped in as she walked in from the porch, the new hire, Austin Dern, following after her.

Dern had changed, too. His dark hair was wet and slicked back from his face, and he wore a long-sleeved T-shirt and jeans, faded and dry. He caught her gaze with eyes the color of slate. Again, she felt as if she'd seen him before, in that weird déjà vu way, but try as she might, she couldn't place him.

Khloe added, "I, uh, I thought we needed help."

"So this is *un*official?" Ava asked, since Joe Biggs was Khloe's uncle.

Biggs kept his eyes on Ava. "I just swung by 'cause Khloe called."

"I was worried, that's all," Khloe interjected as Virginia, spying through the open door, scowled, grabbed a towel, and wiped her hands, then pulled the thick door to the porch shut forcefully, as if she were keeping in the heat and making sure whatever lurked outside didn't get the chance to slip in.

Just swung by on a damned county-issued sheriff's department boat on a foggy night? Because a relative called? Oh, sure. Ava wasn't buying it. Even Virginia, now at the sink again, cast a disbelieving look over her shoulder.

Khloe seemed a little less prickly as she said, "Come on, Ava, if the roles were reversed and I ran outside in the middle of the night and jumped into the bay in November, you would have panicked, too. It's not like when we were kids and snuck out to go skinny-dipping in the damned moonlight!"

In her mind's eye, Ava saw them as they had been, years before, streaking down to the water's edge as the moon cast a shimmering beacon of light across the calm sea. She and Khloe and Kelvin . . . God, what she would give to feel that carefree again.

Khloe was right.

Damn it.

Ava felt the weight of everyone's gaze upon her. From Wyatt to Dern and even to Virginia, whose hands had quit rinsing the dishes, though they were plunged into the soapy water. Everyone waited.

"I made a mistake—that's all." Ava held her hands palm up, as if in surrender. There was just no reason to lie, and she wouldn't have anyway. "I thought I saw my son on the end of the dock and ran out to save him. It . . . it turns out I must've been mistaken. And it's not 'the middle of the night.' " A small point, but valid.

"Feels like midnight," Khloe grumbled.

"The boy's been gone, what, nearly two years?" Biggs asked as Dr. McPherson slipped into the room to stand quietly near the pantry.

"Yes." Ava's voice was careful, her legs suddenly weak. She leaned against the refrigerator, hoping no one would notice. "But I'm fine now, Sheriff," she lied, forcing a smile. "Thank you for your concern and your trouble coming all the way out here."

"Not a problem." But his eyes held hers, and she realized they were both lying. It really irked her to be so submissive, but she knew she had to play her cards carefully or she could end up in a hospital under observation, her mental stability in question.

Again.

Claiming a headache, which wasn't a lie, Ava took dinner in her room, which, she decided, was probably the coward's way out. Too bad. Having Biggs in the house was unsettling, though she couldn't really name why. It wasn't as if he was going to arrest her or anything, but she had the feeling that he, along with everyone else, was against her, or at the very least waiting for her to slip up, make a big mistake.

About what?

Don't let your paranoia override your common sense.

"I'm not paranoid," she whispered under her breath, then clamped her mouth shut. She couldn't let anyone hear her talking to herself. No, that wouldn't do. She needed to regroup and pull herself together and figure out who, if anyone, she could trust.

But as she dunked the crusty bread into Virginia's spicy clam chowder and stared through the window to the dock, she found she had no appetite. On clear nights, from this window she was able to spy the lights of Anchorville on the far side of the bay, even watch traffic moving through the sleepy little town.

Chewing thoughtfully, Ava wondered why Khloe had rushed to call the sheriff. Not 911, but Biggs himself. Because he was her uncle? To avoid an unnecessary trip by the EMTs or to stave off a scandal or any embarrassment? That seemed unlikely.

She stared at the department-issued boat tied to the listing dock, barely visible in the fog.

"Odd," she muttered as she shoved most of the chowder aside. But then everything was and gossip surrounding Church Island certainly wasn't unheard of. In fact, scandal seemed as carved into the walls of this bit of land as surely as the coves and inlets that split the rugged stone outcroppings of the island. She felt a chill and found her sweater, a brown cardigan she'd had forever that she'd left on the foot of the bed. She slid her arms through the sleeves and pulled her hair out of the neckline before cinching the belt tighter around her waist.

Tap. Tap. Tap.

She nearly jumped out of her skin at the sound of knuckles rapping against her door. "Ava?" The door opened and Khloe stuck her head into the room. "Hey, how're you doing?"

"How do you think?" she demanded, her heart knocking wildly. God, she was a nervous Nellie.

"Didn't mean to scare you."

"You didn't." It was a lie. They both knew it. She settled back at the desk where the reddish broth was starting to congeal. "Why did you call Biggs?"

"I told you. I was worried!" Khloe admitted, rubbing her arms as if she, too, experienced a sudden chill. "God, it's cold in here."

"Always," Ava said, "and you're hedging."

Khloe sat on the edge of the mattress. "What if . . . what if something had happened to you and we didn't report it? You could've drowned. Passed out in the water. Been the victim of hypothermia or God knows what else."

"I was okay."

"You were alive. Barely. And really kind of out of it." Thin lines of concern etched her forehead. "I probably really should have called nine-one-one, but I was afraid that they would haul you off and . . ." She shrugged her shoulders, then raked frustrated fingers through her short blue-black hair. "To tell you the truth, Ava, sometimes I just don't know what to do."

Neither did she. "I know."

"So . . . since Uncle Joe is still here, why don't you come down and talk to everyone? Show that you're okay."

"You mean fake it?"

"I mean stop acting crazy. Tell Joe and that psychologist that you know you didn't see Noah."

"But—"

"Shhh! Don't argue." Khloe's big eyes implored her. "Just say you were confused, a little unclear because of the meds you're on and that you realize you couldn't have seen Noah." She didn't add that Ava acting calm and rational would probably help her case, that no one would send her off to some kind of psychiatric evaluation if she pulled this off . . . Oh, hell. "Joe is here unofficially, really. He came as a favor to me—"

"In a department-issued boat."

"It was the fastest way over here. But, really, it's more of a call to check up on you rather than anything remotely official. He even ate dinner with us."

"Really?"

She lifted a slim shoulder. "I would just feel better, since I called him out here, if you'd show him that you're . . ."

"Sane? Have my wits about me? Not suicidal?"

"Whatever. But, yeah." She was nodding. "Just humor me, would you?"

It seemed there was no way around facing the sheriff again. "Fine. Just don't be so quick to call the cavalry next time."

"There's not going to be a next time. Right?"

Let's hope, Ava thought, but didn't answer as she found a

jacket hanging inside her closet and slipped her arms through its sleeves. "I think I'm lucky that Sea Cliff is closed. Otherwise Biggs might have hauled me up there."

"Very funny," Khloe said without the trace of a smile at the mention of the old mental hospital. An asylum for the criminally insane located on the southern tip of the island, Sea Cliff had been closed for a little over six years. Everyone at Neptune's Gate had grown up within five miles of the hospital, which had been permanently closed after one of the most dangerous criminals in Washington State history, Lester Reece, had escaped the thick, crumbling walls and rusted gates of the facility.

Chapter 3

Bracing herself for what would probably be another interrogation, Ava followed Khloe down the single flight of stairs and walked through the dining room where Graciela had cleared the soup tureen and dishes from the table. They deposited Ava's dirty dishes on the counter in the kitchen, then made their way through to the library where Biggs had settled into an easy chair and was cradling a mug in his fleshy hand.

Her cousin Ian, along with Jewel-Anne, had joined Wyatt and Dr. McPherson in the cozy room with its Tiffany lamp shades, cushy old couch, and side chairs. Dr. McPherson worked with Ava's medical doctor, but was Ava's primary counselor. The conversation was a quiet hum, the mood sober. Jewel-Anne, for once, wasn't listening to music, though she had one of her hideous dolls with her. This time it was a Kewpie-type doll with big, staring eyes, exaggerated lashes, and a deep-red mouth curved into a precocious pout. Ava didn't know whether the doll with its tangled yellow curls was supposed to be a child or a teenager. Either way, it was disturbing, especially the way Jewel-Anne held it, as if the damned thing were her child.

Ian didn't seem to notice the doll and kept reaching into his breast pocket where he'd once kept a pack of cigarettes always at the ready. He'd given up the habit a while back, he claimed, though Ava had seen him out near the dock, sneaking a smoke, though why he lied about it was anyone's guess. Long and lanky, topping six feet, with curly brown hair showing a few strands of gray, Ian had taken a job on the island as a handyman a few years back, and Ava had often wondered why he didn't move on, get away from this place. He, like her other cousins, had once owned part of Church Island, or "a piece of the rock," as Ian's father had often said, a reference to an old slogan for an insurance company that fitted his view of the island.

No doubt the cozy little group had been discussing Wyatt's wife and her current mental state, as they all became quiet when she walked into the room.

Great, she thought as the uncomfortable silence stretched, and the knot already tightening in her stomach twisted a little more painfully.

". . . just really needs her rest," the doctor was saying as Ava entered the room. She and Wyatt looked up, a bit guiltily, she felt.

"Ava," Wyatt said, leaping to his feet and quickly crossing the faded rug stretched across the old hardwood of the library. He sent a quick, questioning glance in Khloe's direction as if he were upset that she'd talked Ava into coming down. As he reached Ava, he whispered, "I thought you had a headache."

"I did, but it's a wonder what a couple Excedrin Migraine tablets can do."

"I thought the sheriff wanted to ask her some more questions," Khloe said stiffly.

"I do," Biggs said.

"Good." To Ava, Khloe said, "Let me get you some hot chocolate." But she was too late. As if anticipating Ava's return, Demetria, Jewel-Anne's nurse, appeared with a steaming mug in which tiny marshmallows were dissolving in the thick, hot cocoa. She handed the mug to Jewel-Anne. "I've got an-other cup in the microwave," Demetria offered, some of her severity seeming to have receded, her thin lips stretched into the semblance of a smile. "Just a sec."

"Let me help," the psychologist said, starting for the kitchen.

"Hey, could you grab me a cup of coffee?" Ian asked with a smile at Jewel-Anne's nurse.

Demetria looked about to say, *Get it yourself*, but instead she smiled coldly. "I'll see if there's any made." Turning on her heel, she found her way back to the kitchen as Wyatt, holding Ava's hand, helped her to the sofa. They sat together, side by side, stiffly, and Ava was all too aware of everyone watching them, watching her. Wyatt's fingers remained linked with hers, as if he cared—or was afraid she might bolt.

To where? We're on an island, for God's sake.

Beneath her sweater, her shoulders stiffened and she couldn't help but feel Wyatt was acting the part of doting husband, putting on a show for everyone else, which was ridiculous. Everyone who lived at Neptune's Gate knew their marriage was in trouble. It had been since the night Noah had disap-peared.

Casually, she pulled her hand from his and stuffed it into the deep pocket of her sweater. Her finger brushed something cold and metal . . . a key, she realized as the tip of her index finger scraped the jaw-like serrations on one side.

A key to what? To where? Hadn't she worn the sweater ear-lier today? There had been no key in its pockets, or at least she hadn't thought so.

Demetria returned with a cup of hot chocolate for Ava and handed it to her. Evelyn McPherson, on her heels, returned as well, cradling her own mug.

"No coffee?" Ian asked. At Demetria's shake of her head, he scowled. "But I smell it and . . ." He glanced at Biggs who was taking a long swallow from his cup of coffee. "Goddamn it!"

He pushed himself upright and stormed into the kitchen while Demetria seemed to swallow a smile.

Small, small victories, Ava thought, weary of all their games.

Biggs shifted in his chair, his eyes on Ava. "You saw something and ran out to the dock?"

"I already told you I thought I saw my son and I ran out to save him. I guess I was wrong," she admitted, though she had to force the words. "But I saw something. Someone. On the dock."

From the corner of her eye, she caught Wyatt sneak a look at Evelyn, who stood near the fire, ostensibly warming the back of her legs but really, Ava knew, scrutinizing her patient.

Her throat thickened and she stared into her cup as the marshmallows disintegrated, like foamy, dark waves on the beach.

"I guess I was confused, but I was frightened."

"You thought you were saving someone?" Biggs asked.

"Yes."

"Is she on hallucinogens?" he asked the psychologist.

"I wasn't hallucinating!" Ava argued, then heard a quiet cough and saw Austin Dern standing near the window, ostensibly looking out at the dark night. He caught her gaze in the watery glass for just an instant and gave an almost imperceptible shake of his head.

"I mean . . . Oh, I don't know what I mean." She hated this. She was lying, but Dern's subtle warning had penetrated her anger.

"You know Noah's been gone for nearly two years," Evelyn McPherson said kindly, and tears threatened behind Ava's eyes. "He would be almost four now. He would look much different than when you last saw him."

Ava swallowed hard and nodded.

To the sheriff, the doctor said, "Obviously this isn't a good time."

"Is there ever one?" Ava asked. "A good time?"

"There are better times." McPherson straightened and Joe Biggs took his cue.

"Glad this is all straightened out," the sheriff said.

Really? Ava stared at Biggs as if he'd gone mad, but if he saw the doubt in her eyes, he ignored it. Squaring his hat on his head, he started out of the room.

"Thank you, Joe," Wyatt said, and the big man stopped. "I know it's an inconvenience."

"All in a day's work." Biggs shook Wyatt's hand before walking through the kitchen, his heavy footsteps fading as the back door creaked open.

In her pocket, Ava's fingers curled over the unknown key in a death grip. She didn't know why it felt important. She didn't know who had left it for her, but she didn't think it was some random mistake. The key was significant to something.

If she could only figure out what.

What the hell had he gotten himself into? Dern wondered as he strode down the broken stone path to the stable where the small herd of horses that were now in his care was locked for the night.

The whole island was something out of a Hitchcock movie and a bad one at that, the kind his mother had watched far into the nights to accompany her and her ever-present insomnia.

He glanced back over his shoulder at the house, a huge, rambling beast of a building that rose into the night, its single turret appearing like the long tooth of a monster's lower jaw, piercing the low layer of clouds huddling over the island. Neptune's Gate . . . Whose idea was it to name it that? He supposed the building had been dubbed long ago, maybe by the original owner, a sea captain who had settled here and taken up sawmilling back when the virgin forests stretched over the states of Washington and Oregon for thousands of square miles.

Well, old Stephen Monroe Church begat himself a loony of a

great-great-granddaughter in Ava Church Garrison. Beautiful, almost hauntingly so if you believed in those things. Dern didn't. With her big eyes, as gray as the waters of the Pacific in winter; high cheekbones; and pointed chin, she had the markings of a real beauty, but she was just too damned thin for his taste. Waifishly so. Though it hadn't always been. He knew.

He checked on the horses and felt a little calmer as the smell of dry hay, dust, and oiled leather was layered over the more astringent smells of urine and the earthy scent of manure. The horses rustling in the straw, occasionally nickering, was also comforting. Then again, he'd always felt more at home with animals than he had with people, and today the reasons for his feelings had become clearer than ever when he'd met more of the people housed in Neptune's Gate, a nest of vipers if there ever was one.

Locking the door behind him, he headed up the exterior stairs to the apartment that was now, at least for a short while, his home. Inside was a studio, smaller by half than the library in which he'd witnessed the interaction of the Church family members, the staff of Neptune's Gate, and the sheriff. That's where the lines blurred a bit. Some of the staff were relatives, and even the damned county sheriff was related to Khloe Prescott, who supposedly had been the missing kid's nursemaid and stayed on after his disappearance to care for Ava, who had once been her best friend.

It was like a never-ending riddle.

And he knew they were all liars. Every last one of them. Including the waifish Ava Garrison. He could feel it.

His room was barren, just a couch that folded outward into an uncomfortable bed, a gate-legged table with a stained top, one "easy" chair, and a television circa 1983 or so. A gas stove painted a deep forest green stood a step away from the front door and offered the only heat in the unit. It was also now covered with his still-soaked pair of jeans. On the wood-paneled walls, pictures of seagoing vessels from an earlier era hid holes in the worn paneling.

Home sweet home.

Earlier, upon his arrival, he'd tossed his bedroll onto the couch and packed his few clothes into a tiny closet that fit him just fine. His bath consisted of a shower stall, toilet, and chipped pedestal sink tucked behind a bifold door, and his kitchen was a long closet with a functional sink, tiny counter, microwave, and mini-fridge. From the heat stains on the old Formica counter, it seemed that a previous tenant had once owned a hot plate, but it was nowhere to be found in the tiny, single cupboard that housed dish liquid, two plates, two bowls, and an assortment of jelly jars and glasses. A coffeemaker was tucked into a corner, two cups nearby, but no coffee to be found anywhere.

He heard a scratching sound at the door and opened it to find a bedraggled dog—a shepherd mix of some kind, probably Australian crossed with a bit of Border collie, all black with three once-white feet. They were now covered in dirt. "Who the hell are you?" he muttered, then said, "Hold up." Grabbing one of the two towels from a cupboard beneath the television, he wiped the dog's feet before the mutt wandered inside, made three circles, and dropped onto the worn rag rug that covered the linoleum in front of the gas stove. Head in his paws, the shepherd stared up at Dern, as if waiting.

"Make yourself at home," Dern muttered before snagging his still-damp jeans off the stove and turning up the heat. As his new friend watched, Dern carried his Levi's to the bathroom where he draped them over the shower's frosted glass door, next to his still-wet shirt.

The dog didn't move except to thump his tail when Dern snapped the bifolds shut and returned. "I take it from the way you walked in that you've been here before, right, buddy?" Dern bent down—he couldn't resist scratching the dog's ears—

then twisted his collar around and read a long-expired tag. "Rover?" he asked, rocking back on his heels. "Seriously? That's your name?"

Again, Dern was rewarded with a thump of the dog's wet tail as he unbuckled Rover's collar and checked to see that it really was a dog collar and nothing else. He'd already swept the small apartment for any signs of bugs, the electronic kind. He'd found nothing suspicious, no hidden microphones or tiny cameras anywhere. He'd even checked what served as an attic and searched every inch of the flooring, walls, and ceiling. It was a habit, something he'd done ever since his days in the military. And considering his motives for being here, a good idea.

"All clear," he told the dog as he reattached the collar, then gave Rover another pat before straightening and wishing he'd thought to stock the mini-fridge with a beer or two.

His plan was that tomorrow morning, after taking care of the stock, he would boat across the bay to Anchorville, check out the tone, nose around a bit. If he had the time, he hoped to sift through the local gossip without arousing any suspicion and learn more about Church Island and its inhabitants.

If possible.

Now he walked to the window facing Neptune's Gate and looked up at the gargantuan house. Lights were still glowing in some of the windows, though he couldn't spy Ava Garrison's room from this vantage point. That bothered him a little, especially now, after her surprising dive into the bay a few hours earlier. But he couldn't make a scene about where he lived, about the fact that he needed a spot where he could keep an eye on her, or he would arouse suspicion. As it was, he had to be careful.

After yanking the blinds closed, he double-checked his hiding spot, one of the holes in the wall covered by a picture of a clipper ship riding angry waves. Earlier, he'd carefully superglued a strong, waterproof pocket to the inside of the paneling, as far down the hole as he could reach. The pocket had a Velcro flap, and inside were several items, including a prepaid cell phone that couldn't be traced, at least not easily; an Internet connective device that he didn't want anyone to find; and a small jump drive that held all the information he dared keep on the island. The backup info was tucked far away at a private data backup site on the mainland, one that kept it away from prying eyes. The last item was his gun. A Glock that couldn't be traced to him.

Nonetheless, he never felt completely safe, was always wary.

"Comes with the territory," he reminded himself as he extracted the Internet connection device and the data stick from their hiding spots. After checking the dead bolt, he opened his laptop and connected to the Internet, ready to write his notes on what he'd discovered on his first day under the employ of Ava Garrison.

Unfortunately, at this point, he had more questions than he had answers.

But that would change.

The dog let out a long sigh and closed his eyes.

Dern glanced at the smelly shepherd.

He figured the beast might just be his only friend on the island.

Then again, that suited him just fine.

Chapter 4

She awoke alone.

Again.

Wyatt's side of the bed was cold, as if he'd never joined her.

"Good," she whispered, then made a face at the sound of her relief. It was just wrong. She'd already lost her son and, it seemed, her own identity, so she should be holding fast to her husband and her marriage. But she was seriously in danger of losing both and all she felt was relief.

When had *that* started?

At first, after Noah's death, she and Wyatt had clung together, holding each other, tasting each other's tears. There had been a tenderness and a desperation to their lovemaking that had evaporated over the months with the realization that he wasn't returning, that their boy was gone forever.

Wyatt began staying on the mainland, and when he returned, they rarely slept together.

Despite her need for another baby.

One child cannot replace another. She knew that. But she wanted another child. Someone to love.

Through the closed door, she heard the sound of Jewel-Anne's wheelchair whirring outside her door. Had her invalid cousin been spying again? Jewel-Anne was getting creepier by the minute, and Ava found her patience with her cousin wearing thin. And why the hell would Jewel-Anne be hiding and watching her, eavesdropping on her conversations? Was her cousin that bored? It just didn't make a helluva lot of sense.

Again, Ava's headache raged, and again she felt as if the world were collapsing around her. She was groggy, the remnants of deep sleep dragging her down, but she fought it. She'd always been a light sleeper, but lately . . .

You were drugged. Obviously. Since you have been ignoring the sleeping pills Dr. McPherson prescribed, she probably slipped them into that damned cocoa you sipped so greedily last night. Hadn't she been in the kitchen with Demetria?

She drew a breath. *Don't go there. Evelyn McPherson is a well-respected doctor, a psychologist trying to help.*

Closing her eyes for a quick second, Ava tried to force herself out of bed, to face the day, but it seemed daunting.

You can't just lie here and feel sorry for yourself, can't feed the paranoia that everyone's against you. Get out of bed and do something. Anything!

Throwing off the covers, she forced herself to roll off the mattress and hunt for her slippers. The cozy, rumpled bed beckoned, but she ignored the temptation of dropping back onto the mussed covers, laying her pounding head on the pillow and closing her eyes again to block out the world. What good would that do?

Slippers on her feet, she paused to stretch, listening to her spine pop, feeling a yawn coming on.

Coffee, that's what you need. Two, maybe three cups of Italian roast or any blend with a crazy lot of caffeine.

At the window facing Anchorville, she winced a little as a slim shaft of sunlight pierced through the opening between the nearly closed curtains and cut through her brain like a hot knife. God, her head hurt. But then it always did in the morning.

She flung the heavy drapes aside and stared outside to a day already begun. The sun was up in the east, shafts of bright light hitting the water and sparkling so brightly she had to squint to make out the ferry, just churning away from the shoreline of the town of Monroe—a hamlet, really—on this side of the bay. Little more than a general store with a post office, a café that was open on the whim of its owner, a small inn, and a coffee kiosk surrounded by a smattering of houses, Monroe boasted seventy-eight full-time residents. The few children who lived there caught the ferry to school in Anchorville, and most of Monroe's residents were employed on the mainland as well or worked at the old hotel, which was now a bed-and-breakfast, the only lodging on the island.

Now the ferry was churning away from the island, gliding across the sun-spangled water effortlessly. A few recreational boats were chugging their way from the marina to the open sea.

Instinctively she looked back at the dock, listing in the water, its weathered boards drying in the sun. Nothing looked out of place today; there wasn't a hint of anything amiss, no physical reminders of her boy in his little red sweatshirt and jeans. No one standing at the misty dock's edge.

"You're losing it," she whispered. *Just like they think.*

She turned to try to catch a glimpse of the stable and the apartment where Austin Dern now resided, but of course she couldn't see it from this angle.

Get a move on.

Turning, she spied her morning meds, three cherry-colored pills placed in a cut glass holder the size of an espresso cup sitting next to a glass of water.

Someone, Wyatt probably, had brought them in this morning while she slept. She hadn't heard the person arrive. A chill slid down her spine as she thought of what anyone could do while she slept so soundly. She didn't want to swallow anything that might dull her mind, but Wyatt and McPherson insisted she needed the meds.

"Bull," she muttered under her breath, carrying the glass into the bathroom, tossing the brightly colored pills into the toilet, and flushing them away.

The water was still running in the old pipes when she returned to the room and replaced the medication glass on the nightstand.

Throwing on a pair of jeans and long-sleeved T-shirt, she rummaged in her closet for a pair of beat-up tennis shoes and a green fleece pullover, the pullover something she'd worn for years that now was at least a size too big.

Spying the sweater she'd worn the night before, she scrounged around in the right pocket and slipped out the key that had been left inside.

"Where do you fit?" she wondered aloud, staring at the jagged, worn notches in the blade of the key. There were no identifiable markings on it, nothing to indicate what it unlocked, but she slipped the slim bit of metal into the front pocket of her jeans, just in case she figured it out.

Walking out of her room, she thought she might trip over Jewel-Anne, but her cousin was far too clever to be caught spying and had whizzed away. If she'd really been outside Ava's door at all.

In the kitchen, Ava found the coffeepot and poured herself a dose of whatever blend Virginia had brewed, then grabbed a napkin and a slice of some apple coffee cake that was already cut and left to cool on the counter. The house was quiet for once, not even Graciela's off-key humming or Jewel-Anne's wheelchair disturbing the silence.

Odd, she thought, but then what wasn't? Her entire life seemed surreal these days. She walked through the back door and across the porch to the outside where the autumn air was brisk, a few dry leaves skittering over the lawn, the smell of the sea ever present. Today, in the sunlight, the island seemed peaceful and serene, no hint of the evil that seemed to ooze over the hillsides and seep through the walls of Neptune's Gate at night.

All in your mind, sweetie. All in your mind.

Looking over the bay, she sat on the porch swing and slowly rocked.

The coffee was strong and hot, burning a path down her throat and taking the edge off her headache. Virginia's coffee cake was still slightly warm and filled with cinnamon and cooked apples, probably from the twisted trees in the orchard that still bore fruit.

So what the hell are you doing? Waiting for something to happen? That's not you, Ava. Never has been. You were—make that are—a take-charge woman. Remember? Didn't you graduate from college in a little over three years? Weren't you an entrepreneur who started her own advertising business, making a fortune on e-marketing before you sold the company? Didn't you parlay a nice inheritance into a fortune that allowed you to buy out your cousins and siblings so that you would eventually own most of this island? If it weren't for Jewel-Anne holding out, Neptune's Gate would be yours alone and wasn't that your dream? She bit the edge of her lip and thought. What had become of the woman she'd once been, the one who had set her sights on Wyatt Garrison and never let go? Where was the athlete who'd once run marathons? What had happened to the person who had shrewdly bought out most of her relatives so that she could own Neptune's Gate herself, a woman who had planned to restore this old house to its former grandeur?

She's gone . . . lost when her only child disappeared. A tear rolled from Ava's eye, and she angrily brushed it away. *No more moping around grieving! No more letting others push you around! No more playing the damned victim! Toughen up, Ava.*

And if the past bothers you so much, then figure it out. Find out what happened to your boy and move the hell on.

"Oh, God," she whispered, suddenly afraid to let go.

Come on, Ava! For the love of Christ, do something!

Downing the remainder of her coffee, she nearly cracked the glass-topped table as she slammed her mug down onto its dusty top. She crumpled her napkin, stuffed it into her jeans pocket, then walked down to the dock and boathouse. Inside she discovered only the dingy was still there, but the powerboat was missing, its slip empty, the lift down. She'd always been fascinated with the boathouse as a child, how it smelled brackish from the sea, the way the water was always restless, the hidden attic above where the mechanism for the boat lift was hidden along with a few abandoned mud wasps' nests and a multitude of sticky cobwebs that, filled with the bodies of desiccated insects, dangled and draped over the single dirty window.

She and Kelvin had hidden there as children, away from parents whose fights were as volatile as their passionate affection.

Kelvin. Her heart twisted when she thought of her brother, and she walked swiftly from the boathouse, refusing to let the memories of her only sibling draw her back to that dark place that forever seemed to call her. First Kelvin, then Noah.

Maybe all the members of her family who thought she was crazy were right. There was a good chance that she was certifiable.

Then again . . .

From the boathouse, she made her way up a series of rock steps to the garden, where, in the summer, roses, hydrangea, and heather flourished. Today the garden was weed-choked and neglected, grass growing over the stones. She stopped at the marker, a rock carved with Noah's name. There was no birth date, nor was the day he disappeared etched onto the uneven stone. It contained only his name. She bent and rested on one knee, leaning forward and touching the letters, then kissing her fingers and brushing them over the hard surface. "I miss you," she whispered, then felt as if she were being watched, studied by unseen eyes.

She glanced over her shoulder at the house but saw no one in the dark windows that reflected the sea.

Wyatt was right. She couldn't go on this way. Living in the past. Not knowing what happened to her boy. *You have to find out what happened to him. You. You know you can't rely on anyone else.*

Straightening, she looked down at the dock and scowled. Why was it that she always saw him *there*? It wasn't as if he'd been playing near the boathouse when he'd disappeared, and yet in her dreams or in her waking visions of him, she always viewed his little backside at the edge of the dock, so dangerously close to the water.

Why did her nightmares always take her there?

Through a rusting gate, she walked to the rear of the house where she eyed the stable, barn, and outbuildings. The horses and a few head of cattle were grazing in a pasture, sunlight burnishing their shaggy coats. Curious, Ava eyed the area, searching for Dern, but he wasn't anywhere outside. When she explored the stable and barn and even climbed the stairs to his apartment, she found it locked and no one answered her knock. Dern, like everyone else in the household, appeared to be MIA this morning, which was too bad because she wanted to talk to him, find out more about the man who had pulled her from the bay.

From the stable, she walked to the front of the house and let herself in the front door. No longer was she alone. Virginia was rattling around in the kitchen. Also, Ava heard footsteps on the floor above, then the smooth hum of Jewel-Anne's wheelchair.

No, she was no longer alone.

And she didn't know if that was a good thing.

Or bad.

She wandered to the kitchen where Virginia, balanced on a

step stool, was straightening cans in the pantry, every tin label facing out, the larger cans in the back, smaller in the front. Boxes of pasta, too, were visible, along with an array of spices and the basics of rice, beans, flour, and sugar in square glass jars, all labeled precisely. Glancing over her shoulder, Virginia asked, "You get something to eat?" She righted a crooked carton of chicken stock.

"I pilfered a slice of your coffee cake. It was good."

"That's not much. You want something more?"

"No, thanks."

A stack of tuna cans was twisted to perfection. Virginia glanced at her watch. "Lunch won't be for another couple of hours."

"I think I'll make it. So . . . where was everyone this morning?"

Beneath the shoulders of her housedress, Virginia's shoulders tightened almost imperceptibly and the tins of canned fish suddenly threatened to topple.

"Hey, there!" Wyatt's voice rang through the outer hallway. Ava turned to find him striding toward her. The worry she'd seen etched across his face last night had evaporated, and he even managed a smile. "How're you feeling?"

She shrugged. "Not bad."

"Good." He hooked her elbow with a hand and admitted, "I was worried."

"I'll be okay."

One corner of his mouth twisted upward. "I'm counting on it." But there were still doubts in his eyes, doubts he tried to hide. "So what do you say? Want to go into town?"

"With you?"

"Of course with me. Maybe get some lunch."

"I thought you had to work."

"I'm leaving later this afternoon, but I thought we could get off this island for a while, pick up some groceries or whatever, just hang out."

"Just hang out," she repeated.

"I know, I know." He dropped her elbow and held up a hand as if in surrender. "We haven't done it in a long time, but I was thinking it might be time to, you know"—he lifted one shoulder and his smile stretched a bit—"reconnect."

She glanced upward, toward the landing on the second floor, to make certain no one was listening. Lowering her voice, she said, "So why didn't you come to bed last night?"

"I was there."

"No . . . Really? But . . ." She shook her head and stepped back from him, remembering their cold bed, how the pillow had shown no impression of his head, that the sheets and covers on his side had been neat and unmussed. He couldn't have been there. She would have known, would have felt him. "You weren't there."

"I got up early."

"Wyatt." She lowered her voice further, trying to hang on to her patience. "What is this?"

"You tell me."

"Why are you lying?"

"Good question," he said, his smile fading. "Why would I?"

"You weren't there when I went to sleep or when I woke up."

"That's not exactly news, Ava. Happens all the time . . ." Then he looked away from her and let out a long-suffering sigh. "I was there, Ava. Right next to you. For most of the night. I came in and you were asleep, so I didn't disturb you, and then later, when you were so restless, I got up and spent the rest of the night from about four a.m. on down here, in the den." He hooked a finger toward the room on the far side of the staircase, the place he'd claimed when they'd moved in years before and the room to which he'd often retreated, closing the French doors and drawing the curtains whenever he was working from home, which over the past two years had happened less and less.

"Your side of the bed hadn't been slept in," she insisted.

"Much," he corrected, holding up one finger as his face

flushed a bit. "It hadn't been slept in *much*." Scowling, he said, "Okay, forget about coming into town with me. Maybe it's not such a good idea. I guess we both need our space." Shooting her a final look somewhere between disappointment and anger, he walked back the way he'd come, his footsteps ringing hollowly on the marble floor of the foyer.

She ground her teeth together. *It's your fault, Ava. He was offering an olive branch and you snapped it in half.*

"Uh-oh." Ian's voice whispered through the foyer, and she turned to find him leaning on the wall near the elevator. "Trouble in paradise?"

"What business is it of yours?"

"Touchy, aren't we today, cuz? What's wrong? Off your meds?"

What was this all about? She thought of the pills she'd flushed down the toilet and refused to feel guilty about it. No way, no how.

"You know, it's really not smart to piss Wyatt off," he said idly.

"I don't mean to."

"Sure you do."

Ian was staring at her, and she said, "Don't you have a job or something?"

"Not much of one now. Not since your hubby decided to hire that ex-marine or Navy Seal or whatever he is."

"Dern? I thought he was a rancher."

"That too."

"What do you know about him?"

"That he's trouble. I don't get it. Why Wyatt has to have his spies around . . ." Ian made a face.

Ava felt her paranoia ratchet up a notch. "Why do you think he's a spy?"

"Isn't everyone? Isn't that what *you* think? You're not the only one who can play the paranoid card, Ava."

She glared at him.

"I don't know a whole lot, okay. Only what I found out on the Internet. Dern's had a couple of scrapes with the law. Arrested twice, never even arraigned or convicted."

"Arrested for what?"

"The Internet only gave up so much info, but you might want to ask him."

"Wyatt would never hire anyone with a record."

Ian gave her a look. "I said he was never charged. That doesn't mean he's lily-white, though, does it?" A grin stretched over his teeth. "Then again, who is?" His cell phone jangled and he punched the CONNECT button and strolled away.

As he spoke in hushed tones, Ava hurried up the stairs and walked to her room, but Graciela was already inside, the bed made, the room freshened. "Good morning," she said as she tweaked the recently plumped pillows, then ran a hand over the coverlet, smoothing it.

"Morning . . . but . . . you know you don't have to make my bed." Ava had always taken care of straightening up her own room all of her life and preferred it that way.

"Oh, I know." Graciela nodded as she swung into the adjoining bath. "But since your . . . um . . . your accident last night, I thought I would help out."

Ava walked to the doorway and caught the maid yanking down her towel from a hook near the shower. "I can take care of it myself."

"I know." Graciela's smile was pinned neatly on her pretty face as she gathered a wet washcloth from the counter near the sink, then bent down and snagged a bath mat from the floor. "But Mr. Wyatt, he asked me to." She started to straighten, glanced into the toilet bowl, and stopped.

"Why?"

The girl lifted a shoulder, then flushed the toilet, and Ava realized at least part of the pills she'd tried to flush away had lingered.

Graciela knows you're dumping your meds. . . .

"I didn't ask," Graciela said, and for a second Ava was lost, then realized the maid was answering her question about Wyatt's request.

"When?" she managed as if nothing were wrong. "When did he ask you?"

"Last night." Her dark eyebrows nearly collided, and her smile fell from her lips. "Is there a problem? Did I do something wrong?"

"No, no," Ava was quick to assure her. "It's just that from now on, I'd like to do it myself."

Graciela blinked, appearing a little crestfallen, and Ava felt like a heel.

"I'm sorry," the maid said softly.

"Don't be. It's all right. The room ... looks great." Ava backed into her bedroom, allowing Graciela to pass. "It's fine. Just . . . in the future, check with me, okay?"

"Whatever you want, Miss Ava." Graciela, towels bunched under her arm, swept past.

"It's just Ava," she reminded her, but Graciela, her back stiff, was already walking out of the room.

"Yes, Miss—" Graciela said, then snapped her mouth shut and made her way quickly to the elevator.

For the love of God, Ava, don't pick fights. Don't make mountains out of molehills!

But she returned to the bathroom and peeked into the toilet. If there had been any trace of her medication disintegrating against the porcelain, it had been washed away in Graciela's final flush.

"Not a big deal," she said aloud, as if the maid being onto her wasn't worth the time of thinking about it.

But deep down, Ava knew she was lying to herself.

Again.

Chapter 5

Ava was hurrying down the main stairs of the house when the phone started ringing. One ring. Two. She was almost in the front hallway when she heard Virginia's voice as she answered. "Hello . . . oh, yes . . . hello, Mrs. Church . . .

Mrs. Church? Uh-oh. Ava cringed inside as she ran through the possibilities of who the caller might be: her uncle Crispin's wife, Piper, mother of Jewel-Anne and Jacob? It certainly wasn't Crispin's *first* wife, Regina, the bitter woman who had borne him his first three children: Ian, Trent, and Zinnia. Regina was long dead, the result of an automobile accident in which Uncle Crispin had been at the wheel. He'd survived and shortly thereafter had taken up with Piper. Ava wanted no part of the conversation with Piper.

". . . of course," Virginia was saying, and glanced down the hallway where she spied Ava gathering her purse. Shaking her head and waving her off, Ava hoped that the cook would get the message. Of course she didn't. "She's right here," Virginia said brightly. "Just a second."

With a smile as warm as the frosts of winter, Virginia headed her way. Ava steeled herself.

Thrusting the phone into her hand, the cook announced, "It's your aunt."

Perfect. Shooting Virginia a don't-ever-do-this-to-me-again glare, she yanked the phone to her ear and said, "Hello?"

"Oh, thank God you're all right! I was so worried after Jewel-Anne called last night." Piper. In her mind's eye, Ava conjured her impossibly thin aunt whose flaming red hair shot out of her head like lit firecrackers gone wild, all curly streams that she couldn't tame without massive amounts of hair straightener. Piper's fingers would be splayed theatrically over her more-than-ample chest, her breasts out of proportion to the rest of her tiny body.

"I'm fine," Ava assured her, and sent Virginia's broad backside a withering look as the cook lumbered toward the kitchen.

"Are you? I can't tell you how upset I've been. Ever since Jewel-Anne called me last night, I've been beside myself. I couldn't decide whether to make this phone call or not; then I said to myself, 'Ava is your niece, damn it, Piper. You need to call and see how the poor girl is doing.' "

"I'm good," Ava said dryly.

"Oh, how can you be?" Piper asked on a sigh. "After all you've been through? I know it's none of my business, but if I were you, I'd sell that drafty old house, move off that sorry rock, and start over. Most of Wyatt's business is in Seattle anyway, so why stay on the island and relive that horrible night over and over again? I'm telling you, Ava, you need to do this for your sanity. As long as you stay there, you'll be forever haunted, and that's just not healthy, don't you know? You and Wyatt, you need to have another baby and— Oh my, listen to me ramble. More advice than you ever wanted to hear."

Amen, Ava thought as her aunt tittered.

"Anyway, I just wanted to hear your voice, find out how you were doing, and I'll pass it along to your uncle, too. He's been worried sick!"

Crispin, the brother Ava's father had swindled out of his share of the Church fortune? Ava didn't believe for a second that he cared one iota what happened to her, the last of his brother's progeny.

"Oh, dear, I've got another call. We'll talk later," Piper said, and clicked off.

Ava hung up with relief and then hurried through the kitchen and out the back door before some other relative decided to pick up the phone. Who knew who Jewel-Anne had called or texted or e-mailed or Facebooked or whatever? Ava didn't want to hang around and find out. Besides, she really needed to straighten things out with Wyatt. She'd been short with him. Actually, she'd been a full-blown bitch the last couple of days, always suspicious as hell, always second-guessing his motives. And he, too, was tense. Well, who could blame him? Their fight today was indicative of the state of their marriage. Maybe she should try to start over . . . if it wasn't too late.

Casting a glance at the stable again, she thought about the new man Wyatt hired and told herself to trust that her husband had picked the right man for the job.

She walked swiftly down the back steps to the curving drive and through the massive open gates to the road leading into town. Monroe was less than half a mile down the hill, built upon the shore where the bay fingered a little inland, and Ava figured the walk would help clear her head and keep her focused.

Without meds.

Hopefully the fresh air and exercise, not to mention getting out of that prison of a house, would help dispel the headache that seemed to be constantly lurking inside her brain, ready to rage at any moment.

She slid a pair of sunglasses onto the bridge of her nose and kept to the side of the road where the gravel-covered sparse moss and weeds hadn't quite died with the coming of winter. The air was brisk, the scent of the sea strong as the sun peeked from behind thick, billowing clouds. Farther west, out to sea, a fog bank seemed to hover, as if waiting for a starting bell or some other indication to roll inland. For now, though, the day was clear, the sunlight warm against her skin despite the breath of autumn.

Once in the tiny burg of Monroe, she found her way to the marina and passed boats where fishermen were sorting their catches or cleaning their hulls or fiddling with the engines of their moored crafts.

Moored near the end of one pier was the *Holy Terror*, a walkaround-type fishing boat. Butch Johansen was seated at the helm of his small craft, perusing a newspaper. A ratty baseball cap hid the fact that he was prematurely bald, and a cigarette dangled from his lips. He wore a down vest over a sweatshirt, jeans that had seen better days, and half a week's growth of dark beard.

He glanced up as Ava's shadow fell across him.

Squinting against the sun and smoke from his slowly burning filter tip, he said, "Hey, little sister!" a name he'd tagged her with years ago when she had followed her brother and his best friend along the sheep and deer trails of the island. Most of the time they'd tried to ditch her; most of the time they'd failed. "What the hell are you doin'? I heard you half drowned last night after you went in for a quick little midnight dip."

"Is that what you heard?" She would have bristled, but this was Butch, Kelvin's best friend, someone she'd known for as long as she could remember. He was forever teasing her, and he found the fact that so many people she knew thought she was crazy somewhat amusing.

"Close enough."

"Bad news travels fast."

"In a town this size, *any* news travels at the speed of light."

"Speaking of which, think you could streak me across the bay?"

"Hot date?"

"I'm a married woman, remember."

Butch tossed his cigarette into the water. "If that's what you call it." When she was about to protest, he lifted a hand to stop her, then added, "Okay, okay, I was outta line. It's just that Wyatt and I don't exactly see eye-to-eye."

"Is there anyone you do? See eye-to-eye with, that is?"

His thick eyebrows converged beneath the frayed edges of his baseball cap. "Guess not. At least not since Kelvin." Untying the lines holding the *Holy Terror* against the dock, he added, "Your brother was one of a kind."

She felt a pang of regret. "Yeah, I know." Kelvin's death was difficult to think about, a painful wound that had never quite healed. Though it had been over four years since that horrid night, it was with them all constantly. Climbing aboard, she watched as Butch twisted his cap so that the bill pointed down his back, slid a pair of sunglasses over his nose, then started the engine. "You still miss him."

"Just every damned day. That's all."

She sat on one of the plastic seats as he maneuvered the boat away from the other crafts nestled in this little marina. She missed her brother, too. Soul deep sometimes, though the night he died was partially lost in her mind, her brain not accepting the horror of it all, though she'd been with him . . .

The mouth of the bay was tricky to navigate, as it was guarded by seven black rocks visible only in low tide but lurking under the surface when the tide was in. Treacherous and sharp, they'd been named the Hydra by her great-great-grandfather, and she always shuddered as they passed, for upon those hidden rocks, her brother had died.

Refusing to stare into the gray depths of the sea, she wrapped her arms around her torso. For his part, Butch didn't so much as glance in her direction as they passed the only dark tip currently visible, a stony protrusion thick with barnacles and starfish.

Once in the open water, Butch let the engine out. Churning a heavy wake, the little boat cut through the dark waters where a stiff, salty breeze was whipping up whitecaps, and seagulls soared in the clear blue skies.

Her spirits lifted as soon as she stepped ashore on the dock in Anchorville. It was afternoon now, the sun sinking lower in the western sky, but she spied the boat Wyatt had used earlier tied to its mooring. A sleek inboard cruiser, it boasted a galley and sleeping quarters, though it was rarely used for anything but transport to and from the island.

"You want me to wait?" Butch asked after she handed him a twenty-dollar bill, which he made a big show of not wanting but pocketed anyway.

"No. I'll ride with Wyatt."

"Sure?"

"Absolutely."

Butch cocked a bushy, doubting eyebrow but nodded. At the top of the graying steps leading into the town, she paused and looked out to sea. Spying the *Holy Terror* streaking away from the mainland, she held up a hand and waved, then let it fall. Butch didn't so much as cast a glance over his shoulder.

She checked her watch and saw that it was two-fifteen. The ferry to the island returned at four, so she'd have to be quick if she wanted to finish everything on her agenda.

First stop was to try and catch up with Tanya, a high school friend who had dated Ava's cousin Trent—who just happened to be Ian's twin—for a few years. The relationship had fizzled when she'd met and quickly eloped with Russell Denton, a bad-ass cowboy type who couldn't stay faithful, sober, or away from poker tables.

That marriage had crumbled fairly quickly but not before she'd gotten pregnant . . . twice. Tanya and Russ had been involved in one of those mercurial and toxic relationships that they could never quite end. Eventually, less than a year ago, the divorce papers had been inked. Now a single mother of seven-year-old Brent and his older sister, Bella, Tanya was the owner of Shear Madness, one of the two beauty shops in Anchorville. With her nose for business and ear for town gossip, Tanya was doing all right, or so she'd told Ava. Tanya had left the marriage in possession of the house, an older bungalow built on one of the town's steep side streets, and this little shop. She was one of the few people Ava felt she could trust entirely.

As clouds gathered overhead, Ava hurried to the beauty shop, some five blocks from the docks and wedged between a deli and the best bakery in the county. Her stomach growled as she passed the bakery's open door where she caught a whiff of freshly brewed coffee laced with the scent of warm bread and cinnamon.

The door to Tanya's salon was closed, the lights dimmed, and a sign in the window had been posted with a quickly written note saying that the shop would reopen in the morning.

"Great," Ava muttered, disappointed. Then again, what had she expected? It wasn't as if she'd made an appointment. She glanced into the darkened interior where the walls were painted a soft pink and the decor was an homage to the sixties, with framed black-and-white pictures of women icons of the decade. Everyone from Marilyn Monroe, Jackie Kennedy, and Brigitte Bardot to Twiggy and Audrey Hepburn stared down at the four stations, now empty, their black faux-leather chairs unoccupied.

She grabbed a coffee to go at the bakery, resisted the urge to buy the last cinnamon roll in the display case, then tried calling Tanya only to get voice mail, where a lifeless computer's voice instructed her to leave a message.

She didn't.

Instead, she sipped her coffee and walked to the corner

where she caught a glimpse of the bay and Church Island, still visible despite the fog bank slowly rolling in from the sea. She even made out Neptune's Gate on one end and, just visible on the southern tip of the island, the dark roof of Sea Cliff. The institution had been closed for six years now, forced to shut its doors permanently when the last of its criminally insane inmates, Lester Reece, had escaped. Reece had been a suspect in several local homicides and had been convicted of murdering his wife and her best friend in one of his many fits of rage. His defense team had insisted that he'd been suffering from paranoid schizophrenia, and in the end, Reece had been sentenced to live out his days at Sea Cliff.

Then he'd somehow duped the guards, slipped through the iron gates, and disappeared into the night.

Ava felt a chill when she thought of Reece and his heinous acts. It seemed impossible now to think of him, and the others who had been equally dangerous, living so close to Neptune's Gate. Of course, as a child, she'd accepted it as just a part of Church Island's lore.

"So, who sprung you?" A male voice cut into her reverie, and she nearly jumped out of her skin.

Looking over her shoulder, she caught sight of Austin Dern heading her way. A beat-up backpack was slung over his shoulder, and the shadow of his beard had darkened overnight.

"I'm not locked up."

Yet, hadn't she thought of the house as a prison just an hour earlier?

"If you say so." Not bothering to mask his skepticism, he shifted the backpack higher onto his shoulder. "You coming or going?"

"Coming. Just got here . . . I have a few errands to run and I thought maybe I'd look up an old friend."

"Good idea."

"And you?"

"Needed a few things," he said easily. "I checked in Monroe, but you can't get much more than stale pretzels and pepperoni that's months past its pull date at Frank's Food-O-Mart. The name's kind of a lie, y'know. Not much would pass as food in there."

She felt a smile threaten the corner of her lips. God, when was the last time that she'd grinned or been even slightly amused?

"Frank's, that's the name, right?" he asked, squinting.

"Monroe's answer to 7-Eleven. And you can get corn nuts there," she said, nodding. "If you're desperate. I don't think they have pull dates."

His gaze sharpened on her face as if he'd just discovered something unexpected. "You could be right." He hitched his chin toward the marina, where there were several boats that were used as private taxis to and from the island. "Depending on how long you'll be, we could share a ride."

Shaking her head, she demurred, "Don't wait. I'll probably catch the ferry."

"I don't mind."

He didn't budge, and she wondered what he really thought of her after dragging her kicking and screaming out of the bay the night before. "You sure?"

"Yeah, really. Despite what you might think or may have heard, I don't need a keeper."

"I didn't say—"

"I know." She held up a hand to ward off any further arguments. "Thanks."

He nodded, then started toward the waterfront. "Your loss."

"If you say so," she said, throwing his words back at him, and the sound of his laughter tumbled back at her. Watching him walk down the hill toward the marina, she noted the breadth of his shoulders pulling at the seams of his jacket and the way the faded denim of his jeans fell over buttocks that moved easily.

Heat climbed up the back of her neck, and though she told

herself it didn't hurt anyone to "check out" another man, her gaze slid to the slip where Wyatt had docked the family cabin cruiser.

"Get over yourself," she whispered under her breath, then waited, sipping her cooling coffee until she saw Dern climb into a boat and negotiate a ride. As he settled into a seat, he glanced over his shoulder and up the hill, his eyes finding her before the captain started the taxi's engine and maneuvered his boat out of the marina.

She wondered about him. How he'd found the job on the island.

Nothing sinister in looking for a job.

So why did she feel she'd met him before? That Austin Dern had his own set of secrets? That he wasn't who he said he was?

Because you're a suspicious bitch.

She smiled a little, then as the first raindrops fell, turned up the hood of her jacket and hurried along the side streets. Head bent against the wind, she decided to cut through the park where an elderly woman was herding two dogs on separate leashes. Half-grown whippets were pulling this way and that, nosing the wet grass and charging after a gray squirrel that had the nerve to scamper from one oak tree to the next.

"Harold! Maude! Come along!" the woman said, pulling hard on the leashes, while the thin dogs strained to give chase. They lunged and stood on their back legs as the woman tried in vain to haul them toward a little blue Subaru parked near the curb. "It's raining!" she reminded her pups, though neither Harold nor Maude seemed to notice. "Oh, for goodness' sake. How about a treat? Come *on* now!"

Her dogs didn't so much as flick an ear in her direction. Ava skirted the woman's unruly charges and wound up at the far edge of the park, where a wrought-iron gate was open to the street. She was about to jaywalk when she stopped dead in her tracks.

Her husband was holding open the door to a coffee shop and looking toward the interior. A second later, Dr. McPherson emerged. Wearing boots, a slim skirt, and sleek leather jacket, the psychologist opened an umbrella against the rain, then turned and with Wyatt's hand on her elbow, walked away from the park, heading toward the bay.

Ava stood frozen to the spot.

Her heart drummed in her chest as she watched the couple leave. Wyatt's head bent low under the umbrella, and his fingers never left the crook of Evelyn McPherson's elbow. It was almost as if he were shepherding her along the wet sidewalk, as if he had some proprietary claim to his wife's doctor.

What did that mean? She barely noticed the steady drip of the rain or a teenager who whipped by her, sending up spray from a puddle.

It's nothing, she told herself. *Nothing.*

Yet she was left with the same cold feeling of suspicion that had been with her since leaving the hospital, that everyone she knew wasn't as he or she pretended to be. Not even her own husband.

Fortunately, Wyatt had been so wrapped up in Dr. McPherson that he hadn't noticed his bedraggled wife standing in the rain. Which was just as well. It was far better if no one had any idea about what she was doing on the mainland.

They already thought she was nuts as it was.

If anyone on the island realized she had started seeing a hypnotist, there would be no end to the questions and raised eyebrows.

Trouble was, she didn't really blame them.

Even to her own troubled mind, it sounded lame.

Chapter 6

Once she was satisfied that Wyatt and the good doctor were out of sight, Ava tossed her coffee cup and its cold remains into a nearby trash can, then hiked the remaining three blocks to her hypnotist's studio.

Telling herself it meant nothing that Wyatt was meeting with her doctor, that she had to have a little faith, she hurried down the curved steps to the basement level, then paused at the door of the rambling Victorian home. Once owned by a timber baron, it had been cut into several apartments and was now owned by Cheryl Reynolds, a fiftyish woman who claimed to have a "gift" to not only be able to hypnotize her clients, but also, for a few extra dollars, predict their future.

You've never been one to believe in hocus-pocus or parlor games or hypnosis, have you? Remember going to the state fair and seeing a hypnotist with volunteers from the audience, how they all appeared to sleep, then got up and stomped around, then flapped their arms as if they were chickens? Is that what you want? The first time, this didn't work, right? But still you're back here, hoping for what? Answers about your son? Repressed memories brought to the surface?

Ava's shoulders tightened. She felt a cool breath of wind tugging on her hair and remembered the dream, how real it had been, then yesterday seeing Noah on the dock.

She pressed the buzzer.

Two of Cheryl's stray cats watched from their perches in the retaining wall as Ava waited, second-guessing herself.

Half a minute later, the door opened.

"Ava, so good to see you," Cheryl said as she motioned Ava inside.

Barely five feet, Cheryl hid her curves with a tie-dyed caftan, and her blond curls were banded away from her round face, which was creased with worry. No doubt the story of Ava's latest crazy dive into the bay had reached her ears, too, through the coffee shops and tearooms of the town. "So, tell me," she insisted as soft music whispered through the hallways and the scent of incense couldn't quite mask the thin, sharp odors of mildew and cat urine. "How are you?"

"I keep saying I'm fine, but of course . . ."

"You're not."

"It's the dreams again. I know it sounds crazy, impossible, but I see him. I see my baby." She fought to keep her voice from cracking when she thought of Noah.

Cheryl patted her arm. "Come on in. Let's see what we can do." Waving for Ava to follow, Cheryl led her through a series of connecting rooms to her studio, a converted bedroom painted an icy gray that reminded Ava of the sea in winter. "You can have a seat in the recliner, or if you prefer, the couch." She paused to light a candle.

This was Ava's second visit. The first stab at hypnosis hadn't been all that effective; at least there had been no major breakthroughs, no startling revelations that had helped Ava understand her own troubled mind.

Yet, she was back.

Still restless. Still searching.

She forced herself to settle into the oversized La-Z-Boy and raised the footrest. As she closed her eyes, she felt the warmth of a cozy blanket as Cheryl draped a quilt over her legs. Dear God, she was tired, and here she felt safe. At peace. A relief that was never present at the island.

"So I want you to go deep today," Cheryl said softly as she settled into a nearby chair. "Just relax and go deeper . . ."

Ava was barely aware of the sound of her voice or the relaxing music as she slid beneath the veil. It was a weird sensation, as she wasn't truly asleep, though she wasn't sharply awake either, but hovering between the two states. Dreamlike . . .

"Breathe deeply . . ." Cheryl's voice was gentle, yet firm.

Ava drew in a long breath and the tension seemed to drain from her muscles.

"Now go deeper . . . to your private place . . ."

The place of calm. That's how she thought of it. In her mind's eye, she saw herself in that sunny cove near the waterfall. She was wearing a yellow sundress, her hair pulled away from her face by a simple rubber band. White sand shimmered in the sunlight filtering through the trees and a gentle spray touched her cheeks. The water was clear and cool and . . .

Noah was there, too, she realized. Playing in the sand, his chubby fingers digging through grains that glinted in the sun's warm rays, he was only a few feet from her.

"Baby," she said aloud, and he grinned, showing off his tiny teeth.

"Mommy! See what I find!" He held up a clam shell, golden and glistening, beautiful in its complexity but broken and chipped.

"Careful, honey, that's sharp."

She walked toward him, her shadow falling across his upturned face, and she saw a bit of challenge in his eyes. "That's why it's called a razor clam . . ."

"It's mine!"

"I know, but let Mama see it. Just to make sure it's okay."

"No! Mine!" he repeated, his little chin jutted defiantly, the shell clenched in his fist.

"Of course it is." She knelt beside him, her arm outstretched. "I just want to make sure it won't hurt you."

But he wasn't listening. Instead he was backing up, away from her, holding tight to the shell, blood beginning to show between his chubby fingers.

"Noah, please—"

"No!"

More blood.

She lunged for him, but on short little legs, he turned and sped off toward the water.

"Noah!" she screamed, frantic. "Stop!"

In that mind-numbing instant, she saw her mistake. She took off after him at a dead run, her bare feet pounding the sand.

"Noah!" Her voice caught in the wind as the ocean darkened from aquamarine to slate gray, shifted from a tranquil lagoon to the dark and roiling sea. "Stop! Oh, please! Baby!" Horrified, she watched him step into the water, the waves lapping, foam crashing around him.

She was breathing hard, chasing him, but just as she lunged forward, grasping at him, he turned, eyes round with fear; then his little feet slid off an underwater shelf and he disappeared into the deep water. "Noah!" she cried, desperately. "Baby—"

"And you're waking up," a voice said from a distance.

Sobs erupted from her throat.

"Breathe deeply. And you're opening your eyes—"

Ava's eyes flew open and she found herself half lying in the recliner in Cheryl's studio. Her heart was pounding frantically, her fingers clenched into the chair's leather arms, her mind filled with dark images that brought a soft cry from her lips.

"And you're calm now . . ." Cheryl sounded certain.

Ava slowly let out her breath, the tension draining from her body again as she felt the relief that her horrid dream was passing. She unclenched her fingers, let her shoulders slump. "Oh, God," she whispered, glancing up at Cheryl and feeling tears fill her eyes. Damn she didn't want to cry.

"You relived it."

"No." Shaking her head, she sniffed and slapped her tears away. "That's just it; I don't think I ever lived it the first time. There's no *re*living it."

"That you're aware of."

"Damn it all."

"You okay?"

"Do I look okay?" she asked, then nearly laughed at the absurdity of it all.

Cheryl leaned closer as the candle burned. "It's your fears coming to the surface," Cheryl said, "but what concerns me is that they permeate your quiet place. Before you can completely relax, before we can go deeper, the visions return."

"I know." This was only her second session, and in the first, she'd had a similar experience, yet Ava was convinced that if she could ever get past the mental barrier she'd created for herself, she would remember so much more, find the truth.

"Here." Cheryl offered her a cup of steaming herbal tea that smelled like ginger. "Want to try again?"

Sipping the tea, she shook her head. "Another time." Another swallow. "You have any other clients who have this same problem?"

Cheryl smiled as the door to her room slid open and a skinny tortoiseshell cat slithered inside. "There was a guy a few years ago who had a major mental block, but we got through it. I think we can with you, too . . . You get right to the edge and pull back."

"How is that possible? I thought with hypnosis"—she shivered inside—"that, you know, you could delve past every-thing."

"Everyone's different, Ava. Even the most willing partici-pants sometimes are difficult to reach. We'll try again, if that's what you want."

"Okay." She sipped her tea, then, pulling herself together, paid Cheryl and made an appointment for the next week.

Even though she half suspected the whole hypnosis thing wasn't working, she couldn't give up. At least not yet. As she made her way back to the dock, she wondered if anything could help or if she would forever be trapped in this state of unknow-ing, a hellish purgatory that had no end.

Her recent hospital stay hadn't done more than calm her, and her regular therapy sessions with Dr. McPherson hadn't provided any major breakthroughs. Hypnosis had been a last grasp on her part, a desperate measure, and it, too, hadn't suc-ceeded in opening repressed memories or shrouded truths.

Maybe there are none. Maybe the answers you're searching for will never be found.

That thought was chilling, and it chased her through the nar-row streets and down the barnacled steps to the dock where she found Butch, seated at the helm of the *Holy Terror* as he flipped through the pages of a worn paperback and smoked a cigarette.

"I thought I told you I'd catch a ride with Wyatt," she said as he glanced up to peer at her over the tops of his sunglasses.

"You did." He set the book down and started the engine.

"So?"

"You're a liar, Ava. We both know it." He flashed her a smile that made him look ten years younger, then waved her into the boat. "Climb aboard."

"You didn't have to come back for me."

"I didn't."

"Now who's the liar?"

He snorted, adjusting the brim of his hat. "Wasn't doin' anything anyway. Fishin's lousy."

"So bad that you had to hang around here and wait for me."

"Nothin' better goin' on."

She didn't believe him for a second, but she took the ride.

As she settled into her seat, Butch tossed the ropes holding the boat to its mooring inside the hull, then stood behind the helm. Threading the *Holy Terror* through the other docked fishing and pleasure vessels, he didn't notice as she sank deeper into the plastic cushions and told herself the vision she'd had during hypnosis was nothing, just her active imagination. Again.

She heard the engine begin to race as Butch let out the throttle, and when she opened her eyes again, the marina and Anchorville were behind them and the gray expanse of water between the island and mainland was narrowing.

She told herself she wasn't going back to prison, that she was a free woman, but as the *Holy Terror* bucked a little as the prow hit the wake of a speed boat cruising the opposite direction, she knew she was lying to herself.

Ava wrapped her arms around her middle and felt a cold spreading through her body as Neptune's Gate came clearly into view. It had once been the one place in the world she'd felt safe and secure. She'd worked hard to own all of it . . . well, *almost* all of it. There still was Jewel-Anne's portion. Jewel-Anne was the only holdout, the one cousin who hadn't been swayed by money.

"Why would I sell it? I *love* it here, Ava," she'd said, looking up at her with her pretty, little girl face and seemingly innocent eyes. They'd been in the back hallway, near the elevator shaft, Jewel, for once, without one of her dolls. "It's more important than any amount of money."

"You could live with friends, be in the city—Seattle or San Francisco, even L.A.—instead of being cooped up here on the island." Ava had already offered her cousin nearly twice what Jewel's share of the estate was worth.

Jewel's perfect little mouth had twisted into a wry smile and her eyes had seemed to shine with superiority. "I said I love it here." She'd flipped her hair over her shoulder, turned her wheelchair around, and waited for the descending elevator car. As it clunked to a stop and the doors whispered open, she'd cast one last glance at Ava and vowed, "I'll never leave. This is my home."

Home, Ava thought sourly now as she focused on Jewel-Anne's corner room, the one tucked inside the middle floor of the windowed turret. From inside, one could view the gardens, bay, mainland, and open sea, and it was Jewel-Anne's favorite spot, one where she'd said often enough, "I can see where it happened, you know . . . the place where Kelvin drowned. . . ." Her smile would always turn wistful, then sad, and there was always an unspoken accusation in her eyes.

She'd had to voice it only once. "You killed him, Ava," she'd whispered while staring out the window and clutching the black-haired doll with porcelain skin and one eye that never quite opened. Jewel-Anne's voice had been filled with a quiet, repressed hatred. "He loved you and . . . and you killed him." At that moment she'd looked up, her upper lip curling slightly, her fingers twisting a lock of the doll's straight hair. "You're a hypocrite, Ava. A liar, a murderer, and God only knows what else. You *act* at being a wife, *pretend* to be a loving mother."

Ava had been stronger then and nearly slapped her martyred cousin. "And you're a bitch, Jewel-Anne. I don't care if you are wheelchair bound—you're a straight-up bitch."

"Perfect," her cousin had said. "Because you're stuck with me. I will *never* sell my share of this house to you. *Never!*" Her fingers had stopped moving and hatred seemed to emanate from her small, broken body. She raised a knowing eyebrow and said in a succinct whisper, "The truth is, Ava, I'd rather die first."

Chapter 7

While on the mainland, Dern had bought a fifth of Jack Daniel's, a value-sized bag of Doritos, and twenty pounds of dog food. Not exactly nutrition central, and it did suggest a commitment to the mutt, but so what?

That wasn't the big deal, Dern thought as he set the bottle in one of the near-empty cupboards. Groceries weren't the true reason he'd headed to the mainland. The annoying thing was that he'd learned little on his quick trip.

He'd frequented a grocery store, the liquor outlet, a coffee shop, a sandwich place, and a bar, striking up conversations about Church Island and its inhabitants, and no one seemed to know much other than the same old local gossip he was already wading through.

Yeah, the original owner, a sea captain, had bought up most of the land. Yeah, the place was worth a lot these days, and it was owned almost in its entirety by Ava Church Garrison. All agreed she was "beautiful, and let me tell you, she can be a hard-nosed bitch of a businesswoman when she wants to be. Went completely around the bend when her kid disappeared, ended up in a mental hospital because she tried to slit her wrists or some damned thing. As nuts as the rest of the family." Local consensus had it she was married to a lawyer from the city, and there was more than a good chance he married her for her money and oh, yeah, the Church family? A bunch of loonies; couldn't be trusted. Even that one in the wheelchair, Jewel-Something-or-Other, odd duck, that one. But she at least had a few brains; Jewel was the one relative who hadn't sold her share of Neptune's Gate to her cousin, the only holdout. Funny thing, that.

At a dive of a bar named the Salty Dog, Dern had brought up Sea Cliff Hospital and had suffered a few long looks of reproof. The consensus seemed to be that losing the hospital wasn't a bad thing. In fact, the three men nursing drinks at the Dog seemed to share a sense of relief.

"Sea Cliff?" Gil, an older guy with long white hair and a voice that was gravelly from years of smoking cigarettes, repeated when Dern had asked about the abandoned asylum. "After that nutcase Lester Reece escaped and disappeared, everyone in Anchorville was mighty glad Sea Cliff closed its gates." He'd taken a long sip from his whiskey as some country single had played. Shaking his head, Gil added, "No good ever came from that looney bin. Let me tell you. That place was more of a prison than it ever was a hospital."

The wide-girthed, silent man who had been seated on the bar stool next to Gil had nodded his agreement before burying his nose into a half-full beer glass.

"Fuckin' nut jobs in there. Wouldn't have gone there if I was dyin'!" a third man interjected, a scrawny guy with gapped teeth in a worn flannel shirt and baggy jeans who slid his glass toward the bartender. "Hey, Hal, I'll have another."

Just then the phone rang and the barkeep said, "In a sec, Corky," then swept the receiver to his ear and propped it there with one shoulder as he drew another Budweiser from the tap.

"I heard the local shrink Dr. McPhee—I think that's her name—used to work out there." Dern nodded toward the plate-glass window with its glowing neon sign filling half the space that overlooked the bay and, farther out, the island.

"McPherson." Gil shook his head of white hair. "Maybe. Don't know."

The scrawny guy cackled. "Yeah, McPherson, uh-huh, that's right. My aunt went to see her there a while back. They had clinics for the public, outside the gates of that damned place."

"On the island?"

"Yep. But they closed, too. Anyway, Aunt Audrey, she didn't like anything about Sea Cliff. It bothered her being so close to the hospital. Quit after three sessions."

"So where'd McPherson go?"

Corky lifted a shoulder. "Got an office somewhere around here."

"In Anchorville?" Dern asked.

"Near Third Street. But she still ferries herself out to the island." He was nodding, agreeing with himself. "The woman who owns most of it, she's a real head case. Went off the rails when her kid drowned."

The muscles in the back of Dern's neck tightened a bit.

"Went missing," Gil corrected. "No body was ever found."

Corky snorted. "If the kid was alive, he'd have shown up by now." He snagged the beer that Hal scooted across the scarred bar. "Thanks. Y'know, some folks think Lester Reece came back after he escaped and was behind the kid's disappearance."

"The prisoner at Sea Cliff?" Dern asked, trying not to show too much interest, though anything about the island caught his attention.

"Yup." Corky took a long swallow from his glass.

"Conjecture," Gil disagreed. "Reece, too, is probably dead."

"Nah-ah," Corky disagreed. "People 'round here, they seen him."

"Recently?" Dern asked.

"No way." Gil pulled a disbelieving face. "No one saw him since right after his escape."

Corky complained, "But Old Remus Calhoun—"

"Is a bald-faced liar. Likes to stir things up." Gil seemed convinced that the rumors were false. "Remus claims he saw Big Foot, too, and swears when he was in Scotland he caught a glimpse of Nessie." He took a long swallow from his drink, then wiped his mouth with his sleeve and said, "What're the chances of that?"

"So no one saw Reece again? After his escape?" Dern asked, and the silent guy shook his head and even Corky gave it a rest.

"Most likely drowned tryin' to get away from the island— y'know like those guys who used to try and break out of Alcatraz," Gil thought aloud. "One of 'em Churches claims they seen him swimmin' away that day."

"Which one?" Dern asked.

"Oh, damn . . ." He paused, thinking. "He was the brother of that invalid girl up at the island. What's his name? Jim or Jack or . . ."

Corky snorted with an edge of disgust. "Jacob."

"Yeah, that's it," Gil agreed. "The computer geek."

Silent Guy nodded again.

Gil added, "Old Lester, he's kinda like our own version of Elvis, though. People keep thinking they see him, just like they did with the King for years, but nah, he ain't around. No more'n D. B. Cooper is." He let out a hard laugh that morphed into a coughing fit. As he hacked, his sallow face flushed a sudden deep red.

"You okay, Gil?" the barkeep asked as Gil got control and took a long sip of his drink.

"Yeah." Gil cleared his throat.

"Maybe ya should switch to menthols," Corky advised.

"And maybe you should shut up." Gil sent Corky the evil eye, but the smaller man didn't seem to notice or care as he burrowed his nose into his drink.

Dern finished his own draft and didn't ask any more questions about Church Island or its inhabitants. But he thought he'd have a talk with Jacob, who, now pushing thirty, was off and on the island, always "going to school." He spent a few minutes just listening as the others talked, and the conversation turned naturally to the coming crabbing season, then the latest football news. He drained his drink, set some bills on the bar, and left the three men still arguing about the Seahawks' chances of making it to the play-offs. Gil was certain Seattle would pull through, but the silent guy just shook his head and motioned for another drink. *Ever the optimist,* Dern thought caustically.

As the door closed behind him, he heard Corky's shrill voice still bitching about "that fuckin' idiot of a coach."

Now, back on the island, with the old dog curled up in front of the wood stove, Dern thought about Ava Church and decided most of the rumors about her had a modicum of truth. She was gorgeous with that thick, dark hair, and beneath the sadness in her eyes, there was a spark of intelligence and more than a bit of rebellion. She'd apparently been a dynamo, a self-driven woman, before fate had beaten her down.

She was attractive, even sexy, despite the ugly scars he'd seen running up her wrists, evidence that some of the town gossip was spot-on.

He decided against pouring himself a drink and went out to check on the stock. He'd tried to run down Jacob, but once again, the guy wasn't around, the door to his basement apartment locked tight.

Wyatt was waiting for her.

Seated in the den, the television turned to some news channel, he looked up when Ava walked through the archway to the kitchen and set the remote on the table. "I heard you went into town."

She nodded. "So did you."

"I know. I invited you, remember? Lunch?"

"Wyatt—"

"You made it pretty clear that you didn't want to go with me because you didn't believe that I'd come to bed last night."

She felt her temper ignite but knew renewing their fight wouldn't solve anything. She held up a hand before the old debate heated up again. "Let's not go there again."

He seemed to smolder for a moment, then said, "Okay, you're right. Arguing's not going to help." Some of the tension left his features. "No big deal. We can have lunch another time. I was just surprised to hear that you went into town."

"It was kind of a whim," she said, hoping to smooth the waters. "I just needed to get out. Tried to see Tanya, but she wasn't around. How about you?"

"Business," he said. "Checked in with Outreach."

Outreach was a small offshoot of the Seattle firm for which he worked. So they were both equivocating, stepping around the truth. When had they gotten so distant, so far away that they needed to avoid the real issues in order to communicate? He must've felt it, too, that fine line of trust between them fraying, as he was staring at her as if she were a complex puzzle he couldn't quite piece together.

"You could have come with me," he said softly. "I asked."

"I know. I just . . . I thought we needed a little time apart, even though we get plenty." She glanced around the room with its cozy furniture and big windows. "But I did need to get out of here, you know, had to see something besides these four walls."

"I suppose." Then nodding, he added, "Yeah, I get it. You could go stir-crazy here."

"Some people think I already am."

He snorted a laugh, walked up, and hugged her fiercely. "I know," he whispered against her hair. "We're working on that." He'd always been strong and athletic, and whenever he'd held her, it had felt that he'd never wanted to let go. Now the scent of his aftershave reminded her of what it had been like to fall in love with him. Tears burned the edges of her eyes, but she blinked them back. "Next time, come with me," he said.

"Okay," she agreed, fighting the urge to break down and cling to him. *But, really, do you trust him? Even now as he's lying to you?*

She let go of him and started to step away, but his hand stayed on her arm. "What's happened to us, Wyatt? We used to be . . ."

"Closer?"

"I was going to say we used to have fun with each other."

"I know." He kissed the top of her head. "We will again soon. I promise."

He had the brains not to add, *when you get better,* but it was there, standing between them like an invisible barrier, one they couldn't really define, much less scale.

"I'll hold you to it," she said, lying through her teeth as he reached for his jacket, which had been slung negligently over a nearby chair.

"Good. Now, look, I have to go to Seattle—it's just for a night, maybe two, depending on how receptive my client is to negotiating his way out of a lease; then I'll be back. In the meantime, you can always reach me on my cell."

She nodded.

"And I've asked Dr. McPherson to stop by again."

"I already have an appointment with her later in the week."

"I know, but I saw her today in town. She asked about you and so we set it up." He lifted a shoulder. "Couldn't hurt, now, could it?"

She was surprised that he brought up the psychiatrist. "So you just ran into her?"

"Not really. Once I learned that I'd be away, I called her, met her for coffee, and suggested she spend some time here."

"She's busy."

"Not *that* busy," he disagreed. "Besides, the mainland is just a boat ride away. Turns out, she liked the idea." His expression turned serious. "She wants to help you, Ava, and she might just be able to if you'd stop fighting her."

"I don't fight her."

He pressed a finger to her lips. "Just try. Okay?"

When he withdrew his hand, she asked, "Do you think I'm crazy, Wyatt?"

"Confused."

"Don't slide away from the issue."

He let out his breath. "I think you need help. Psychiatric help. And so do all the doctors at St. Brendan's. You're the one who wanted to be released, to come back here, to . . . face your demons." Touching her lightly on the shoulder, he added, "But you can't do it alone, Ava. And no one else here is qualified to help you. Not me or Graciela or Khloe, not even Demetria, though she's a nurse. We just don't know how best to deal with this. But Dr. McPherson does." His smile was troubled, his eyebrows drawn together. "You have to trust us, Ava. We're all here to help you, but we just can't do it if you don't help yourself. And going to a hypnotist . . . really?"

Her breath caught in her throat. Denial leaped to her lips.

Before she could protest, he reminded her, "You have to remember that Anchorville is a small town. Maybe not as small as Monroe, but small enough." With a glance at his watch, he swore under his breath, then kissed her forehead. "Got to run. Butch is probably already here."

"Butch?"

"Johansen," Wyatt clarified, and Ava's heart sank. "Kelvin's friend. He ferried you back and forth to the island, right?"

"Yes."

While slipping his arms into his jacket, Wyatt was nodding, as if he already knew the answer. "I called him. Asked him to pick you up and then wait for me once you got home." Wyatt eyed her speculatively. "He didn't mention it?"

"No." She shook her head and felt a pang of betrayal.

"Well, he's my ride to the mainland. I thought I'd leave the cruiser here, in case anyone needs it." Was there just the hint of cruelty in his gaze, a smidgeon of superiority? Or did she imagine it as he found a raincoat in the front closet and grabbed his small bag, just big enough for his computer, toiletries, and a suit.

And then he was gone, the door closing with a soft thud. She peered out the window and saw the *Holy Terror* moored at the marina.

What the hell was that all about?

Why hadn't Butch said anything?

He'd never liked Wyatt, never gone to any lengths to hide it, and yet . . . She clenched her fists, digging her fingernails into her palms. *You're overthinking things. Let it go. Wyatt's your husband. Do NOT second-guess his motives.*

But she couldn't help herself.

Wondered if she would ever really trust him again.

Bothered, she took the steps two at a time to her room and once inside, checked to find that the unidentified key she'd discovered in her sweater pocket was still tucked away in the jeans she'd worn yesterday. Made of tarnished metal, the key appeared old, as if it had been fashioned for an ancient door lock. Too big for a trunk or a newer cupboard or cabinet. She tried it on her door, then, because she heard Graciela on the stairs, slipped it into the top drawer of her desk, under some papers, and told herself she'd figure out what door it unlocked later. She had no idea how it had gotten into the pocket, and that, too, was a mystery to be solved.

Maybe it had been a mistake. An oversight.

Yeah, right, like maybe someone slipped his or her key into your pocket . . . as if maybe that someone had been wearing your sweater? Or was hiding it quickly? Or did someone drop it unknowingly?

Into your pocket? Seriously, Ava. Someone meant for you to have it, and at least it's something to do. An action to take.

An action it was high time she did take.

Walking to the window, she caught a glimpse of Wyatt heading toward the marina and flagging down Butch, who, waiting in the *Holy Terror,* waved back.

"Great," she said under her breath, and chalked off another person she'd allowed into the "Can Be Trusted" column of acquaintances in her life.

Staring through the glass, she watched Wyatt settle into the very seat she'd occupied earlier as the *Holy Terror* headed into the waters of the bay. Ava was left with the unsettling truth that she couldn't trust anyone associated with the island. Worse yet, she couldn't shake the feeling that Wyatt, the man she should trust above all others, wasn't the man she'd thought she'd married.

Then again, was she the girl he'd fallen in love with?

Not a chance, she thought as she caught a glimpse of her ghostlike reflection in the window's watery glass. That girl had died long ago. . . .

Then who the hell are you?

She swallowed hard and felt a rising sense of panic. Somehow, somewhere she'd lost herself. Not that she'd been a sweet innocent when she'd met Wyatt, but in the years since, she had definitely changed. No longer was she the hardheaded, sometimes even ruthless, businesswoman. Okay, maybe she was still hardheaded, but once she'd been athletic and bold, nothing like this shell of a person who stood at the window now.

She placed her hands on the pane, as if trying to grab hold of something of the woman she'd once been. Staring through the pale ghost of her reflection to the surly sea beyond, watching as the boat her husband was aboard grew smaller, she felt a silent rage steal through her blood, a fury at the impotent person she'd become.

"No more," she whispered, her hand sliding down the glass to clench into a fist. No more weakling crippled by her own fears.

It was time to take control of her life again. If that meant going against all of her "well-intentioned" relatives, then so be it.

It was time to fight back. Hard.

Chapter 8

The next day, Ava felt stronger, ready to take on the world, a part of her that had been missing surfacing for the first time since she'd been released from the hospital.

If she'd had nightmares during the night, she couldn't remember anything about them this morning, though there was a lingering worry hovering around her brain. She tried to shake it off. Today she wasn't going to let any stupid dream shackle her, remembered or otherwise.

Tossing off the bedcovers, she got to her feet, ignoring the headache pounding at the base of her skull as she showered, then slipped into her favorite robe and cinched the belt around her waist.

With her hair barely towel-dried, she walked to the bedroom window, threw back the curtains, and opened the blinds. Her stomach clenched, anxiety twisting her nerves, but when she stared through the old glass this morning, she didn't see her son standing on the dock. There was no terrifying image of her boy teetering over the dark, swirling water.

"Thank God," she whispered, one hand still wrapped around

the cord of the blinds, her shoulders slumping with sudden, nearly overwhelming relief.

Maybe she was getting better.

This morning as she peered through the window, she saw a rising mist and the shivering fronds of dew-covered ferns. The damp stone pathway split, one branch leading to the private apartment in the basement, the other curving past the garden and toward the closest pasture. It was that walkway that wound around to the side of the house, the one that was just visible from her bedroom. She caught a glimpse of Austin Dern rounding up the horses. Dun, palomino, black, and bay, the animals were shrouded in the thickening fog and seemed to appear, then fade as they followed the tall man out of her range of view toward the stable at the back of the house.

She hurried out of her room, past the stairway and down a short hall to one of the unused guest rooms. Its door stuck a little but finally opened to display a bed that hadn't been slept in since the summer and a side table with books collecting dust. Portraits of her great-grandparents had been hung here years ago, their stern, unsmiling visages glowering down on anyone who stepped across the threshold.

The air inside was still, smelling of dust and disuse, odors that couldn't quite be freshened with the fragrant sachets tucked in the empty bureau drawers. Even the scented candles placed in front of an antique mirror had lost their aromas.

She crossed to the window where sheer curtains draped over blinds that had been closed for months. With a flick of her wrist, she snapped them open and stared through the dirty glass. From her vantage point, Ava viewed the outbuildings located behind the house and the fields of wet grass that sprawled past the fence line to the brush and thickets of fir and hemlock that crawled up the hillside.

Dern was working with the horses near the stable.

Hidden by sheer curtains, she studied the man who had been

her rescuer, the man Wyatt had hired, yet had neglected to mention. With broad shoulders and a long stride, Austin Dern seemed comfortable with the horses, as if he'd been around livestock all of his life; the stereotypical Hollywood cowboy wearing disreputable jeans, a beat-up sheepskin jacket, and cowboy boots. In need of a haircut and a shave, he opened a gate and shooed the horses through. The only thing missing from the image was a Stetson and an accompanying drawl.

He looked up then, as if he were suddenly aware of her interest. The hairs on the back of her neck lifted as if a cold breeze had swept over her nape. Again the eerie feeling that he was familiar brushed her soul.

"You're imagining it," she whispered, then stepped away from the window and told herself she hadn't seen him somewhere in her youth. . . .

She remembered the feel of his strong arms surrounding her, the pressure of his wet body against her as he'd dragged her from the sea.

It all seemed surreal now, as if it had happened to someone else.

Surely, if she'd met him before, she could recall . . . ? From the shadows of the unused room, she watched Dern as he walked into the stable, Rover, a stray shepherd that had just shown up a few years back, at the rancher's heels. For a split second, she thought about trusting him, then quickly cast the thought aside.

No one. You can't trust anyone. Especially not a stranger who'd just shown up and been hired by Wyatt. Nothing is as it seems . . . remember that.

There was no use fantasizing about the newcomer. She knew nothing about him except that he'd saved her.

It bothered her that Wyatt had hired the man without filling her in. Typical!

She dragged her gaze back to the dock where she'd been certain she'd seen her son teetering on the slippery boards, dangerously close to the deep water, the misting fog swirling around him. Her heartbeat accelerated at the memory.

Had it been an hallucination brought on by anxiety? Or had it been a result of those damned pills she'd been prescribed?

She *knew* her son hadn't disappeared on the dock . . . right? So why the morbid fascination with those damned slippery boards jutting into the bay?

What the hell was wrong with her?

Just because the police had suggested Noah fell into the bay didn't mean it was true. Of course not!

Her head began to throb again and she snapped the blinds shut before returning to her room.

Walking into the bathroom, she splashed cold water on her face. Over the running water, she heard a quick rap on the door. Sometimes she felt as if her room were Grand Central Station.

"Coming!" Snapping a hand towel from its ring, she dabbed at her face as she stepped into the bedroom and found Graciela letting herself in. "Miss Ava?" she said, her practiced smile intact. "Virginia wants to know if you want breakfast?"

"I'll get something later."

Graciela's smile fell away. "She says the coffee is ready."

"Good." Ava waited.

Graciela didn't budge.

Or take the hint.

"I'll be down in a little bit. I'll grab something then." Who was the boss here? Still the stubborn maid lingered. Ava tossed the towel onto the foot of her bed. "Is there something else, Graciela?"

"*Si* . . . yes." She frowned a bit as if reluctant to convey the message.

"What is it?"

"I thought you might want to know that your cell phone's been ringing downstairs."

"My cell?" Ava glanced quickly around the room for her phone. "I didn't hear it."

"It's in the main hall, by the door, in your purse."

"The hall?" Ava's gaze shifted to the chair where she'd always plopped her purse before bed each night. Sure enough, her bag was missing. "Thanks. I'll get it," she said to the maid, whose returning hint of a smirk suggested that she knew Ava was losing her mind. "Just give Virginia the word about breakfast, okay?" she said as Graciela swept out of the room, the door thudding shut behind her.

Good riddance. Graciela did nothing wrong and yet there was something about the pretty little maid that got under Ava's skin.

Ava sure as hell didn't remember leaving her purse downstairs. Not that it was a big deal, just another indication that she wasn't thinking clearly and that the holes in her memory now included smaller rips in the seam along with the bigger, gaping tears she couldn't sew back together.

But she was certain, feeling as she did today, that the only way back to being herself was by staying off the medication the doctors had prescribed. All those lousy pills did was dull her, and she had to be clear and mentally focused so that she could find out exactly what had happened to her boy and why she was haunted by visions of him.

Quickly she ditched her robe and dressed in a fresh pair of jeans and loose-knit sweater. She was pushing her head through the neckline when another series of raps against her door preceded Demetria poking her head inside.

"Hey!" Ava said sharply. "I'm getting dressed here."

"Oh." The nurse didn't seem the least bit concerned even though she mumbled a lifeless, "Sorry." She was carrying a small paper cup and a glass of water. "Your pills."

"Just put them on the nightstand." Ava pulled her hair out of the neck of her sweater and shook her curls free. "I'll take them later."

"You know, they really need to be taken on a schedule to keep your med levels even."

"Let me guess—to avoid any mood swings?"

The nurse's lips pursed a bit. "Precisely," Demetria agreed.

"And the mood swings are bad because . . . ?"

Demetria regarded her warily. "I assume you remember jumping into the bay the other night? I think it would be a good idea to avoid another life-threatening situation, don't you?"

"I'm better."

"It's only been—"

"Long enough!" Ava snapped, then tried to rein in her temper. Any signs of volatility would only bolster the nurse's case. "I know I haven't been the most stable person around. So, if I start doing swan dives into the bay again, then *maybe* I'll consider taking the pills. But let's just see how it goes."

"Dr. McPherson won't be happy."

"And I live to make her happy," Ava deadpanned. Demetria was still holding out the damned cup, so she gestured to it. "Don't worry about those. I'll call the doctor and tell her what gives."

"Couldn't you do that after you take your medication?"

Jewel-Anne's nurse was really getting under her skin, and it was all Ava could do to keep her voice level. "Just leave the pills on the nightstand."

"Why do you have to make things so difficult?" Demetria burst out, as if she couldn't hold it in any longer.

"I was just thinking the same about you." She strode by the nurse, bumping her arm to send the pills flying.

"Watch out!" Demetria dropped to her knees and started frantically searching for the meds. "Now look what you've done!"

Ava was already heading down the stairs, her footsteps muted by the soft runner that flowed down the center of the old, wooden steps. She wasn't going to be dragged into an argument this morning. Demetria was one of those self-righteous know-it-alls whom Ava couldn't stomach. Fine for Jewel-Anne, who somehow had manipulated her nurse into believing that Demetria was in charge.

A weird relationship that.

Ava wanted no part of it.

Downstairs she was met with the sounds of Virginia's off-key humming over the sizzle of frying bacon, both emanating from the kitchen while a steady rain beat against the tall windows flanking the massive front door.

Graciela was right: Ava's purse was just where she'd said it would be, tossed carelessly onto a small bench in the foyer. She must've left it there yesterday . . . but she couldn't remember. Deciding it didn't matter, she scooped up the bag and scrounged through the interior to find her cell planted deep in a zippered pocket.

As the scents of warm coffee and crisp bacon caused her stomach to rumble, she unlocked the keypad and scrolled through her messages. All told, she'd missed three calls—two from Tanya and the third only identified as a "private call." Also, she'd received one text from Tanya:

Give me a call ASAP.

"Okay, okay." Punching the RETURN DIAL button for Tanya's number, she started up the stairs again.

Sharp footsteps caught her attention. "Miss Ava?" Virginia's voice called after her.

Nearly missing a step, she turned and spied the cook just as Tanya answered. "Hey, I wondered if you'd ever get my message! Make that messages! For God's sake, don't you ever check your phone?"

"Hi. Hang on for just a sec, would ya?" Ava said into the cell as the cook, four steps below, stopped dead in her tracks at the base of the stairs.

"Oh, I'm sorry," Virginia said quickly, eyebrows pulling together as she realized that Ava was talking on the phone. "I didn't realize you were busy." Backing toward the kitchen, Virginia gestured toward the rear of the house and said softly, "Breakfast is ready, in the morning room."

Ava was about to argue but rather than get into another debate, she said simply, "I'll be right down," before mounting the stairs again. Once out of earshot, she turned her attention to her phone conversation. "Sorry, Tanya, everything's happening here at once."

"NBD." *No big deal* in Tanya-ese. "I got your message. Sorry that I missed you at the shop. Plumbing issues at the house . . . flooded basement, broken pipe—oh, don't get me started!"

"Sounds bad."

"It was, in this case the you-know-what was running downhill all right, right into my laundry room . . . Ugh! I shudder just thinking about it, but Al from Al-Wright Plumbing came to the rescue and in a few days, when things dry out, everything will be back to normal. So he says. For now, I have to do all the laundry from home at the shop where I've got the small stack unit. Things could be worse, I suppose."

"A lot," Ava said as she walked into her room and shut the door behind her.

"Oh, God, Ava, I'm such an idiot!" Tanya said. "It's nothing . . . just dirty socks and underwear, a little inconvenience. I mean, after what you've been through . . ." She let that thought slide and added, "You know, I'm just so, so sorry."

There was a click on the line, as if someone else were trying to reach her. Ava ignored the call. "It's okay." But it wasn't. They both knew it.

Leaning against the door to her room, she felt the weight of her loss dragging her down, but she couldn't go there, not today, not when she was finally feeling proactive. "I was just hoping we could get together for . . . coffee, or lunch, or maybe drinks. Whatever."

"I'd love it! Anytime . . . well, I'd have to work it in. You know, between the salon hours and the kids' schedules and everything else. That'll be a trick. With school, soccer, and—if you can believe it—ballet for Bella, it seems like I'm in the car half the day. You should see my gas bill!"

Hauling children to their activities, it sounded like heaven to Ava, but she didn't voice it. She said, "You're the busy one these days, so you name the time."

"Okay . . . let me see . . . I've got my appointment book and personal calendar on my computer . . . so how about . . . Oh, gee . . . there's a chance I can meet you tomorrow. I've got an hour for lunch, but it would have to be late, like two or two-fifteen? Is that okay? I've got a cut and color that might run longer than it should."

"Works for me."

"Okay, just stop by the shop."

"Twoish. Got it. Bring pictures of Bella and Brent."

"Got 'em in my station already. Yeah, I know, I'm one of *those* moms." She laughed and Ava relaxed a little.

"See you then." She was about to click off when Tanya's voice stopped her.

"Wait! Hey, Ava, this entire conversation has been all about me. What about you. Are you okay?"

There was that damned question again.

"I, uh, heard what happened the other night," Tanya added in a rush. "Is everything all right?"

"Right as rain," she said quickly as she heard footsteps on the stairs, then added under her breath, "I'll tell you all about it when we get together."

"Promise?"

Tap. Tap. Tap.

Knuckles rapped on her bedroom door.

Good God. Again?

"Cross my heart," she whispered automatically as she disconnected. Growing up, they always said those three words when they weren't joking. It was their unwritten rule that whenever either of them said *Cross my heart,* it meant that whatever they were saying was the God's honest truth. Then to the door, she yelled, "I'm coming," as she clicked off her phone while simultaneously flinging open the door.

Jewel-Anne, seated in her chair, fist raised as if to knock again, was planted on the threshold, her wheelchair blocking the doorway and making it impossible for Ava to pass.

"Your breakfast's getting cold," she stated flatly. Her doll, a redhead with green eyes, tucked into a special bag that was snapped to the side of her chair, seemed to stare up at Ava with her thick-lashed eyes. Jewel-Anne flipped out one of the earbuds of her iPhone, held firmly in her other plump hand.

"I already told Virginia I'd be right there," Ava said a tad testily.

"I just thought you should know." Jewel-Anne was prim today, supercilious as ever. "And Trent texted me. He said he's trying to reach you, but you won't call him back."

"He didn't—" She remembered the private number on her cell's tiny screen. "So he couldn't get me and called you?"

"I guess." As if disinterested, she shrugged a shoulder.

"Why?"

"Maybe because you didn't answer and he knew he could get hold of me." Jewel-Anne said it as if Ava were a bona fide idiot. There was a lot of that going around these days. Too much, in fact. "He's got a new phone number," she added, then rattled it off.

Having delivered her message, Jewel-Anne flipped her hair over her shoulder, then pressed a button, reversed, and turned her wheelchair deftly on the landing before whirring away. "You're welcome," she called over her shoulder as she passed by the nursery . . . the closed door to Noah's room.

Ava shook her head as she made her way downstairs again, read the menu on her phone, and called the number she had for Trent.

Sure enough, she got a disconnect message.

She was about to try the number Jewel-Anne had rattled off, one of the few memory skills that hadn't abandoned her in the past few years, but as she reached the first floor, the phone rang in her hands. "Hello?" she said, reading the caller ID message of "private caller."

"So you *are* alive," Trent teased.

"Against my own best efforts, some people think."

"Ah-ah-ah, careful. I might be one of those." But he chuckled in amusement.

"Probably are." Of all of her cousins, Trent, Ian's twin, was the one with whom she felt the most connected. Trent, "the sane one" as he referred to himself, was half an inch shorter than Ian, but what he lacked in height, he made up for in looks and personality. "The lady slayer" he'd called himself in high school, and his self-aggrandized opinion of himself hadn't been far from the truth.

Just ask Tanya.

Or several other of her friends in high school. "So, I'm fine," she insisted, and let him think what he wanted. No doubt he got reports from his half sister and twin about her "condition" or whatever it was they called it. "Piper already called me."

He groaned. "Stepmommy Dearest."

"Exactly."

"Let me guess. She acted as if she were worried sick about you."

"That's about it in a nutshell."

"But I don't have to worry about you?" he asked.

"Why don't you be a freethinker and assume that I'm *not* insane."

"Where's the fun in that?"

"Huh."

He laughed and they talked as she walked the length of the foyer to the back of the house and the solarium, which offered a wide view of the stables, fields, and hills surrounding Neptune's Gate.

"Just take care of yourself," he said as the conversation wound down, and she walked into Wyatt's office. Cradling her phone against her shoulder, she snagged a pen from the cup on his desk and scribbled Trent's new phone number onto the palm of her free hand. "Remember, Ava, you're living in a nest of loonies."

"Funny, that's exactly what they all think I am."

"Then you fit right in."

"Don't think so," she said with a laugh.

"So prove them wrong."

I will, she thought as she hung up, then transferred his number into the contact list in her phone. But first she had to prove it to herself.

Chapter 9

Ava dutifully ate a quick breakfast of congealing fried eggs, cold bacon, and toast soaked in butter, all washed down with coffee. Afterward, she grabbed an apple and a banana from a basket on the morning room sideboard, then hurried up the stairs to her room again.

More clearheaded than she had been in weeks, she dug around in her closet, found her laptop, and settled herself in a chair by the window. What she needed to do was figure out where everyone had been the night of Noah's disappearance. She'd wondered about it often enough in the past but hadn't had the strength or presence of mind to figure it out.

Of course, the police had done something similar, but Sheriff Biggs and his underlings hadn't tried too hard, she thought, because they'd worked under the supposition that Noah had wandered outside and drowned. After cursory statements from everyone in the house, a search by officers and volunteers of the island and divers who had scoured the waters of the bay near Neptune's Gate's private dock, they'd decided that her son had slipped off the dock and drowned, his little body carried out to sea with the tide.

Except that the tide had been coming in at the time he'd been discovered missing.

She'd checked.

But no one had listened to her, and she really couldn't blame them—she'd been a maniac: frantic with fear, wild with desperation to find her son, and suffering a breakdown in the process . . .

No wonder no one took her seriously. In the ensuing two years, she hadn't given up faith that her baby would be found, but her fractured mind hadn't been able to focus or concentrate.

Until now. She glanced to the bedside table and the tiny cup holding the pills Demetria had picked up from the floor and placed on the table.

Tranquilizers to calm her.

Antidepressants to lift her spirits.

She carried the container into the bathroom. Once more she threw the meds down the toilet, but this time she made certain they all flushed away. She supposed the intensity of this headache might be from stopping the pills cold turkey, but she didn't care; she'd suffer through the withdrawals or whatever they were.

Once satisfied that there was no trace of the pills left, she returned to the bedroom, drank down half the water in the glass, and left the empty pill cup on the table, not that anyone would believe her, but she went through the motions anyway. Next, she quickly braided her hair away from her face so that it wouldn't get in the way as she typed and dived into her project.

She remembered the night that her life had changed forever. The Christmas holidays had been in full swing and the house filled with people—those who worked at Neptune's Gate as well as those guests who had been invited to be a part of the festivities. Ava started listing everyone who had spent the night as well as those who had just dropped by. One by one, she placed their names on a legal pad with a pencil she'd found in the desk drawer, but she couldn't be certain that she'd recalled everyone, not with the way her memory was these days. Nonetheless, she transferred the list onto her computer.

Her fingers moved awkwardly over the keyboard at first, the keys feeling unfamiliar, but she kept at it, typing carefully, making mistakes and corrections until muscle memory took over. "Just like riding a bike," she told herself, and soon she was in the rhythm of it, creating columns of names, relationships, where each person had claimed to be when Noah disappeared. She'd gone over it with the police again and again but had been so brokenhearted she hadn't been able to do much more than grieve.

Now she looked down at the spreadsheet she'd compiled. Would it help?

No way to tell until she tried.

Three hours later, a headache throbbed behind her eyes as she sat in her desk chair. She rotated the kinks from her neck and stared at the chart and timeline she'd created on her computer, one made primarily from her own recollections and conversations with others over the past few years.

She could see the house as it had been that night. . . .

The foyer had been festooned with fir garlands winking with white lights and threaded with gold ribbon. A twenty-foot tree had stood at the base of the steps, its boughs laden with winking lights, ornaments, and red bows, its upper branches nearly reaching the second story of the open stairway.

A steady stream of Christmas songs had been playing from speakers located all over the house, familiar notes audible only when the din of conversation, laughter, and clink of glasses had receded.

The mood had been festive, the only moment of sadness when, at dinner in the dining room, Ava had glanced to her right, to the seat her brother, Kelvin, had always occupied at family gatherings. Of course he was missing, his chair occupied by Clay Inman, who was an associate of Wyatt's, a junior partner in the firm. Inman's family lived somewhere in North Carolina, if she remembered right, and he'd had nowhere else to celebrate the holidays. He'd innocently taken Kelvin's chair. No one save Ava, or perhaps Jewel-Anne, who had caught her eye at one point during the meal, had seemed to notice.

By nine o'clock, Noah had become cranky and she'd carried him upstairs, rocking him a bit and placing him in his crib.

"No," he'd objected, and pointed a finger at the twin bed that had been delivered just that week.

"I don't know . . ."

"Big bed, Mommy!"

"Okay, okay." She'd given in, a mistake she'd regretted immediately. "But you go to sleep."

She'd tucked him in and waited in the rocker as he'd closed his eyes, feigning sleep. Then he'd opened one eye again.

"Sleep," she'd repeated firmly, and settled into the rocker.

Twenty minutes later, he'd given it up and was breathing regularly. Ava had gotten up from the creaking rocker, leaned over the twin bed, and whispered, "Merry Christmas, big guy," as she'd brushed his dark curls from his forehead and planted a gentle kiss upon its soft skin. "I'll see you in the morning."

He'd offered up the ghost of a smile though his eyelids were closed, sooty lashes lying upon his cheeks. She remembered stopping at the door and looking over her shoulder to double-check that his blanket was covering his body and the night-light was glowing softly under the window situated between his crib and bed.

Her heart ached as she thought of that last, final glimpse she'd had of her son. The pain was palpable and she picked up the pencil again, twisting it anxiously as the memories rolled through her brain.

She'd been in a hurry.

Satisfied that Noah was asleep, she'd left his door ajar as she'd walked out of his room. Then she'd gathered the skirt of the red dress she'd bought for the occasion and hurried down the stairs to join her guests. She remembered pausing on the landing, thinking she'd heard Noah call "Mommy?" but as she'd waited, straining to listen, his little voice hadn't drifted to her over the cacophony of sounds rising from the first floor, and she'd told herself she'd imagined it.

"There you are!" Wyatt had called up to her, and she caught sight of her husband standing at the foot of the stairs, a drink in his hand as he grinned up at her. "We've got guests!"

"I know, I know. I was just putting the baby to bed."

She hurried down the rest of the stairs and said good-bye to Inman and a couple of others who had gathered near the front door, slipping into coats, scarves, and gloves before being ferried back to the mainland.

The guests came and went and she engaged in small talk and made certain that the drinks were flowing, the candles remained lit, each guest was involved in a conversation, the music never died, and her smile was clearly in place. For over an hour, no one checked on Noah. She'd had the baby monitor set up, an audio system with remote speakers in their bedroom as well as the den and morning room. They'd installed a video monitor as well, but the camera had been angled toward the crib; it hadn't been redirected toward the twin bed because Noah hadn't moved to it yet.

Both had proved useless. That night the audio monitor had been muted by the noise level of the party, and the camera had offered no clues. It wasn't outfitted with a tape, and even if it had been, it was unlikely with its limited view that any image would have shown.

The guilt that had been with her since that night was still her companion.

How many times had she wished she'd returned to her son's room?

How much mental self-flagellation and anguish had she borne thinking that she'd ignored her child when he'd called for her, when he'd needed her most? That one, stupid decision might have been the difference between . . .

She closed her eyes for a second and felt her throat thicken with the tears that were always just under the surface. No. Crying wouldn't help. Neither would railing at the heavens.

She knew.

She'd already tried those two tacks and had beaten herself up for ignoring her heart and rushing back to Wyatt and the party. . . .

"God help me." Her fists clenched on either side of the keyboard and she lowered her head.

Concentrate.

Don't let the heartache overcome you.

And yet the pain was always there, scraping at her soul, reminding her that it was her fault he'd gone missing. Her damned fault.

And now you have to find him.

No one else will.

Swallowing hard, her eyes burning, she set her jaw and forced her thoughts again to that last night.

The party had wound down early, a little after eleven, but for the most part, those who had remained in the house were still hanging out downstairs. Wyatt had been in his study, sharing a glass of rare Scotch with Uncle Crispin, father to the bevy of Ava's cousins.

Trent and Ian had been playing billiards in the rec room that was located half a floor down from the main living area, and their sister, Zinnia, had stepped through the French doors to the garden to take a call on her cell. Through the half-open door, they'd felt the cold of winter and heard her chewing out her most recent boyfriend, the guy who'd refused to spend the holidays on "some fuckin' rock in the middle of nowhere." He'd ended up jetting off to Italy, which royally pissed off Zinnia. Fueled by several Irish coffees and a temper she'd never learned to control, Zinnia had let the boyfriend, Silvio, have it, according to both her brothers.

Aunt Piper had kicked off her high heels and was reading in the sitting room while her son, Jacob, had walked outside to smoke a cigarette on the front porch. Ava remembered catching a glimpse of him through the window. His body had been in shadow, but the tip of his cigarette had glowed red in the darkness.

Jewel-Anne had already gone upstairs for the night; she was the only member of the family who'd admitted to being on the second floor, though she'd sworn she never went near Noah's room. Later, she said she was certain his door had been shut.

Ava remembered leaving it slightly ajar, and it was heavy enough not to have blown closed. Someone had to have shut it on purpose.

"Who?" she whispered as she wrote it on the legal pad and circled it, over and over again. Next to it, she wrote WHY?

Sheriff Biggs and his detectives had thought there was a chance Noah had gotten out of bed himself and wandered down the long hallway to the back staircase, therefore avoiding being detected by anyone downstairs. From those steep back steps, the authorities surmised, he could have climbed upstairs to the third floor or even to the attic, though a search of the upper floors had found nothing. The police had then surmised that the boy could have gone to the kitchen and out the back door in a moment when all the staff were elsewhere or just didn't notice him. There was the chance, too, that he'd wandered around the basement, but, like the attic, a search of the underground rooms had provided no clues to Noah's whereabouts.

Of course, there was the chance that Noah had been abducted, though in the following days, no ransom call or note had been received, and Sheriff Biggs had fallen back to his original theory that the boy had wandered outside and gotten lost.

Now the pencil in Ava's fingers snapped. "No way." She just didn't believe it, though Biggs had his reasons. Excuses, she thought.

Ava had always thought the idea that no one had seen Noah escape outside was lame, but it was true that the back door to the porch had been left open sometime in the evening. The screen door had been banging in the wind, a sound no one had noticed during the festivities. Only later had Virginia mentioned the noise. "I did hear something," she'd admitted, "but I thought it was farther away, like the barn or the stable window. There's always something rattling or banging around here."

Most of the night, Virginia had been in the kitchen. Khloe and her husband, Simon Prescott, had been working that night, Khloe helping out in the kitchen while Simon had taken turns with both their ranch hand, Ned Fender, and Butch Johansen, ferrying the guests to and from the island.

Graciela had helped prepare and serve the hors d'oeuvres and drinks, while keeping the room picked up and tidy. She disposed of used napkins, dirty plates, forgotten flatware, and empty glasses.

Demetria had spent some of the night attending to Jewel-Anne and had spent the rest on her own. Ava remembered her speaking with Ian and sipping wine with Wyatt, even talking to Tanya while Jewel-Anne was elsewhere.

All of the help was alibied for the most part, though the alibis had loose timelines only guessed at as people kept coming and going, on the island, off the island, in the house, out of the house . . .

But not up the stairs.

Few people admitted to leaving the first floor of the house, and the handful of those who had said they'd climbed the main stairs by the Christmas tree or used the elevator had claimed they had been looking for another restroom. Each person had sworn they'd never been on the second floor after Ava had put her son to bed and had alibis to confirm their statements.

So who?

Frustrated, she flung the pieces of her useless pencil into the trash can near her bed.

The guest list hadn't been that large, really. Inman, of course, and Tanya who had elected to drag Russ to the party even though they'd been separated at the time.

"We're trying to work things out," she'd said by way of explanation. "For the kids."

It had been a failed attempt. Less than two months later, Tanya had filed for divorce and Russell had left Anchorville permanently.

There had been a few other guests as well, friends who'd known her parents, people whose roots were planted in Church Island soil as hers were. Most of those locals had left early, before she'd shuttled Noah off to bed. Her son had sagged against her, all the while saying, "Not tired, Mommy. *Not* tired!"

Oh, how she ached to hear his little voice now. Even a protest was better than this nothingness, this not knowing. Closing her eyes, she leaned back in her desk chair and tried to make sense of it all. She'd relived the night Noah had disappeared thousands of times in her head and never come up with any answers, any clues to what had really happened. And now . . . now she had a chart and a timeline, which wasn't much and probably not more than the police had developed two years earlier.

What was the name of the lead detective who had interviewed her? Simms or Simons or . . . *Snyder*, that was it! Wes Snyder. In his midforties with a fleshy face and a cue-ball head that he shaved close. Snyder had been kind enough, serious and intense, a whole lot smarter than Joe Biggs, and yet, he, like everyone else, had come up empty, without any real theories of what had happened to Noah. There was talk of kidnapping, but that, too, had been negated, the FBI never stepping in. Eventually even Snyder had given up—like all the rest.

Except you, Ava. You can never let this go.

Eyes open again, she snagged a pen from a cup on her desk, then wrote Snyder's name on the legal pad under a previously scribbled *Joe Biggs*.

From her cell, she dialed the sheriff's department and asked for Detective Snyder, only to be told he was out for most of the day. She left a message on his voice mail, then slammed the phone down. It seemed as if she were being purposely thwarted at every turn. Everyone was against her.

Her head was pounding, her muscles tighter than bowstrings, her stomach rumbling loudly. She popped a couple of Extra-Strength Excedrin, downed a glass of water, then broke off pieces of the banana she'd snagged earlier and chewed on them thoughtfully.

Her jangled nerves eased a bit, but she knew she needed to get out of the house, to think things through. Clicking off her computer, she tucked it, along with its case and her scribbled notes, inside her closet.

The old house was beginning to make her feel claustrophobic. Throwing on an old Mariners sweatshirt, she headed out of her room, only to stop at the staircase. Her gaze skated along the open landing that wound its way around the staircase to land at the door of Noah's room. Only once since her release from the hospital had she found the nerve to push open that door and peer inside. Then the grief had assailed her and she hadn't been able to enter. Since then the door to the nursery had been firmly shut, the room left exactly as it had been, the only disturbance being its weekly cleaning.

Today she felt compelled.

Before she could second-guess herself, she strode to her son's bedroom, twisted the glass doorknob, shoved open the door, and stepped inside.

Her heart pounded.

Her hands were clammy and cold.

The only light in the room was from a window where the shade was half drawn. The gray day seemed to seep into the room, draining color from the sailor print coverlet on the twin bed and dulling the once-vibrant sheets. Her throat tightened.

She felt ill with grief.

Hidden deep beneath the smells of furniture polish and dust, she thought she detected the faint aroma of baby oil . . . but that was probably her mind just playing tricks on her again.

Swallowing hard, she snapped on the tiny mariner's lamp and noticed the mobile suspended over the crib. Tiny, smiling sea creatures hung lifeless. Heart in her throat, she switched on the mobile and the tiny smiling crab, seahorse, and starfish began slowly rotating to a tinkling bell and a few notes of a familiar lullaby.

She remembered Noah as a baby, lying on his back, his eyes following the slowly moving sea animals, or as a toddler, standing by holding on to the rails, trying to reach the suspended animals.

"Ava?" Wyatt's voice cut into her reverie.

She jumped about a foot, hitting the spinning starfish and sending it bobbing, the rest of the mobile wobbling wildly. Turning quickly, she found her husband standing in the doorway, light from the hallway throwing him in relief. "You scared me!"

"Didn't mean to." Wyatt forced a smile that didn't touch his eyes. His coat was slung over one arm and in the other he carried his small bag. "I just wondered what you were doing in here."

"Remembering," she said, running her fingers along the top

rail of the crib where marks from Noah's baby teeth cut into the smooth wood.

"Is that a good idea?"

"God knows."

"I . . . I, uh, had a little more work to do, but I was hoping that . . . we could just hang out later tonight. Have dinner in the den, maybe watch a movie?"

"A house date?" she asked, and he nodded, his smile seeming sincere for the first time.

"That's what we used to call them."

"I remember."

"Good." He nodded and she felt a rush of relief, a fragile sense of hope that what they'd once shared hadn't been completely destroyed. "Ava?" he said softly.

"Yes."

"He's gone." He cleared his throat. "Noah. He's not coming back and . . . I think it would be best if you would accept it."

Shaking her head, she straightened her shoulders. "I can't and I won't."

"Then you're not going to get better."

"I just want to know the truth, Wyatt."

"No matter what?"

She felt that cold fear coiling inside her again, but she steadfastly tamped it down. "No matter what."

His gaze held hers for a second, his lips tightening. Then he slapped the doorjamb in frustration. "Do whatever it is you have to do, Ava. You're damned well going to anyway." He strode away without another word, his footsteps fading.

"I will," she vowed to the empty room as she softly turned off the small lamp near the empty bed.

It looked like the "house date" was off.

Chapter 10

Pissed at the world in general and Wyatt specifically, Ava stormed outside where the salty breath of winter rolled in from the sea. The argument still filling her mind, she passed lacy ferns and broad-leafed hostas that huddled in the shade as she followed the winding, overgrown stone path that cut through the garden.

She just needed to do something, *any*thing to get her life back on track. Set to walk off her frustrations on her way into town, she noticed the horses grazing near the fence line and came up with a better plan.

As a kid, she'd loved riding her favorite mare at a full gallop across the dew-dampened fields and into the dark woods surrounding the estate. She'd spent hours following the old deer and sheep trails that snaked through the woods and along the coastline, exploring every inch of the island, even getting to know those places her parents had declared "forbidden." Despite her mother's warnings, she'd followed her favorite paths that took her past the dungeon-like walls of the old asylum and upward along the cliffs that fell hundreds of feet to the roiling surf that crashed against the shore. There were old cabins, a waterfall, the rock quarry with its mines, and other just as taboo spots.

Ava had made a point of visiting them all.

She passed through a gate and across the twin ruts of an access road to the fence line where the horses were grazing. Whistling, she caught the attention of Jasper, a bald-faced bay gelding. The horse lifted his head, flicked his dark ears, and snorted.

"Come on," Ava urged, wondering why all the males in her life were so obstinate. "It'll be fun. Promise." Slowly, as if it pained him, the gelding approached.

"About time," she whispered, and reached over the fence to rub the bay's forehead. Jasper snorted, his breath warm as it clouded in the cool afternoon air. "I missed you, too. Come on, let's go for a ride."

For once, Jasper didn't put up any resistance and followed Ava into the stable. Minutes later, she'd thrown a faded blanket and a saddle over his back, cinched the girth tight, and slid the bridle over his head.

Within minutes, she'd swung herself onto his back and guided him outside. She glanced at the house once and spied Simon working in the garden, and when he lifted his head to look in her direction, she quickly urged the horse away from the fence line. The fewer people who saw her, the less she would have to explain, and she was sick and tired of explaining her every movement. Besides, she didn't know much about Simon, just that he and Khloe had a tumultuous, if passionate, marriage, and that at one time he'd worked in communications in the army.

Once through a final gate, she took the gelding into the open field again, leaning forward over his sleek neck. "Let's see what you've got, old guy," she encouraged, and urged Jasper into a canter.

Immediately the horse's gait lengthened into a smooth lope,

his hooves digging into the wet grass, propelling them past thickets of hemlock and fir that soared high enough that their tops were lost in the low-hanging clouds.

Faster and faster the gelding ran, until the countryside was a blur, the cold air rushing past, tangling her hair.

A bubble of laughter rose in her throat. How long had it been since she felt so free? So exhilarated? God, it seemed like forever! At the creek that cut a jagged path through the center of the field, Jasper didn't break stride, just splashed through the flattened banks, spraying muddy water as he ran.

To the south, the abandoned asylum was visible, a concrete and stone fortress that was built on the sheer bluff over the ocean. Weathered iron railings sagged while streaks of rust colored the gray walls in reddish rivulets. Broken windows were boarded over and a flagpole stood tall, a lone sentinel, its rusting chain rattling in the wind.

A shadow crossed the wall walk and for a split second she thought she saw someone atop the thick rock wall and then, in an instant, the image disappeared into the darkening gloom. She shivered. Sea Cliff now seemed an eerie place, one she didn't want to think about now, not when she'd felt a burst of freedom and happiness for the first time in years.

"No buzz-kills," she whispered, the words thrown back in her throat from Jasper's canter and the rising wind. Tugging on the reins, she forced the horse to slow as rain began to fall in earnest. They slipped into the forest of hemlock and fir and walked through the dripping boughs, the smell of the wet earth mingling with the salt air.

She saw Jasper's steaming breath and felt a chill as the solitude of the island surrounded her. This was a lonely place, cut off from the mainland, but the isolation had never bothered her. In the past it had given her strength and peace of mind. Of course, that was before the tragedies . . .

The path wound ever upward where the trees gave way to a

headland with a breathtaking view of the strait. From this point, other islands could be seen, dark peaks jutting out of the ever-shifting waters of this arm of the Pacific.

The last time she'd been here had been the morning after Noah had gone missing. She'd searched every building, every niche in the house, and finally she'd ridden through the woods to this very spot and had looked out to the sea, afraid she'd see his small body in the restless waters. She'd even attempted to climb down the dilapidated stairs that switched back and forth sharply to a bit of beach and dock that hadn't been used in decades. Her jaw clenched. She'd been so frightened the night Noah had disappeared, so spurred by her need to find him, that she'd attempted to climb down the stairs that night.

The wind had buffeted her, the sea crashing below. She'd held her flashlight tightly in one hand, her other fingers steadying herself on the rickety, wobbling banister.

Slowly, carefully, she'd descended, a litany of prayers tumbling through her mind.

Oh, God, please let me find him.

Please let him be okay . . . please, please, please . . .

"Noah!" she'd yelled, her voice ripped from her throat, the roar of the sea deafening. "Noah!" Then, more quietly, "Oh, baby, please . . . come to Mama . . . please."

Her hood had flown off, her hair flying in front of her face.

Step by step, she descended the unsteady stairs. One step. Two . . .

At the landing, she'd taken a deep breath, turned, then inched her way down the second short flight. All the while, the old staircase had groaned against her weight.

But she had to go down.

Had to find him.

Where was her baby? *Where?*

"Noah!!!"

Heart beating with dread, she'd eased onto the third landing, turned a hundred and eighty degrees, then stepped down.

Bam!

Rotting wood splintered.

The damned step collapsed.

Screaming, Ava had pitched forward. Her foot caught in the yawning hole, twisting her ankle.

Frantically she'd scrabbled for the rail.

Her flashlight flew from her hand, spinning, its beam of light spiraling wildly as it tumbled into the darkness.

"Help!" she'd screamed, one foot dangling, her fingers clawing into the unsteady rail, her head nearly to the next landing. "Help!"

Another blast of wind and the staircase shuddered, groaning against the rocky face of the cliff.

With all her strength, she'd clawed her way upright, pulled her foot through the step, and, determined to reach the bottom, to find her boy, had continued down in the darkness, carefully sliding her hands down the rail, feeling her way, unsteady but relentless.

The pain in her ankle had been excruciating, but it was nothing compared to the ache of despair she'd felt as she'd reached the beach, where, of course, there was no trace of her son.

None whatsoever.

She'd spent the rest of that night on the beach, huddled against the cold, crying softly as the surf rushed and pounded and the gods of all that was evil in the world laughed at her.

The next morning, once the storm had died down and the coast guard had found her, she'd caught snatches of phrases that had hounded her ever since.

"Out of her mind, poor thing . . ."

". . . wonder if she'll ever be right again . . ."

". . . imagine . . . a terrible loss . . . she's strong, but who could survive this . . . ?"

All well meaning. All voiced with more than a hint of concern. All worried as hell.

At the time she'd ignored them. Because at that time, Ava

had still fervently believed Noah would be found somewhere on the island. Safe. Scared. But alive.

Over the ensuing hours and days and weeks and months, her hope had dwindled, and now here she was, unsure if she would ever see her son again, at the top of the cliff-side stairs that had been barricaded since that night. The steps still clung to the wall of the island, bleached and faded, in worse shape now than they were two years earlier, the warning sign and surrounding fencing meant to discourage anyone intent on climbing down.

A sharp wind tossed her hair around her face while the rain drizzled steadily and low-hanging clouds obscured the horizon. She squinted to the west, where the strait stretched out to the Pacific. A few small islands barely visible and strung out like the ghostly spines of a giant underwater creature seemed to rise and sink with the ferocity of the tide.

Almost of its own accord, her gaze moved closer to the mouth of the bay, and she felt an involuntary shiver.

Her heart clenched when she thought of her brother and the night that had taken his life.

Dismounting, she let go of the reins, allowing Jasper to pick at the grass, his bridle jangling as he moved. She didn't know why she'd felt compelled to ride here, to face a distant pain she'd rather forget, to ultimately destroy her fleeting elation, but she had.

She walked to the edge of the cliff where she stared at the mouth of the bay. Her throat tightened. Submerged in the depths beneath the deep water was what locals referred to simply as the Hydra. Invisible to the naked eye on the calm waters, but ever changing beneath a swift current, the neck of the bay was narrow and dangerous to those boat captains who weren't familiar with the tight channel.

Ava knew only too well about the hazards of the entrance to the bay. Goose bumps rose on her arms as she stared at that long passage, to the spot where the rocks were hidden and part of the jetty had become submerged.

Chilled, she wrapped her arms around herself and in her mind's eye, she saw the day as it had been then, nearly five years earlier, a day not unlike this gray afternoon—except an unexpected squall had unleashed all its fury upon Kelvin and his most prized possession, a new, sleek sailboat, out for its maiden voyage. . . .

Chapter 11

On the day of the outing the sky was darkening ominously as a storm gathered, dark clouds roiling, sea undulating madly. The four of them were all on the new sailboat: Kelvin, Jewel-Anne, Wyatt, and Ava.

"Get us home!" Jewel-Anne shrieked, her eyes round with fear, her face pale in the swirling rain. She clung to the rail.

"I'm trying. Batten down the fucking hatches and go inside!" Kelvin yelled.

"And be trapped? No way!"

"Jewel, please!" he snapped.

"Just hurry!" She clung on, as stubborn as a barnacle.

"Get inside!" Ava yelled as the wind keened, and the boat lurched violently.

"Shit!" Kelvin worked the helm as Wyatt dropped the sea anchor from the stern, hoping to keep the boat steady, but the waves were lashing at the *Bloody Mary,* spinning her wildly in the sea.

"Bring her around. Bow into the waves!" Wyatt screamed, then swore as a monster wave crashed over the stern and the boat shuddered wildly. "The storm's blowing inland! Bow into the waves!"

"Nooo!" Jewel-Anne wailed as she stared at the rising wall of water. "Get us in! Hurry!"

"We have to ride it out!" With Ava's help, Wyatt struggled with the trysail. Meant to help in a storm, the damned thing seemed as useless as the motor that Kelvin had tried and failed to start.

"Oh, please! Just get us home!" Jewel-Anne was crying now, her legs sliding around as she struggled for purchase, her arms wrapped around the rail.

Wyatt shouted, "We can't get across the bar!"

"Then we'll all die!" She blinked wildly. "All of us, including the baby!" Her gaze found Ava's, beseeching her, speaking to Ava's most maternal instincts.

"She's right!" Ava said, thinking of her unborn child. *Her* child. *Wyatt's* child. "We have to get to land."

"Even if we get across the bar and into the bay, which we won't, we won't be able to dock," Wyatt pointed out. His jaw was set, rain sliding down his face, his hair plastered to his head.

"For the love of God, get that damned sail down!" Kelvin demanded fiercely, his calm shattered with the magnitude of the storm.

Wyatt grimaced at the size of the next wave. "Keep her at ninety degrees!"

"I can't. Shit!" Kelvin fought the wheel, and the rocks guarding the bar loomed larger. "Hang on!"

With a roar, the wave crested and drenched the boat. Icy water surged around Ava, who, already nauseous, fought to cling on. The small craft bobbed wildly, spinning with the force of the raging ocean.

Hair flying around her face, soaked to the bone, Jewel-Anne screamed as she clutched the rail near the helm. Her eyes were wide with fear, her skin ashen. "You have to hurry!" she cried, as if they could outrun the storm.

Kelvin ignored her, his jaw set as another wave slammed over the deck and the boat listed slightly.

"Get below deck!" Wyatt ordered.

Jewel-Anne was beside herself. "You're going to crash! For the love of God! Kelvin! We're all going to die! Watch out!"

"Shut up!" Kelvin didn't so much as glance at her. Rain plastered his hair to his head; his arms strained at the helm. "Just shut the fuck up!"

Stomach churning and freezing from the water, Ava gripped the rail and strained to see shore, a light, anything to guide them. What had started out as a whimsical tour had turned quickly into this disaster, and now Kelvin was straining to get the boat to shore without hitting the rocks that surrounded the island.

"We're not going to make it!" Jewel-Anne screeched as the wind howled, and the boat rocked.

"Get your fuckin' life jacket on!" Kelvin insisted.

"I can't!" Jewel-Anne was hysterical, her face as white as death. She grabbed his arm and nearly doubled over as the boat rocked crazily. "We're all going to die!" Wailing, she dropped into a pathetic puddle at Kelvin's feet.

"Get her away from me!" he told Ava. "Now!"

"Don't you touch me!" Jewel-Anne was screaming again, glaring at Ava as she clawed at Kelvin's arm.

"Come on, Jewel-Anne," Ava said, but Jewel-Anne clung to Kelvin's legs.

He tried to kick her away as he struggled to keep the craft afloat. *"Get her below deck!"*

"Nooo!" Jewel-Anne was having none of it.

Ava pulled on her cousin's arm. "Come on, Jewel!"

"Leave me alone!" She scrambled to her feet, then grabbed the railing and nearly pitched headfirst into the swirling, storming sea.

"Jewel-Anne!" Wyatt leaped at the floundering woman while Kelvin tried to steady the boat in the huge trough. "Get the hell below deck!"

Jewel-Anne seemed not to hear him.

"Come on, Jewel," Ava said as calmly as she could, though the boat was pitching crazily and her stomach was roiling, acid climbing up her throat.

"Jesus!" Kelvin yelled over the scream of the sea. "Get below!"

"So I can be trapped like a rat when you capsize?" Jewel cried.

"I'm not going to— Oh, fuck." He turned his attention to the helm.

"It's safer in the cabin," Ava said tautly, trying to sound strong and convincing when her own heart was racing, adrenaline and fear pumping through her bloodstream.

"Liar!"

"Let's go, Jewel-Anne!" Ava grabbed her cousin's arm, the fingers of one hand curling over the slippery sleeve of Jewel's jacket while she located a life vest below the deck seating with the other. God, her cousin could be bullheaded. "Put this on. Now!" She slapped the vest into her cousin's hand. "Leave Kelvin alone. Let him steer us in." She tugged on Jewel-Anne's arm as the boat lurched.

"No!" Jewel lost her footing and cried out in pain as she fell.

"Get her the fuck out of here!" Kelvin roared, trying like hell to control his own panic as he navigated in the trough in front of a gathering wave.

Jewel-Anne whimpered and scrabbled away from Ava, looking as awkward as a crab on its back upon the wet deck. The hood of her jacket had blown off, and she was still not wearing the damned vest dangling from her fingers. "You stay away from me!" she hissed, panic rising in her eyes, rain lashing at her face and hair. "Oh, God, oh, God, oh, God! We're all going to die!"

Ava's control snapped. She lunged forward and hit the slick deck. On her knees, she grabbed her cousin's arm and shook it angrily. "For the love of God, Jewel, calm the hell down!"

Jewel screamed, "Shut up!"

Smaaack! Without thinking, Ava slapped her cousin across the face. "Get a damned grip!" she yelled over the screaming wind. "No one's gonna die. Pull yourself together!"

Startled, Jewel-Anne stared at her as the boat pitched crazily. "You bitch!"

"Both of you. Stop it! Do something, for Christ's sake!" Wyatt screamed over his shoulder. He was still wrangling with the useless sea anchor.

Rain lashed down on them, running off their jackets and hoods, their life vests little peace of mind against the vicious, angry sea and the rocks now mere feet away, the sea whirling around them. Ava pulled herself upright and tried to drag Jewel-Anne to her feet, but her heavy cousin was a dead weight, nearly impossible to force to her feet on the slippery, unstable deck. "Come on, come on," she muttered as the wind screamed and the storm raged. Sheer terror gave her strength, and finally Jewel-Anne was standing again, bracing herself near the helm.

Despite the fact that all hell was breaking loose around her, she rubbed the red mark on her face. "Bitch!" she hissed at Ava. "This is all your fault!"

Wildly, the boat pitched and rolled, barely staying afloat.

Jewel clung to the railing, her eyes suddenly trained on the sea. "WATCH OUT!"

Ava followed her cousin's gaze.

Her heart nearly collapsed as she saw the rocks. Black. Jagged. Menacing. "Sweet Jesus," she whispered, fear scraping down her soul. They were too close! This trough was just too damned close to the rocks!

Jewel-Anne threw herself at Kelvin. "Turn about! Kelvin! Turn about!"

Kelvin ordered, "Do something with her! *Now!*"

"Hang on!" Wyatt shouted as another mammoth wave swelled wildly to crest above the boat. He lunged forward, grabbed Jewel-Anne, and pulled her close. "Stop this! Now! Get your life vest on!"

Too late.

The wave crashed down, a deafening wall of water. Ava's feet went out from under her.

Bam!

Her head crashed into the gunnel.

Pain exploded behind her eyes. The world started to turn black. Blindly she scrabbled for something to hang on to. A torrent of icy water nearly crushed her, taking her under, flooding her mouth and lungs.

The boat groaned and shuddered.

Ava came up coughing and blinking, unable to focus. This was it. They could never weather the storm. She thought of the baby and wished to high heaven the little unborn person would have had a chance . . .

Don't give up! You can't!

She focused on her brother.

Kelvin, jaw set, eyes filled with the look of the doomed, was braced against the helm, fighting the storm and losing. As if they were alone in the world.

Wyatt!

Oh, sweet Jesus, where was Wyatt?

And Jewel-Anne?

Coughing and spitting, Ava grabbed hold of a length of line unraveling from somewhere and held on as the boat rolled with the swells.

Where the hell was Wyatt? Dread beat inside her heart. "Wyatt!" She could barely see. Water rushed over the deck. She wouldn't believe that she'd lost her husband. He had to be here! And where the hell was Jewel-Anne? Frantic, she started yelling for help, silently praying that they hadn't washed overboard.

Oh, God, oh, God, oh, God . . .

Please, let them be safe.

Her panicked gaze searched the decking. She screamed her husband's name, but the roar of the sea pounded in her ears, the sound as immense as her fear. Her voice was but a whisper.

"Wyatt!" she yelled, still coughing as the boat listed dangerously and the rocks . . . the damned rocks were so close. . . . *"Wyatt!"*

SSSCRRRAPE! The horrid sound of stone tearing through fiberglass rumbled through the sailboat.

The *Bloody Mary* shuddered.

Ava clung to the rope. *God, help us!*

Another monster wave cascaded over the gunnels and decks. "Hang on!" Kelvin yelled.

Up the sailboat lifted, masts groaning as Kelvin tried to turn the prow from the trough into the next monstrous wave.

The keel scraped the sharp rocks. Shrieking as if in pain, the keel split open and the sea swarmed over the decks, flooding into the lower part of the boat, bringing it down, the craft pitching and bobbing even as it sank into the hurtling depths.

Another wave rose, swelling beneath the broken *Bloody Mary*, lifting the boat high, and then, in a mighty rush, pushing it once more into the spiny rocks so sharply that it capsized.

Flung into the frigid water, Ava was swallowed by the sea. The line wrapped tightly over her palm, the nylon rope that had saved her, now pulled her deeper into the ocean and tied her to a certain death. Her damned life vest couldn't save her.

Frantically, she tried to untie herself. Her fingers fumbled. *Come on, come on!* Her lungs were beginning to burn. The line wasn't knotted, just twisted, and she couldn't pull her fingers free.

Come on, Ava, you can do it! Don't give up!

Her lungs were on fire now, her fingers getting clumsier as the sea tossed her in its wild current. Pieces of debris swirled around her and the line only tightened.

Panic tore through her.

If she didn't get air soon—

Bam!

She was thrust into the rocks. The side of her face and ribs cracked against the jagged, barnacled rock.

A rush of air bubbles rose from her lips.

Pain ricocheted down her spine.

She could barely think. Blackness surrounded her, pulling her under. Her senses dulled, seducing her to just let go. . . .

No!

With one last effort, she forced the line from her fingers, ripping it away with her free hand, scraping off her skin, breaking her nails; then as the nylon finally gave way, uncoiling around her, she kicked. Hard!

Straining to reach the surface, her body beaten and exhausted, she knifed upward, fighting the raging current, uncertain she would make it despite the foam vest.

Suddenly, she broke the surface. Gasping, she dragged in a lungful of air just before the next huge breaker pounded down. She rode the wave, letting the tide push her over the rough rocks and across the bar, into the bay.

Limp, tossed around and beaten up, the wind and sea raging around her, she caught a glimpse of the lights of Neptune's Gate winking in the distance. Warm patches of gold glowing through the gloom.

Her heart clenched.

The expanse of turbulent sea was daunting. If she could only swim to shore . . . less than a mile . . . but first . . .

She tried to tread water, to search the white-capped, undulating surface to search for Wyatt, Jewel-Anne, and Kelvin.

Surely they were alive.

They had to be.

Hadn't they been wearing vests?

"Hey!" she yelled, but her voice was drowned by the storm. Her eyes searched through the odd shapes riding on the surging tide, the flotsam from the *Bloody Mary*. She saw no one. *Oh, please,* she thought desperately. *Wyatt, please . . .* Her throat clogged as another strong, freezing wave pushed her farther inland.

She closed her mind and held her breath, tried not to think that her brother, cousin, and husband could be lost. That she alone could have survived. If she made it.

"Hey!"

A hand suddenly touched her arm, snapping her out of her reverie.

Ava gasped in shock, her feet slipping a little as she left the memory and slammed into the present.

Austin Dern was glaring at her. He had a death grip on her upper arm.

And he looked pissed as hell.

Chapter 12

"What're you doing here?" she demanded, yanking her arm away and stepping backward.

"Watch out!" He grabbed her again, his strong fingers curling over her upper arm and yanking her forward. For the first time, she noticed that she was less than a foot from the precipice, even closer to the dilapidated stairs.

A fresh spurt of adrenaline fired through her blood while a hundred feet below, the surf surged and sprayed, suddenly roaring in her ears. Caught in her reflection, she hadn't noticed how near the precipice she'd edged. Only a few more steps and . . .

Heart suddenly racing, she whispered, "Oh, Lord. I didn't . . ." Her heart thudded in her ears. What if he hadn't come along? What if she'd taken two steps backward and fallen? Letting out a pent-up breath, she finally shook off Dern's hand, stepping away from the cliff and toward the horses. Now there were two, Jasper and Cayenne, a sorrel mare, Dern's mount. They were grazing on the sparse grass, their bridles jangling, their tails moving in the breeze.

"What the hell are you doing up here?" he demanded.

"Nothing. Just thinking."

Thick eyebrows pulled over his intense eyes, he was glaring at her with a don't-give-me-any-crap look. "Can't you think somewhere a little safer?"

She lifted a shoulder and cleared her throat. "I was just out riding, getting some fresh air and . . ." *Why do you feel compelled to bare your soul to him? It's none of his damned business.*

"This is a helluva spot for a daydream. Looked like you were about to go over."

"No." She glared right back at him. "So why are you here?" she demanded.

"I was missing one of my horses. And the dog"—he hooked his thumb toward the shepherd nosing around the brush near a stand of hemlock—"led me here." His gaze held hers. "Seems like it was a good idea."

"I'm fine."

"Really?" One of those dark eyebrows cocked skeptically.

So alpha male. "Yeah, *really.*" Maybe she'd been only a step or two from the edge, but she didn't much like this guy's attitude. "You don't have to make it a habit of saving me."

"You're sure?"

"Yes." Then, as another unpleasant thought occurred to her, "Don't tell me my husband hired you to be . . . what? Some kind of babysitter or . . . bodyguard?"

"I just came looking for the horse. Didn't mean to step into this mess, whatever the hell it is."

She felt her temper simmer. "No matter what you may think because of the other night and here, just now"—she motioned vaguely to the edge of the cliff face—"I really don't need a keeper."

"If you say so."

"I do."

He shrugged, seemingly unconvinced, his eyes still narrowed suspiciously, but he stepped away, palms raised. "No harm, no foul." He grabbed the reins of Cayenne's bridle. "Just bring the horse back, and next time maybe you could leave me a note or something."

"I looked for you when I took Jasper. You weren't around. And I really didn't think I needed permission to take my horse out."

He let a beat pass and she knew what he was thinking, that she *did* need someone's okay to go riding on her own, that she wasn't in control. That she was a damned lunatic.

"You've got a big place here. I might not always be in the stable or barn, but I've got a cell. If you give me a heads-up, I could get the horse ready for you."

"Seriously?" she said. "No matter what you've heard, I am able to saddle a horse. With my eyes closed. I might be the only one who holds this opinion, but trust me, I can do it." Before he could answer, she added, "The way I see it, this is my house, my land, and my friggin' gelding."

"I was just saying—"

"I *know* what you were saying, Dern!" She grabbed Jasper's reins, swung into the saddle, and left the damned ranch foreman or whatever the hell he was, staring after her.

Dern ground his teeth.

This wasn't going well. Not well at all.

Having been put squarely in his place by the very person he needed to get close to, Dern watched Ava ride away. Her back was still stiff with outrage as she half stood in the saddle, her rounded, jean-clad butt raised a bit as she leaned over her horse's neck and urged the bay into a gallop.

Dragging his gaze from her backside, rubbing the back of his neck in frustration, he told himself she was bad news. He'd blown it. Big-time. Apparently she wasn't keen on the whole knight-in-shining-armor-coming-to-her-rescue routine. Well, hell, he didn't blame her. It wasn't a comfortable role, one he'd never much practiced.

He let out his breath and was barely aware of the wind kicking up or the promise of more rain that was thick in the air. His thoughts were centered on the mystery that was Ava Garrison.

He wondered what she was like in bed and how often she slept with that prick of a husband of hers. There was definitely something off there. He'd noticed it in the way they avoided each other's eyes. Yeah, no marital bliss happening here on good old Church Island.

Why he cared, he couldn't imagine.

He didn't even *like* her. In fact, from what he'd learned, she was an A-1 bitch—that is, when she wasn't in a psychological meltdown as she had been since her boy had gone missing.

And yet he was faced with the sorry, unlikely fact that he was attracted to her.

"Slow down," he muttered under his breath. This was all wrong. He couldn't afford to be interested in any woman right now, and Ava Church Garrison was as off-limits as they came: married, a head case, rumored to be the worst kind of bitch when she wasn't in a puddle over her kid. Definitely not worth the trouble.

But there it was.

Women had always been his downfall, but then better men than he had fallen beneath the charms of a beautiful woman. And, unfortunately, he liked them with some fire, women who could go toe-to-toe with him.

Frightened, out of it, wet-as-a-drowned-rat Ava Garrison the other night, hadn't been a problem. Sure she'd been beautiful. But vulnerable. Needy. Definitely not his type. This new Ava, though, the one who looked like she could verbally chew him up and spit him out, now that was a different story. Wrong as it was, he loved a challenge, and man, oh, man, she presented one.

He kept his eyes on her disappearing form. She was at home astride the gelding, hadn't been lying when she said she knew her way around a horse and probably a stable. He watched as she slowed the horse a bit before disappearing into the woods and wondered just what it was that made Ava Garrison tick.

What the hell is it about her that's starting to get to you?

It wasn't just her looks, he decided, though her expressive eyes crackled with intelligence, or at least they had today. And then there were her lips, full and pulled tight over not-quite-perfect teeth in her exasperation with him. Her dark hair had been damp from the rain and curled a bit as it escaped from the braid at her nape. Though a bit on the skinny side now, she still had the body of an athlete, a runner, with slim hips and small breasts and legs that went on forever. He'd seen pictures of her a few years back, before she'd lost her son, and she'd looked the same, only stronger, her waist trim, her abdomen taut.

He knew from his background information that she'd run track in high school and college, a long-distance runner who had also completed at least one marathon in her early twenties, maybe more.

He'd talked to people who had worked with her. The descriptions that had emerged were simple:

Determined.

Driven.

A perfectionist.

And to some, soulless.

A far cry from the weak, shattered woman he'd dragged from the icy waters of the bay just a few nights before. If he didn't know better, he'd have sworn they were two people, because this afternoon, he'd caught a glimpse of that hard-nosed businesswoman, the one who demanded excellence, the one with the razor-sharp tongue.

At least she wasn't sleepwalking anymore.

When she'd come back from wherever her thoughts had taken her, her gray eyes had snapped with fire, her cheeks had been flushed with anger, her lips flattened in disapproval. Her chin had jutted, her jaw clenched.

Trouble was, he found her a whole lot more interesting than the woman he'd hauled from the bay. He'd watched her that night, the shivering, almost cowering victim who'd clasped her hands between her knees, worried her lip, and looked away when those who purportedly loved her had interrogated her.

Now he turned his thoughts from her with an effort. He was alone on this high ridge, the wind off the Pacific churning up white caps on the ocean and buffeting the trees surrounding this open space. He'd found the missing horse and supposed he should get going, too.

Mission accomplished.

At least for the day.

He climbed into the saddle and from atop his horse, glanced out to the sea again, trying to locate the spot he'd found her staring. Murky water, varying shades of gray, rushed through the entrance to the bay, over the submerged, hidden bar that the locals spoke of with respect and a little fear. A string of rocks guarded the entrance, tiny dark islands poking out of the water, waves crashing and spraying over their jagged tops.

So why had she been gazing so intently at the black rocks? They had nothing to do with her child's disappearance, and she was fixated on the night her son was last seen. Rubbing the back of his neck, he realized this had to do with her brother's death, a totally unrelated event.

Kelvin Church had died in a tragic boat accident, and she'd been there, had barely survived herself. That tragedy had also left Jewel-Anne Church in a wheelchair, where she'd been ever since. And within days of the tragedy, Ava and Wyatt had welcomed their son into the world.

As he whistled to the dog, he wondered if the two traumatic events in Ava Garrison's life were tangled together and how much they contributed to her current state of mind. Today she'd been lucid, sharp enough to put him in his place.

Just how long would that last?

Starting back for the house, he adjusted the waistband of his jeans. The cold barrel of his gun, hidden under his jacket and shirt, pressed against his skin, reminding him that he didn't have a lot of time to waste. With Wyatt off the island and Ava so pissed at him, she'd want to keep off his radar. He had a little free time, and there was still some daylight, enough for a quick change of plan. Pulling up on the mare's reins, he turned toward a path leading away from the sea and into the woods where it connected to the overgrown lane running south to the old mental hospital.

It was time for him to return to Sea Cliff.

Riding through the damp woods, with the smell of wet earth mingling with the salty sea air, Ava tried and failed to shake the image of Dern's overly concerned visage. What the hell did he think he was doing following her up to the cliffs?

He saved you, didn't he?

Maybe. She didn't think she'd have taken a fateful step over the edge, but who knew? If she had fallen to her death in the sea, everyone at Neptune's Gate would have shaken their heads and looked sad and whispered that they knew she'd decided to end it all.

She made a sound of exasperation and slowed Jasper to a walk. So Dern had found her up at the ridge, so what? It wasn't as if he were following her, appointing himself her personal bodyguard. And surely Wyatt hadn't hired the man to keep an eye on her.

Paranoia . . . Don't let your fears get the better of you . . .

But as she rode out of the woods and glanced to the south, toward Sea Cliff, she wondered if the image she'd witnessed earlier, the dark figure on the wall walk, had been Austin Dern.

But what would he want with the old asylum? He's a ranch hand. That's all. His only crime is that he keeps trying to save you from yourself.

She narrowed her eyes and blinked against the drizzle as she pulled her horse up and stared at the crumbling concrete. She heard a low howl that caused her skin to crawl before she realized it was probably a coyote.

Nothing more sinister.

And no dark figure appeared on the ledge of the old hospital walls.

"Idiot," she muttered, and leaned forward over Jasper's neck again. "Let's go home, boy."

The big gelding didn't need any more encouragement. His strides lengthened and the wet grass flew by in a rush beneath his hooves. Cold air stole her breath, and as they reached the creek, she saw Jasper's ears prick forward. Rather than splash through the flattened trail area, he headed straight for a deeper chasm. Instinctively, Ava let out the reins, just as she felt his muscles bunch. With Ava leaning over his neck, he sailed over the swift stream, landing with a thud on the far side.

The second his hooves hit solid ground, he took off at a dead run toward the stable. Ava gave him his head. She should have felt that same sense of elation as she had earlier, but now her mood had darkened, all of her worries and fears crushing down on her. How wrong she'd been to think she could outrun her problems. Impossible. She knew that.

As they neared the house, she pulled on the reins and glanced up to the window of the unused guest room. The blinds were open even though she remembered seeing them closed earlier.

Graciela was probably just cleaning and left them open.

Still she focused hard and tried to see into the darkened window, but there was no one. Nothing.

Ignoring the lingering feeling that she was being observed by unseen eyes, she rode to the stable and dismounted. Taking the reins in one hand, she unlocked the series of gates that led to the stable door.

At the entrance, she couldn't help but glance over her shoulder, half expecting the rangy cowboy to appear from the trails threading through the woods.

Of course he didn't.

Silently mocking herself, she removed the bridle, saddle, and blanket; then she cooled Jasper down and offered the gelding a special ration of oats. "You deserve it," she said, reaching under his forelock and scratching his forehead. He snorted, his warm breath dispersing a few remaining oats before he sucked them up through sensitive lips. "Maybe we'll do this again sometime," she murmured before checking to see that all the horses had water and snapping off the lights.

She'd barely kicked off her boots on the porch and stepped inside the kitchen, cutting toward the main stairs, when she heard her cousin's voice.

"Out riding?"

Damn! She should have used the back steps.

Other than being flat-out rude and pretending not to hear Jewel-Anne, she had to face her cousin.

Her stockinged feet slipping a little, Ava paused at the archway to the den where an old movie was flickering on the television screen, giving off the only light to the small room.

Her cousin was waiting. Eyebrows lifting over the tops of her glasses, Jewel-Anne took in Ava's wet jacket and windblown hair. One of her ever-present dolls was at her side, and her knitting needles clicked rapidly in some kind of weird tempo in her fingers, the variegated shades of rose and pink being knit into something tiny, no doubt another cute little sweater for one of her babies.

Ava yanked the rubber band from her head. "It felt good."

"To ride? In the rain?"

"Drizzle." She shook out her braid. "Not really rain."

Jewel-Anne rolled her eyes, then turned back to the TV. "Same difference."

Don't get into this argument. Remember: She's an invalid. You have no idea how she feels trapped in that damned chair.

"See anyone out there?" Jewel-Anne asked, almost innocently, and Ava was about to report that she'd run into the ranch hand when she realized her cousin was talking about Noah. When Jewel-Anne turned to look at her again, a beatific smile curved her pale lips, an almost perfect replica of the smile on the doll sitting next to her.

A trick of your imagination.

Nonetheless, her blood ran cold. "No one," she lied.

"Didn't think so. Oh, here you go, Janey." Jewel-Anne took the time to rearrange the doll beside her so that Janey's face was turned toward the television where the flickering blue light from the screen cast weird shadows over its lifeless features. Janey sat as if mesmerized by the movie.

"There . . . all better," Jewel-Anne said to the doll, and began knitting again, her gaze returning to the images on the screen.

Wow, Ava thought. *This is just weird. Jewel-Anne blames me for the accident that took Kelvin's life and put her in a wheelchair, and this is what she's become.*

Ava started for the stairs, but Jewel-Anne's voice chased after her. "I thought maybe you saw Dern again."

"Again?"

Click, click, click.

Ava retraced her steps as Jewel-Anne added, "He went out riding after you did. I saw him. So did Simon." She glanced away from the television for just a sec. "Thought Dern might have chased you down."

Ava refused to rise to the bait, but she had questions. "Do you know anything about him?"

Jewel-Anne thought for a moment, her needles stopping their frantic cadence. "I think Dern got the job through someone Wyatt knew. Like a friend of a friend or something. I don't really know." She started knitting again. *Clickity click, clickity click.* "Why don't you ask your husband?"

"I did."

"And?"

"I think he said Dern had worked for a client of his."

Jewel lifted a shoulder, her smarmy smile in place. "So, there you go."

"I just wondered which client."

"Does it matter?" She looked up, her expression perturbed, and before Ava could continue, she said, "Look, if you don't trust Wyatt—"

"You're putting words in my mouth," she interrupted. "I just thought Dern looked familiar."

"Familiar? How?"

"I can't really put my finger on it, but I feel like . . . I don't know, that I've met him before . . . or maybe he just reminds me of someone."

"Maybe you should just ask Dern." Jewel-Anne blinked. "Unless you're afraid to."

"Afraid to? Of course not."

"Didn't think so." But her smile said differently, and again her long needles started flashing in her small fingers. "I know; you're just confused."

Ava didn't bother answering. It was useless. The woman was exasperating and seemed to love playing mind games, always trying to goad Ava.

Taking the stairs two at a time, Ava tried to outrun that niggling sense of guilt that had nagged at her ever since the boating accident over four years earlier. While she'd come out of the disaster relatively unscathed, Jewel-Anne had been tossed around the sea like a rag doll, her body battered against the rocks, her spine cracked, and only Wyatt's strength as a swimmer had saved her.

There was a reason the younger woman was bitter.

Ava was never comfortable around her, but she really didn't have the heart to ask her cousin to leave.

"Are you out of your mind?" she'd said the last time Ava had brought up the touchy subject of buying out her cousin. Jewel-Anne had then let that little statement sink in before adding, "And where would I go, huh? Got any ideas? An institution maybe? That would be easier for you, wouldn't it? Not seeing me? Not being reminded." She'd hit the button on her chair and stormed away, her chair humming along the old hardwood as she'd made her way to the elevator from the morning room.

Wyatt had been in the room and cast a now-you've-done-it glance at his wife, though he'd held his tongue. He, of course, had insisted the handicapped woman stay at the house. Easy for him, as he was gone more than he was here; he didn't have to deal with Jewel-Anne very often and rarely spoke to Demetria, the nosy, dour nurse. The idea was that Demetria would help Jewel-Anne become more independent, but as Ava saw it, the opposite seemed to be coming true.

And just after the accident, Ava hadn't been opposed to having her cousin stay in the house—far from it. Noah was born nearly two months early, only days after Kelvin's death, and his care had been all-consuming for Ava. The baby had been her absolute joy, and so when Jewel-Anne had been released from the hospital, Ava hadn't argued about whether her cousin and nurse could stay at the house. Why not? There was more than enough room. She'd been sleep deprived with the newborn, bereft over her brother's death, and, yes, feeling more than a little guilty for proposing the sailboat trip in the first place, something Jewel-Anne never let her forget.

At first there had been hope that she would recover the use of her legs. Jewel-Anne's condition had never been declared medically permanent. But after nearly five years and no visible improvement, that hope had faded, and Jewel had become a fixture around Neptune's Gate.

Ava tried not to let her cousin get on her nerves, but sometimes Jewel-Anne's attitude made it hard. Truth be told, the girl had simple needs: the freaky dolls; her Elvis collection, some of which were still on vinyl and played on an ancient stereo in Jewel-Anne's room, the one Jacob had hauled down from the attic once his sister had learned it was stowed away there; old movies on television. When Demetria wasn't pushing her charge into occupational and physical therapy, Jewel-Anne pored over newspapers, gossip magazines, and online blogs about celebrities. She was into reality shows and did get out once in a while, insisting on having different colors streaked into her hair every couple of months. She had her hair cut and colored at Tanya's shop on the mainland, where she kept up on the local gossip.

Sometimes, Ava wondered if Jewel-Anne and Tanya's conversation ever included Ava as the topic, but she decided not to worry about it, even though Tanya was known to tweak a story or two to add a little drama to her information. But Tanya was a trustworthy friend, whereas Jewel-Anne was not.

Still, Ava thought as she reached the second floor, it seemed that her cousin used every chance she could to dig at Ava. She wondered if she would ever get over her anger over the sailboat accident, would ever stop placing the blame at Ava's feet.

Probably not, Ava thought with a grimace. Jewel-Anne was forever zipping in and out of places, nearly running into Ava or startling her or just getting on her nerves. She appeared to receive a great sense of satisfaction in irking Ava. Sometimes Jewel-Anne was childlike, almost impish, as if she were no older than eleven, and other times she was calculating and shrewd and adult.

And she was a liar.

Ava knew that for a fact.

Chapter 13

"I just don't see what we have to discuss anymore," Ava said an hour later. She was seated in the family room near the window, wishing she were outside again. It was nearly dark now; last summer's lush hydrangeas were dark sticks visible through the glass. A fire had been lit, and Dr. McPherson sat in a nearby chair.

"It's been only a couple of days since your last hallucination," she said in that soft-spoken yet authoritative voice that bugged the hell out of Ava.

"I wasn't hallucinating. I saw him."

The doctor, not a hair out of place, nodded. "And I hear you've been refusing your medication."

"Who told you that?"

"Or that you're making a habit of flushing it down the toilet."

"Is this entire household part of some covert spying operation that I'm not aware of?"

"No." She shook her head. "Everyone's just concerned."

"And taking notes, counting pills, reporting back to you . . . or maybe to my husband." Ava let out a sigh and stared at the fire. "Look, I don't need this anymore."

"By 'this' you mean . . . ?"

"These sessions and the medications and all of you observing me like I'm some freak in a sideshow." She climbed to her feet and warmed the backs of her legs at the fireplace. Somehow it made her feel stronger to stand, to look down at the psychologist who seemed to be the epitome of everything Ava used to be but was now not. Evelyn McPherson's hair was pulled away from her face in a tidy knot and showed off her classic facial features that were as wrinkle-free as her jacket, blouse, and skirt. Dressed in gray, with a scarf of black and pink, her boots, briefcase, and purse all coordinated. Ava tossed a glance at her own reflection in the mirror over the fireplace: zero makeup, hair that was still crinkled from its earlier braids, jeans, and a sweatshirt that was two sizes too big.

She used to look like the psychologist.

Hell, she used to *be* that same kind of woman, but even more so. No kind, patient smiles for Ava Church. Nuh-uh. Not when she was known in financial circles as a ballbuster.

"I heard you went riding today," the doctor said.

"Yes."

"Alone."

"Who told you that?"

The doctor shook her head, and the anger that kept flaring up was white-hot now. "Sorry. I didn't realize it wasn't an authorized horseback ride," Ava said through gritted teeth.

"I was just concerned."

And she looked it, with her concerned expression. Ava almost bought into it. Almost.

"I appreciate that you've been trying to help me. But it's over. I'll handle this my way. So, this session and any further ones are over."

"Denial is one of the signs of—"

"Paranoia? Schizophrenia? Some other kind of -ia? It doesn't matter."

"Ava."

"You're not hearing me." Feeling the heat of the fire against her calves, she took a step closer to the coffee table. "Maybe I am crazy. It's possible." Before the psychologist could interject, she held up a finger. "But it's my crazy and I'm owning it."

McPherson's brow furrowed.

"There's nothing more you need to do for me," Ava said, then glanced out the window to the night beyond, a darkness that was beginning to crawl across the island.

Khloe tapped on the half-open door.

"I hope I'm not disturbing," she apologized in the doorway as both Ava and Dr. McPherson turned toward the sound, "but the door was ajar . . ." She was actually carrying a tray with a teapot and two cups.

"It's fine, Khloe. We were about finished anyway," the doctor said calmly.

Not for the first time, Ava felt as if she were in some weird movie out of the fifties where the staff was all in collusion, eavesdropping at doorways, offering tea as a ruse to listen more closely . . .

This was her good friend Khloe, from high school, offering up tea and sharing knowing looks of conspiration with the psychologist.

Bizarre, that's what it was.

Or paranoia? Maybe Dr. McPherson was right . . .

At least Khloe wasn't dressed in a maid's uniform. Slipping into the room in jeans and a sweater, she said, "I thought you might like something before dinner." After carefully setting the tray on the coffee table and holding the top of the pot in place, Khloe began to pour.

"I'll pass," Ava said as Evelyn McPherson picked up one of the steaming cups.

"You sure?" Khloe straightened and they met eye-to-eye. Once friends. Now . . .

"You know I don't drink tea." *Except on occasion with*

Cheryl, the hypnotist. "Coffee, yeah. And I used to drink Diet Coke like water. Remember? In high school?"

Khloe arched a brow. "That was a long time ago," she said as the smell of orange pekoe mingled with the scent of wood smoke. "Did you want a soda? Mom has a case stored in the pantry and I could find some ice."

"No." Ava's cold tone stopped Khloe short. Tamping down her temper, Ava added, "I just want to be treated like a normal human being. Can you do that?"

"Of course," Evelyn said evenly.

"You've never been 'normal,' Ava," Khloe said at the same moment.

Ava's lips parted, but the tiniest of smiles crossed Khloe's lips. For a second, Ava saw her as she had been so many years ago, when their biggest problems were getting dates to the prom and figuring out how to get the hell out of Anchorville.

Khloe picked up the tray.

"I just don't want people tiptoeing around me, or coming into my room unannounced, or insisting I have breakfast when I'm not hungry," Ava said, desperate to be understood. "Just once I'd like to be able to . . . I don't know . . . *sleep in* or something. I don't want anyone worrying whether I've had my orange juice or taken my pill. I just need to be left the hell alone!"

"Ava," the doctor reproached.

"No, it's okay." Khloe's gaze held Ava's, and it was as if she were seeing her friend for the first time in a decade. "I get it."

"Good," Ava said with feeling.

Khloe nodded, then, as if she realized she was suddenly getting much too personal, too close to the friend she'd once been, she swallowed hard, turned, and walked swiftly from the room.

Ava knew they all had a reason to worry, but she was getting better; she was. And she wasn't going to take any more of those damned meds!

Leaving the doctor still holding her teacup, Ava stalked from the room and headed for the stairs. She caught a glimpse of Khloe's backside as she disappeared through the kitchen door. They'd been great friends in high school. Sure, they'd had the usual spats, and Khloe had taken a while to forgive Ava for dating Mel LeFever for a time. But they'd gotten past it and spent graduation together, though Ava could still recall the night that Khloe had accused her of stealing the one boy she cared about. Of course, everything changed when Khloe and Kelvin had gotten together. Mel LeFever was a distant memory and Khloe had fallen head over heels for Kelvin.

Khloe and Kelvin . . . "Double K" they had called themselves, and Khloe had eagerly accepted an engagement ring from Ava's brother only a few months before his death in the boating accident. Ava had been thrilled for both of them, and then the tragedy struck, and Ava gave birth to Noah and the world was vastly different.

Directly after Kelvin's funeral, a broken Khloe had left Anchorville for a few months, but when she returned, Wyatt hired her as Noah's nanny. At the time, Ava hadn't been sure she needed a nanny at all, and her relationship with Khloe had become strained. Kelvin was gone, and maybe Khloe, after listening to Jewel-Anne's vitriolic rambling about the boat accident being Ava's fault, had pulled away from Ava emotionally. Their relationship wasn't the same. But Ava's protests to Wyatt about Khloe fell on deaf ears.

"It'll be good for her, let her know that she's still a part of the family," he'd said. They'd been waiting in his car for the ferry: him behind the steering wheel, tapping its rounded top to some rhythm running through his head; her staring through the windshield to the bay from the passenger seat. The sun had been out that day, bright rays sparkling on the water, fishing and pleasure boats dotting the bay. The windows had been down and the breeze had helped cool the warm interior of Wyatt's car, salt air mingling with the new car smell that still lingered.

Noah, strapped into his car seat, had let out a soft coo from the backseat and Ava had reached around to touch his soft cheek. "Hey there, big guy," she'd whispered, happier than she'd ever been.

"A little help with the baby wouldn't be a bad thing."

"I think that's the father's job."

"But his father"—he'd touched the tip of her nose fondly—"is gone a lot. And that's the way it's going to be for a while until I can convince the partners that my time is best spent in Anchorville."

"Then do it. You're a lawyer. You should be able to present a strong argument."

Wyatt had laughed, that deep, throaty laugh she'd loved. "Yeah, well, remember, they're attorneys, too."

"Oh, so they're onto you."

"Mmmm. Just consider hiring Khloe. The way I see it, it's a win-win for everyone."

"I don't know. She's not trained."

"Not professionally, but neither are we." He'd flashed that damnably boyish grin again and pushed her lightly on her shoulder. "Come on, Ava, she's the oldest of six kids. She was always helping Virginia out growing up, right?"

"But a nanny? Do we need one?"

From behind the wheel of his Mercedes, Wyatt had glanced over at her. "We still need a little time together, alone." He smiled at her just as the ferry, churning water in its wake, pulled up to the dock. "We could have some fun, you know. Noah's going to need a little brother or sister."

"Someday," she agreed, smiling despite her reservations.

"The sooner the better. You and I both know these things take time." His eyebrows wiggled suggestively. "Maybe we can start tonight?"

"Dreamer," she'd said, but laughed as he'd put the car into gear and guided the sedan onto the flat deck of the ferry. As they'd ridden to the island, she'd relented.

Within two weeks, Khloe had come to work for them, along with Virginia. Eventually she'd begun dating again and married Simon Prescott, a landscaper who had once worked intelligence and communications in the military, then took a job in Anchorville before landing here on the island. So Simon had moved in with Khloe and things had been steady for a few months.

And then the unthinkable had happened.

At Christmas time, Noah had disappeared.

Everything had changed. Khloe, rock-steady while Ava broke into a million pieces, had somehow graduated from good friend to nanny to caregiver.

Ava had been so bereaved that she hadn't noticed it happening, only knew that she'd spent hours clinging to Khloe and crying, relying on her friend for consolation and care. Wyatt, himself destroyed, hadn't been able to help his wife as she'd tumbled from despair and grief to a darker condition that no one would acknowledge outright but was the start of her hallucinations, her inability to define what was real and what was not.

"Mrs. Garrison?" She was nearly to the top of the stairs when a gruff male voice caught her attention. Turning, she found Austin Dern at the base of the stairs. "I think this is yours." He was holding her phone in one hand. "You must've dropped it up on the ridge."

"Oh." She hadn't even missed it, and as she hurried down the stairs, she thought of the two times she'd dealt with him alone, once in the bay, another time just a step or two from the edge of the cliffs. "Thanks." She plucked the phone from his fingers and started for the stairs again, then stopped. "You know, I think that considering the fact that you might have saved my life twice, you could call me Ava."

He frowned as he thought about it, and she tried to ignore that whole sexy cowboy aura that surrounded him. Unshaven jaw, tanned skin from hours outside, crow's feet fanning from his eyes as if he squinted against the sun, long, lean body covered in faded denim and plaid—definitely *not* her type. "If that's what you want," he agreed.

"I do." Her gaze touched his, and she realized his eyes were a dark brown and guarded. For a split second she remembered the length of his body pressed close to hers in the cold water. Her nightgown had been molded to her body, showing off every inch of her skin. His arms and hands had been strong, holding her tightly, helping her stay afloat. "Please."

He considered, then nodded. "All right . . . Ava." Again his gaze found hers, and what she saw in their depths was as frightening as it was arousing. She suspected that Austin Dern, when he set his mind to a task, didn't give up until it was accomplished. Her throat tightened, and she nearly stumbled on the step as she tried to back up.

She hurried up the rest of the stairs and quickly walked into her room. Closing the door behind her, she felt flushed, almost jittery, and attributed it to a lack of food. It couldn't be her reaction to the man. No way. She was not that kind of woman.

Oh, yeah, and just what kind of woman are you these days? Do you even know?

Ignoring her rapidly escalating pulse and the questions that seemed to plague her, she dug in the closet for her computer and notes and flopped onto the bed. She hit the START button on her laptop, and as the machine booted up, she wound her hair away from her face and snapped it into a haphazard ponytail.

Before she could even get into her program, there was a soft knock on the door, and without waiting for her to answer, the door cracked open and a hand slipped through. Clamped tightly in the female fingers was a sweating can of Diet Coke.

Ava almost laughed.

The arm lengthened and Khloe poked her head around the edge of the door. "I found one hidden in the back of the fridge.

I think Mom was saving it for herself." She slipped into the room and leaned against the panels of the door. "Shhh . . . don't tell anyone. Mom gets pretty tweaked if she can't get her caffeine fix." She walked across the room and handed Ava the soda.

"Thanks." Ava popped the top, hearing the click and distinct hiss of a can being opened.

Khloe hesitated by the edge of the bed. "I just wanted to tell you that I know things are weird around here. Sometimes I think we should all just get the hell off this island, but, well . . . that's kind of impossible and I know things are going to get better."

"You mean, *I'm* going to get better."

"All of us," Khloe said. She let out a sigh and looked out the window. A sadness seemed to overtake her. "Well, I've gotta run. Simon'll be home soon." She glanced at her watch and said, "Oh, God, he might be home already. Wish me luck."

"You got it."

Khloe was half out the door when she added, "And the Coke, that's our little secret, right?"

"Right."

Our little secret, Ava thought as she took the first swallow from her can.

"Watch out!" Khloe cried as she was pulling the door shut, but not before Ava heard the high-pitched hum of Jewel-Anne's wheelchair. "What're you doing here?"

Eavesdropping again, that's what.

So much for secrets.

They were impossible to keep with her cousin in the house.

Ava was about to climb off the bed and give Jewel-Anne a piece of her mind when her phone vibrated. After digging it out of the pocket of her jeans, she saw Wyatt's face and number on the tiny screen.

"Hey," she answered, settling back against her pillows.

"Hey back at you." The anger she'd heard in his voice earlier had dissipated. "I'm sorry for the fight."

"We're married. It happens," she said, though of course it was happening more often than not lately.

"I just wanted you to know that the house date has to be postponed. Meetings ran late and I've got a drink with a client, so I won't be home until late."

She'd pretty much figured the house date was off anyway. "Which client?" she asked lightly, keeping the suspicion from her tone.

"Orson Donnelly. Donnelly Software?"

Ava was familiar with the name. The guy had made a fortune in the ever-expanding software industry, developing programs primarily for start-up businesses. But lately, Donnelly and his son had parted ways and the son thought he was entitled to his share of the business or something.

"Yeah, I've got to talk him off the ledge, so I don't know how long it will take. Don't wait up."

"Okay."

"And, Ava?"

"Yeah?"

"I love you."

He hung up before she could respond, and she was left with the phone in her hand, not even able to say to the empty room, "I love you, too."

Chapter 14

"I swear I had a Diet Coke in here," Virginia muttered to herself, her shoulders deep into the refrigerator. No one else was in the kitchen, at least not that Ava could see.

Hearing footsteps, Virginia straightened and slammed the door shut. "Guess I'll just have to restock."

The dinner dishes were still piled in the sink, the dishwasher half emptied, the smell of clams, garlic, and tomato sauce heavy in the air. Three filled plates were covered with Saran Wrap, and two plastic containers were packed with the extra red clam sauce, the leftovers from a meal that Ava had devoured. For the first time in days, she'd had an appetite, and the warm bread, Caesar salad, and spicy pasta had been delicious. Enough so that she'd managed to get through dinner without getting furious with Jewel-Anne or perturbed with Demetria. She hadn't even bristled at Ian's remarks about her being "lucky" enough to own so much of the island even though he'd sold his share to her long ago. His resentment was usually masked, but once in a while he couldn't help reminding her that she'd "played her cards right." He'd always made his statements as if they were a joke and he was just teasing her, but she knew beneath his smile was the grim belief that somehow she'd taken advantage of him and the rest of the family by buying them out.

Tonight she'd ignored him.

"Are these for Khloe and Simon?" she asked, indicating the covered plates.

"Mmm. And the new man . . . Dern." Virginia was walking into the pantry where she scrounged around the shelves and returned carrying three cans of soda. "I thought he might appreciate it." She opened the refrigerator door again and slipped the Diet Coke onto the shelves. "Bachelors, you know." As the door shut, she gave Ava a knowing stare. "Never cook for themselves."

"Let me run it down to him," Ava offered, and when Virginia seemed about to object, she added, "Payback. He found my cell phone earlier and returned it to me."

Virginia shrugged. "One less trip for me."

After sliding into a jacket, Ava grabbed the plate and headed for Dern's apartment. It had been her plan all along, to find some excuse to talk to the man again, find out a little more about him. As she walked swiftly along the path to his quarters, she tried to convince herself that she needed more information on the man because he was her employee, someone who had shown up rather abruptly, and she just had the feeling that there was more to him than met the eye. It wasn't because he was attractive, for God's sake, and even if he was, she was a married woman . . . maybe not happily married, maybe even a hair's breadth from separating and even divorcing her husband, but married just the same.

The fog was hanging low tonight, the security lamps shrouded in a fine mist, and the sound of the sea was a muted rush in her ears. Closer to the stable, the smell of horses filtered through the briny smell of the salt water from the bay and she noted the patches of light from the window of Dern's quarters.

Her boots rang up the old steps, and she heard Rover give a sharp bark as she climbed the stairs to his apartment. Before she was on the landing, the door opened and Dern, backlit by an interior lamp, filled the doorway.

Upon seeing Ava, Rover went nuts, barking and spinning in circles behind Dern's jean-clad legs.

"Built-in security system," she said, hitching her chin toward the excited shepherd as she handed the new man the plate. "This is from Virginia. She has this thing about making way more food than anyone could ever eat."

"Really?"

"Consider it a perk of being hired at Neptune's Gate. Trust me, Virginia won't let anyone starve while they're here."

Rover was whining and sitting on the floor, his nose in the air, his tail sweeping the old oak planks.

"Looks like someone misses you," Dern said, stepping out of the doorway and allowing Rover to shoot past to whine pathetically as Ava leaned down to pet him.

"Yeah, well, he's a traitor." Smiling, she ruffled the dog behind his ears. "Any port in a storm." She glanced up. "He was a stray who landed here, and Ned took him in, so he kind of comes with the apartment. Virginia puts food out for him on the back porch of the main house, and there's even a dog door cut into the panels of a door off the back porch. I bought a bed and tucked it near the back stairs, but he prefers it here or in the stable or even outside. Isn't that right, boy?" she said to the dog, and his tail thumped faster against the decking. "Yeah, I thought so."

"He seems to like you."

She laughed. "He even trusts me. Now, that's unique on this island."

Dern raised a dark eyebrow.

"I know, I'm suffering from some kind of persecution complex or something." She straightened and Rover slipped down the stairs, past her to the outdoors.

"Persecution complex?"

"Or something," she reminded. "The diagnosis changes weekly. But you probably know that." She watched the dog sniff around the closest fence post, then relieve himself against it. "I'm sure Wyatt told you all about me when you were hired."

"He only said you'd had a hard time with the loss of your son. Come on in. I need to set this down." He carried the plate inside, and Ava followed him into the apartment as Rover squeezed inside again by her legs. She hadn't been over the threshold of these living quarters over the stable in a long while, but little had changed since the last time she'd visited. The same pictures hung on the walls, the rag rug was just as she remembered, and the furniture, worn the last time she'd seen it, was a little more tired than it had been. There were a few things belonging to Dern in the unit, but nothing that suggested he intended to stay for a long while.

"Is there anything more you need here?" she asked, but he shook his head and held up the plate.

"This'll do."

"Well, let me know if you find you need something."

He nodded. "I will."

"Good. I'd better get back. The spaghetti probably needs to be heated up in the microwave as it is." Leaning down, she gave the dog one last pet. "Oh, and by the way, 'Rover' was Ned's idea. He showed up without tags and no one in Monroe claimed him, so Ned dubbed him Rover." She straightened. "You know Ned, right? Isn't that what Wyatt said?"

"Never met the guy. I worked for a guy who knows your husband. Donnelly found out his son, Rand, wasn't cut out to run a ranch, so he sold it out from under him. Left me out of work. Donnelly hooked me up with Wyatt." One side of his mouth lifted into a crooked smile. "It's really no big mystery. Ask your husband." Before she could respond, he added, "Let me guess. You already have." Crossing his arms over his chest, he said, "As I said, contrary to what you seem to believe, I wasn't hired to keep an eye on you."

She nodded but hesitated at the door. "So why is it I have a feeling we've met before?"

"I must just have one of those faces."

"No. That's not it."

He raised a shoulder. "Well, I can't explain it, because I'm sure if we'd met before, I would remember you. You're not the kind of woman I'd be likely to forget."

She felt a little tingle zing through her bloodstream, then told herself she was treading in dangerous waters. "I'd better go. Let you get to your meal. Bye, Rover," and then she was out the door. Not that he tried to stop her.

She wondered if he was watching her, peering through a slit in the curtains or the blinds, then shook off the idea. It was dark, even with the few security lights shining, so if he was watching, he'd only note that she was making a beeline for the back of the house.

As soon as she was out of the pool of eerie light cast by the lamp nearest the house, she turned and walked through the garden, to the memory stone that Wyatt had placed for Noah a year after his disappearance.

"Get rid of it," Ava had insisted at the time. "It's like a gravestone and he's not dead."

"It's just a memory plaque. When he returns, we'll make note of the date or remove it altogether."

She'd been furious at the time, but once the smooth stone, etched with Noah's name was placed in the garden, near a climbing rosebush that wound upon a trellis, she'd found surprising comfort in running her finger over her son's name or just kneeling near the rock and remembering holding him, feeling his warm arms around her neck, hearing his high-pitched laugh. God, she missed him . . .

She passed by the stone tonight, slowing and reaching down

to touch the tiny memorial. "I will find you," she promised. "Wherever you are, honey, Mommy will find you." Her throat tightened, but she didn't break down, wouldn't let herself.

Straightening, she walked through the back door to the old staircase that wound its way from the basement, up three flights, and past the attic to the widow's walk at the top of the house. The stairs had originally been built for the staff, but there was no hard-and-fast rule. Still, most of the time everyone who lived or worked at Neptune's Gate used the elevator or main staircase, and as she creaked open the door, she smelled the dusty, musty odor of disuse.

Her stomach clenched as she realized the last time she'd climbed down these stairs to the basement was the week of Noah's disappearance. She, along with dozens of others, including the police, had searched the house from top to bottom, and she'd clambered down the old staircase at least a dozen times, her hope dwindling with each search.

Now, heart beating with the memory, she slapped the light switch and headed down the heavy plank steps. At the bottom of the staircase, she found another light switch, hit it, and suddenly the labyrinth of unfinished rooms was partially illuminated by five or six bare, dusty bulbs, one of which flickered out while the rest gave off a dim, feeble light that washed over the junk that was stored down here: shelves of empty jars, broken picture frames, and old sports equipment, even a slot machine that no longer worked.

Aside from Jacob's bachelor apartment with its own exterior access and a wine cellar that Wyatt had insisted be built five years ago, the area was unfinished and had been so for nearly a century. She passed the glass door to her husband's wine room with its perfect blend of temperature and humidity, and out of a sense of due diligence, she tried the mysterious key in the door, which was just plain silly. The room was new, its lock shiny and large. The key she'd found was old and the wrong shape. Of course it didn't work, but as she tried to force the key into the lock, she looked through the glass door and noticed the labels on a few bottles before giving up.

She turned her attention to the main area of the cellar, a space that had been dug out and created with the rest of Neptune's Gate.

The ceiling was low, and several times she was hit in the face by cobwebs that clung to her hair, leaving a sticky residue that couldn't be brushed off. "Yuck," she muttered, wiping her hands quickly over her face.

As she passed through aisles of clutter, she saw her grandmother's sewing machine draped with its cover next to a pile of out-of-date textbooks from half a century earlier. Her uncle's bow and arrows were hanging near a pair of hip waders and crab pots complete with floats. Nearby, next to the Nordic-Track, she nearly tripped on a set of dumbbells and weights.

She'd always hated it down here.

If the dampness and the smell of mold wasn't enough, the knowledge that this space was shared by mice, rats, wasps, and God only knew what else was unnerving.

But she felt compelled to check it out.

Her heart clenched when she spied a plastic tub of baby clothes, marked and labeled with Noah's name. Next to the container were a few of his toys. She spied a fire truck with a broken wheel and a set of blocks, still in their box. Fondly, she touched the hemp-like mane of a rocking horse he'd never really used.

Her knees nearly gave way as she pried off the plastic lid and almost reverently dug through the sleepers, layette blankets, and jackets, clothes she'd boxed up before he'd turned two. She'd stored them on the shelf of the closet of one of the guest rooms, but obviously someone had taken it upon themselves to bring them down here. Her throat was thick as she fingered a tiny little pajama set made to look like a tuxedo, and she had to blink away tears when she remembered propping him under the Christmas tree that first year and taking twenty or thirty pictures with the new camera they'd bought just for the occasion. She opened one of the plastic bags and smelled the scent of the special baby soap she'd used to wash his clothes.

"I miss you," she said, then, hearing footsteps overhead, refolded the tux, slipped it into its plastic sleeve, and returned it to the tub. Clearing her throat, she crammed the lid onto the plastic bin and returned it to its shelf.

She couldn't spend much more time down here or she'd be missed, and she didn't want to explain herself.

Reaching into her pocket, she grabbed the key again and began searching for old lockboxes or desks or drawers, anything with a lock. It seemed a nearly impossible task, as a hundred years of broken, forgotten, or outgrown clutter surrounded her. Generation after generation of Churches had stored unused items between the old walls of the basement.

Starting at the far end near the ancient furnace with its huge ducts, she searched through the discarded junk and uncovered one lock after another.

First, she slipped the key into the lock of a rolltop desk.

No go.

Next, two trunks from another century.

Uh-uh, but there was evidence of mice or rats on the clothes from a long-ago era that smelled vaguely of mothballs.

Shuddering, she reminded herself to have this place cleaned.

She uncovered an attaché case and diary, both locked, but their keyholes were much too small, and as she walked through the dingy place, she became more and more creeped out. It was like picking her way through the ghosts of her ancestors, and a chill crawled up her spine, a chill that had nothing to do with the cool temperature within.

Don't let your nerves get the better of you.

Spying a dusty secretary desk in the corner of a room that

had only been framed in, she threaded the key into the lock. For a second she felt triumph, but the key wouldn't budge one iota. "Useless," she told herself. She'd been in the basement nearly an hour, and she still had no idea where the damned key belonged. Maybe it had nothing to do with Neptune's Gate at all.

She stood in the middle of the room and tried to concentrate, to come up with a logical idea for what the key was used for.

"Nothing," she said, the musty smell of the low-ceilinged room heavy in her nostrils. *The damned key is probably just part of a prank. Right up Jewel-Anne's alley.*

"But why?" she wondered. Was the girl bored, or just mean-spirited?

Shaking her head, Ava moved on. She found a vanity with a mirror that folded out into three sections. Her image in the dusty, speckled glass appeared worried and wan, on edge. "Well, duh," she whispered to the woman in the reflection. In her mind's eye, she saw her grandmother, seated on this faded, padded bench in her bedroom on the second floor—the same bench where Wyatt had been known to crash—and looking at herself in the mirror. Grannie always wore her hair wound into a knot, a perfect twist of snow-white hair, but at night, she'd let it down and stroke it in front of the mirror, her white locks still thick as they curled past her bony shoulders. Ava had been allowed inside the room that smelled of Joy, an expensive jasmine and rose fragrance rumored to have been favored by Jacqueline Onassis, or so Grannie had bragged as she'd turned her head in the mirror to view her profile, then push up the bit of a sag beneath her chin. She'd also been allowed to brush Grannie's hair, a privilege that wasn't bestowed upon any of her other grandchildren.

A cool breath of stale air touched the back of her neck and Ava shivered. She could almost hear her grandmother whispering, *Don't give up, Ava. You're a Church, a fighter. And don't be played for a fool . . . oh, no, that would never do . . .*

BANG!

Ava gave an involuntary cry and jumped from the bench at the sound. Something hard had fallen onto the concrete floor. Banging her knee on the vanity, shaking the mirror in the process, she dropped the key as she whipped around, looking through the shadowy, draped clusters of furniture.

"Who's there?" she said, her heart thumping, her nerves as taut as bowstrings.

But nothing moved.

Everything was still.

Aside from her wild, galumphing heart.

"Show yourself!"

Her throat was dry as she squinted through the two-by-fours of the unfinished wall and past the odd shapes of discarded furniture.

No one appeared.

No sound or smell indicated she wasn't alone.

But she had the distinct feeling that someone was hiding in the shadows. Watching.

She strained to hear and thought, just briefly, that she heard the sound of music, an ancient Elvis hit, probably whispering through the dirty air ducts overhead.

She forced her breathing back to normal levels.

She hadn't imagined the sound.

Something definitely had fallen.

And not on its own.

Still eyeing the shadowy room, she bent her knees and felt along the cracked floor for the key. When she didn't immediately find it, she used the flashlight app on her cell to illuminate the area and found that the key had slipped beneath the vanity. She grabbed the tiny piece of metal and straightened, her face turned toward the dusty mirror.

An image moved in the reflection, a dark shadow that quickly darted across all three mirrors.

Whirling, her skin crawling, Ava forced her eyes in the direction of the movement, reversing it in her head as it would move opposite of what she'd seen. Toward the stairs. "Who are you?" she demanded, straining to hear footsteps.

Nothing.

Oh, God.

Maybe it was her imagination, her sick mind playing tricks on her. No. She'd seen something! She had!

Her throat dry with dread, she moved forward, shining the beam of her phone flashlight into all the hidden corners where someone could hide.

What if he's got a weapon? A knife? Or a gun?

A cold fear settled in the pit of her stomach, and her entire body broke into a cold, damp sweat as she edged her way through the shadows and dust, following her flashlight's tiny beam, ready to jump out of her skin if the light caught in someone, or some*thing's*, eyes.

Dear God, she was really freaking herself out. She made her way toward the stairs but stopped when she saw Noah's toys. The rocking horse was moving, back and forth.

Her heart pounded and she looked over her shoulder, half expecting someone to jump out at her.

Someone was in the basement.

"I know you're here," she warned. "What is this?"

But no one answered. All she heard over her own shallow breathing was the creak of the floor overhead.

There was nothing more she could do down here, and truth be told, she wasn't in the mood to sit in the semidark trying to coax some sicko from his—or her—hiding spot.

"Fine. Sit down here if you want. But I'm locking the door!" Heart beating a frightened tattoo, she mounted the stairs, and only when she'd reached the top, did she take a breath.

She closed the door to the stairs and was about to make

good on her promise to lock the door when she heard the distinctive whine of Jewel-Anne's wheelchair. A second later, her cousin, earbuds in place, buzzed around the corner. Upon spying Ava, Jewel-Anne appeared surprised for just an instant, then smiled slyly and shook her head. "You were in the basement?" She pulled a face as she stared at Ava's shoulders and hair, popping out one of her earbuds, the soft notes of Elvis's "Suspicious Minds" sounding tinny and faint. "What for?" Jewel-Anne wrinkled her nose. "It's nasty down there."

Ava tried again to flick the cobwebs from her mussed hair. "How would you know?"

"What?" Jewel-Anne whispered, stricken for an instant. Wounded. Her fingers clenched over the wheel of her chair and she blinked hard against tears. "Low blow, Ava," she said roughly.

Ava felt like a bit of a heel.

"We're caught in a trap . . ." Elvis warbled almost inaudibly.

Then her cousin's lips pursed self-righteously and she lifted her little chin defiantly. "You know, Ava, I haven't always been in this chair. If you hadn't insisted we go out boating that day, Kelvin would still be alive and I'd be able to walk!"

"You've got to stop laying the blame on me," she shot back, sick of Jewel-Anne's warped view. "The accident wasn't my fault."

"Keep telling yourself that," Jewel-Anne said before reversing her electric contraption and calling over her shoulder as she rolled out of sight, "Maybe someday you'll convince yourself."

Torn between fury and, yes, guilt, Ava sagged against the door frame. Intellectually she knew that Jewel-Anne was completely wrong, but sometimes it sure felt like someone was to blame. That emotion she totally understood.

Chapter 15

Dern hadn't counted on Ava Garrison being as sharp as she was.

From what he'd understood, she was a basket case, one step out of the loony bin, but the information had been wrong. After hauling her out of the bay on the first night, he'd discovered that she was far more intelligent and intuitive than he'd been led to believe. In fact, he decided as he kept to the shadows as he made his way back from the main house to his apartment, she was a force to be reckoned with.

"The best laid plans . . . ," he muttered under his breath as he quickly climbed the stairs, unlocked the door, and stepped into his temporary home.

Rover was anxiously waiting for him and giving him the evil eye as only a dog can do for being left to his own devices. "You can't always come along, y'know." Dern scratched the shepherd behind his ear and was, it seemed, immediately forgiven. The old dog grunted in pleasure as Dern scratched his back.

"Our secret, okay?"

As if he understood, Rover let out a soft woof, then, when Dern straightened, padded over to his spot by the fire and settled in. "Good boy," Dern muttered as he fired up his laptop and stuck his connection device and jump drive into the appropriate USB ports.

Within seconds he was connected to the Internet and double-checking all the files he had on Ava Church Garrison as well as Church Island, Neptune's Gate, and the people who had lived and worked on this miserable scrap of an island. The history of the island was in one file, ties to Anchorville in another, and there was another dedicated entirely to Sea Cliff. His jaw tightened as he thought about the crumbling asylum. He'd scaled a fence and walked through the old hallways where staff members and patients had once worked and lived. Aside from a thick layer of dust, stagnant air, and a general feeling of neglect, the building was intact. On the outside, however, where the wind and rain buffeted the walls, the feeling of abandonment was more pronounced. Picnic tables were rotting, their paint peeling, the dappling of seagull droppings ever-present.

With his collar turned toward the elements, he'd walked around the outdoor area inside the fence. The old familiar paths in the grass had become overgrown, barely visible with the new growth of weeds and the concrete walkways had cracked.

Disuse and despair, that's what remained.

Sea Cliff hadn't been built as a prison, and yet that's what it had come to symbolize.

At least for Dern.

He just had to keep up the charade.

For as long as it took.

He started to second-guess his reasons for being here but quickly dismissed any lingering doubts. Ava Garrison wasn't going to ruin his plans. If she became more of a problem, he'd just deal with her.

It wasn't as if she were the first woman to get in his way.

She wouldn't be the last.

That thought stopped him short because he had a tiny, niggling suspicion that dismissing Ava Church might not be so easy to do.

The dock was empty.

Even through the shifting fog, Ava saw that her boy wasn't standing near the water.

"Mommy!" His voice called to her, and she threw off the covers. Naked, the breath of winter's air caressing her skin, she reached for her robe, but it was caught on the hook of the door and wouldn't budge.

"Mommy . . . ?"

Oh, God, he sounded frightened. "Noah! I'm coming." She flung open her bedroom door and found herself in the boathouse where the smell of diesel and brackish water filled her nostrils. Why was Noah here? Her eyes searched the murky waters, but all she saw was her own naked reflection and that of a man standing behind her, just over her left shoulder. Austin Dern, his eyes full of secrets, met her gaze in the undulating surface. He, too, was naked, and when he reached for her, placing a hand around her torso, strong fingers pressing into the flesh over her ribs, she gasped.

"Mommy?"

Noah's voice again. She turned and Dern disappeared, like a puff of smoke as she reached for the door of the boathouse and stepped outside. Dawn was streaking the morning sky as she raced barefoot up the path to the porch and inside. Taking the back stairs, she ran to the second floor and heard Noah's tiny voice calling her.

"I'm coming, baby!" she yelled, flying along the hallway, her feet slapping the wooden floors, the spindles of the railing near the front stairs rushing by in a blur.

At Noah's door, she heard him sobbing. "Oh, honey," she

said brokenly. Her heart leaped at the thought of seeing him again. It had been so long, so damned long . . . She yanked on the doorknob.

Nothing.

Again, she grabbed hold of the glass knob and twisted hard. It didn't budge.

"Noah?" Oh, God, had he stopped calling for her? "Mommy's here, just on the other side of the door. You didn't lock it, did you, sweetie?"

She pulled with all her might, her muscles straining, her shoulders aching. Through the door, she could hear his sobbing, his soft little cries.

Her heart shattered into a million pieces. "I'm coming!" Closing her eyes, she grabbed the door handle with both hands, twisting and throwing herself backward.

The glass knob came off in her hands, cutting her palms and fingers. "Noah?" she called, and heard him whimper.

Looking through the hole left by the broken knob, she saw into her son's room where all had gone quiet except for the tinkling notes from the mobile as it spun slowly over his crib. The tiny seahorse and crab seemed to be laughing at her, and she knew in her heart that her son was gone again.

Falling onto the floor, she lay in a shivering puddle of despair and terror. "Noah," she whispered brokenly, her tears mingling with the blood dripping from her clenched fists, "where are you? *Where?*"

"Ava!" Wyatt's sharp voice cut into her sobs. "Ava! Wake up!"

Strong fingers wrapped around her shoulders, and she blinked hard against the sunlight streaming through the windows. Wyatt was leaning over the bed, shaking her gently.

"What?" she whispered, then sat up and scooted into the pillows toward the headboard, away from him. The dream, so real, clawed at her brain; she actually looked at her hands for any trace of blood, but they were unmarked, not so much as a scratch upon them. A dream. Only another dream.

She pushed her hair from her face, trying to get her equilibrium, to come to terms with the fear and disappointment. As frantic as she'd been to get into her son's room, at least in the dream she'd known him to be alive.

"Are you okay?" her husband asked.

She looked up sharply at him. There was that damned question again.

"You were having a nightmare. Crying out. I thought you'd want to wake up."

She squeezed her eyes shut. It had been so damned real. If she tried, she could still hear Noah's plaintive, frightened voice.

Hearing the whir of Jewel-Anne's wheelchair, her eyes flew open again. She saw that the door to her room was open. Wyatt was the only one inside, but through the doorway, she could see both Jewel-Anne and Demetria, hovering. Ava sent an angry glare at the nurse, who herded Jewel-Anne and her contraption out of sight. "I could use some privacy," Ava said.

Wyatt was already walking around the foot of the bed. "I heard you screaming and I ran in here. I wasn't thinking about anything but seeing that you were all right." He closed the door gently, then leaned against it. Worried eyes assessed her, and she pulled the covers up to her chin.

"I've had bad dreams before. A lot," she said, her voice less sure than her words. She felt a quivering inside, and she swallowed back the panic that rose within. Maybe they were right. Maybe she really was cracking up.

"You were in the guest room?" she asked, striving for normalcy.

"No, I came in this morning. Caught a ride with Ian. I left you a text. Didn't you get it?"

"No . . . I . . ." She found her phone on the bedside table. She must've turned it off. Suddenly she remembered working on the computer until falling asleep. She hadn't bothered turning off or charging either the phone or the computer. She'd even let the computer go into sleep mode, had left it on the bed next to her. Glancing at it now, she noticed that the screen was still dark, but that didn't mean that someone hadn't seen that she'd been reconstructing the night Noah disappeared. Hit one button and the computer would come to life. Wyatt could have waited until the screen went dark again before waking her. But he would have had to have timed it just right or gotten incredibly lucky because he couldn't have predicted her nightmare.

No, it was unlikely he'd seen the screen.

So her secret was safe from him. He couldn't know how desperately she was still trying to force together the jagged pieces of that horrible night.

"You've been here a while?" she asked.

"Dr. McPherson said you were very definite about needing your space, that no one was to disturb you. You'd made that clear."

"You talked to her? Already this morning?" She picked up her phone and turned it on. "What time is it?" The face of her phone read ten-thirty. She couldn't believe it. She hadn't slept in past seven in years, since she was a college student, and only then after pulling an all-nighter the night before. A tiny light on her phone was blinking, indicating she'd received at least one message while she was dead to the world.

"How about I bring you some coffee?" Wyatt said, and her head snapped up at his kindness. A simple offer, and yet she was touched.

"Thanks. But I'll be right down."

"I'll be in the office." He smiled. "Join me."

"Okay." Her heart lifted a little. Maybe there was still a chance for them after all. They had loved each other. Passionately and fervently. "Forever," she'd whispered after saying "I do" in the garden at the small ceremony where she'd pledged to be his wife forever.

So why was it she felt she couldn't trust him? Couldn't trust any of them? She knew the answer to that and wouldn't go there, not yet. She plugged in the phone and saw that aside from Wyatt's text, there were two other calls, one from Cheryl, rescheduling their next hypnosis session, and the other from Detective Snyder. It looked like a third call had come in, but the number was unfamiliar and no message was left.

Hmmm, she thought. *Could it have been a wrong number?*

While the phone was charging, she confirmed with Cheryl for a session the next day, then dialed Snyder's number, got his voice mail again, and left a message asking if she could stop by the station the next day and go over information about Noah's disappearance. Phone calls made, she then threw on her clothes, ignored anything remotely concerned with makeup, and hurried downstairs where she found Virginia already starting on lunch by peeling potatoes at the kitchen sink. "Good morning," she greeted her.

"'Morning." After finding a mug in the cupboard, she poured coffee from the glass pot in the coffeemaker, then heated it in the microwave.

"I was told not to call you for breakfast," Virginia said, glancing over her shoulder.

"It was fine."

"There are muffins or bagels, I think."

"I'm good," she replied, and snagged a chocolate biscotti from a glass jar tucked into a corner of the counter. "This'll do."

"Humph. Not much of a breakfast." Virginia clucked her tongue as she peeled the thin skin off another potato, and Ava, determined to smooth things with her husband, headed to his office on the first floor.

She found him seated at his desk in front of his open laptop, his cell phone cradled between his shoulder and cheek while he scribbled notes on a yellow legal pad. As she entered, he held up one finger, and when she tried to back up, he shook his head and waved her into a chair near the French doors that led to the veranda. She tucked one foot under her other leg as she settled into the chair, took a long swig of coffee, then dipped her biscotti into her mug.

"Sure . . . I'll be there . . ." Wyatt glanced at the small desk clock situated on the corner of his desk. "Let's see. How about four?" His gaze shifted to Ava and he rolled his eyes as he listened to a long diatribe on the other end of the phone.

Smiling, she turned her attention to the window where the glass was still heavy with moisture, the sun just beginning to warm the panes.

She'd just swallowed her last bite of biscotti when he finally hung up. "Sorry," he said, "had to do a little lawyer hand-holding. Orson Donnelly again." He leaned back in his desk chair until it groaned in protest. "Between you and me, he's a real pain in the ass."

"He's the one who gave you the reference on Dern?" she asked.

"Yeah. Dern worked for Donnelly's son before Orson sold his place. He mentioned the guy was out of work, and since Ned had already taken a hike and Ian was a . . . less-than-enthusiastic rancher, I called him, had him fax over his credentials, double-checked with Donnelly that Dern wasn't the reason his ranch was failing, and hired him." He cocked his head to one side. "You have a problem with the guy?"

"Just curious as to how he just showed up one day. Everybody else who works here I knew before they were hired, or in Simon's case, because he married Khloe." That much was true. She'd known Graciela because she was a friend of Tanya's younger sister, a local who had grown up in Anchorville.

Demetria, too, had lived across the bay but had worked at Sea Cliff before hiring on as Jewel-Anne's personal caretaker. Even Ned had been a friend of Uncle Crispin's, whom he'd hired on years before.

So Dern was the outsider.

"I thought I'd give Ian a break." One side of his mouth lifted. "Maybe now he'll have a chance to find his true calling." He leaned forward and, placing his elbow on the desk, said, "Want to talk about your nightmare?"

"Nope."

"It was about Noah again."

She didn't bother answering, didn't need to.

"That's one of the reasons you're on medication. So you can rest. Get quality sleep. My uneducated guess is that either the prescription isn't working, or you're not taking your meds."

"Hmm," she said.

Frustration darkened his face. "You'd rather hallucinate, or nearly drown, or scream your way through some terrifying dream than take the meds?" When she didn't respond, he said, "I know you don't want to feel doped up. I understand that. But you're not doing yourself any good or the rest of us, who have to be on edge worrying about you, listening to you scream in the night, or fishing you out of the drink before you drown. If Dern hadn't been nearby the other night, I shudder to think what would have happened to you."

"I can swim."

"Ava." He shook his head in disbelief. "If you hadn't drowned, there's always hypothermia and . . . you weren't yourself. Who knows if you'd really be able to save yourself!" He made a sound of exasperation. "I just don't know what to do anymore."

"How about trying to back off a little?"

"Seriously? And risk you hurting yourself?"

"What are you really suggesting, Wyatt? That I go back to

St. Brendan's?" She hadn't even been home a month and he was trying to wash his hands of her. "Is that what you want?"

"No!" He looked at her sharply, his hazel gaze drilling deep into hers. "Of course not. But I'm running out of options here." His fingers splayed into the air, as if he was about to fend off any other objections. "I just wish you could quit fighting me. I lost a son, too, you know. I'm just trying like hell not to lose my wife as well."

Her throat closed and tears threatened her eyes as they always did when he was kind to her. "He's alive."

"I want to believe that, too. Really. But whether Noah's alive or . . . not, he's gone, Ava. You have to accept that. He's not coming back. If he'd been kidnapped that night, then why hasn't anyone contacted us? Why no ransom note? And . . . and if he was sold to another couple who was so desperate for a child, why hasn't he been found? There were pictures of him plastered all over the media. The newspapers. Television. Radio. The Internet, Facebook, and MySpace and you name it. We tried everything. You remember what a circus it was!"

She did. Those first few days filled with hope and despair and panic and the soul-numbing fear that they'd find his body.

Wyatt's face was lined with concern. "You have to face facts, Ava. Noah is gone. It kills me, too."

"But last night, I heard his cries."

"You were dreaming!"

"No, they were coming from his room."

"It was just the wind or . . . or this old house creaking or God knows what, but something was permeating your mind, infiltrating your subconscious and twisting it into some kind of weird manifestations within your dream."

"I know what I heard," she said, and from the corner of her eye she saw Jewel-Anne zipping toward the elevator. Jewel slid a glance at the open door of the den but didn't meet Ava's eyes.

Wyatt caught the exchange and pushed back his chair. He

rounded the desk and softly but firmly shut the door. Then he crossed the floorboards to stand directly in front of her. "Ava, please, I'm just trying to keep things together."

"I'm not trying to thwart you, Wyatt," she said, her voice raspy with emotion. "I just have to do whatever I can to find out what happened to Noah."

"Even if it means sacrificing your health? Our marriage?"

"I don't want to sacrifice anything, Wyatt. And I shouldn't have to. I just want to find our child. Let me do it."

She walked out without waiting for his answer.

Chapter 16

He wasn't getting it, Ava thought the following morning as she grabbed her jacket, slid her arms through its sleeves, and walked outside. Wyatt wouldn't let himself see her need. He didn't understand her and therefore wouldn't, or couldn't, help her. Ever since she'd returned from St. Brendan's, neither she nor Wyatt had brought up the D-word. It was almost as if by silent, mutual agreement they'd decided to try to make the relationship work, that no papers would be filed.

But it wasn't working.

They both knew it.

Wyatt had kissed her good-bye before he'd headed to the mainland yesterday, but the kiss had been a quick buzz on the forehead, nearly an afterthought. A duty.

Theirs was a complicated relationship, and maybe always had been. Maybe she'd been young, naïve, and hadn't wanted to peel back the layers and look too closely at their marriage. She pocketed her phone, grabbed her purse, and was on her way outside when she ran into Ian on the first floor.

"I'm going into town to pick up Trent," he said. "Need anything?"

"Trent's here?" Ian's twin lived in Seattle.

"In Anchorville. He texted a couple of hours ago and asked if I could come get him. He said he tried to reach you, too, but you didn't answer."

She must've missed the call that had come in.

"Ask your husband. He invited him."

"Wyatt didn't say anything," Ava said.

Ian lifted a shoulder. "That's just what Trent told me. I don't think it's a secret. No big deal."

Ian was probably right and she decided not to start planting suspicions in her own mind. It was crowded enough as it was. "All I want is a ride across the bay, if you're going."

"You got it. So what is it this time, business or pleasure?" he asked as they walked toward the boathouse together.

"What do you think?"

He laughed. "That there's not much of either going around right now."

As they passed by the dock, she glanced at the graying boards and tried to convince herself that she hadn't seen Noah the other night, that it had all been just a trick of the fog and her own willing mind.

Blue smoke and mirrors.

Ian ferried her across the bay and offered to pick her up later, but she declined and left him to meet his twin at the Salty Dog.

First stop: the Anchorville Police Department, where she was meeting with Detective Wesley Snyder.

"You know, Ms. Garrison, I'm sorry, but we don't have any new leads," Detective Snyder said from the other side of his cluttered desk. He was a tall man, his suit coat sleeves riding up his arms. Light gleamed off his bald head, and he looked at her from a face etched with genuine concern. His "office" was a cubicle, one of several with half walls that separated it from other, identical semiprivate offices. Though the walls were padded, the sounds of jangling telephones and other peoples' conversations, the thud of footsteps, and the hum of printers and fax machines seeped into the space.

Ava was perched on the edge of one of the uncomfortable visitor's chairs and trying to find a way to get through to the one man in the sheriff's department she considered an ally. "I just thought that if I saw your notes, what you'd pieced together, and compared it to what I have, maybe I could find something that was missed earlier . . ." She saw the answer in his eyes.

"I'm sorry. I can't do that. We've been over this before."

"I'm Noah's mother."

"Doesn't matter. I'm not allowed to let anyone outside of the department see what we've got. It could compromise the case. You know that."

"It's been two years."

He ran a hand behind his neck. "I know, but I can't break the rules. However, if you have anything you think might help, by all means leave it with me."

"I don't have any hard evidence, if that's what you mean. Just what I remember from that night."

He found a thick folder on his desk and opened it as he plucked a pair of reading glasses from his jacket pocket, shook the bows open, and shoved the half-lenses onto the end of his nose. "Let's see." Flipping several pages over, he stopped halfway down the stack, grunted his approval, and pulled several pages from the clip that held them fast. He scanned the pages, then slid them across the desk.

She recognized her statement from the night of Noah's disappearance. "This is what we've got from you. Oh, and I think this, too . . ." He dug a little deeper in the file and found a few more pages, this time part of an interview that had been recorded and transcribed. Most of the information was the same as what she'd compiled over the last few days. He said softly, "Was there something more you wanted to add?"

She started to feel foolish as she recalled when she'd made this statement. They'd been at the house, in the dining room, and Detective Snyder's little recorder had been sitting on the table as the interview had progressed, its pinpoint, red light flashing as she spoke. She'd told him all about the party the night before, where everyone had been in the house, what she remembered of the night. It was the very same information she'd put together again.

"No," she admitted, feeling the heat climb up her neck as she sat back in the chair. "This is what I remember."

He replaced the pages and his eyes above the half-lenses were kind. "Well, if you think of anything else, please, let me or someone here know. And I promise, I'll keep you in the loop if anything new develops." He stood then, indicating the interview was over, and she left feeling deflated.

Of course the police wouldn't listen to her; not without some hard evidence, something beyond conjecture, or her own visions, or her own damned needs.

She walked out of the station and took a deep breath. Clouds were rolling in off the Pacific, dark and gray. A blustery, relentless wind was chasing along the waterfront, and the temperature seemed to have dropped ten degrees since she'd entered the police department. Tightening the belt of her sweater coat, she walked the seven blocks to Tanya's salon.

Raindrops were just beginning to splash against the sidewalk as she ducked under the striped awning of the Shear Madness salon. A small bell tinkled as she pushed open the door to the small shop. Along one wall was a row of three stations, each complete with pink sinks, pink chairs, and small faux crystal chandeliers sparkling overhead. The first station was occupied, a woman leaning back in the sink while her beautician washed her hair, the smell of recently used chemicals heavy in the air.

"Hi, Ava," Hattie, the stylist, said as she glanced over her shoulder. "Tanya's in the back." Then to her client, "Okay, that's good," as the woman sat up and Hattie started gently toweling her head.

Ava picked her way over hair clippings that hadn't yet been swept up, past the two empty chairs, and a huge photograph of Marilyn Monroe on a back door where she knocked and found Tanya standing in the middle of the unfinished back room. A toilet, sink, and stacked washer and dryer were framed in. The rest of the space was still open, and from the temperature, without any heat vents.

Tanya was still wearing the gloves she used to color hair and a dark apron over a long skirt and sweater. She was standing square in the middle of the concrete floor. "Hey, hi," she said, turning to look over her shoulder as Ava stepped into the unfinished room. "I was just trying to figure out for about the millionth time how to cram in a manicure and waxing station back here, maybe a tanning bed or massage table. Trouble is, I need a hallway to get to the washer and dryer and still have room for a back door and . . . oh, who knows . . ." She peeled off her gloves in frustration and tossed them into a basket near the washer. Then she turned to Ava and gave her friend a hug. "It's good to see you. And you don't need to hear about my space/construction/contractor problems. Besides, I'm going cross-eyed just thinking about them. Maybe I should just leave things as they are. C'mon let's go eat! I'm starving!" She was already untying her apron and reaching for a jacket hanging on a bracket on one of the exposed two-by-fours.

"Perfect."

"Guido's?"

"You read my mind."

Tanya opened the door to the salon and poked her head inside. "I'm taking off for an hour or two, Hattie."

"Got it. I'll hold down the fort," was the muffled reply.

Tanya let the door to the salon close and, as she zipped her jacket, led Ava to the back exit. She snagged a pink umbrella from a stand, then unlocked the door and held it open for Ava.

Outside, rain was pelting the broken asphalt of the alley that ran the length of the tightly packed buildings. A black cat, belly low, scurried across the alley to hide beneath the loading dock of a furniture store. Beyond, the sky was an ominous, dark gray.

Ava flipped up the hood of her sweater and mentally kicked herself for not bothering with a jacket as Tanya fought with the umbrella. Together, half running, they skirted puddles, parked cars, and trash bins, then turned onto a side street, where they caught up with the sidewalk. Three blocks later, they jaywalked across a narrow street to an Italian restaurant tucked into a storefront. Guido's, an Anchorville institution, had been run by the Cappiello family for as long as Ava could remember.

Inside, the restaurant smelled of garlic, tomato sauce, and warm bread. The floor was black-and-white tile, and a flag of Italy was proudly mounted over the arch leading to the kitchen. The walls were painted with fake windows opening to scenes from Italy. Seascapes of the Italian coastline or panoramas of hills of vineyards were interspersed with "views" of the Colosseum or Trevi Fountain or some other recognizable Italian landmark. Tanya picked a booth that cuddled up to a picturesque "window" with a view of the Leaning Tower of Pisa.

"This is my favorite," she explained, peeling off her jacket. "From here I can see the door. I always like that. My dad was a cop, you know, and always faced the door. Just in case."

"You're a hairdresser."

She shrugged. "Old habits die hard." She picked up a plastic-coated menu, scanned the items, and said, "I'm going to have the linguini with pesto. Oh, God, I shouldn't. I've been dieting all week . . . no more than, like, a thousand calories a day, but the pesto, it's all homemade and organic and just a-MAZ-ing!" She snapped her menu closed. "Trust me."

"I do," Ava said without thinking. It was true. Tanya was one of the few people she knew she could trust.

"Oh, God, I should really have a salad. With some kind of light dressing or no dressing or . . . oh, hell!"

The waitress, a slim girl in a black pencil skirt, white blouse, and red tie carried two glasses of water to their table. "Can I get you something to drink?" she asked.

"A glass of Chianti," Tanya said quickly, then checked her watch. "No, I can't. Got one more color job this afternoon." She glanced across the table at Ava and pulled a face. "Wouldn't want to mess up Mrs. Danake's streaks. Okay. No. I'll have a diet soda. And a house salad. You know, I *want* half the items on the menu. Oh . . . damn, I should be shot, but I'll have a side of the pesto linguini."

"Lunch size?"

"Perfect." She rolled her palms to the ceiling where a fan was slowly turning and intoned, "I had no choice."

"A cup of the minestrone soup and the same pasta," Ava ordered.

"Oh, wait. We could split an order of the linguini," Tanya said, brightening. "Half the calories."

Ava smiled. "Fine with me."

Tanya, pleased with herself, turned to the waitress. "Could you do that, split the pasta, but maybe the dinner size?"

"Sure."

"And I'll want bread sticks with my salad."

"A basket of bread is complimentary."

"Awesome." As the waitress disappeared, Tanya leaned back against the hard bench. "I *hate* dieting. It's such a pain. What I really want is a three-course Italian meal, complete with sausage on the side and tiramisu for dessert, and then top it all off with a cigarette." She sighed loudly. "I'm afraid those days are gone forever."

"Sounds like what we had when we came here in high school, after a game. Maybe you should join the cheerleading squad again."

Tanya laughed. "Shhh! No one knew I smoked."

"Shhh . . . *everyone* knew you smoked."

"Don't tell my mom, okay?" she said with a sly grin. It was her joke. Tanya's mom had been dead for six or seven years.

"I think she knew."

"Yeah, she did. I borrowed one too many Salem Lights from her purse and she got wise."

Ava chuckled. "So you promised me some recent pictures of the kids . . . ?"

"Oh! Yeah. Got 'em." Tanya grinned from ear to ear, then began rummaging in her bag until she found her phone and started a slide show on the phone's small screen.

Ava leaned across the table. "They're so big."

"Bella's nine and Brent just turned seven. Already in first grade. She's in fourth and has a boyfriend if you could call it that. You know when one of her friends whispers that some boy likes you and then all of the sudden they're quote 'going'? I ask, 'Going where?' and she just looks at me as if I'm from another planet. But nine. Really? A boyfriend? Isn't that the time you're still hating the opposite sex?" She shook her head. "So now I get to monitor the TV and the computer or before I know it she'll be quoting one of those ridiculous reality stars."

Flipping through a few more pictures, Tanya said, "Here's a recent one of Brent, who, wouldn't you know, wants to be a cowboy." She wrinkled her nose.

"Like his dad," Ava said, and looked at a picture of Brent wearing a Stetson that was at least three sizes too big and what appeared to be a brand-new pair of cowboy boots.

Tanya scowled. "Anything but that." She moved through the rest of the pictures quickly, showing off images of Bella dancing or riding on a boat or playing soccer, while Brent was with a mottle-colored dog, or on a horse, or looking so small in a football uniform. "I'm not big on this, either. I think he's waaaay too young, but Russ paid for the sport and supposedly it's not tackle and I don't know. It's hard raising kids these days . . ."

The minute the words were out of her mouth, she pulled a face and looked contrite. "God, Ava. I'm sorry. I'm so dumb sometimes!"

"No, it's okay," Ava said quickly, but it was a relief when the waitress appeared with their drink orders, saying their meals would be there in a few minutes. She turned her attention to another booth, where a couple was so in love, they'd squeezed into the same side and were making cute little jokes about tossing coins into the fountain painted onto the wall next to their seating area.

"Young lust," Tanya said, and the moment passed.

"So, how are you and Russ getting along?"

"Let's see . . . He's an ass. I don't know what the hell I was thinking. Marrying him was kind of a rebound thing, you know, after Trent. Russ knew all about how I felt about Trent, and he never seemed to believe that I was over him." She twirled her straw in her drink. "Maybe he was right. I mean, Trent . . . he's . . . got 'it,' whatever that is." Her ice cubes danced as she added, "I saw him the other day, you know."

"Who?"

"Trent. He was here. In town. Well, at the marina."

"Really? I know he's here now. Ian said so and was going to

meet him, but when I talked to him on the phone, he never mentioned being in Anchorville."

"Okay," she said with a shrug.

"You're sure you didn't see Ian?" Ava questioned.

"*I* can tell the difference," Tanya said with a snort. "I dated Trent for over a year and he was my first, you know. I'd never done it with anyone before. So, yeah, I think I can tell him apart from his twin. It's not like they're identical."

"They look a lot alike."

She lifted a shoulder, unconvinced.

"You talked to him?"

Tanya shook her head. "Nah. I was surprised to see him and didn't look my best and"—she grimaced—"I should have said hi or something." More rapid twirling of her straw. "And he was such a big presence in my marriage, you know, I figured I'd leave it be. Russell and I are still arguing about money and . . . even though just talking to Trent might not lead to anything, it might get back to Russ and fan all those old jealous fires." She gave a mock shudder. Then she looked back at Ava again, focused on the here and now. "I know it shouldn't matter. I shouldn't let anything Russ does change my life, and I try not to, believe me. But he's still the father of my kids and I still have to deal with him. It's just easier sometimes if I don't rock the boat."

"Come on, you have a life to live, too. You can't let Russ control you. That's emotional blackmail."

"Maybe." She shot Ava a look. "So tell Trent to call me when you see him."

"How about I give you his new phone number." She found a pen in her purse and a napkin on the table, then found Trent's number in her phone and wrote it down. Sliding the napkin across the table, she added, "This is really none of Russ's business."

"Tell him that." Tanya tucked the napkin into a pocket of her jeans. Sighing, she glanced over at the young couple, then at the painting of the leaning tower. "I remember being 'in lust' with Russ, but I'm not all that sure we were ever 'in love.' Not like you and Wyatt—Oh, here we go!"

The waitress deposited their first course on the table, then added a basket of warm bread wrapped in a napkin. Ava tested her soup and Tanya fished out a bread stick and dunked it into her dressing before twirling it deftly to remove the excess dressing before taking a bite. "Oh my God, this is good." She washed her bite down with diet soda, then said, "So tell me about the other night. You know, when you took your little dive into the sea."

"I jumped," Ava corrected. "And it was off the dock, in the bay, not exactly the ocean."

"Why did you do it?" Tanya asked, dipping her bread stick in the dressing again.

"I thought I saw Noah again. I know it sounds crazy, and . . . maybe it is, but I know what I saw." She sighed. "You think I'm ready for the loony bin, too."

"Of course not. But there are a lot of mental . . . issues in your family. I mean, kind of a crazy streak that goes through the generations? You told me that."

"I know."

"Didn't your great-great-grandmother throw herself off that widow's walk at Neptune's Gate?" she asked. "And Trent's father had some kind of mental blackout while he was driving, right? Killed his wife?"

"Uncle Crispin. His first wife."

Tanya looked at Ava, and they both knew what the other was thinking: the rumor that the accident wasn't really an accident at all, that Crispin had already been involved with Piper and a divorce would just be too expensive. Nothing had ever been proven, but the taint still remained.

"We've got our crazy stuff," Ava admitted. "I'm just the craziest right now."

"You came unhinged when Noah disappeared. You can't be blamed for that. You freaked. I would, too."

Ava thought a moment, then said, "Tanya, can I tell you something?"

She leaned forward. "Oh, goody. Some deep dark secret?"

"When Noah went missing, we searched the entire island. I even went down the ridge stairs and spent the rest of the night there."

She nodded.

"But now, when I see Noah, it's always at the dock. There's nothing that connects the boathouse or the dock or anything to his disappearance, but there he is. It just feels so damn real."

Tanya stared at her friend, and Ava braced herself for another lecture about how she was fantasizing, wishing her boy alive and tricking her mind into creating images of him, creating false hope, but Tanya reached across the table and took Ava's hands in hers. "Okay, then let's say he's alive," she said, nodding slowly.

Ava could scarcely believe her ears. Someone was actually listening to her. "But he looks the same as he did the last time I saw him, two years ago. He hasn't changed."

"You trying to talk me out of this now?"

"No! But it doesn't make any sense."

"Maybe you just need to figure out what the hell's going on."

"Meaning?"

"Either you're hallucinating or you're seeing a ghost . . ."

Ava yanked her hands back, not liking where this was going.

"Or someone's messing with you, yanking your chain."

"But how?"

"I don't know. Psychotropic drugs? Hallucinogens?"

Ava thought of the pills she was asked to ingest. "Either way, you're saying that my visions of Noah are all in my head. That he's not really there."

"You said it yourself. He's not the same age. I'm just saying that whatever happened to Noah, your visions are something else."

Her insides turned cold. "You mean, someone wants me to believe he's alive when he's not?"

"I don't know about that. I mean, you're seeing Noah, right? Not purple dragons or palm trees growing out of icebergs or your dead mother or even Kelvin. Just Noah. I'm not sure any drug can induce a specific manifestation. No, you're putting Noah in there. But the hallucinations might have a cause." She grabbed her fork again.

"You're saying someone *wants* me to see him."

"No, I'm saying someone *wants* you to think you're crazy. And *you're* using Noah. Or, more accurately, your own grief is using Noah's image."

"But why would anyone do that?"

"You tell me. Who would have the most to gain if you were out of the picture? Or institutionalized?"

"Or dead?" Ava suggested, taking Tanya's logic to the next level.

"No, not dead." Tanya was shaking her head so violently, her curls bounced around her head. "That would be easy."

"What do you mean?"

"Killing someone. Easily done. Weapons, assassins, pills, whatever. You can get killed a thousand different ways. It's the getting away with it, that's the problem. So, if you want to keep your hands clean, maybe you just drive the person crazy. Gaslight 'em."

"You're starting to really worry me," she said with a smile.

"Har, har, har. Tell me I'm wrong. What if someone really wants you to believe you're going off the rails . . . way off the rails?"

"To get rid of me?" she asked skeptically.

"Get you out of the picture, anyway." She tucked into her linguini.

"Who? Why? Church Island?"

"That's a good guess."

"I don't even own all of it. And believe me, it comes with its own problems. Big, big problems."

"Then name something else. I'm just sayin'," she muttered around a forkful of pasta. Her eyes seemed to glaze over. "God, this is good!"

Chapter 17

Trent didn't answer.

Not on the new number he'd given her nor on his old cell number, which she tried again out of desperation. No voice mail had been set up on the new phone, so she texted him, asking him to call her as she hiked up the side streets to Cheryl's studio.

Had Tanya really seen him recently? Especially since he'd been in Anchorville?

And if so, what did it matter? He'd never really said where he was calling from, but since he lived in Seattle, it was possible he'd arrived unannounced. It wasn't impossible, just out of character. One more thing that didn't seem right and tickled Ava's radar.

Deep in thought, she pocketed her phone and felt a light mist against her face. The rain had stopped for the most part while she'd been in the restaurant with Tanya, but now the temperature had dropped again and a thick blanket of fog had rolled in.

The narrow streets were deserted, no pedestrians out, only a few cars rolling by. Here and there she saw patches of light, warm spots glowing in the gloom of coming evening. Twice she felt as if she were being followed, as if she'd heard the scrape of footsteps on the pavement behind her, and twice she'd been wrong. When she'd looked over her shoulder, she'd seen nothing but wisps of fog and a deepening night.

"Get over yourself," she said just as a dog started barking crazily. She jumped before realizing the sound was coming from at least a block away. Still, she glanced behind her and for just a split second thought she saw movement near a tall fir tree, but as she stared at the conifer's wide trunk, she realized she was seeing only a broken branch that nearly scraped the ground as it was buffeted by the wind.

Stop it!

She turned and hurried up the next block and a half to Cheryl's studio. Though she still felt as if hidden eyes were watching her, following her every move, she ignored the warning prickle at the top of her scalp and just walked a little faster, past a parked car and a dripping wall of arborvitae before crossing a final street.

Three cats scattered as she reached the entrance to Cheryl's basement and tapped on the door. Rain was pouring from the sky now, the day nearly dark as night, her sweater coat failing her completely, dampness seeping into her shoulders.

Cheryl, dressed in another tie-dyed caftan, opened the door and shepherded her through the bevy of rooms. "You're going to be soaked to the skin," she said as Ava slid onto the recliner.

"Is that a prediction?"

"I don't predict. Just open doors to the mind." But she chuckled as she lit a candle. The room began filling with the scents of lavender and thyme, and soft, soothing music could be heard over the drip of rain gurgling down a downspout mounted outside near the single window in the room. "So let's get to it, shall we?" She unfolded a blanket and spread it over Ava's legs before taking her own chair and starting the session.

Within seconds, Ava was relaxed, the edges of this dark basement room fading away, and she was with her son again in summer, when sunlight danced upon the water and Noah ran and giggled near the shore.

Happily he played in the sand, a small plastic boat in his hands . . . a boat that was the perfect replica of the *Bloody Mary*. "Where did you get that?" she asked him, and he looked up at her, his smile wide enough to show off his perfect little baby teeth. "Uncle Kelvin," he said clearly. "He gaved it to me."

But that was impossible. Kelvin died before Noah was born. Her son never had the chance to meet him. "It was Uncle Kelvin's boat?" she said, clarifying. Maybe someone else had given the toy to her son.

But Noah was shaking his head, his blond curls catching in the sunlight. "He gaved it to me." He looked up then, his eyes much wiser than his age. "Why don't you believe me, Mama?"

"But I do—"

He frowned suddenly. "You don't believe anyone."

"Noah, that's not true. Why would you say such a thing?"

He looked up at her innocently and said, "Daddy told me."

"Daddy?" she whispered as the sun seemed to go down and her son faded from her sight. "Noah?" she called as darkness descended, and she found herself on the deck of the *Bloody Mary*, the storm raging. Sails whipped wildly and the wind screamed. Rain lashed the deck as the boat pitched and rolled. Jewel-Anne screamed as if in horrid pain. . . .

And then she was with Noah again, her perfect little son, a child she never thought she'd have after her series of miscarriages. So precious. A miracle. Born right after the storm. She hardly remembered much of the pregnancy, had thought she'd had the flu in the early months.

"Three, you're coming around . . . Two, you're surfacing, coming closer . . . One . . . And you're back," she heard, awakening to find herself in Cheryl's studio. She looked down at her arms, empty. No baby to hold.

"You were in the boat again," Cheryl said softly. "You were screaming."

"I know." Ava felt weighted down and weak. There was so much she couldn't remember about that night, so much grief and sadness. She'd tried through her sessions with Cheryl to learn more about the tragedy of Kelvin's death as well as her son's disappearance, hoping the hypnotist would unlock some memory her brain refused to recall. Now, though, she wondered if it was maybe best that she couldn't recall all the details of that horrifying night.

Both Khloe and Jewel-Anne seemed to have trouble forgiving her for suggesting the boat ride that day. God knew she'd mentally beaten herself up about it, even though she knew it wasn't her fault. But sometimes it felt like there was something else. Something just out of reach, if she could just remember.

"You okay?" Cheryl asked, concerned.

"There's that question again."

Cheryl smiled, but it didn't quite touch her eyes.

"What?" Ava demanded.

"Nothing."

"Yes . . . something."

Cheryl glanced away for just a moment, then said soberly, "It's just that I think you should be careful."

"Okay . . . scary. Why?"

"Things aren't always as they seem or what we want them to be. There's a lot of bad blood out on the island. You know it. I know it. And sometimes I can't help myself. I worry about you."

Ava thought about Tanya's comments but said, "Don't," to Cheryl, touching her surprisingly cold hands. "I am careful, in my way."

"Good," Cheryl said fervently.

"Maybe we could get together, next week?"

"Yes . . ." But Cheryl's thoughts were clearly elsewhere, and Ava left feeling more unsettled than when she'd arrived.

Cheryl closed the door of her basement and leaned against it, waiting for Ava to head down the street. Her expression was sober. Dealing with Ava Garrison was always difficult, and sometimes Cheryl didn't know if she helped or hurt her.

"Help her . . . you always help," she reminded herself as she walked back to the room where they'd just ended their last session. A few of her cats swarmed around her feet and she smiled, then reached down to pet each head. Merlin, her long-haired stray, slipped into the next room, his gray tail twitching a bit. Cheshire, her overweight tabby, and Olive, the skittish tuxedo cat with white toes, white chest, and white whiskers splashed upon her black coat, trailed after her.

"Watch out," Cheryl scolded as she entered the room, closed the door, and went about straightening up. She folded the blanket that had been tossed over Ava's legs and put her notebook into a desk drawer. She blew out the candle, then snapped out the light at the doorway. The studio was instantly dark, not so much as a frail beam of light falling through the window.

Hissss!

The sibilant sound whispered through the warren of rooms in the basement. One of her cats . . . in the hallway, from the sounds of it. Probably scared himself. "Merlin?" she called, walking to the open door where the hallway, too, was dark.

Odd.

She didn't remember turning out the light.

"Here, kitty, kitty." She slapped at the light switch, but nothing happened. The hairs on the back of her scalp lifted, but she told herself it was merely a burned-out bulb. "Damn." Where were the extra bulbs? Down here and around a corner, in the utility room.

Feeling along the edge of the wall, she heard Merlin again and this time he growled, low and throaty.

Cheryl's heart began to thud. Her nerves tightened and she told herself not to let her imagination run wild. *The cat's skittish. Always jumping at his own shadow. Remember that. Nothing to worry about. Just get the bulb for the hall fixture and grab a flashlight so that you can replace it. There's one in the utility room over the sink—*

Another growl and a hiss, then a deep yowl and the quick, soft footsteps of the cat running off. Cheryl waited, ears straining. She didn't hear anything over the rapid-fire beating of her heart, so she ran her fingers along the wall, guiding herself, mentally walking these halls as she always did.

One foot in front of the other, her breathing a little faster than normal, she rounded a final corner to the utility room, stepped inside, and threw the switch.

Nothing.

The room, without a window, remained black.

The circuit breaker again.

This wasn't the first time, but the damned breaker hadn't flipped since last winter and she'd told herself she didn't need the expense of fixing it. Now that she knew what it was, she realized the fan on the furnace wasn't blowing any air; the basement was nearly silent.

Breathing a little easier, she rummaged in the drawer near the utility sink as the acrid smell of feline urine swept up her nose. Definitely time to change the litter box again. Fumbling, she found the flashlight, her fingers first encountering pencils, stain sticks, and a box cutter on which she nicked herself before grabbing the heavy cylinder. With her thumb, she pushed the switch and the flashlight's weak beam appeared, giving only feeble light.

It would have to do.

A few more steps with the uncertain beam directed at the wall and she found the breaker box screwed into the wall opposite the dryer. This junction box had been dedicated for her set of rooms, which included her apartment on the first floor and this lower level. As she pried open the box, her bloody finger left a smudge on the metal door.

Sure enough, the main switch had blown.

Never before had this occurred. Yeah, one or two breakers had switched off, but not the main switch. What the hell? She reached up to hit the button when she felt a drop in the temperature in the room.

Just a few degrees.

And she heard some street noise, the sound of a car driving past. As if a window in the basement had been left open.

Again, the feeling of something being not quite right crawled up her spine on whispery, cold legs. She reached for the circuit breaker switch and heard the scrape of leather against cement, a footstep behind her.

No!

She threw the breaker, but it was too late. The laundry room was suddenly awash in flickering fluorescent light, the tubes throwing off a weird bluish color just as strong hands slipped around Cheryl's throat.

Someone was choking her!

Panic invaded her body.

She tried to scream, to kick, to fight, but the steely fingers tightened and suddenly she couldn't breathe. Heart pounding painfully, her lungs on fire, she struggled like a wild thing, flinging her fists backward, throwing her head back, kicking and flailing, to no avail. Whatever maniac had her was strong.

Determined.

Deadly.

Please, God, no!

Her lungs felt as if they would burst, and she knew her eyes were bulging, sensed the tiny veins within popping. *No, no, no!* This couldn't be happening . . . not to her . . . not . . . to . . .

Blackness swam before her eyes and she was suddenly released, allowed to drop onto the floor. She gasped for breath, but the sound was a rasp, broken and wheezing, as if her larynx had been crushed. For a second she thought she might live, and then in her weakened vision, she saw the blade.

Long and deadly, glinting with malevolent intent.

Fear congealed in her brain.

Who . . . ?

The blade came down and slipped across her exposed throat. All she felt was a slight burning sensation, but as she lay dying, she knew that her attacker had left, heard the sound of footsteps fading, and then one of her cats meowed softly . . . gold eyes glowing in front of her face.

Cheshire . . . oh, sweet kitty . . .

And then there was nothing.

Chapter 18

Dern kept his distance.

There were just too damned many people from the island in town today. He'd seen them. Ava's husband, Wyatt, was in town, meeting with the psychiatrist. Odd, that.

And Ian had sailed into the marina a couple of hours earlier. Spent some time in the bait shop and coffeehouse, looking as if he were waiting for someone.

And then there was Mrs. Garrison.

He'd been careful with all of them. Didn't want anyone to know he'd been in town. Didn't need the wrong eyes catching a glimpse of him. If a witness noticed that he was keeping Ava Garrison in his sights, it could spell trouble. Big trouble. So he'd kept to the shadows, collar up, baseball cap low over his eyes as he'd viewed her leaving the police station. He'd hung back as she'd walked to the beauty salon, then nearly missed it when she and the hairdresser, Tanya Denton, had ducked out the back entrance and hurried along an alley to have lunch at that Italian place. Nearly two hours later, she'd left her friend back at Shear Madness while she'd trudged up the hill to the hypnotist's quarters.

Yep. Mrs. Garrison had been busy today.

By the time he'd observed her leaving Cheryl Reynolds's hillside home, it was dark. He managed to catch up with her a bit later at the marina, though he still kept to the shadows.

Even from a distance, he could tell that she was upset as she walked beneath the streetlights, sipping from a paper cup with an emblem of a local coffee shop, her mouth pulled into a tight line.

Eventually, nearly forty minutes after leaving the hypnotist, Ava was able to catch a ride to the island by good old Butch Johansen, sea captain of the *Holy Terror.*

So her little foray into town was over for the day.

He watched until Johansen's boat disappeared into the fog, and then he walked to the far end of town and down through the trees to the edge of the bay where he'd docked his small boat.

Now that it was dark, if he worked things right and his luck held, no one would know that he'd ever left the island.

"Geez, Ava, I didn't realize you'd be so bent!" Butch cast her a sidelong glance as he helmed the *Holy Terror* toward Church Island.

"I thought you hated Wyatt."

Butch was squinting into the night as the boat chugged and bounced over the choppy waters of the bay. "I don't like him, but I don't discriminate. I give rides to anyone, including Wyatt." He gave her a look. "At least I didn't marry the guy."

She was bundled up in one of his old waterproof jackets that smelled of cigarettes and the sea. "I just thought you would have said something to me."

"And get you all riled up?" Scowling beneath his ever-scraggly beard, he added, "You were riled enough as it was." Another glance sent in her direction.

"Fair enough." She was tired of fighting, tired of second-guessing, and tired of being suspicious of everyone she knew. It was exhausting.

With the boat's engine grinding loudly, he crossed the bay, slowing near the dock at Neptune's Gate. The second and third stories of the old mansion were dark, though lights were visible from the first floor and even the small window of Jacob's basement apartment.

"Just so you know," Butch said, "I'm supposed to pick up Wyatt in about an hour and bring him back to the island."

She glanced out to the cold, dark water. "I didn't really know when he'd be back."

As he lashed the boat to the dock and let the engine idle, she unzipped the oversized jacket and slung it over the back of one of the seats. "Thanks," she said, paying for the ride.

"Any time, Little Sister," he said with a quick smile.

She headed up the stone steps leading to the front door. As she pushed open the door, she caught the scent of roast pork wafting from the kitchen and saw the door to Wyatt's den slightly ajar. Tossing her purse onto the table in the foyer, she straightened her still-damp sweater coat before walking to her husband's office . . . to find Jewel-Anne behind his desk, sitting in the near dark, only the computer screen giving off any light in the room where the shades were already drawn for the evening.

At the sound of footsteps, Jewel-Anne looked up sharply and tried to maneuver away from the desk toward the door, but it was too late. One wheel got caught against the leg of Wyatt's desk chair, which had been pushed aside.

"Busted," Ava said softly, leaning against the door frame and crossing her arms over her chest.

"I left something here and I just wanted to see if I could find it."

"You left something on Wyatt's desk? Maybe dropped it on the keyboard of his computer?"

Jewel-Anne was nodding; then as her gaze met Ava's, she gave it up. "Okay, so you caught me. I was snooping."

"Snooping."

"Things are . . . weird around here."

"Really." This from Jewel-Anne?

"I overheard you and Wyatt fighting and"—she glanced at the doorway off the front hall and lowered her voice—"I thought you should know. I heard him, too."

"Him?" Ava froze. "Wyatt?" she asked, but she knew, even before Jewel-Anne whispered the words.

"Noah. I heard the baby crying. I heard him."

Ava's knees quivered. Was this some trick? She pressed one palm against the top of the desk for support. "You did not."

"Yes, I did! I heard something and it sure sounded like a baby crying to me!"

Okay, for once take this at face value. "What are you looking for on the computer?"

She shook her head. "This room is where I thought the crying was coming from."

"No."

"Noah's room is right above this one," Jewel-Anne stated flatly.

"Yes, but . . ." As she began to argue, her gaze moved to the ceiling. She pictured her son's room directly above.

"The heat ducts." Jewel-Anne rolled over to the space under the ceiling duct, which connected to the duct that opened into the nursery. "I remember playing here when we were kids. We would talk through the vents and try to 'spy' on each other."

Ava remembered all too well the games they'd played, all the cousins, how they'd run through this house, chasing each other, playing hide-and-seek or, yes, spying on each other.

"I always tried to hear what Jacob and Kelvin were doing," Jewel-Anne admitted. "And this was a good spot to hear what was happening upstairs."

From the corner of her eye, Ava noticed a shadow pass near the door, but Jewel-Anne, oblivious, was still babbling on. ". . . so I thought I might look here and see if there was anything . . ."

She let her voice drift away as Ava placed a finger to her lips, silently sending a message for Jewel-Anne to be quiet. Then, as her cousin watched, Ava crept to the doorway and peeked outside.

Of course there was no one loitering in the hall. Not a soul around. Graciela's soft humming was drifting down from the upper floor, and the sound of pots and pans rattling in the kitchen could be heard, but nothing else.

"What?" Jewel-Anne whispered, her eyes huge behind her glasses.

"Nothing. I guess. But . . . you know what? I appreciate that you're trying to help. I'm glad that someone can confirm that I actually heard a baby crying, but you probably shouldn't be snooping in Wyatt's office."

Jewel-Anne's neck arched defiantly. "Because this is your domain?" She yanked back hard on her wheelchair and faced the door. "I thought you'd be glad that someone believes you!"

"I am. But . . ."

"But what?" Jewel-Anne demanded.

"This is Wyatt's private office. He's not . . ."

"What? Come on, Ava, when have you ever cared about his privacy or anything else about him?"

"He might not like it. That's all."

"Sure."

"I do appreciate it, Jewel. And the heat ducts . . . that's something."

"I know a secret," she suddenly said.

Ava lifted her brows, noticing that Jewel-Anne seemed coldly sober and adult, as if she'd stripped off her little-girl mask for the first time in years. "What kind of secret?"

"Wouldn't you like to know?"

"Jewel-Anne," she murmured, exasperated.

As quickly as it had disappeared, the mask returned, Jewel-Anne's expression becoming sly and secretive. She poked a button on the arm of her chair, switched on her iPod, blasting Elvis's "Puppet on a String," and threw Ava another knowing smile as she zipped through the French doors leading to the main hallway.

Jacob was just rounding the corner from the family room and nearly collided with his sister. "Watch out! Jesus!" He jumped back and dropped his iPad. It hit the floor with a sickening *crrrrack*, then slid noisily toward the stairs. Stricken, he yelled, "Crap, if this is broken!" then scooped up the device, examining it closely. "Shit! The casing's split! All my notes and research and papers are on this thing. God. Damn. It!" he exploded, his face turning the color of his hair as Jewel-Anne whirred off and Demetria came running from the dining area.

"What's going on?" she asked, breathing hard.

"My damned iPad is ruined!" Straightening, his mouth a tight line, he ran his finger over the crack on the electronic tablet's shell. "Why the hell can't you get along with Jewel-Anne, huh?" he demanded, seething as he glared at Ava. "She's in a fucking wheelchair, for the love of God. Can't you cut her a goddamned break?"

Ava gazed at him incredulously. "This is my fault?"

"You're just always so right, aren't you? The fucking bitch who runs this damned island! You know, Ava, it was fine when you were smart, when you *knew* what you were doing. You could be a bitch. But now you're too fucked up!"

"What the hell is this?" she shot back, her temper sparking white-hot.

"You can't tell us what to do anymore!"

"Tell you what to do? When have I—" She caught herself up, realizing Jacob was a half beat ahead of her in this conversation. "You know what? I don't remember telling you to do anything, but I'm going to start. And here it is: move out. Just go. Find another place to hole up and do whatever it is you do, but leave Church Island. Make it today."

"What?"

"I don't know what took me so long. Too much care, maybe. Too many pills."

"You're throwing me out?"

"Yeah. I think I am."

Demetria stepped in. Holding up a hand as if her palm could quell the quarrel, she said. "Now, wait. Both of you should maybe just take a moment."

Jacob didn't pay her any attention. "I'm your driver," he pointed out, hooking a thumb at his chest as he glared at his cousin.

"I can drive myself," Ava said.

"So now you're firing me, too?" His eyes narrowed angrily. "You're un-be-liev-able!"

"No," Ava said, standing her ground. "Actually, for the first time in a long while, I think I'm finally real. And I don't like what's going on here."

"I have school!" he blurted, clearly unsure how to handle this new Ava.

"So get an apartment in Anchorville," she suggested. "It's closer to the damned campus anyway."

"Who's going to keep this place running? I'm the person who makes sure the Wi-Fi works. I've installed the special equipment you need out here. Everything from the damned boat lift to the televisions and computers, even the security system. We're on a damned island, Ava, in the middle of fuckin' nowhere! I even pulled out the microwave and put in a new control panel for Virginia last week. You need me here!"

He was right, but there was no way she was going to admit it. She took a step forward, closer to him. "Contrary to everything you believe, you're not indispensable, Jacob. We'll muddle through without you."

"Jesus Christ, you really are a bitch. Everyone's right!"

That stung a bit, but she didn't so much as blink.

"You can't kick me out!" he insisted, a finger pointing at her accusingly, his chin jutting in rebellion. "You don't own the whole damned island, not even all of this house. Jewel-Anne owns part of it, too. So unless *both* of you throw me out, you're stuck with me. The last time I saw Jewel-Anne, she didn't look like she was going to play on your side."

"Whoa," Demetria said.

Rather than argue further, he strode toward the back hallway.

Ava was left with Demetria, whose eyes followed Jacob's departure across the wide foyer. "I've *never* seen him that mad." Reaching behind her neck, she unclipped her hair. It fell in straight, lank waves around her face. "I'd say he has a few unresolved issues, too."

"Too?"

"He's not exactly the Lone Ranger when it comes to emotional problems." Leaning forward, she let her hair fall around her face, then clamped it into a fist, straightened, and clipped it tightly behind her ears again. She headed away from Ava and toward the back stairs and the elevator. "Sometimes I swear this house is worse than Sea Cliff ever was," she called back. "And trust me, that place was a nightmare."

Chapter 19

Jacob, keys in hand, stepped into his apartment, snapped on the lights, blinked twice, and said, "What the fuck, man?"

Dern was waiting for him, sitting on the edge of the unmade twin bed. The place was a sty. Wrinkled clothes were piled on the floor and bed, soda bottles and cans littered every surface, and the remains of several microwave meals, forks still embedded in the dried food, were an open invitation to the rats that probably lived in the cracks of the cement walls. The room reeked of old pizza, which probably just covered up the musty old basement odor. There was one window and it had been painted black, and a flat screen dominated the wall at the foot of the bed. Beneath the television was a collection of controllers and headgear for the video-game console cut into a closet that, Dern learned, had a back door leading to the rest of the basement.

"What're you doing?" Jacob ranted, placing his iPad onto a shelf already covered with disks and a lamp equipped with a black light. "How'd you get in?"

"Door was open."

"No way!"

It was a lie. Dern had used his lock-pick set and tension wrench and had massaged both locks open in less than two minutes.

"You can't be in here!" Panicked, Jacob glanced at his computer, its screen blank, perched on a makeshift desk created with sawhorses and a large sheet of plywood. Half a dozen sets of wires were connected to the desktop, and each split off to separate devices, including a backup hard drive, tower, modem, and secondary monitor.

"I'll call the police—this is trespassing and breaking and entering!"

Dern tossed Jacob his cell. "And while you're at it, have them take a look at your computer and explain all the porn sites you've been surfing."

"Hey, wait a second . . ."

Dern was bluffing, but Jacob didn't know it and the look on his face said it all. "It's . . . not kids or anything. Legitimate websites."

"Explain it to the cops. I don't really care."

"What the hell are you doing here? What do you want?"

"Been looking for you."

"I was . . . at school."

Dern let that one pass. "I thought maybe you could clear up some things for me."

"What things?" Jacob asked suspiciously. He walked to his desk and made sure the monitor was dark.

"I want to know how things work around here. You're the security guy. Right?"

"Not officially." Jacob seemed nervous. On edge. "No."

"But you have cameras set up, right?"

Jacob lifted a shoulder. "Some. I guess."

Dern already knew this much but decided not to let on. "Can you show me what you taped the night Ava ran off the dock?"

"Only at the house . . . I, uh, don't have any cameras set up at the dock."

"But you must have something for the boathouse? You know, in case there's vandalism."

Jacob asked carefully, "Why do you care?"

"I'm keeping the herd safe, the buildings repaired, just want to know what I'm dealing with."

Unconvinced, Jacob took a seat at his desk chair. Reluctantly, he clicked his computer back on. "I don't think this is part of your job description."

"It's pretty broad. Humor me."

"And you won't tell anyone about the . . . you know . . ."

"The porn. No."

Taking a deep breath, Jacob shoved an empty cup and notepad aside as he moved his computer mouse and accessed the information Dern asked for. The larger monitor glowed to life, and with a few clicks of the mouse, a split screen appeared. The views were limited: the front porch, back porch, exterior of the boathouse, and what appeared to be a larger, panoramic view outside of the garage that showed part of the stable and the parking area. The bottom half of the staircase leading to Dern's apartment was also visible in the wider field of vision in this view of the back of the house.

Jacob again made some adjustments, clicking through a menu, until he found the date he wanted. "Okay, so here we go," he said, more to himself than Dern. Rapid-fire images flickered through the screens, people coming and going in frantic, choppy pictures until he slowed the action down at the date in question and fast-forwarded to twilight.

Dern felt his insides tighten.

On the monitor surveying the back porch, the door flew open and Ava, appearing frantic, her feet bare, her nightgown billowing behind her, rushed past. Seconds later, she appeared on the boathouse screen and ran along the dock, only to disappear again. He saw his own image, first at the bottom of the stairs to his unit where he stiffened, turned his head, and then took off, around the edge of the house and out of the camera's view. Then, he, too, appeared on the boathouse screen, now only in stocking feet, his long legs flying as he ran outside the camera's range.

A few seconds passed and he figured this was when both he and Ava were in the water.

The camera's lens returned to a very small section showing the beach near the boathouse, but only the lower half of their bodies were visible, his jeans soaked, her nightgown gossamer and dripping, her legs distinct as he helped her toward the house.

Two seconds later the door to the porch was flung open and Khloe Prescott barreled across the porch and down the handicapped ramp before disappearing from the screen.

"You want more?" Jacob asked, staring up at where Dern stood looking over his shoulder.

"That'll do."

"Then we're square. Right?"

"One last thing. I heard you thought you saw Lester Reece escaping from Sea Cliff."

"I don't 'think' I saw him. I know I did."

"How?"

"Because I was hunting. Yeah, I know, at night and yeah, it's illegal, not even in season. I heard something in the water, turned my spotlight on the water's edge, and I saw him, man. I swear! It was Lester Fuckin' Reece. Scared the shit out of me!"

"How did you know who he was?"

"Everybody did! He was a fuckin' legend around here. And not a good one."

"So what happened?"

"I took off, that's what happened. Forgot about the fork-n-horn that I had a bead on. Just hopped in my truck and got the hell out of there!"

"Even though you had a gun?"

"A bolt-action Winchester. But, shit, I wasn't going to shoot him with it!"

"And you didn't take a picture of him? On your phone?"

"Like I had all the time in the world. He freaked me the fuck out! He freaks everyone out."

"Thought you might want bragging rights."

"What I wanted was to get the hell away from that psycho. He's killed, what, five or six people? I wasn't about to stick around and be his next fuckin' victim. I just left, man." Jacob seemed sincere, a little on edge, as if he'd really been spooked that night. "Why the hell do you care?"

"I don't. Just heard about it and wondered."

"Well you can quit wondering. I saw the bastard. Plain as fuckin' day! Now leave me alone!"

"I thought Trent was coming," Ava said after dinner as they sat around the fire, the television on mute. Jewel-Anne, with one of her weird dolls propped next to her, was seated in her chair near the window, her knitting needles moving at a frantic pace, clicking over the hiss of the fire. Wyatt, newspapers spread around him, reading glasses propped on the end of his nose, was seated on one end of the couch and Ava on the other. Ian had taken a seat in the recliner and was cradling a drink between his hands.

The whole scenario seemed false. Almost set up.

"Trent must've been held up," Ian said with a shrug. "Probably business."

Ava said, "He's a pharmaceutical rep. How much business could he have in Anchorville?"

"He's got a lot of clients." Ian swirled the ice cubes in his bourbon before taking a gulp.

"There are two drugstores in town."

"And a hospital, one urgent care, and a couple of clinics,"

Wyatt said, glancing at his wife over the top of his reading glasses.

Ian nodded. "Clients need to be wined and dined, y'know. He'll probably call and want a ride back here around midnight." Ian tossed back his drink.

"Maybe he'll stay in town," Jewel-Anne said as she continued to knit. A tiny smile played upon her lips, as if she knew something the rest of them, or at least Ava, didn't.

Footsteps approached and Demetria appeared. "You ready?" she said to Jewel-Anne. "A little PT before bed?"

"Prayer time?" Ian asked with a sarcastic smile.

"Physical therapy, again?" Jewel complained. "Didn't I do enough today at the center?" But she was already shoving her knitting needles and yarn into the bag that was snapped to her chair.

"It's only a few stretching exercises," Demetria said, and followed her charge as Jewel-Anne straightened the doll and pinned a martyred frown to her face before rolling out of the room.

"Is she always in a bad mood?" Ian asked, crushing one of the ice cubes with his teeth. "Well," he said, slapping his knees before standing, "this is just about all the excitement I can handle for one evening." With that, he carried his empty glass toward the kitchen, leaving Ava alone with her husband.

"I heard you went into town today," he said.

Her insides clenched. "I did. Lunch with Tanya."

Wyatt snorted. He'd never liked Ava's friend. "You didn't take anyone with you?"

Was there a hint of accusation in his voice, or just concern? "I figured I could handle it."

"Good . . . I just worry. That's why Khloe's stayed on. To help you."

"I'm fine," she said for about the millionth time. One of his brows arched. "Okay, maybe not 'fine,' but I'm stronger than I was even a few days ago, so don't worry. Let me be the judge of what I can or can't do."

"I know you think I'm being overprotective."

"You are."

"But you've given me reason to worry, Ava! Come on, you know that. And Dr. McPherson isn't convinced that you're capable of making all the right decisions."

"She told you that?"

"Yes."

"Shouldn't she be talking to me?"

"Of course. She'd tell you the same thing."

That much was true, Ava thought. Good old Dr. Evelyn was pretty succinct about what she thought Ava was and wasn't capable of accomplishing. "So she wouldn't think I would be able to make a *sane* decision about having lunch with my friend?"

"I think the issue is leaving the house, *alone*. Going into town, *alone*. Meeting people, *alone*."

"Then, there isn't any problem because I was never alone. I got a ride from Ian over to the mainland and rode with Butch back. I ate with Tanya." She didn't mention Detective Snyder or Cheryl.

"And when you got home, you picked a fight with Jewel-Anne and Jacob?"

"Ah . . . Demetria speaks."

"It was Jewel-Anne who told me."

"Hmm. Did she also tell you that she was in your office and I wanted to know why?"

"Something about the way noise travels through the vents," he said.

"She claimed she heard the baby crying, too," Ava said.

"What?" he said. "Oh, for the love of God, Ava! She was playing with you. She's always had this . . . *thing* about the boat accident and she's still trying to get back at you. It's childish. Ignore it."

"I believed her when she claimed she heard Noah," Ava stated firmly.

He held up his hands as if he had no time for such nonsense, and asked, "So, how did you get into it with her brother?"

"Jacob got all mad at *me* when his sister nearly ran him over with her wheelchair. He broke his iPad or something and came unglued, really unleashed on me—" She started to say more, then stopped short. "Why am I explaining this all to you, like you're my father or something? Ask him! You're my husband. You're supposed to be on my side!"

A deep flush crawled up his neck and his lips flattened over his teeth. "And you're supposed to be on mine, Ava," he pointed out. "I'm not the enemy."

"Really?" she challenged.

His answer was to stalk out of the room.

That night she dreamed again. This time she heard the sound of a child's footsteps outside her door. She threw off the covers and ran outside her room to the night-darkened hallway. Tiny pools of illumination, from the night-lights that had been installed after Noah's birth, guided her. "Noah?" she whispered. "Noah?"

Did she see him rounding a corner? Was that his soft sigh over the hum of the furnace?

She hurried from one room to the next, trying doors, finding some locked and others opening to dark, empty spaces, where beds were made and windows were shuttered.

Where was he?

Not here . . . not here . . .

Her heart wrenched painfully as she hurried down the stairs, her bare feet slipping a little on the runner.

Where is he?

Who has him?

Noah!

There is no enemy. It's all in your mind.

"Noah!" she cried desperately, and heard her own voice echo back at her. "Noah!" Where was he? Her knees trembled, and clinging to the newel post, she let herself slide into a puddle at the base of the stairs in the foyer. Her heart ached, pounding with dread in her ears.

"Ava . . . Jesus . . ." Wyatt was leaning over the balcony rail on the second floor. "Oh, God . . . hang on!" She heard his footsteps pounding down the stairs, felt the vibration in the post, and still she clung to it. "Come here . . ." Strong arms surrounded her, held her close.

"It's Noah," she said, tears streaming down her face. "I heard him, Wyatt. I heard my baby."

"Oh, honey, no . . . he's gone."

"Don't say that!" She tried to pull away, but he held her close.

"Shhh . . ." With little effort he picked her up and carried her to the elevator; then, holding her close and whispering into her hair that everything would be all right, he pushed the button for the second floor.

In less than a minute, they were at the bedroom, and as he carried her to the bed, she swore she heard the sound of his heartbeat, strong and steady while her own heart was breaking into a thousand pieces.

"Ava, it's gonna be all right," he said, though she doubted he believed his own words. "Shhh." He kissed her damp cheek as he laid her onto the comforter. "It's another dream, nothing more." Brushing the hair from her face, he looked into her eyes, and in the dark room, she saw compassion and something more in their depths.

"I just miss him so much," she whispered.

"Me too." His face was twisted with emotions that were as raw as the night. "And I miss you, Ava. I miss us."

"I know."

"Do you?"

"Yes," she whispered, her voice cracking as his lips found hers, and the sweet, delicate kiss deepened into something more, something wild and aflame. The back of her neck burned hot with a passion she'd thought was dead forever, and when his tongue pressed against her lips, she parted them willingly. Anxiously. Eagerly. Her arms wound around his neck, and he slid into the bed with her, pushing off the covers, nudging her knees apart with his. The bedsprings creaked, and something deep inside her broke as she clung to him and closed her eyes and mind to the doubts, the pain, the fear.

She felt his hands on her body, sculpting her, touching her breasts, causing her nipples to harden. Her back arched in anticipation, and he, with one hand splayed over her spine, pulled her tight against him.

Strong, corded muscles pressed urgently to hers, and she gave in to the heat coursing through her blood, the need pulsing deep in the darkest, moist parts of her.

Don't do this, her mind insisted. *Making love to him is dangerous. Trusting him is lethal.*

But he's my husband, she silently argued as her spine tingled and her breasts swelled. *I loved him once.*

This is madness. Treachery. Yes, there was a time when he brought you to the edge, over and over again, caused your body and soul to ignite in passion, but that was a long time ago. He's not the same, Ava, and neither are you.

He growled against her ear, his hands tangling in her hair, and for a split second as she gazed at him, she saw something different in his gaze, a fleeting glint of victory, as if somehow he'd won.

Something deep inside her brain ruptured and in another instant she saw that Wyatt wasn't Wyatt at all, but a stranger, a man she'd never known.

With that revelation, she expected her ardor to cool, her

mind to pull herself out of this emotional vortex, but her heart continued to pound. Her blood was still hot with desire as it coursed through her veins, and she wrapped her arms around her unknown lover, who kissed her hard. Passionately. His mouth ground anxiously against hers, his lips hot, his tongue creating a magic as it flicked and teased, trailing over her fevered skin.

Her breasts tightened and she cradled his head to her as he kissed and laved each nipple.

Desire ran in ripples throughout her body and she wanted more . . . so much more.

He took her hand, showed her how to pleasure herself and him, and she pushed her body against him, her spine arching, her hips moving . . . God she wanted him . . . all of him . . . and when she finally opened her eyes to stare into his, she realized that this man, this figment of her imagination who had induced such fire in her blood and heat deep within, looked a helluva lot like Austin Dern.

Chapter 20

No one was in the bed with her.

Of course.

The side of the bed where Wyatt, or whoever, would have lain wasn't mussed. There was no impression on the mattress, no warmth radiating from a recently vacated space. No smell coming from the sheets.

It was all in Ava's fractured mind.

Again.

She was so weary of it all.

Worse yet, her body felt as if someone had touched her and caressed her, though that's as far as it went. Other than a little puncture on her finger that she didn't remember getting, she showed no signs that she'd done anything other than sleep and toss and turn in the night. No sense of sexual release was present, no soreness between her legs, no stains on the bed where she lay.

Once again, all in her mind.

Though it was still dark, the house was stirring. Light seeped in under the crack in the doorway, and she heard the sound of dishes rattling. Outside, a seagull cried as the wind buffeted the house, the gusts rattling the old panes in the windows.

Her erotic dream wouldn't quite leave. It chased after her, nagging at her mind as she showered and dressed, even causing her to stop for a second and stare at her reflection as she was brushing her hair into a ponytail. A sex dream. With Wyatt. And Austin Dern.

She made a growling sound, pure frustration, before snapping the rubber band into place and brushing her teeth. She rarely remembered her dreams, but this one seemed branded in her brain.

Outside her room, in the open hallway, she walked past several doors until she came to Noah's room and pushed open the door. At least she could cross the threshold now without falling apart.

The room was just as she'd left it the other day, and though she told herself it was time to put his baby things away, she didn't have the heart. She imagined him in the room, cooing and talking nonsensically to himself. How often had she played in this room with him, seen his little hands stretch out to her? If she closed her eyes, she knew she could still smell him. To reinforce the image, she walked to the bureau and opened the canisters and jars of baby shampoo and ointment that had sat unused for so long, their sweet scents bringing back memories. She sniffed one small tub of cream.

A floorboard creaked.

She glanced into the mirror over the bureau and saw Wyatt's reflection as he stood in the doorway.

Startled, she nearly dropped the tube of ointment but managed to set it softly on the shelf.

His eyes were dark with emotion. "Don't do this to yourself. To me. You're only torturing yourself, you know."

"It's not a bad thing to remember."

"Do you think it's a good thing to live in the past, to hold on to false hope, to ruin your life and everyone else's because of some ridiculous and painful conviction, this . . . this fantasy of yours that our son is somehow still alive and will come back to us?"

"I can't give up hope."

"You can't live a lie!" He stepped forward and placed his hands on her shoulders. "Ava, please . . . quit fighting us."

"Us?"

"All of us who love you, who want to help you. Please." A muscle worked in his jaw, and he lowered his head so that his forehead touched hers. "Quit fighting *me*."

Something inside of her broke. "I don't mean to."

"It hurts, I know. But we have to move on."

"I can't."

"Of course you can. It's hard, but you have to do it."

She leaned her head against his shirt, heard the steady beat of his heart and wondered if he was right. She was the one resisting the comfort he offered.

"I have to ask this," she said, afraid she might sound foolish, "but did you come to bed last night?" She tilted her head to look up at him. "To our room? Our bed?"

His jaw worked. "Yes," he admitted. "I heard you cry out, so I came in. I wondered if you'd remember."

She felt a sense of relief. At least she hadn't imagined that which was so real, but still, something felt off about it. "Did we . . . ?"

He chuckled without any humor. "No. Not really. I, uh, didn't think it was the right time."

"So you just left?"

"I didn't want to wake you."

She raised a skeptical eyebrow.

"You've been . . . pretty stressed, and besides, last night I wasn't even sure you knew who was with you."

"What?" Her heart started pounding.

"You were dreaming. Talking in your sleep."

Oh, Lord, had she actually called him someone else's name? Dern's? Please, please no! She felt a flush of heat climb up her neck.

"Did you see the rose?"

"No. What rose?"

"The one I stole from the vase in the hallway and placed under your pillow."

"No . . ." She shook her head, remembering how she'd patted the bed next to her, feeling for warmth.

"Then it's still there." He kissed her forehead. "God, I hope we can make this work, Ava," he said with a smile, but she heard the note of resignation in his words, as if he had already given up on the notion they could work things out. "I'll see you later," he said. "I'm just running into the office in Anchorville for a few hours. I should be back by midafternoon."

"All right," she said, still trying to sort things out as he left. She waited until she heard the front door slam, then hurried in the direction of her room. There had been no rose in her bed. None. She would have found it.

"Now who's crazy?" she whispered, entering the bedroom to find Khloe straightening up, the bed made. Lying upon the neatly smoothed quilt was a single white rose, its petals barely edged in pink, like those usually kept in the hallway vase.

"Where'd you find that?" Ava asked, motioning toward the crushed flower.

"In the bed, that's where! You could have warned me for Christ's sake. I pricked myself on the damned thing."

She held up her right hand, and sure enough a bit of blood was blooming on her index finger. Khloe stuck the finger into her mouth, then headed for the adjoining bath. "You have Neosporin, right?" she said, her words a little unclear, as she was obviously still trying to staunch the blood flow with her lips. "And bandages?"

"Think so."

Didn't Khloe know? She'd been in that bathroom as often as Ava.

She heard the sound of the medicine cabinet door creak open, and while Khloe rummaged around in the bathroom supplies, Ava walked closer to the bed and picked up the rose.

"This wasn't in here last night," she said.

"What? The flower?" Khloe called through the open door.

"Yeah."

"Then when? Oh, damn!" She walked into the room wrapping a small Band-Aid around her finger. "Never was ambidextrous . . ." She spied Ava with the rose in hand. "Careful. Graciela's supposed to pull off all the thorns before putting the flowers in the vase, but she never bothers, claims we should buy thornless."

"But the thornless variety isn't named the Church Isle White or developed by my great-grandma."

"Guess not."

"So really, this was in the bed?" Ava asked.

"Right under your damned pillow. Surprised you didn't get lacerated by it. Jesus!"

Ava glanced down at the scratch on her own finger and Khloe caught the move. "Oh. Looks like you did."

"I guess." Ava wasn't convinced.

Khloe shook her head. "How else do you explain that?" She pointed her bandaged finger at the mark on Ava's.

"I can't," she said, and that in and of itself was disturbing.

Fifteen minutes later, she was downstairs, where she grabbed coffee and, upon Virginia's urging, a container of some berry-flavored yogurt and found out that Wyatt was already in town.

"Said he'd be back before noon," Virginia said as she took stock of the pantry and scribbled the missing contents on a notepad. "I can't believe I'm out of chicken stock again. How can that be possible?"

Rather than answer, Ava hurried upstairs, grabbed her laptop, and headed down to the library. With Wyatt gone, she figured she'd have some time to herself.

Jewel-Anne usually took her breakfast in her room, then hung out there until physical therapy with Demetria in the late mornings; Jacob was off at school or hiding in his dungeon of an apartment; the staff was busy; and Ian, if he wasn't fishing, usually had coffee in town before returning to the house. He spent a lot of time in the boathouse and the small apartment attached to it, though he actually slept at the main house in a room on the third floor, preferring "the luxury of central heating" to the drafty studio with its ancient woodstove.

So she had some time when she wouldn't be disturbed and could actually escape the four walls of her bedroom. Besides, the wireless Internet connection worked better down here, closer to Wyatt's office where the modem was located.

She spent several hours organizing her notes, eating the yogurt, drinking coffee, and adding in news stories she hadn't previously read on the Internet until she heard sirens, distant and faint, their plaintive wails echoing across the bay. She felt a chill but ignored it and switched off her computer. As her laptop wound down, she caught sight of a picture of Noah taken only a few days after his birth. She pushed her computer aside and walked to the library shelf where she picked up the photograph. "Funny little man," she said of the red, swaddled baby lying on the couch. Hers had been a difficult delivery, not that she remembered much of it. That blessed event—so soon after Kelvin's death—was tucked away like so many others and probably for good reason, as her son had nearly died in the process. The months counting down to his delivery had been trying as well, and sometimes she'd been in a full-blown panic that this pregnancy, too, wouldn't go to term. As it was, Noah was born earlier than expected, but he was healthy.

Ava had the same kind of blurry images of the hospital and

doctors trying to stay calm, of bright lights and pain, as she had of the boating accident that had taken Kelvin's life. Those same kind of disjointed, frightening memories, but at least Noah had been born.

She looked at the picture, felt her throat tighten, then set the picture aside and walked to the window to view the garden where the small memorial stone and bench had been placed. Then she moved through the library and down a few steps into the recreation room and around the billiard table that had stood in the center of this area for as long as Ava could remember. Her grandmother had referred to the table as "that gawd-awful monstrosity" with its fading green cloth and dark oak rails.

Through the French doors, she walked outside to the garden and that scrap of space dedicated to her son. As dry leaves, kicked around by the wind, skittered across the path, she sat on the bench and looked down at the marker. Her son wasn't buried here, but on this cloudy, blustery day, it was the place where she felt closest to him.

"Where are you?" she asked herself, then spied other marks in the wet earth. Large footprints, obviously belonging to a man, were visible along with the tracks from Jewel-Anne's wheelchair.

More often than not, when Jewel-Anne rolled herself outside, she wound her chair through these garden paths. No matter how overgrown or bumpy the path was, she would bring one of her dolls with her and talk to them as she rode through the dripping rhododendron and overgrown hydrangeas. Ava had often seen her at this very spot, staring at her son's marker, set only a few feet from the back of the house.

Now she rubbed her hands together against the chill of November. The holidays were fast approaching, and her insides froze a bit as she projected to the future and another lifeless season. All her life she'd looked forward to the yuletide, but after losing Noah, everything had changed. *Every* thing.

She glanced out toward the bay where the whitecaps swirled and the gray waters ran far too deep.

Why was it that everyone other than herself was content to let Noah's memory fade, to just accept that he'd "disappeared." They'd explained it to her, of course. There had been no ransom note, no small body had been found, very few leads—and all of those long exhausted. Even Wyatt had accepted that he would never see his son again, and that's why he'd suggested this memorial.

She glanced down at the rock etched with her son's name. Everyone's acceptance of the fact that Noah was gone frustrated the hell out of her.

Over the rush of the wind, she heard the back door open and the whine of Jewel-Anne's wheelchair on the ramp.

Great. So much for time alone.

Ava was just climbing to her feet when her cousin wheeled along the pathway to the garden. Bundled up in a thick jacket, her brunette doll wearing something similar, Jewel-Anne rounded the corner.

"What're you doing here?" she asked. These were the first civil words she'd spoken to Ava since their argument in Wyatt's office.

Ava considered not answering her but really didn't have the energy for that kind of game-playing and one-upmanship. "Thinking."

She rolled along the uneven path and stopped at the bench, her gaze focused on the stone. "Me too. I guess it helps. I miss him, too, you know," she added, almost to herself, and Ava felt a little of the ice around her heart melting. "That's why I come here. Because somehow Noah seems closer."

"Yeah." Ava's voice was husky, raw with emotion. "I thought you had physical therapy."

"I blew it off." She slid a glance up at Ava. "It's not as if it's doing any good."

"But the doctor said—"

"The doctor," Jewel-Anne snorted. "What does he know? He just writes me prescriptions and suggests occupational therapy or a shrink or things to keep me busy, but none of it means crap." Tears filled her eyes, and she brushed them hastily away before saying, "You're a good one to talk. You *never* do what you're supposed to. Oh, by the way, Khloe told me to remind you that you've got another appointment with the shrink. She's on her way."

Ava's heart sank at the thought of another session with Dr. McPherson. The last thing she wanted to do was sit around and talk about her "feelings" with the psychologist. Then again maybe she could shock her with the sex dream.

Jewel-Anne's phone beeped and she pulled it out of her jacket pocket. "Oh, great," she said as she read the text. "Mrs. Marquis de Sade wants me in the ballet studio. Pronto." She scowled at her phone, then tucked it into her pocket. "I guess I'd better go or she'll come looking and be all pissy." Deftly, she maneuvered a quick one-eighty with her chair and rolled away toward the house.

Ava watched her leave and wondered about all the times she'd spied Jewel-Anne in the garden, the wheels of her chair glinting in the sun. She'd often wondered what it would be like to be confined to the chair and had felt compassion and, yes, even guilt that her younger cousin was wheelchair bound, but then Jewel-Anne would say or do something so heartless and downright cruel that all of Ava's empathy evaporated.

Give her a break. At least try. What would it hurt?

Alone again, Ava knelt down and ran her fingers over her son's marker. Thank God there was no little body lying in a casket beneath the leafless, thorny rosebushes whose blooms had perished months before.

And that was a blessing.

So to think that she was closer to him here was an illusion.

Swallowing hard, she closed her eyes for a second, tried to

get a grip on things. Again, she felt as if she were being watched, as if she wasn't alone in the garden, that there was another presence. Her skin prickled and it wasn't from the cold. She opened her eyes, her gaze scouring the overgrown shrubbery. She found no one other than a seagull swooping toward the bay.

And yet . . .

Looking over her shoulder at the house, she thought she saw movement in one of the upper windows, a curtain shifting in . . . Noah's room?

Her heart clenched.

Who would be in her son's room?

It's nothing. Maybe Graciela dusting or . . .

But she was already moving, her footsteps hurrying, faster and faster, up the steps, through the back door, running through the kitchen and nearly knocking over Virginia and a hot tray of biscuits, dashing through the hallways and taking the front stairs two at a time.

At the second floor, she didn't hesitate, just ran like wildfire to Noah's room. The door was ajar.

Heart in her throat, breathing hard, she stepped inside. More memories washed over her and her oh-so-willing mind's eye wanted to see him in his crib, but he wasn't there.

But . . . her heart jolted when she spied the shoes.

Noah's shoes.

Left as if he'd just kicked them off.

No!

Stepping into the room, she smelled the scent of salt water, and then she noticed the shoes were wet, water puddling on the edge of the carpet.

Eyes rounding in disbelief, she edged closer, snatching up the tiny red sneakers with the Nike logo. They smelled salty from the seawater and her throat closed. "Noah." Nearly collapsing, she thought of her son, conjuring up his image. In her fractured mind's eye, she witnessed his tiny body floating downward in the cold waters of the bay, his hair caught floating and swirling in the ebbing tide, his eyes, wide in his little white face, staring up at her, silently accusing her.

"Baby!"

One little hand reached up for hers, but she was like stone, unable to move.

"Mama!" he cried, and she let out a scream.

"Noah!"

But he wasn't with her; she wasn't on the edge of the bay but in his room. "Oh, God, what's happening to me?" she whispered as the image of her son faded and she turned only to find she wasn't alone.

A man stood in the doorway, filling it, his dark silhouette blocking her escape.

Chapter 21

"Dear God, you scared the hell out of me!" Ava cried, one hand flying to her throat. The man in the doorway wasn't some sinister figure hell-bent to scare the wits out of her but the ranch hand her husband had hired.

"Didn't mean to," Dern said, his gaze drifting from her face to the tiny pair of shoes dangling from her fingers and dripping salt water onto the carpet.

"They're Noah's," she said. "I found them here, on the floor near his closet."

"But they're wet."

"Salt water," she said, her throat tight. What had Tanya said? *What if someone really wants you to believe you're going off the rails . . . way off the rails?*

Well, that someone was doing a damned fine job of it. But who would do something so cruel, so pointedly painful? And why? If someone was definitely trying to freak her out, they were doing a damned good job of it. She thought of the people who lived here, all of whom had access to this room. Her stomach knotted as she remembered her argument with

Jewel-Anne and her fight with Jacob, though they weren't the only suspects, just the two who shot to the top of the list.

"Are you all right?"

"Do I look all right?"

One side of his mouth lifted. "I think you're a whole lot tougher than you give yourself credit for."

She only wished it were so.

Dern took one little sneaker from her hand and sniffed it. "You're right. Salt water."

"Someone put them here. Wanted me to find them."

"Why?" He seemed genuinely confused.

"So I'd seem crazy. Or crazier."

"Who?"

"Damned good question." She snorted a little and wrapped her arms around herself. "I'm not the most popular person on the island."

"But you're the boss. Everyone here has to report to you."

"Except for my relatives."

Dern placed the wet shoe on a side table, walked to the closet, and opened the door. All of Noah's clothes were hanging on tiny hangers or folded into the shelves built into the closet. His shoes were placed in a neat row, none out of place, no space left for the wet red Nikes.

"Is everything else where it's supposed to be?"

After placing the second shoe down beside the first, noting the pair made a wet smudge on the table's glossy, recently dusted top, she walked to the closet and resisted touching the little outfits her baby had worn. "I think so. I haven't looked in here in a long, long while . . . not since I went to—" She caught herself just as the name of St. Brendan's was about to roll off her tongue. "Before I left for a while."

She wasn't kidding anyone. No doubt Dern had heard the rumors that she'd spent time in a psychiatric ward, but she wasn't going to confirm them. At least not yet.

"Why would anyone do this?" He was shaking his head, his dark eyebrows drawing together, one hand rubbing at the stubble along his jawline as he thought. "Maybe it was an accident."

"An accident? Someone accidentally had my son's shoes and dropped them in the ocean and then brought them up here and left them neatly by the closet?" she asked, unable to hide the sarcasm in her tone. "No, someone deliberately did this. Left them where I would find them."

"Why?" he asked again.

"I don't know. It's some kind of sick prank!" Anger crawled up her back as she picked up the shoes and started for the door. "Don't you see? Someone's getting their kicks by tormenting me."

He caught her elbow with his hand. "Don't."

"Why the hell not?" she snapped, fury and frustration burning through her.

"Because there's bad news."

"You mean *more* bad news," she threw out, but her sarcasm died on her lips when she saw how serious he'd become. His eyes were somber and dark. "What?"

"I got a call from Ian. That's why I came to the house, to find you."

She waited, a new anxiety building.

"He said that you know a woman named Cheryl Reynolds."

"I do."

His grip on her arm tightened slightly and his jaw tightened a bit. "She's dead, Ava," he said softly.

"*What?*" The small shoes fell to the floor, thumping and bumping along the gallery.

"It looks like she may have been killed."

"Murdered?" Cold despair slid through her guts. "No . . . this . . . is wrong." She wouldn't believe it. "Another sick, twisted idea of a joke!"

"I don't think so," he said, and her anger slid away. "I called a friend I know at the marina. He said rumors are flying, and he saw cop cars and an ambulance race up the hill earlier."

This had to be wrong. *Had* to! "But I just saw her," she protested even as she remembered hearing the distant wail of sirens earlier.

"I'm sorry," he said.

"No . . . I don't want to hear this . . ." She couldn't, wouldn't believe that Cheryl was dead. No, not just dead, but *murdered*? Heart drumming, denial pounding through her brain, she dug her cell phone from her pocket and started to call Ian when the phone rang in her hand.

Tanya's name and number came up on the screen.

"Hello?"

"Oh, God, Ava, did you hear?" Tanya jumped in. "About Cheryl? That someone killed her? Right in her own home?" She was frantic, and the pit in Ava's stomach turned sour. "I can't believe it, just can't. Nothing like this ever happens in Anchorville!"

"Slow down," Ava suggested, though Tanya was only voicing her own thoughts. "You're serious?"

"As a heart attack!"

"Okay . . . okay, so what happened?"

"No one knows. The cops are being pretty closemouthed, but I hear things, y'know, at the salon, and it sounds like some intruder just walked in and killed her. God. My client, well, Ida Sterns, tends to exaggerate, but she said they found Cheryl in her basement with her cats all around. One of them was even lapping up her blood!"

"Ugh!"

"But it's true that Cheryl's dead, Ava, and someone freakin' killed her!" Tanya seemed near to hyperventilating. "The whole town's on edge, just like they were when Lester Reece escaped from Sea Cliff. It's nuts! Oh, Lord, I've got to run and pick up the kids, but . . . I know you see Cheryl. I just thought you should know. Oh, I'm getting another call. Shit! It's Russell! Just what I need! God, what does he want? Oh, crap. He probably heard about Trent."

"What about Trent?" Ava headed downstairs and into the foyer, toward the tall windows flanking the door. Dern was right behind her and stopped when she did. She looked through the glass to the gray day beyond. Across the water, the town of Anchorville was spread upon the shore, and there were strobing red lights on the hill near Cheryl's house.

Dear God.

Tanya was still talking about Trent. "We just had a couple of drinks. NBD. Look I've got to go!" And with that she clicked off.

Numb, Ava turned to Dern. Something must have shown in her face because he grabbed her arm again, steadying her. "I'm sorry," he said, and as he stared down at her, his fingers warm through her sleeve, she flashed on her dream. She remembered the stranger in her bed, the imagined lover sliding over her naked body with his own, the strength of him pressed against her abdomen, the fire of intense, hard-edged sexual desire shining in his eyes. The hands that had splayed over her spine, fingertips touching the cleft in her buttocks, had been strong, determined, and now, standing in this room, she felt that same wanton desire that he'd evoked, a curiosity about his prowess in the bedroom, a need to experience all that he'd promised.

If only in her mind.

She drew her arm from his clasp and put some space between them. "It's just so hard to believe," she said, clearing her throat and knowing her embarrassment was evident in the heat of her cheeks. She thought of Cheryl again and realized how little she really knew about her. She'd been married twice, but Cheryl had never mentioned that she'd had children, nor had Ava ever seen any pictures of children mounted on the walls or placed upon the small tables of Cheryl's studio. "I just don't understand why anyone would want to harm her."

"That's always the question," he said as they heard the elevator hum to life, and soon Jewel-Anne and Demetria met them in the foyer.

"Did you hear?" Jewel-Anne asked. She was ashen, her eyes round behind her thick glasses.

"About Cheryl?" Ava asked. "Yes."

"It's so unbelievable . . . But it's all over the news." Jewel-Anne was fingering her iPhone.

"You knew Cheryl?" Ava asked, and was rewarded with a perturbed look.

"Anchorville's a small town, Ava. Of course I knew her. Everyone did." She bit her lip. "Does anyone know where Jacob is? Is he on the island? He'd want to know." Before anyone answered, her fingers were flying over the tiny keyboard as she, presumably, texted her brother.

"It's awful," Demetria whispered, shaking her head as if to deny the tragedy. "There hasn't been a murder around here in years. Since Lester Reece was convicted. You don't . . . think he's come back, do you?"

"No!" Khloe cut in quickly, coming from the kitchen.

Jewel-Anne stiffened in her chair. "I doubt it," she said. "He . . . he just seemed to disappear."

"Probably with help from his daddy," Khloe cut in.

Was it Ava's imagination or did Dern's mouth tighten, almost imperceptibly? In a heartbeat, the expression had vanished, just like Reece had years before. Despite the rumored sightings of Anchorville's most infamous criminal, Lester Reece had either died or somehow managed to elude the police. If it was the latter, then Khloe was right. If Reece had escaped justice, no doubt he'd turned to his tight-knit family. Reece was the son of a local judge who had finally stepped down amid rumors of adultery and graft, but he'd denied his son nothing. Privileged and handsome, Lester had also had a cruel streak that had eventually escalated to murder. Though Reece had been convicted, his clever, high-priced attorney had found psychiatrists who declared him to be mentally unstable and he'd ended up at Sea Cliff rather than behind prison bars. He'd escaped from the hospital and his disappearance had cost the hospital administrator, Ava's uncle Crispin, his job.

"He was seen recently," Demetria insisted. "By Corvin Hobbs. Just a few months ago."

"Who would believe Corvin?" Jewel-Anne said curtly. It was true. A local fisherman, Hobbs was known for his tall tales and affinity for Johnnie Walker.

"Looks like we've got company," Demetria said as she peered through the window.

Ava followed her gaze and saw a boat cutting through the water, its wake a white, churning tail. She recognized the family craft with several people inside. Not far behind was a second boat boldly marked as belonging to the sheriff's department.

As the first boat slowed before pulling into the boathouse, Ava recognized Ian at the helm. With him were his twin, Wyatt, and, of course, Evelyn McPherson.

They had just disembarked when the boat from the sheriff's department pulled up to the dock. A woman helmed the craft. With her was Detective Wesley Snyder. The only person missing was the sheriff.

"Perfect," Ava said, glancing up at Dern. "Looks like we're going to host a party."

"Wonder why?" His scowl was deep.

"Because they all figured out that I saw Cheryl yesterday. They probably hope that I saw something that will help with the investigation." Deciding to get out of the line of fire, Ava headed for the stairs to the second floor.

Dern followed. "It may be more than that," he said as he joined her in the upper hallway.

"Meaning?"

"Maybe you were the last person to see her alive."

"You think they might consider me a suspect?" Ava asked in disbelief. "I hardly knew her."

"I don't know. But someone's messing with you. Big-time."

She heard a step on the landing and saw Graciela, dust rag in her hand, wiping down the stair railings. She, too, was staring out the windows as the entourage from the boat landing walked up the hill to the house. "What's going on?" she asked.

"Looks like we have company," Ava said.

"And the shoes?" Graciela swept Noah's sneakers from the floor. "What're they doing here?"

"I found them. In his room."

"Wet?" Graciela asked, eyeing Ava as if she were untrustworthy.

"Yes."

"But they weren't in the closet?" She seemed confused as she lifted the tiny Nikes by their heels.

"No! Not in the closet." Ava snagged the shoes dangling from the maid's fingers.

"But why?"

"Oh my God!" Khloe's voice preceded her footsteps, and when she rounded the corner below them, she was stuffing her phone into the pocket of her sweater. "Why didn't you tell me about the murder?" she demanded of Ava.

"I just found out myself."

"Ian called me a few minutes ago," Dern explained as he and Ava retraced their footsteps downstairs.

Ava brushed past Khloe and opened the door. Wyatt was just climbing the front steps. "I've got bad news," he said, his face grim as he walked inside and brushed a kiss across her cheek. He smelled of the ocean and something else . . . the slight tinge of cigarette smoke.

"We heard," she said as the twins arrived behind him. Trent gave her a bear hug. Of all of her cousins, he was the closest to her.

"What a mess," he said as Ian and McPherson stepped through the door. "Ian says you knew the victim."

"Everyone did." Ava shut the door behind them. "Cheryl lived in Anchorville for years."

Unzipping his jacket, Trent said, "But I thought Ian mentioned that you saw her professionally?"

So much for keeping things to herself, Ava thought, and caught Dern staring at her. "I thought hypnosis might make me remember and . . . and that maybe I would recall something that might help me find Noah." So now the secret was out.

Wyatt zeroed in on the shoes dangling from Ava's fingers. "What're these?" Lines of concern and frustration etched his forehead. "Noah's?"

"I found them in his room. They're wet. Salt water."

"What?" he whispered.

"Someone put them there. For me to trip over."

"Why would anyone . . . ?" At the sound of footsteps on the porch, he said, "We'll talk about this later." The doorbell chimed hollowly. "Right now, we've got to deal with the police."

Chapter 22

"So it looks like you were Cheryl Reynolds's last appointment of the day. You may have been the last person to see her alive," Detective Snyder said from his seat on the couch in the library. His partner, Detective Morgan Lyons, stood near the closed French doors to the hallway, as if she expected someone to try and interrupt them. Wound tight, Lyons managed to exude a take-charge aura despite her small size. She was younger than her partner by over a decade, somewhere in her midthirties, Ava guessed. Trim, with wild brown hair that seemed determined to escape the knot she'd pinned at the base of her skull, she watched Ava with guarded eyes.

Everyone other than Ava had been ushered into other rooms of the house, and she, over Wyatt's protests, was talking to the police alone.

"You really shouldn't," Wyatt had advised her. "Without legal counsel."

"You mean, without you?" she said.

His eyes darkened and he'd gripped her arm and pulled her out of earshot of the detectives. "I mean a criminal attorney, Ava."

"But I don't need one. I've done nothing wrong." She'd stared up at him only to find doubt in his eyes. "You believe me, right?"

"Of course," he'd snapped, then released her.

She'd walked with the two detectives into the library. Now, both of the officers were looking at her. Bald, no-nonsense Snyder and skeptical Lyons with her large eyes and tight lips. "I told you when I left her, Cheryl was in the doorway to the basement where her studio is. I don't think anyone else was downstairs, but I can't be sure. I was, um, being hypnotized, so I wasn't really aware of what was going on around me, but I didn't see anyone else there. Just Cheryl and her cats."

"Did she lock the door behind you?"

"When I arrived? No." Ava thought hard. "But I can't be sure."

"What about when you left?" Lyons asked.

"I don't remember her locking the door. Didn't hear it click or anything. All I recall was that it was dark. The streetlights had come on." But they came on early this time of year; the clocks had been set back to standard time earlier in the month, and the afternoons were incredibly short.

Snyder asked, "You said it was after five?"

"Uh-huh. The session was scheduled for four-thirty, and I remember hurrying to get there. I'd had a really late lunch with my friend. It took up most of the afternoon. So I got to Cheryl's a few minutes late. Maybe four thirty-five. By the time I left, it was five-thirty or so. Really getting dark."

"Your sessions usually lasted an hour?" Snyder adjusted the digital recorder that he'd placed on the table between them.

"Give or take," Ava admitted. "Cheryl isn't . . . wasn't one to be rigid about time."

Snyder asked, "And you were there because . . . ?"

"For the same reason I came to see you earlier," she said,

showing a little irritation. "I'm trying to find out what happened to my son. I've had memory issues, and I was hoping hypnotism might unlock something in my subconscious, something I can't recall."

"But you remember everything about your session?" Lyons clarified from the doorway. "The 'memory issues' weren't a problem yesterday."

Ava had to bite back a smart retort. "No. I remember what happened before and after being hypnotized. Just not during." Ava glanced up at the stiff-backed detective. "I'm not really in touch with what's going on around me when I'm under."

Snyder said, "But Ms. Reynolds was in the room with you the whole time."

"I think so, yes, but I can't swear to it."

Snyder frowned. "Could someone else have come in?"

"To the room? I doubt it." She tried to remember if she'd felt any change while under hypnosis.

"What about to the rest of the house?"

"I don't know. I think Cheryl rents out the upper floors, so I suppose someone could have come or gone . . ." Ava frowned.

"And the basement?" Lyons pushed.

"I was there in her office, but there are other rooms, so it's possible. The door between the hall and the room I was in was closed while I was in a session. All I can tell you is that I don't remember hearing anything out of the ordinary," she said with forced patience.

Before Detective Lyons could ask another question, Snyder clarified again, "You were her last scheduled appointment."

"I don't really know what her schedule was," Ava answered.

"She didn't talk about seeing anyone else?" Lyons asked.

"No."

The questions continued and Ava went over everything again. And then a third time: What time had she arrived? How long had she stayed? When she left, did she see anyone suspicious on her walk to the marina? Ava answered as best she could: No, she didn't know of anyone who would want to harm Cheryl. She'd known the deceased casually about ten years, been a client more recently. She'd had a session less than a week earlier and then the last one yesterday.

"And you got a ride back to the island nearly forty-five minutes after your session?" Lyons asked after over an hour of what was beginning to feel more like an interrogation than a simple questioning.

"Yes. I picked up a latte at a shop in town, The Local Buzz, and then caught a ride from the marina with Butch Johansen. He's a friend of mine and captain of the *Holy Terror.*"

For the first time, a hint of a smile brushed Detective Lyons's lips.

"So you didn't notice anything out of the ordinary?" Detective Snyder asked.

"No," she said, and then decided to go for broke. "One thing: I did feel like someone was watching me. From the time I left Cheryl's until the time I got on the boat, I just had this weird sensation that someone was . . . following me." She saw both detectives straighten a bit.

"Who?" Lyons asked.

"I don't know. And look, I'm not even sure about it. It was just a feeling I had." She caught Detective Lyons looking at her wrists, just visible beneath the cuffs of her sleeves, and when their eyes met, she said evenly, "I know the rumors about me. That I'm crazy. And they're true. I wasn't myself after my son disappeared, but I'm not mentally *ill.* Can I tell you one hundred percent that someone was following me? No. Just like I can't tell you that no one else was in Cheryl's house when I left there. Did she seem troubled? Maybe. She warned me to 'be careful,' that things 'weren't what they seemed to be.' She said something about there being 'bad blood' out here on this island and that she was worried about me."

The detectives exchanged glances. "Why was she worried?" Snyder asked.

Ava shook her head. "Maybe because I keep pushing to find Noah, my son."

"And that would put you into danger?" Lyons asked.

"I'm just speculating. I don't really know."

The detectives asked a few more questions but still seemed dissatisfied when they finally called it quits. Snyder pressed his card into her palm. "If you think of anything else, give me a call."

"I will," she promised, but knew it was as empty as the rooms at Sea Cliff. She tucked the card into the front pocket of her jeans and felt something inside her pocket . . . cold metal. She was reminded that she'd never found the lock for the damned key.

Maybe there was none.

Maybe, after all of this, the key was meaningless, just something she'd found one day and slipped inside her pocket. After all, her memory had some major holes in it.

And that, as ever, was the problem: She just couldn't remember. She was close, or at least she thought she was, to recalling something important. Something vital. It was like a cloud on the horizon, wispy and thin, shifting into a shape that didn't quite form into a clear picture. She just couldn't seem to get there.

Maybe it was time to do something about the key. Maybe someone in the house knew what it was about. Maybe the same someone who'd left Noah's shoes for her to find. Now, she picked them up from where she'd set them down and headed out.

It was time to figure out who that someone was.

"She's hiding something," Lyons said later, once the detectives had boated across the bay and driven to the department. She snapped her keys out of the ignition of the department-issued cruiser, a tank of a car complete with big engine, a screen separating the front and backseats, and that undisputed aroma of stale cigarette smoke.

Snyder climbed out of the car and walked with her up the cracked cement path that split twin patches of lawn and past the flagpole that held Old Glory and the Washington State flag with the first president's face stamped across its emerald-green field. Both flags snapped in the same stiff breeze that had buffeted the detectives as they'd cut across the bay.

Stride for stride, Snyder and Lyons reached the door, and by training, Snyder held the door for her, though, by God, he knew she didn't expect anything the least bit "macho" or "condescending." She'd been adamant, though he'd explained it was just common courtesy. Didn't matter, though.

Today, however, she did mutter a quick, "Thanks," under her breath as they stepped into the long, flat building whose roof seemed to forever leak and smelled vaguely of some pine-scented disinfectant.

Snyder was tired, the muscles in his lower back aching, the result of an old football injury that flared up whenever he spent too many hours on his feet and not enough in his La-Z-Boy in front of his sixty-incher and SportsCenter. "You think Ava Garrison killed Cheryl Reynolds?" he asked as he reached into his pocket for his pack of cigarettes. The pack was empty, save for one Marlboro that he kept just in case he really needed a hit of nicotine, a rush that e-cigarettes just didn't deliver. The damned things might be great for avoiding lung cancer and emphysema and the like, but they just weren't the same as a real smoke. "What's the motive?"

"I didn't say she did anything," Lyons snapped. She was touchy. Maybe that time of the month, but he didn't dare suggest it. She might come unglued and go all ape-shit on him and accuse him of not being PC. Well, hell, he *knew* that. He'd crossed that line before. Truth to tell, he liked the woman, even if she was a little on the high-strung side. "But who knows what she said when she was under hypnosis?" Lyons went on. "Maybe she didn't like someone knowing so much about her."

"Then why go?"

"I'm saying maybe she's hiding something. Might have something to do with the case; maybe not. Just sayin'."

They walked into the cubicle that Snyder called home, and he began peeling off his jacket. His computer was still running with information on the Cheryl Reynolds case, along with pictures of her basement; her dead body was visible on the monitor. They were still waiting for the autopsy, but it was a formality. The bloody gash across the front of her throat was evidence enough for him to know it was a homicide. He hung up his jacket and slid his arm out of his shoulder holster as Lyons checked her smartphone for the thousandth time today. It was all business, he trusted, but man was she addicted to that thing.

"I'll be right back. Gonna hit the ladies' room." Texting now, she walked off, toward the back of the building.

Over the last few hours, they'd talked to all of the hypnotherapist's clients, especially those she'd seen the day she died. All of Cheryl Reynolds's friends and acquaintances had been astounded that anyone would do anything to hurt their own personal hypnotic guru.

Snyder had also managed to speak with each of the two ex-husbands, but so far they were both off the primary suspect list: One lived over fifty miles away, was remarried, and had been at work all day; the other, a more likely suspect, lived in Seattle and though out of work had been "hanging out" with his friends at a local bar. The bartender had confirmed. Both the alibis seemed solid enough.

So far.

As a landlord, Reynolds had no tenant disputes.

Nor, apparently, any angry ex-lovers.

He rubbed the kinks from his neck as he reviewed his notes.

According to the will they'd found in a desk drawer, the heirs to Reynolds's meager savings account and her interest in the rambling old house included an out-of-state niece who was nine, the only child of her now-deceased sibling, and the local animal shelter, which, according to the terms of the will, was supposed to house her "babies"—a total of seven cats—until they died. He'd seen at least five of the felines when he'd first been called to the scene. Who the hell knew where the other two were? The first quintet had already been taken to the shelter; they'd round up the others today or tomorrow.

Cheryl Reynolds's cell phone, home phone, and computer records were being checked, but so far no red flags had popped up.

The house didn't appear to have been robbed . . . or at least it didn't look like it at first pass, but the crime scene team was still working the house and surrounding area.

It was still early in the investigation.

There was a lot of ground yet to cover.

Friends and neighbors might have seen or heard something.

A fingerprint might be found.

Someone might remember seeing a car or person out of the ordinary. Her taped interviews might unlock a clue. . . .

Lyons reappeared at the opening to his work space. She was tucking her phone into her pocket and had a package of peanut M&M's she must've grabbed from the vending machine located in the lunchroom near the lavatories. "Biggs brought up the idea that this could be the work of Lester Reece," she said.

"The missing Lester Reece," he reminded her, though he didn't add that he didn't think much of the sheriff's opinion. J. T. Biggs was a mediocre lawman at best. "Why would a killer who escaped from Sea Cliff hospital return to the one town where people would remember and recognize him?"

"He was in a *mental* hospital. Determined to be certifiable."

"Paranoid schizophrenic, or something."

She slit open the package of candy with her thumbnail. "The guy's nuts with a capital N. He could do anything."

"Nah." Snyder wasn't buying it. "I was around for that one. You weren't. Lester Reece wasn't any crazier than any of the other sick bastards we lock up. He just had a much fatter wallet and a damned good attorney." Frowning at the image of Cheryl Reynolds on his computer screen, he added, "If you ask me, Lester Reece is fish food."

"He killed his ex-wife, right?"

"Deena and her friend . . . what was her name?" he said, then snapped his fingers. "Mary or Marsha or . . . Maryliss, that was it. Thought I'd never forget it. Maryliss Benson. They were best friends, but at one time Reece had an affair with the friend, so who knows if his intended victim was the ex-wife or the ex-girlfriend? Cruel, privileged son of a bitch. Thought he was above the law."

"Reece was a lady-killer, literally."

Snyder snorted. "He was involved with a lot of women around here before anyone realized what a whack job he was. Even then, a few still hung out, got off on his fame or infamy or whatever the hell you want to call it."

"Oh what a tangled web we weave," she said as she popped a few of the peanuts into her mouth.

He laughed. He hated to admit it to himself, but he liked Morgan Lyons, all bristly five-foot-four inches of her. Sassy, smart, with a quick wit and a sharp tongue, she held her own with most of the veterans around the department even though she'd been hired less than a year earlier. For the five years previous, she'd worked for the Oregon State Police and had never really copped to why she'd jumped ship there. All he knew was that she was a good detective and too good-looking for his own good. As tightly packed as she was wound, she had breasts too big to completely minimize, a nipped in waist, and an ass that caused him and the rest of the male population to fantasize what she'd be like in bed.

He, of course, knew better. He had the two ex-wives to prove it, so Detective Morgan Lyons, sexy as she was, was off-limits. Beyond off-limits.

He wasn't that crazy.

Not anymore.

He'd trained his dick to be a little smarter. At least he hoped he had.

Besides, she was rumored to have a serious Bad-Ass of a former husband. The guy just happened to be an ex-cop who had a bad temper and was into authority trips. And, oh, yeah, he had a hard-on for guns, all kinds of guns. From assault rifles to Saturday night specials, the guy collected firearms.

Could be a lethal combination.

"How about we get a cup of coffee?" she suggested.

He glanced at his watch. "It's kinda late."

"Quit being such a pussy. Haven't you heard of decaf? I'll buy you whatever fancy coffee drink you want and we'll talk to the barista. Check out Ava Garrison's story."

"You don't seem to think much of her." He grabbed up the jacket he'd just shed.

"I think she's a crackpot. She admitted it herself in the interview. And I saw the scars on her wrists. Not something a sane person would do." She crushed the remainder of her bag of M&M's in a fist and said, "I'll even buy."

He smiled. "Forget the latte. After we talk to the people in the coffee shop, let's head on over to O'Malley's. For a beer. And I'll buy."

"You're on." She almost smiled back.

Almost.

Chapter 23

"How'd it go?" Wyatt asked as Ava walked out of the library after her interview with the police.

"Horrible. From what they can piece together, I might have been the last one to see her before she was . . . before she died, so that's why they were questioning me. They thought maybe I'd seen or heard something." Shaking her head, she admitted, "I don't think I was any help at all." She was still holding Noah's shoes.

Wyatt noticed the shoes and asked, "What's going on?" as she walked past him toward the stairs. Then, "Where are you going?"

"I want to find out who left these in the nursery."

"Oh, Ava . . ."

"What?" she asked, and when he didn't immediately respond, she guessed, "This is really embarrassing for you. Your wife is a nutcase and that bothers you."

"I just worry about you, Ava."

"So worried that you hired a psychologist to monitor me?"

"To help you," he reminded tightly.

She started to walk away again, but he jumped forward and caught her by the crook of the elbow.

"Just think, okay? Don't do anything that you'll regret."

"Too late for that!" she snapped, and he winced as if stung.

"Is everything all right?" Evelyn McPherson asked, rounding the corner. Her eyes were clouded with worry, her fingers cradling a coffee cup, her boots clicking softly on the hardwood.

"Cheryl Reynolds is dead," Ava pointed out. "How in the world could everything possibly be all right?" Ava's nerves were strung tight from the police interview.

"I'm sorry. You're right. How're you doing? Maybe we should talk," the psychologist suggested in a soft tone that bugged the hell out of Ava.

Ava glanced at the woman in her designer boots and slim skirt, a soft sweater completing the ensemble. "I don't think so." She turned, despite hearing her husband plead, "Ava, please . . . don't."

Oh go to hell! she thought, but kept her mouth shut. For now. Leaving Wyatt and Dr. McPherson in the hallway, she strode into the den where the family and staff had collected. They were all there, scattered around the room. Her relatives. Those who worked for her. Everyone who lived or was employed at Neptune's Gate, even Austin Dern, leaning against the bookcase in the far corner of the room.

There had been soft conversation over the hiss and pop of the fire, but it died away as soon as Ava stepped past Demetria, who stood near the doorway.

"How're you doing?" Trent asked, offering her the first sincere smile she'd seen in hours. He'd poured himself a drink and was warming the back of his legs on the fire. Ian stood next to him, a drink in his hand as well.

"Not great," Ava admitted as she heard footsteps behind her.

Wyatt and the good Dr. McPherson. Joining the party. Together.

Perfect.

"When are you ever great?" Jewel-Anne asked.

So it was going to be Antagonistic Jewel-Anne today.

Well, fine.

Bring it on.

Mr. T slunk through the shadows in the back of the room to finally settle down, hiding beneath the couch and peering out at everyone.

Jewel-Anne was huddled near the window in her chair with a doll, this one with straight black hair and wide, blankly staring blue eyes that opened and closed as it was jostled. Her knitting needles were quiet for once but were poking out of a ball of yarn visible in the pouch strapped to the wheelchair.

Next to her stood Jacob, looking like a biker-dude wannabe in his black leather jacket and camouflage pants and wearing half a dozen silver rings that only highlighted the tattoos across his fingers. A three-days' growth of beard added to the illusion that he was tough, that he wasn't the computer nerd he truly was.

Ava said to Jewel-Anne, "A friend of mine died yesterday. And she didn't just have a heart attack. She was murdered. So, no, I'm not okay."

Jacob asked, "Why were the cops all over you?"

"Because I saw Cheryl yesterday."

"As a friend or a hypnotist?" Jewel-Anne asked, her eyebrows rising over the rims of her glasses, though her surprise was clearly less than authentic.

Ava set Noah's now-nearly-dry shoes in the middle of the coffee table.

Ian's gaze followed her movement. "What's going on?"

"Aren't those Noah's shoes?" Khloe, cradling a coffee cup, asked. She sat with her husband and mother on a sofa tucked into the corner. Simon was holding her hand, and he seemed to glower up at Ava.

"Yep." Ava looked across the room and noticed Austin Dern standing quietly in the corner near the bookcase, almost in the shadows. Again, Ava was hit by a hint of familiarity. Had she met him somewhere before? *Don't go there. Dangerous waters. Very dangerous waters.* "They were in his room," she told them.

"Isn't that where they're usually kept?" Khloe seemed genuinely confused. "You still have a lot of his clothes."

"I don't keep them wet. Not dipped in salt water."

"What?" Khloe stared at Ava as if she were making it up, but at least Graciela, who, too, had touched the shoes earlier, was nodding. She stood near the entrance to the hallway leading to the kitchen and looked as if she'd rather be anywhere than in this room.

Catching Graciela's agreement, Khloe said, "Let me get this straight. You think someone *deliberately* dunked a pair of Noah's shoes—*those* Nikes—in the bay and then left them in the nursery for you to discover?"

"Maybe someone was trying to freak me out," Ava suggested.

Jacob snorted. "You don't need any help in that department."

"Hold on," Wyatt cut in, glaring at Jacob, and even Dern seemed about to protest. Wyatt threw a glare at the ranch hand and muttered, "This doesn't make any sense."

"I know. I was trying to tell you that when the police arrived earlier," Ava said. She scooped up the small shoes and walked them over to Wyatt, who stood in the doorway. "Here. Feel them. Smell them!" She grabbed Wyatt's hand and dropped her baby's first serious pair of sneakers into her husband's palm.

"Shit, maybe he should taste them, too," Jacob suggested, then, when Jewel-Anne hit his knee with her fist to shut him up, clamped his mouth closed.

"Jesus," Wyatt whispered; then he did smell the damp leather. "You found them in the nursery?" he asked, though it had already been stated. "You were in Noah's room again?"

She bristled. Why was he turning this around?

When she didn't respond, Wyatt asked again, "Why did you go into his room?"

"It's not as if the nursery is off-limits," Trent pointed out. "Ava can go anywhere she wants."

Wyatt ignored him. "It just seems strange that after not going into his room for months, now you're in there all the time."

"I saw someone in his room!" Ava didn't bother hiding her annoyance. "I was in the garden with Jewel-Anne earlier. She left and . . . and I looked up at the house and saw someone in the window."

"Someone?" Wyatt repeated.

"He, she . . . was behind the curtains, but they were in Noah's room!" Even to her own ears, Ava sounded desperate. As if she were grasping at straws to explain herself. She felt every pair of eyes in the room focused on her and almost heard the unspoken thoughts whispering between them, thoughts suggesting that she'd really gone off the deep end this time.

Demetria. Graciela. Virginia. Even sullen Simon. Along with Khloe and everyone related to her. Ava tried not to sound overly anxious, but it was tricky. She reined in her emotions with an effort and somehow managed to keep her voice steady. Holding out a palm to ward off any interruption, she said, "I was alone. And . . . I just got this feeling that someone was watching me. You know how you sense someone nearby when you can't see them?" No one responded, but she caught a knowing, almost conspiratorial glance between Wyatt and McPherson. Nonetheless, Ava forged on. "When I looked up at the window to Noah's room, I saw a shadow behind the curtains."

"A shadow? Or a phantom?" Jacob sniggered.

"Let her speak," Dern ordered. Arms folded over his chest, he hitched his chin at Ava. "Go ahead."

Encouraged, she said, "So, I ran up to the nursery, and when I got there, whoever it was had left."

"Poof." Jacob tossed up his hands as if there had been a small explosion.

"That's when I saw the shoes, by the closet," Ava declared, skewering Jacob with a glare of her own.

"Big deal." Jewel Anne this time.

"Maybe it is," Trent cut in. "Let's go with what she says. So, then, who did it? Who took the shoes, dropped them into the water, and then brought them back to the nursery for Ava to find?"

When he said it like that, Ava felt silly, as if she were making a mountain out of a molehill. Cheryl Reynolds was dead and she was worried about wet shoes? No wonder everyone thought she was losing it. . . . Trent didn't pick up on her change of heart and gestured to Wyatt, Ian, and himself. "Not any of us. We were on the mainland. You too," he said, indicating Evelyn McPherson. "By process of elimination, that leaves the rest of you."

"If anyone was really in there," Demetria countered. She was standing in the doorway to the hall leading to the kitchen. Half in and half out of the room, as if she didn't know whether she was included or not. Just like Graciela.

Despite second-guessing herself, Ava wasn't going to let the conversation travel down that dangerous path. "*Some*one put the shoes there."

"The last time I saw those shoes," Khloe said solemnly, "they were in your closet, Ava."

"In *my* closet?" Some of her bravado slipped.

"You kept them there because they were Noah's favorites. Remember?" Khloe was nodding, as if encouraging her to recall.

"I . . . I don't think so."

"On the top shelf, next to his favorite books."

No, this was wrong. But there was a grain of truth in there somewhere. She remembered reaching up to get a purse and had seen them. . . .

"I saw the shoes in the closet this morning," Graciela put in, looking at Ava as if she truly were a mental case. "That's why I asked you why they weren't in the closet when I saw you with them. I meant *your* closet."

Oh, God. This was all turning around. "If . . . if you saw them in my closet this morning, who took them out and . . ." It was getting clearer now what was going on here. She was being railroaded into thinking that she'd stolen the damned shoes herself, dunked them in the bay, then put them in Noah's room on purpose, when she was having one of her spells, the kind she never remembered. "You all think I did it," she whispered, disbelieving. But a part of her, that splintered part of her mind, suddenly wasn't so sure.

"No one said that," Wyatt assured her, yet there was a hint of irritation beneath his placating words, as if he wanted her to snap out of her funk, to remember, to return to the woman she'd once been, the one he'd married.

"What about security cameras?" Dern asked, and his gaze traveled to Jacob. "You know, they've got those things now, not just audio monitors but videos as well."

Jacob lifted his shoulders as if to say, *Not my responsibility.*

"We didn't have them when Noah was an infant," Ava said, shaking her head. "I wish we had, but, no, there are no monitors in place." So, just like when her child disappeared, there was no film of anyone walking into his room and snatching him up. Her heart started to ache again, and she closed her mind to that life-altering mistake.

Everyone was still looking at her.

In for a penny, in for a pound, she thought, drawing from some inner strength. They already thought she was nuts. Maybe it was time to really prove them all right. She caught Dern's dark gaze, saw his reservations, the questions in his eyes, but plunged on.

"I know you all think I'm losing it."

"No one said that," Wyatt said again.

"I see it in your eyes," Ava said.

"You did jump into the bay the other night," Jewel-Anne reminded her. Prim and self-righteous. "And you hallucinate."

"Maybe."

"No 'maybe' about it," Jacob said.

This wasn't going well, but then what had lately? "Then what about this?" Withdrawing the key from the pocket of her jeans, she held it up, then put it on the table next to the damp shoes.

"A key?" Jewel Anne said with a little disbelieving laugh. "What's it to?"

"I don't know. I thought someone might tell me."

"Because . . . ?" Jewel-Anne prompted.

"I found it. In my pocket, and I didn't put it there."

She felt rather than saw Wyatt's shoulders slump, and from the corner of her eye, she noticed that the psychologist's lips had pursed a little.

"Is it important?" Trent asked, and for the first time since she'd seen him, he, too, seemed unsure of her, of where she was taking the conversation.

"I have no idea where it goes, what lock it opens."

"Maybe it doesn't open anything," Ian offered up. "It looks old." He crossed the room, plucked the key from the table, and, eyeing it, said, "If it bothers you and you don't know where it belongs, why don't you just throw it away?"

Wyatt's eyebrows shot up, silently encouraging her to do just that.

Ava couldn't. Not yet. "I think it could be important. That someone left it in my sweater for a reason."

Ian rolled his eyes. "Really? It's just a key. No one snuck

into your room and slipped it into your sweater in the dead of
night while you were sleeping. Enough with all this old cloak-
and-dagger stuff. If someone wanted you to have a key, they
would have handed it to you and said, 'Here, this is the key to . . .
whatever' or 'Did you lose this?' or 'Hey, I found this. Know
where it goes?' " He glanced around the room at all the somber
faces. "It's no great mystery, Ava, and it has nothing to do with
your quest to find Noah. It's just a damned key that you probably put in your own pocket and forgot." To make his point, he
tossed the key into the fire. "There!"

Ava gasped.

Ian added, "Problem solved."

Wyatt was already crossing the room. "That isn't neces-
sary." He threw Ava's cousin a dark look. "For the love of
God, what's wrong with you?"

"What's wrong with *me*?" Ian threw back. "What's wrong
with *you*? You're the one married to the nut job!"

"This is my house and I won't stand for it!" Wyatt roared.

"Then get your facts straight. This house isn't yours. It's hers."
He hooked a thumb at Ava. "And that's why you allow yourself
to be so pussy-whipped, whether you want to be or not!"

"You're done," Wyatt said in a dangerous tone. Using the
tongs meant to move wood around in the fireplace, he carefully
fished out the key, scraping it through a thick bed of ash to the
edge of the grate. The key recovered, Wyatt showed Ian a menacing look.

"I'm really sick of all this drama," Ian responded with a
snarl. "It gets us nowhere." He took a swallow from his drink
and, with an effort, pulled himself together. "Look, Ava, I'm
sorry about Noah. I really am. And I understand why you won't
give up and want to find him. I do. But . . . the other stuff? The
jumping into the bay, the shoes . . ." He pointed to the pair on
the table, then hooked his thumb toward the fire. "Some stupid
key . . . It's nothing, okay? You keep telling all of us that you're

not hallucinating, that you're not even the least bit neurotic, but really? Don't you see? Shoes, keys, midnight plunges into freezing water, it's not what a sane person would do."

Ian looked around for support, but no one else said a word. Thankfully.

"We all feel it, Ava," he went on, undeterred. "And I for one applaud you for not giving up on your boy, but your methods of trying to find him, of insisting someone's deliberately trying to set you up, they're not normal and it's not right. No one thinks so, but they're either afraid of losing their jobs or afraid you'll throw them off the island, so they don't speak up."

He crossed the room and placed a hand on her shoulder. "Let all this go."

With that, he left.

Jacob said, "Ian's right. I don't know about the rest of you, but I'm sick of all this weeping and crying and accusations. All the damned hysteria!" Throwing up a hand, he turned to Ava. "Your son is gone. Period. You'd better learn to move on and deal with it!"

Khloe gasped. "Jacob," she protested.

Ava felt as if she'd been sucker punched.

"What? That shocks you? Seriously?" Jacob looked from one of his half siblings to the other. "We *all* feel this way."

Wyatt nearly leaped across the room. "You're done here, too," he said, looming over Jacob. "Get outta here. A woman is dead, for God's sake!"

"Hey!" Jacob held up both hands palms out. "Talk about over-reacting. Don't kill the messenger, okay? I'm just keepin' it real!" He looked around the room and, when no one came to his defense, spat, "Figures." Then he stomped out, his army boots thudding loudly. The cat, startled, shot through the doorway to the kitchen, nearly colliding with Demetria.

Khloe's cell phone went off and she answered, holding the phone to her ear as she walked out of the room for privacy.

Ava had had it. Maybe Ian and Jacob were right. Maybe she was overreacting, making mountains out of molehills.

Seeing shadows and evil when they didn't exist.

But she doubted it.

Cheryl Reynolds's murder was proof enough of that.

Chapter 24

Snyder climbed onto his bike, adjusted the strap of his helmet, and started peddling back to his apartment. He took a lot of crap for riding his ancient ten-speed, but because of it he'd dropped nearly thirty pounds and lowered his blood pressure and cholesterol levels. So he put up with the rain, cold, and bad jokes from his coworkers.

On a whim this evening, he took a detour, riding down past the marina, smelling the brackish water and the underlying odor of diesel. He stopped to look across the whitecaps rising in the bay to Church Island, that bastion of the Church family.

Fog was rolling in, a thick mist that obscured his view, just as all the bullshit swirling around Ava Church Garrison was clouding his mind, taking him away from the evidence in the Cheryl Reynolds case. It was already dark anyway, but on a clear night, he would be able to see the smattering of lights of Monroe, pick out the ferry dock, and even view patches of light from the windows of Neptune's Gate, that behemoth of a house. He'd noted, though, that only the first two floors were ever illuminated. Never had he seen any lights in the upper floor; although, from Anchorville, he had only one view of the home—just the front.

And it was a long ways away.

Except for the time he'd gone to Church Island after the Garrison boy's disappearance, he'd never given the house or its inhabitants much thought. He'd heard the rumors, of course, but for the most part he'd ignored them.

Now he turned down a narrow side street and cut around an idling truck double-parked and belching exhaust as the driver tried to quickly unload beer kegs for the nearby tavern.

Riding along a street that paralleled the water, Snyder kept his eye on traffic, but his mind was spinning, just as it always did when he biked. He decided what he really needed was a motive and the murder weapon. Both the barista at The Local Buzz and Butch Johansen confirmed Ava's story, and he just couldn't see her as a cold-blooded, violent killer.

Then again, he'd been wrong before.

Lester Reece was a prime example of that. He'd been the lead detective on that one.

With a sigh, he looked at his watch. He was a firm believer in the "first forty-eight" theory, meaning that if the killer couldn't be found in the first two days after the murder was committed, the chances of finding him or her and solving the homicide plummeted. Now, he felt the clock ticking; it had been twenty-four hours since someone had taken Cheryl Reynolds's life.

Stopping at Ahab's, a small fish market that had existed for nearly a hundred years and looked like it, Snyder picked up the last of the fresh local oysters. The place, with its glass cases, shaved ice, and array of seafood, hadn't changed since the last time it was remodeled, about the same time refrigeration came into vogue, it seemed. Faded signs from the thirties, forties, and fifties still hung on the thick wooden walls that once had been painted white, and more often than not, butcher paper taped to the windows announced the catch of the day. Large vats of run-

ning salt water held live razor clams, Dungeness crab, and oysters in their cold shimmery depths. Outside, in a converted car-
port, a blackened crab pot stood ready to cook whatever sea
creature a patron chose while seagulls and seals patrolled the
lapping waters of the bay for castoffs.

Snyder made small talk with Lizzy, who had to be near
ninety and had been a fixture at the market for as long as Snyder could remember. Her face was lined, her glasses thick, her
hair wiry and snow-white beneath her ever-present net, but she
was agile and sharp and knew most of what went on in town
before it occurred.

Scooping six oysters and ice into a plastic bag, she said, "You
cracked Cheryl Reynolds's murder yet?"

"Still under investigation and no comment."

"No surprise there. Odd one, Cheryl was. Always dressed as
if she was goin' to one of them love-ins or something."

"I guess."

"She was kinda peace, love, dove, and all the sixties or seventies crap. If you ask me, it's what happens when you fraternize
with weirdos."

"You think Cheryl hung out with a bad sort?" He couldn't
help but look around her shack of a business situated on the
wharf where all kinds of riffraff were known to hang out. Half
the drug busts made in Anchorville occurred within fifty yards
of the docks.

Lizzy read his mind. "Oh, well . . . down here it's different,
and I *don't* invite any of my customers into my house! Besides,
I got Jimmy and his dogs right next door at the bait shop."

Snyder had met Jimmy, Lizzy's grandson, who, in his fifties,
always seemed stoned. He'd also petted George and Martha on
their big heads when he was picking up bait or a fishing license
next door, and he doubted either Labrador retriever could
gather up the energy to scare off would-be assailants.

"Here ya go!" Lizzy rang up his purchase, snapped up the

twenty, and slammed it into the ancient register that still actually dinged as the drawer closed, then dropped his change into his hand.

"If you ask me, you should be lookin' at Lester Reece," she said as Snyder zipped his plastic bag of oysters into his backpack.

"He's dead."

"Don't believe it. Uh-uh." She walked around the counter and switched off the glowing neon OPEN sign. "And Cheryl, you know, she knew him."

"She did?"

"Sure. Well, actually she knew his mother. A client of hers. And another one who's not all there, if y'know what I mean." She rotated a long finger near the ear with her hearing aid. "Stuck with the judge even though he ran around all over the county. If it was me," she said, grinning to display perfect dentures, "I would have shot the SOB."

"Then you'd be in trouble."

"No way. Justifiable homicide in my book!"

Chuckling, he left just as another patron, head bent against a gust of wind, tried to enter.

Lizzy blocked the door. "We're closed. Come back tomorrow."

"But—" the man protested as the door was slammed in his face and the interior lights were doused. "Oh, man," he said as much to himself as anyone else. "Stella is gonna kill me!"

Snyder swung onto his bike and started heading uphill to his apartment, which was on the north end of town.

By the time he'd cracked a beer, shucked the oysters, and turned on the big screen, his cell phone was ringing. Morgan Lyons's name and number showed on the screen. "This had better be good," he said as he answered.

"I just finished going through Cheryl Reynolds's list of clients. Found it on an old disk for her computer. Guess whose name came up?"

"Not in the mood for games." But he felt a small rush of adrenaline, a little taste of expectancy.

"How about Jewel-Anne Church?" she said, and the rush in his blood died a quick death.

"She's a cripple. I don't think she killed anyone."

"The correct term is *handicapped* or even *handi-capable*, but that's not the point. She wasn't always in that wheelchair, you know. And this was before the boating accident that caused her paralysis."

"Okay."

"You don't think it's important."

"Only in the fact that everyone Reynolds ever knew is a potential suspect, but, no, I don't think just because she's related to the last person known to see Cheryl alive and was her client a while back that Jewel-Anne's in the running. Unless you have something else."

"Nah."

"Didn't think so."

But it did bother him that on the very day Ava Garrison had come to the department wanting to get more information on her son's disappearance that she'd gone for a session with Cheryl. A coincidence? Probably. People from the island undoubtedly consolidated their trips. But Snyder always paid attention when something was out of the ordinary, a little out of sync. So he'd keep his eye on the rich lady who owned most of Church Island, and he'd keep on file the fact that the handicapped cousin had been a client of the hypnotherapist. Into the phone, he said, "Anyone else on the list who's a little more interesting?"

"Not yet, but I'll keep you posted."

"Do that," he said, and stepped outside to his postage-stamp-sized deck, where he fired up the barbecue and cooked the oysters. He knew that the shellfish bathed in butter and sprinkled with a blend of Italian cheese wasn't going to help his cholesterol numbers, but he figured he only lived once and he'd eaten enough rabbit food in the past week to satisfy himself, if not his doctor.

Tonight, he was going to enjoy himself and watch some football, as the Seahawks were playing against the Steelers, and he loved it when the Hawks took it to Pittsburgh. During his eight-year marriage to wife number two, he'd inherited a brother-in-law from Pennsylvania. The guy was a bastard, one of those freaks who thought betting on the games was all there was to life, so Snyder took great pleasure in beating him. Tonight, the matchup promised to be a good one with the Seahawks favored by three. One lousy field goal.

He found his favorite TV tray in the hall closet and set himself in front of the television with his beer and oysters and half a bag of chips, but even as Seattle pulled ahead in the fourth quarter, he found himself losing interest as he polished off the last of the chips. In his mind's eye, he kept seeing Cheryl Reynolds lying in a pool of her own blood, a herd of cats mewing and slinking around her.

It was weird as hell.

Dern finished with the livestock, patting each silky nose as he poured a ration of grain into their mangers. The horses snorted and shifted in their stalls, rustling the straw as they buried their noses into the oats.

The stable was warm and dry, and aside from the odd light cast by the fluorescents, inviting. It smelled of horses, grain, dust, and oiled leather, all scents he remembered from his grandparents' ranch where he'd grown up.

Life had been simpler then, or maybe he was just being nostalgic; because that's when it had all started, this restlessness, this need to change his own destiny.

With Rover following after him, he snapped off the lights and turned his collar to the driving rain and wind. A squall had kicked up and would probably last most of the night. Glancing toward the main house, he wondered what was going on inside. Lights glowed from the windows on the lower level, and here and there a room on the second floor cast out a patch of gold as well. He'd avoided the house for most of the evening. After the detectives had departed and the Church family had gathered in the den, he'd made his excuses of work to be done and left.

He couldn't hang too closely. They'd question him and get suspicious, so he had to keep his distance. Though they treated most of the staff like family, he was the new kid on the block, and he didn't want to raise any questions about himself or his past by appearing too interested.

Climbing the stairs to his apartment, he wondered if he'd made a mistake in coming here. Yeah, it had seemed the perfect opportunity at the time, but now, after spending time with Ava Garrison, he couldn't help but think he should get out now — before he was found out, before he got himself in too deep.

She was intriguing. A basket case, yeah, but sexy as hell, and beneath her sadness was a sexy, smart woman to whom he was attracted whether he wanted to be or not.

"Idiot," he growled under his breath, and the dog gave off a soft "woof" as if in agreement. On the landing, he petted Rover's head and gave himself a quick mental kick. He couldn't get too comfortable here, and there was no time for second-guessing himself. He was on a mission and that was that. Ava Garrison and her huge eyes be damned.

If she got hurt, well, that was all part and parcel of the business.

"Damn it all to hell anyway." After unlocking the door to his studio, he stepped inside and froze.

Something was off.

He felt it.

But nothing appeared out of place. The book he'd been reading was still on the small table near the couch, two glasses and a dirty plate left in the sink had not been disturbed, there were toast crumbs on the counter, and his jacket was still hanging off the back of a kitchen chair just as he'd left it, and yet . . .

It wasn't so much what he saw as what he sensed . . . even a thin thready scent of something above the lingering odor of bacon and onion fried earlier in the day.

Calm down. No one's onto you.

He thought about checking his hiding spot but decided against it for fear there was a camera hidden somewhere. Only after shedding his jacket and searching the place from stem to stern for microphones, cameras, or anything else that might have been planted did he relax a little and lift the picture from the wall to double-check that nothing had been taken or compromised.

Assured that he wasn't being monitored, he pulled out his unmarked cell and made the call.

He was getting jumpy; that was it and it wouldn't do.

Not before his mission was accomplished.

He punched a familiar number.

A woman's voice answered. "I was wondering when I'd hear from you," she said.

He nodded, as if she could see him. "Just want to let you know that everything's going as planned."

"I heard that a woman was murdered in Anchorville."

"That's right." He didn't dare say more.

"Be careful," she warned in her familiar tone that reminded him of warm summer nights and starry skies.

"Always."

He clicked off before the conversation got too personal and wondered who the hell had been inside his apartment.

More importantly: Why?

Ava suffered through another private session with Dr. McPherson, and of course the psychologist was encouraging, even saying that she thought Ava could be making a breakthrough, that as her mind healed, Ava's memory would return—the same old song and dance Ava had been hearing ever since she'd been released from St. Brendan's.

"I want to wean myself off my medication," Ava told her, but the therapist hadn't budged even though she suspected Ava wasn't taking her meds.

"That's the ultimate goal, of course. But for now let's not do anything drastic. You really do seem to be getting better."

"Am I? I saw my son and jumped into the bay the other night. And now everyone seems to think I'm gaslighting myself."

Ava hadn't added that she'd snagged the damned key from the hearth and now kept it with her at all times. Foolish? Maybe. Paranoid? Most definitely. Obsessive? Yeah . . . really obsessive, but she kept the key with her anyway, could feel the thin metal in the pocket of her jeans right now. As for her son's wet shoes, she knew someone had taken them from her closet, dipped them in seawater, and left them for her to find just to give her an emotional jolt. She'd returned them to the top shelf of her closet. For now.

"You've been under a lot of stress," Evelyn had said, leaning closer, "but I do think you're improving, on the right path. I know you want off the medication and we'll work toward that." Her smile seemed sincere, but the worry in her eyes never quite disappeared. Probably because it was masked with guilt. "This is going to take some time. We all have to be patient."

Of course, she didn't know that Ava wasn't taking one damned pill, and the headaches she'd been warned would result from going cold turkey off the meds hadn't been all that bad. She would survive.

After the session, Ava quietly left the room even though inside she was running. She crossed through the kitchen where Virginia was still cleaning up after a meal and found some hot

water for a cup of peach-flavored tea that claimed to be soothing. Since she was still supposed to be on the prescribed medication, which wasn't supposed to be mixed with alcohol, Ava
had gone along with the ruse, all the while thinking a glass of
wine or even a margarita might be better for her anxiety.

Nonetheless, she played her part, dipping the tea bag into a
cup of hot water, watching as Graciela slipped her arms through
the sleeves of a long jacket and tucked her hair into the collar.
Virginia had the radio playing softly, some pop-rock song from
the eighties barely audible over the running water as she rinsed
a baking dish.

"Need a ride?" Ian offered Graciela as he walked into the
kitchen and set his glass on the counter. He and Trent had been
playing pool. Ava had heard the faint click of billiard balls and
laughter as she and the psychologist had talked in the den.

"I'm fine." Graciela flashed him a thankful smile.

"I'm going into town anyway," he said. "Out of cigarettes."

"Okay then," Graciela acquiesced.

"I thought you quit." Ava tossed her tea bag into the trash
under the sink as Khloe sauntered into the kitchen.

His gaze was cool. "That's why I'm 'out.' " When she didn't
ask the question, he added, "I'm a big boy. I think I can decide
what's good for me."

Ava blew across her teacup. "Tar and nicotine?" she asked,
unable to keep from ribbing him a little.

"And arsenic and ammonia or whatever. Probably just
about all the carcinogens you can think of."

"They're your lungs," Ava said, but Virginia, wiping her
hands on her apron, snorted her disapproval.

"Disgusting habit."

"Come on, Mom, you smoked for years." Khloe set a few
more cups into the sink, and when Virginia seemed about to
argue, she added, "*For years.* Virginia Slims, I remember."

"That was years ago, before I knew better!" Virginia said,
obviously in a bad mood at being called out.

"Well, I still don't." Ian, placing a hand on the small of Graciela's back to steer her toward the back porch, gave them all a quick wave. "I'll be back in half an hour. Just gonna drop Graciela off and stop at the Food-O-Mart."

Ava was carrying her cup toward the front stairs when she saw Dr. McPherson and her husband standing close, heads together and whispering. She carefully backed up behind a wall, then stopped to listen but could only hear a few words.

". . . about Noah . . . I know . . . ," the doctor said.

Wyatt's response was muffled completely, as his back was to the doorway.

". . . some kind . . . breakthrough . . . Kelvin . . . I'm sure . . . patience . . . with Ava . . ."

Again Wyatt's response was unclear. Sick of eavesdropping, Ava rounded the corner and found them still close together, Wyatt's hand on the doctor's shoulder as he leaned closer to hear her.

Ava had had enough.

"So . . . what's the diagnosis?" she asked, walking into the hallway. Wyatt looked up sharply over his shoulder and his expression darkened. "I heard my name, so I assume you were discussing my 'condition.' "

"It's true," Wyatt admitted, straightening. "I was asking about you."

"Isn't that highly illegal?" she asked, and Evelyn McPherson actually blushed. "Isn't there something about physician/patient confidentiality? You're a psychologist; I think that covers you, too," she said to Dr. McPherson before her gaze moved to her husband. "And you're a lawyer, so you know it, too. So, what's going on here?"

The cords on Wyatt's neck stood out a bit. "I don't like what you're insinuating."

"Yeah? After you suggested I get an attorney before talking with the police? After you and Evelyn here are all over each other whenever you're alone?"

"Ava, no," Evelyn said, shocked.

"Don't," Wyatt warned, but Ava was done with all the game-playing, the pretenses, the damned lies.

"You're saying," Ava said to the doctor, "that you aren't having an affair with my husband."

The woman took a step back and shook her head. "No. Never."

Ava raised a skeptical eyebrow.

"What the hell are you talking about?" Wyatt burst out. "Are you out of your fucking mind?" He appeared absolutely scandalized by the suggestion. "I'm only with Evelyn because she was recommended, had worked with you at St. Brendan's. I thought hiring her would help you! Don't turn it around on us."

"On us," Ava repeated. "Why does it feel like two on one here, that you two are ganging up on me?"

Evelyn said, "I would never . . ." Her words sounded heart-felt, but her eyes gave her away when she looked to Wyatt for support.

"Maybe I don't need you any longer," Ava suggested.

"In my professional opinion, you're improving due to your sessions."

"I'm not so sure," Ava said curtly.

Wyatt stepped in. "Of course you are." He grabbed Ava's free hand and rotated it, palm up, to show the ugly lines running up and down her wrists. "Look what you did. After Noah left. You were so bereaved, so messed up." His eyes held hers. "Don't slip away again. Keep seeing Dr. McPherson." His fingers dug into her arm in his repressed fury.

But the psychologist had regained some of her equilibrium. "If you would prefer another therapist, I could recommend someone. Elliot Sterns is very good — "

"No!" Wyatt was adamant. He dropped Ava's wrist. "You stay. You've been helping her. She needs you."

"I think that's my call," Ava said.

Evelyn was nodding. "It is."

Wyatt glanced from one woman to the other, then said to his wife, "Dr. McPherson is just placating you right now, trying not to upset you, but the truth of the matter is that I'm your guardian, Ava."

"What?" she asked, nearly choking.

He plowed stiff, agitated fingers through his hair. "After the suicide attempt, I had papers drawn. Don't you remember?"

Vaguely, in the back of her mind, she recalled a meeting with a judge, but she'd been out of it, hadn't really understood what was going on.

"Dr. McPherson stays, Ava," Wyatt said with a renewed authority. "Unless you want to see yourself back at the hospital."

Ava set the teacup down on a side table with shaking hands, then grabbed hold of his elbow and pulled him farther into the hallway so that their conversation wouldn't be overheard. Lowering her voice, she dropped his elbow and said, "You'd commit me?"

"Only as a last resort," he assured her.

"You're threatening me?"

He bristled slightly, his lips flattening over his teeth. "God, Ava. I have to make certain you're safe! That part came with the territory when I said 'I do.' "

"Safe?" she repeated. "What are you talking about? I'm not going to hurt myself, if that's what you're afraid of."

"Look, it would be for your own good."

"You don't have to be my keeper, Wyatt. That wasn't part of the 'territory.' " She stared at him hard, tried to see what was behind his eyes. "One of the things I do remember is that you and I were on the verge of divorce just before I wound up at St. Brendan's."

"You didn't just wind up there," he reminded her. "It wasn't a choice. You were committed because you tried to kill yourself! Pills and a razor. Do you remember that?"

"No!"

"Then you're still sick, Ava. Very sick." He touched her shoulder lightly, almost lovingly, but she knew it was all fake. An act.

"I'm never going back to the hospital."

He didn't respond, just held her gaze with his own, that slightly superior, condescending stare she hadn't noticed before she'd married him. Though he didn't utter a word, she felt the *We'll just see about that*, hanging silently in the air between them, and a dread, as cold as the bottom of the bay, settled into her soul.

Chapter 25

Ava needed to get out. The bedroom walls were closing in on her and she couldn't stand being in Neptune's Gate a second longer.

In the bathroom, she found a rubber band and snapped her hair into a quick ponytail. Though she wasn't on house arrest, she felt a prisoner in the old walls of the home she'd loved so much of her life. Tonight, though, she needed a break. She caught a glimpse of her reflection, the circles under her eyes, the tension in the corners of her mouth, the pale color of her skin, and she cringed.

No more of this being a weakling!

No more being a victim!

No more being pushed around!

She changed into a pair of running pants and top that she'd worn years before, then found her waterproof Windbreaker, complete with reflective tape. She didn't have to worry about her husband giving her any grief about running in the dark, as Wyatt had already asked Ian to take him, along with Dr. McPherson, over to the mainland.

"You're going out?" Khloe asked as Ava, shrugging into her jacket, hurried down the stairs. "Now?"

"For a little while."

"To Anchorville?" Concerned, Khloe glanced out the tall windows in the foyer to the darkness beyond.

"Just to Monroe."

"It's raining," Virginia said as she walked into the foyer, untying her apron.

"I won't drown."

Virginia eyed her speculatively and Ava was reminded of how recently they had all thought she would die in the waters of the bay. "Look, I've gotta go."

Before anyone else put up an argument, she grabbed a flashlight and a baseball cap, then headed out the door. Everyone thought she was crazy anyway, so let them shake their heads at her insanity for running in the rain and dark. She really didn't care.

She bounded down the steps and found the gravel path leading to the drive. From there, she started jogging, slowly at first, feeling the cold air against her face and realizing as the rain splattered against her fingers that she'd forgotten gloves. Too bad. She wasn't going to retrace her steps and explain herself all over again.

Down the hill to the main road she jogged, her running shoes slapping the wet asphalt, the beam of her flashlight bobbing ahead of her, her lungs feeling the bite of cold air.

And yet it felt good to run, to feel her calves and thighs, to breathe deeply of the salty air. The road followed the curve of the bay, running like a flat ribbon along the shoreline and into Monroe, where a sprinkling of streetlights gave off a watery blue illumination.

Slap, slap, slap!

She increased her pace slightly, her eyes trained on the weak beam of her flashlight, her legs stretching, her breathing regu-

lar. Cold rain ran down her neck, but she didn't care. The feeling of freedom, the exhilaration of actually doing something,
was worth it.

So where was Noah?

She didn't believe he was dead. Wouldn't go there. But if
not, then whoever had taken him hadn't done it for ransom. So,
it had to be someone who wanted her son, and it was definitely
someone who was either at the Christmas party as an invited
guest, a member of the staff, or someone who had snuck into
the house and avoided being seen by anyone.

Unless the kidnapper had an accomplice.

She'd thought of that before. And if there was an accomplice,
then it came down to someone she knew or Wyatt knew. The
names of the people who'd been at the house that night ran in
circles through her brain: Jewel-Anne, Jacob, Trent and Ian, of
course. Zinnia, Aunt Piper and Uncle Crispin, Wyatt, and
every member of the staff, most of whom were still employed
at Neptune's Gate. And then there were the others: Butch Johansen and several of Wyatt's clients and acquaintances. Tanya
and Russell . . . Oh, God, there were too many to consider.

*What about Evelyn McPherson? Had she been there? It
would have been before she became your psychologist . . . even
then, were she and Wyatt seeing each other?*

No . . . Ava had met Evelyn McPherson at St. Brendan's
where she'd been introduced as her therapist . . .

A distant memory sliced through her brain . . . something she'd
forgotten. The room was crowded, people coming and going from
the party, music playing, glasses clinking, laughter and conversation filling the air. She'd been hurrying down the stairs, her hand
trailing along the banister where garlands had been strung, and as
she passed by the highest branches of the Christmas tree, she saw a
woman through French doors to the darkened den. The panes on
the doors reflected the lights of the tree that dominated the foyer,
and beyond the glass, a heavy-set woman she'd not met stood in

profile. At first Ava had thought the woman was alone, maybe talking on her cell phone, but she'd been focused on something outside of Ava's field of vision. That woman, whose appearance had altered significantly since, must have been Evelyn McPherson.

Had Evelyn turned to glance up the stairs as Ava had hurried down? Or was she imagining it now? And why hadn't the doctor appeared on any of the lists that Ava had created since Noah's disappearance, or the people questioned by the police, or—The toe of her running shoe caught on the edge of a pothole and she was jerked out of her reverie.

She tripped, falling forward, dropping the flashlight as she broke her fall with her hands. Gravel and rough asphalt tore at her skin and ripped the knees of her running pants as she slid, then caught herself.

"Damn!"

She watched as her flashlight rolled down the rest of the hill, sending a wobbly, spinning beam shimmering against the wet pavement. Palms stinging, knees aching, Ava climbed to her feet and was thankful no one had seen her clumsy fall. Her back pained her a bit, but otherwise the bruises were mainly to her ego.

Wiping her skinned hands on her jacket, she looked around, half expecting Dern to appear. The last few times she'd nearly hurt herself, he'd come racing to the rescue, but the night remained quiet and dark, only the sound of the lapping tide heard over the rush of the rain.

"Stupid," she muttered, then took off after the flashlight that had finally come to rest at the edge of a gutter, its lamp half submerged in a puddle.

Catching up to the damned thing, she picked it up and wiped it off on her jacket, then walked into the small town, past Frank's Food-O-Mart where two teenagers in stocking caps and heavy jackets were seated on the curb, under the overhang of the roof while smoking cigarettes and drinking Red Bull.

Down two blocks, she moved past the only inn in town and

into Rose's, the small café that was luckily still open. Rosie, the owner, manager, and waitress, was behind the counter, swiping a rag over the old Formica counter.

"I'm closing in fifteen minutes," she said, squinting a bit before recognizing Ava. With a toothy smile, she added, "Ms. Church! You know my hours are flexible. Come on in!" Rosie was never going to remember Ava's married name. Now she dropped her rag and grabbed a plastic menu. "Haven't seen you in a while." A slight woman with a bit of a rounded back, Rosie was somewhere in her seventies and had owned the place for as long as Ava could remember. "Sit anywhere you want. The joint's not exactly jumpin'."

She was right. The small restaurant was nearly empty. A huge man who looked as if he'd be a lot more comfortable in a tavern sat at the counter, his belly pressed against the top Rosie had so recently swabbed. Next to the guy, a kid of about ten was picking at the fries on his plate, the remains of a hamburger in evidence.

"How're ya doin'?" Rosie asked.

"Okay."

"You sure?" She handed the menu to Ava.

"Yeah, I am. But don't ask my family. They all think I'm nuts."

Rosie chuckled and coughed a little, a smoker's rattle that she ended by clearing her throat. "That's what families are for, don't ya know? To love each other to death, all the while ripping their hearts out. Can I get you anything to drink?"

"Glass of wine. White. Chardonnay, I guess." To hell with the ruse of taking her meds.

"Comin' right up. Hey, you want the last piece of pumpkin pie . . . huh? Better snap it up or old George there, he'll get it." She hooked a thumb at the other customer.

Thinking about the possible caliber of the house wine, Ava said, "How about some cheese and crackers?"

"Only got saltines."

"They'll do."

Rosie was nodding. "They're for the chowder and oyster stew. Clyde made the stew this mornin'. But we're fresh out."

Clyde was Rosie's husband. They'd been married, off and on, for forty-plus years and currently lived in the apartment over the café.

After a wineglass was deposited on the table, she murmured a quick thanks and took a sip, decided it was passable, and looked out the big plate-glass window as Rosie went back to the counter. From her corner booth, Ava gazed across the black water to the lights of Anchorville, thick strands of illumination around the shoreline that were spattered more sparingly up the hillside.

Of course, the distance across the water made it impossible to see anything in the town clearly, but she stared in the general direction of Cheryl's studio. Cheryl's worried image came to mind and the last words she'd uttered to Ava resonated through her brain.

"I think you should be careful. . . . Things aren't always as they seem or what we want them to be. There's a lot of bad blood out on the island. You know it. I know it. And sometimes I can't help myself. I worry about you."

Cheryl had ended up dead. Murdered. Not the other way around. The danger, apparently, had been to Cheryl rather than to Ava. Odd. Ava frowned, thinking backward to their session. Why had Cheryl been so upset? Was it something Ava had said while she was under hypnosis?

Twisting the stem of her wineglass between her fingers, Ava watched the Chardonnay swirl in the goblet bowl. The motion of the clear liquid reminded her of water sloshing, and a lightning-quick memory burned through her brain.

The day Kelvin died came back to her once again, the painful events of that boat trip somehow tangling up in her head with Noah's disappearance. Sometimes she felt there had to be a connection between the two; her mind seemed to always try to link both tragic events. She'd never been able to discover what held them together, so she always came to the inevitable conclusion that the only thing tying the two events together was the emotional loss she'd suffered at losing both her brother and her son.

Back when Kelvin was alive, there were fewer people living at Neptune's Gate and the family had been estranged. Ava had already bought them out, and aside from Jewel-Anne, they had all left the island, most thinking "good riddance" to the rock in the Strait of Juan de Fuca, which separated Vancouver Island in British Columbia from Washington State.

They'd only returned for her brother's funeral, and a few, including Ian, had offered to "help" and stay on.

"We're closing!" Rosie's shrill voice broke into Ava's thoughts, and she looked up quickly to see the glass door opening.

Austin Dern was pushing his way inside, and he didn't pay any attention to the owner's screeches.

"Did you hear me?" Rosie demanded, hands on her skinny hips.

"I'll just be a sec." He walked to Ava's booth and slid across from her.

She said to Rosie, "It's okay. He's . . . a friend."

"Humph!" she snorted, but didn't argue.

"Why am I not surprised that you're here?" she asked as he shed his jacket. "It seems any time I leave the house, you show up. Ready to rescue me."

A smile tugged at one corner of his mouth, and she noticed that his lips, beneath his five-o'clock shadow, were blade thin. "Something tells me you don't need to be rescued."

"You're right. Despite what my family seems to think." She took a long gulp of wine, then said, "Buy you a drink?"

He glanced at the counter where Rosie was refilling napkin

holders and sending him looks definitely meant to kill. "I get the feeling the bar's closed."

"What's your deal, Dern? Why are you chasing after me?" She pointed at him. "And don't give me some garbage about how you just happened to see me leaving or anything like that. And I don't really believe in guardian angels, so that won't fly, either. Since I don't remember hiring you as my bodyguard, there must be some other reason you keep following me."

Rosie chose that moment to sidle over with a small plate of sliced cheese and three small packs of saltines. "Anything for you?" she said halfheartedly. "Bein' as you're a friend of Ava's and all."

"How about a beer?" When she lifted an eyebrow, he added, "Whatever you've got on tap."

"That would be nothin'," she said, lips pursing a bit.

"Then a Bud."

"That we got."

At the counter, George instructed his kid to zip up his jacket, then after snagging a couple of leftover fries from the boy's plate, left some bills on the counter and lumbered outside.

Rosie closed the door behind them and locked the dead bolt.

"About as warm and fuzzy as a mad porcupine," Dern observed.

Ava felt her lips twitch just as Rosie deposited the bottle of beer and a glass onto the table. "Anything to eat?" the waitress asked, almost as a dare.

"I'm good," Dern said.

"Clyde's closin' the kitchen." She gave Dern another once-over, then, with her rounded back as stiff as she could make it, turned and swept through a gate that separated the dining room from the cramped area behind the counter.

Ava agreed. "Not the cuddly type."

Dern ignored the glass and took a long pull from his bottle.

Ava watched him swallow, the movement of his Adam's apple, then forced her gaze back to his eyes. He, of course, was watching her right back.

"So you didn't answer my question. Why is it I feel that you're following me? And don't," she said, holding up a finger, "even suggest that I'm being paranoid."

Setting his bottle down, he shook his head. "Wasn't going to. It's true. I've kept an eye on you. But no, I'm not following you. I saw you jump into the bay, then I was missing a horse, and then I did see you leave for town. I was going to walk down myself, get some fresh air and a couple of things I need."

"Huh." She wasn't buying it.

"Beer, toothpaste, and coffee." When she didn't say anything, he added, "Life's essentials."

"But instead of stopping at Frank's, you showed up here."

"I did see you come in." He lifted a shoulder. "Thought we could talk without half a dozen of your relatives eavesdropping."

"Is that what they do?" she asked, and a slow, crooked smile crept over his lips.

"Yes."

She couldn't deny it.

Leaning back in his chair, he nodded. "Not that it matters. Every family's got its quirks."

"What about yours?"

"You really want to know?" He seemed skeptical.

"Sure."

Lifting a shoulder, he said, "It's all split up. Folks divorced when I was around ten. Never saw my old man after I hit high school."

"Siblings?"

"A sister in Baton Rouge, a brother who's God knows where. We lost touch around fifteen years ago." Dern's eyes darkened a bit. "Not that we were that close anyway."

"No cousins?"

"None that I ever knew. Guess I grew up a loner. Learned how to fend for myself."

"So you're . . . not married?"

He snorted as if the question landed somewhere between funny and ridiculous. "Not anymore." Lips twisted a bit. "We were high school sweethearts, if that term's still in use. It didn't work out."

"Why?"

"Too young, probably." Again a shrug. "I was in the army, came back from a tour and was slapped with divorce papers. Decided not to fight it, as she'd already started living with someone else, and I went back to school."

"No kids?"

He shook his head. "Probably a good thing in retrospect."

"And then what? After college you became a ranch hand?"

Again, the flash of a self-deprecating grin. "Isn't that the normal progression?" He finished his beer. "Just found out that I work better with animals than people. So, what about you?"

"You don't know my life story?" She shook her head and finished her wine. "I thought it was all public information, common knowledge."

"I'm not from these parts, remember?" When she didn't respond, he added, "I worked for Rand Donnelly on a ranch outside of Bend, in Central Oregon. Grew up farther east, near Pendleton." He reached for his wallet. "Didn't you check my references?"

"I didn't even know you were hired."

"Seriously? I thought you were in charge."

"Once upon a time, maybe." When she picked up her purse and pulled out her billfold, he slapped a couple of bills onto the table. "I got it."

"I said I'd buy you a drink."

"Next time it's definitely on you." As she climbed to her feet, she saw him take notice of the rips in the knees of her jogging pants.

Before he posed a question, she said, "Let's just say that on my way down here, I embraced my inner klutz."

"You're okay?"

Again that question. "A few scrapes, but I'll survive," she insisted.

He held the door for her and they walked outside. Her waterlogged flashlight wasn't of any use, but Dern had an app on his iPhone that offered up enough illumination.

They trudged up the hill together, following the main road in silence. As they turned into the lane, Rover was waiting for them and tagged along after Dern as if he'd known the man all his life. Ava couldn't help but ask herself why she felt more comfortable with this stranger. After all, Dern was a man she'd met only a few days earlier, yet she somehow thought she was more in touch with him than she was with her own husband.

A man you'd planned to divorce, remember? Before Noah had gone missing, they had been separated most of the time, the Christmas party planned as they tried to fend off what had seemed inevitable. Then, once their son had vanished, they'd clung to each other only to have the tattered fabric of their marriage unravel further. Through their grief and fear, there had been serious discussions about ending their marriage . . . or at least that's the way she remembered things.

Now, hands deep in her pockets, her breath fogging in the cold air, she remembered her erotic dream in which Wyatt had morphed into Dern and she'd made love to him. Wildly. Without inhibition. Feeling his calloused hands slide over her buttocks and up her rib cage.

Or had it been Wyatt?

He left the rose for you, remember? Feeling the tiny prick on the edge of her finger with her thumb, she closed her mind to all the bizarre possibilities. She would never make sense of her dreams, and besides, she was being distracted.

From finding Noah.

She couldn't let it happen, she determined as the wind blew off the sea and seemed to send an icy draft through her heart. Her single intent was to find her son. Period.

Chapter 26

"I think I've met you before," Ava said the next afternoon in yet another session with Dr. McPherson. "I mean, before Wyatt hired you. At the time you went by Eve." They were in the den, and Ava, rather than make a scene, had agreed to the session, more to get information rather than give it.

Rather than arguing, the therapist was nodding as she sat in a chair, her hands clasped at her knees. "We've been over this, remember? We discussed the fact that I met you at the party you hosted at Christmas, the night that Noah went missing."

Ava's heart stuttered. "When?"

"At the party. Then again when you were still recovering at St. Brendan's," Evelyn said so patiently it grated on Ava's raw nerves. "That's where your husband asked if I would agree to see you as a patient once you were released from the hospital. He knew I had an office in Anchorville."

"I would have remembered," she said, but a hint of a memory sizzled through her brain, something so quick and fleeting she couldn't hold on to it.

The doctor's smile was ingratiating. "You're still blocking

that night out, Ava. It's coming back in bits and pieces, but there are still holes. I'm here to help you fill the gaps."

"Okay, let's start with the first one. You were introduced to me as Eve Stone."

She nodded. "I had been married, but it didn't work out. My divorce wasn't quite final at Christmas, and I hadn't officially gone back to my maiden name until a few months later."

"You looked different."

"Amazing what losing fifty pounds and lightening your hair can do."

Was this right? Had she ever heard this story before? "And you came with . . . ?"

"Actually, your cousin Trent invited me."

"Trent?" This didn't sound right.

"We knew each other in college."

"At U-Dub?" Ava asked, using the familiar name for the University of Washington in Seattle.

"Oregon. We were both psychology majors for a while." An amused smile tugged at the corners of her lips, and for a second, Ava stared at her. Had she been wrong about this woman all along? She'd been insistent that she wasn't involved with Wyatt and now . . . now Ava nearly believed her. "I went on to Washington for grad school," the psychologist added.

"Trent didn't." That much was true, but Ava felt as if something was left unsaid, that there was still a piece that didn't feel right.

Evelyn reached into a side pocket of the large bag she'd plopped onto the chair next to her. "I did a little soul-searching last night, and I really don't think I can help you if you can't trust me." She pulled a business card from the pocket of her purse and slid it across the coffee table to Ava. "Here's the name and number of Dr. Rollins. He's in Seattle, of course, but I've worked with him and he's familiar with the island and your family. He used to work at Sea Cliff when your uncle was running the hospital."

The name was familiar, and the image of a large African American man came to mind. Smooth, mocha-colored skin, oversized glasses, white beard, and short-cropped hair, if he was the man Ava remembered on her few visits to the hospital. "That's where I met him. At Sea Cliff. He still has patients in Anchorville and shares an office with a couple of other doctors. Dr. Rollins is in two days a week."

Ava picked up the business card.

"It's imperative that you trust your therapist," Dr. McPherson said earnestly. "So that you don't hold back. I would be glad to make the referral and consult with Dr. Rollins or whomever else you choose. I'll do whatever it takes to make the transition more comfortable for everyone. Whatever you want." Dr. McPherson almost seemed relieved. "I'm not sure anyone will be willing to come to the island, but you can suggest it."

Ava glanced at the card with Dr. Alan G. Rollins's name, number, address, and e-mail listed. "And Wyatt is okay with this?"

"I haven't told him." Her smile seemed sincere, though it all could be an act. "As you said, this is *your* life. I'm *your* doctor."

"But he hired you. He claims he's my guardian."

Evelyn lifted a shoulder. "He could stand on ceremony, I suppose, but I don't think he will." Getting to her feet, she slung the strap of her bag over her shoulder. "He only wants what's best for you, you know."

"So he tells me." Ava clutched the business card in her fist.

The therapist's eyebrows pulled together, and she touched Ava lightly on the shoulder as she passed. "Let me know what you want to do," she said, then walked quickly out of the room.

Ridiculously, Ava felt abandoned. Now that she could be free of the psychologist her husband had chosen for her, the woman she suspected of sleeping with him, Ava wasn't so certain she wanted to let go.

Don't second-guess yourself. You know what you saw!

"But maybe I was wrong," she whispered, walking to the bookcase where a number of family pictures were displayed. Her gaze landed on a picture of Wyatt holding Noah on the beach, the wind ruffling Wyatt's hair, Noah's eyes squinted against the stiff ocean breeze. Ava's heart squeezed as she picked up the photograph and traced the outline of her son's face.

Sad, she replaced the picture and saw that it was next to a snapshot of Jewel-Anne astride the palomino mare with Sea Cliff rising on the hill in the distance. In the shot, Jewel-Anne was grinning from ear to ear, her body round in the saddle, a shadow of the person taking the picture falling in front of the horse. The photograph had been taken before the accident that had robbed her of the use of her legs, and back then, Jewel-Anne could actually grin. Heavy for her height, she'd been pretty, her face unmarred with the lines of unhappiness that had formed since the accident.

Setting the framed picture aside, Ava walked to the window overlooking the garden where the tracks of Jewel-Anne's wheelchair were visible in the gravel and the ferns shivered in the wind. What if, as everyone believed, Ava truly was paranoid? She thought of her recent session with the therapist. What if Wyatt and Evelyn McPherson weren't involved? What if Ava's tormented mind had conjured up her husband's infidelity?

A wife always knows.

Someone had told her that a long time ago.

But that someone may just have been wrong.

Later, in the rec room that smelled of furniture polish, Trent confirmed that Evelyn McPherson Stone had been his date at the Christmas party. "Come on, Ava, you remember me introducing you to her," he said, racking the balls on the pool table. She didn't.

"In the kitchen. We came in through the back door and caught hell from Virginia for it." He centered the triangular rack, the colorful balls spinning on the dark green felt. "You were hurrying through, too, looking for something—more glasses, I think? Anyway, Virginia was mean as a snake that night. She told you something about not being able to work this way."

As he whipped the rack off the neatly positioned balls, Ava tried to bring back the memory. From the kitchen, she heard the sound of Virginia's off-key humming. Vaguely, she recalled the cook's rebuke and her unusual bad mood. At the time, Ava had attributed Virginia's scowls to the fact that she had to work that night and her daughter had remarried Simon; Virginia hadn't been happy about it.

Yes, Ava had hurried through the kitchen, nearly knocking into a waiter carrying a platter of hors d'oeuvres. He'd spun deftly away, not losing a single appetizer from his silver tray, but Virginia had been beside herself, struggling to keep her tongue inside her head.

"It all happened near the pantry and the back staircase," he recounted. "I remember because Virginia was all bent out of shape and had shooed us out of the room so the caterers could work. Man, she was in one helluva mood."

"That's right," Ava said as the image grew stronger. She remembered being distracted, looking for the extra wineglasses as Wyatt was about to make his annual holiday toast. Somehow they'd ended up three glasses short, and Ava had remembered the extra stemware boxed in the shelves near the pantry in a closet where they'd stored odds and ends, everything from extra keys to lightbulbs to holiday decorations.

In her search for the glasses, she had come across Trent and he'd been with a woman she'd never met before: Dr. McPherson. "You introduced her as Eve."

"I know. I still call her that. It's how we were introduced

way back when at a party before a Ducks football game," he said, referring to the University of Oregon athletic team. "We were tailgating, I think."

Is that what he'd said at the party? It didn't sound right, but she couldn't completely remember, and now, as he leaned across the table, trying for what seemed an impossible shot, she recalled shaking the woman's hand as they were introduced.

He flashed her a smile. "You'll remember it all soon, right? It's coming back to you." He leaned over the table, snapped back his cue stick, and sent the ball spinning. *Crack!* The billiard balls spun to all sides of the table.

"I hope."

"Be patient."

"I think I have been."

"Never your strong suit."

She couldn't argue that fact as he took the next shot, sending the cue ball into a cluster of other balls. The five spun into a corner pocket.

"It's just that there are holes in my memory, and they don't seem to be closing."

"They are. Just not as fast as you want."

She wasn't so certain. "Ever since Noah disappeared . . ."

"Before that," he said, eyeing the balls remaining on the table. "After Kelvin died."

She held up a hand. "That's not right."

"Sure it is. That's when you started having . . . mental issues."

"*Before* the baby was kidnapped?" *No. No. This was all wrong.*

Trent's head snapped up. "Not kidnapped, Ava. There was no ransom note." He walked closer to her. "No one contacted the family after Noah went missing."

"What do you think the word *kidnapped* means? Someone *took* Noah. Out of his bed!" Her heart was beginning to pound a little more wildly. "That happened."

"He went missing. Yes. We don't know how."

"He was two years old. He couldn't just get out of bed himself and . . . and what . . ." Her heart turned to ice as she imagined her child climbing out of his bed as he had at least once before and wandering around his room, walking into the hallway. "I don't know what you mean," she finished. But she did. Then another thought occurred to her. "You think that *I* had something to do with my child's disappearance?"

He dropped his pool cue. "Of course not!" he said, rounding the corner of the table to give her a supportive hug. "I don't believe for a second that you would knowingly do anything to hurt Noah."

"Knowingly?" she whispered, appalled, her despair palpable. Did he really believe . . . She caught a glimpse of the scars on her wrists; that memory, too, was blurry and repressed. After her son's disappearance, hadn't the police zeroed in on her? Hadn't Biggs thought she might be involved? Not only had she been the last person to admit to seeing her son, but also in most cases, she knew that family members were the first suspects. . . .

"That's not what I meant." Trent was irritated. "Don't twist my words around, okay?" His quick anger flared for a second; then he sighed and shook his head. "Come on, Ava. Don't do this." He gave her another fierce hug, silently reminding her of their long-lasting bond, one that started in childhood.

Now, though, she felt his tension, sensed his hesitation, a lack of conviction. For the first time, she recognized a fissure in that once-solid connection, a crack in her relationship that she feared ran far deeper than she'd ever suspected.

Dern was getting in too deep.

That much was obvious to him as he strode across the wet grass to the stable. With the dog at his heels, he glanced at the looming house and wondered about Ava Church Garrison and wondered why she fascinated him so much.

A mistake.

He couldn't get even remotely involved with her, and it wasn't just because she was married. No, there were deeper reasons, the very essence of why he was here working for the damned woman.

Yet he was having trouble maintaining his distance from her, and he could tell himself over and over again that he'd followed her into town last night because it was part of his job, but that would be a lie, and he wasn't into kidding himself. He was intrigued by her—more than he should be. She was troubled, haunted, but beneath those sad eyes and worried, full lips, he saw another person, a glimpse of the strong, vibrant woman she'd once been.

And that was the person he wanted to get to know, to draw out, the only human on this godforsaken island he felt remotely close to.

Wrong, Dern. Ava's not an ally. She, too, is an enemy.

"Oh, hell."

Remember why you're here. Do not let her good looks or her act get to you. She's not the victim here, and you know it.

As the dog sniffed around the grain bins, he let himself into a stall where he'd penned the palomino mare this morning. He'd seen her limping slightly earlier in the day and had checked out her right foreleg, finding nothing. Now, as she snorted her disapproval, he straddled the leg and looked at her hoof once more, checking that there were no cracks or bits of gravel or thorns in the frog or sole, that the hoof was intact. Gently, he prodded and searched, and the mare did no more than flick her ears. Nor did she show any discomfort as he examined her foreleg, finding nothing suspicious in the coronet, sesamoid, and pastern. All seemed sound, as did her knee and shoulder. "So what's with you?" he asked, and she snorted as she turned her head to look at him, a pale blaze showing on her blond face.

He wasn't a vet, but he'd been around horses all his life. He led this one from her stall to the field where she lifted her nose high into the air, let out a sharp whinny, and took off at a dead run for the rest of the herd. A blond streak, without the hint of a limp, she only slowed when she reached Jasper's side.

"You think she was faking it?" Dern asked the dog as he watched for a few minutes and decided the mare was going to be all right. "We'll keep an eye on her, what'd'ya say?"

Wagging his tail slowly, Rover cocked his head, as if in so doing he could fully understand.

"Don't worry about it. Come on." Whistling, he headed back to the stables where he intended to check on the tack and repair a broken hinge on one of the stalls.

Just so he looked like he was performing the job he was hired to do.

But that, too, was an act.

He, like everyone else on this damned rock, wasn't what he claimed to be, and it was only a matter of time before someone figured it out.

Then all hell was sure to break loose.

He thought of Cheryl Reynolds, left in a pool of her own blood.

His jaw tightened.

Maybe hell had already arrived.

Chapter 27

With a flick of her wrist, Ava tossed her night meds into the toilet, then flushed. She watched the pills swirl away and felt a second's satisfaction. "Good riddance," she said, and turned back to her room where she half expected stern Demetria, or bossy Khloe, or forever-sneaking-around Jewel-Anne to be silently observing her.

But she was alone in her room, aside from a short appearance by Mr. T, who must've taken a wrong turn. The cat slunk away, heading in the direction of the back of the house. "Not that way," Ava whispered under her breath. The cat would find out soon enough that the door to the back stairs was always closed, and he'd have to deign to slink down the wide staircase, just like everyone who resided here.

She was bothered and restless, and the thought of turning in for the night wasn't comforting. Ever since she'd had her talk with Trent, she'd stayed in her room and been on the computer. Her back was sore, her shoulders aching, her mind spinning with what she'd learned.

She'd started out rereading the accounts of Kelvin's death

and remembering her own experience in the icy water; then she'd tried to tie her brother's death to Noah's disappearance. Of course she'd found no connection other than her own obsession of "seeing" her son near the water's edge at the dock.

Glancing out the window to the boathouse, she wondered what she was missing, what link existed between Kelvin and Noah. Her brother had never known his nephew, of course; Kelvin had died a short while before Noah's birth.

She snagged her favorite sweatshirt from her bedpost, tossed it on, and hurried down the stairs to the foyer.

Wyatt's den was still dark. He'd called to say he was returning later tonight, and their conversation had been short and stiff. A million questions remained unasked, just as many answers remained hidden in the silence. For one thing, she didn't relish the thought of discussing Evelyn McPherson's resignation as her therapist. Time enough for that later.

As she crossed to the door, she heard the sound of a television, muted through the walls, and above it, the distinct click of billiard balls. Her cousins were playing pool. Good. It would keep them busy.

The kitchen was dark, Virginia having gone back to her apartment after dinner. Demetria was nowhere to be seen. Khloe and Simon had left for Anchorville earlier, and Jewel-Anne was probably already in her suite with her creepy dolls and the Internet, her latest passion being online games, while listening to endless Elvis tunes on her iPod. Weird. Weird. Weird.

Oh, come on, Ava. Do you really think Jewel-Anne is any stranger than you with your obsession with your son's disappearance and your conviction that everyone is out to get you?

With her paranoia chasing her, Ava slipped through the front door and felt the cold of the night slap her full in the face. Quickly, she rushed across the porch and down the front steps toward the dock. The wind swirled, causing dry leaves to skitter and dance over their damp counterparts. Shoving her hands deep into the single pocket of the sweatshirt, she half jogged down to the end of the dock. Alone, she stared at the dark, roiling water. So often in her dreams, she'd seen Noah standing in this exact position.

Not just when you were asleep. You woke once and saw him here, too.

She looked across the bay to the lights of Anchorville and then back to Monroe, which was farther down this shoreline on this side of the water. The few streetlamps glowed a hazy blue, and the winking neon sign in the wide glass at the front of Frank's Food-O-Mart, the stalwart throwback to the fifties, was visible. To the west was the open sea and behind her the house rose upon the hillside.

Why had Trent suggested Kelvin's death was somehow linked to her son's disappearance?

Because Noah was born so close to the time that Kelvin died. You gave him his middle name in memory of your brother: Noah Kelvin Garrison . . .

But there was more, another reason she tied the two events, something slippery and elusive, like a deep-water eel that kept coming close only to slither away into dark crevices.

There was something she was missing, she just knew it, but she couldn't quite remember what it was. *Think, Ava!*

What is it?

Her eyes strayed to the darkened garden and the area where her son's marker had been placed. A place she'd visited often, an area where Jewel-Anne hung out. It was weird, her cousin's fascination with the marker.

"You're not the only one who's grieving," Jewel-Anne had told her when Ava mentioned her fascination with the marker. *"I miss Noah, too, Ava!"*

As Ava stared at the garden, an icy finger of dread scraped down her back. There was something about that spot. . . . *Oh . . . dear . . . God . . .*

The wind touched her face, but she barely noticed. Clouds rolled over the moon.

The hairs on the back of her neck lifted one by one.

"No way," she whispered, but it was too late. A wisp of a thought, the edge of a very real nightmare, touched her brain. "Noah."

Her heart turned to ice.

All the spit dried in her mouth.

Was there something under that flat piece of marble etched with her son's name?

Was there a deeper, darker reason the marker had been placed there, in the garden? Was it not so much a memorial, but a *headstone?*

"No . . . oh, please no . . ." But the horrid idea had taken root and she couldn't dislodge it.

She had no memory of the stone being planted between the manicured shrubs, but now, in the deep darkness, she was certain there was a reason that particular spot in the garden had been created. The marble, the bench, the greenery surrounding a simple shrine . . .

"Oh, please," she murmured. "Oh, no, no, no . . ." But she began to move. Fast. Heart in her throat, she ran, her feet slapping the dock, the old boards thudding as she sped to the boathouse. Quickly she shouldered open the door and flipped on the light. The boat was in its slip, raised out of the water, life jackets hanging from hooks on the walls, oars and fishing poles propped in the corners.

No shovel.

Nothing she could use to dig.

She yanked the door shut, hesitated, told herself that she was acting like a lunatic, that there was no reason for the surge of panic shooting through her. Nothing had changed. Everything was as it had been.

Then why did she have the overwhelming notion that the wide spot in the garden dedicated to her son's memory might be something more, something sinister?

Her pulse pounding in her ears, adrenaline spurting through her blood, she tried to quiet the frantic feeling that was overtaking her, pushing her to the limits of her sanity.

Her baby wasn't buried under that marker. He couldn't be!

And yet her mind conjured up all kinds of horrid scenarios in which her son had died and someone had hidden his perfect little body.

Heart thundering, she turned and ran through the garden toward the lane. Wet cobwebs brushed her face, but she didn't care. She reached the lane and splashed through puddles, striding around the back of the property to the greenhouse. She had to know, *had* to! No matter what. Tears blurred her vision as she rounded a final corner and found the entry to the greenhouse unlocked, the door ajar.

Frantic, she slapped on the light switch and winced at the sudden burst of bright illumination. Broken pots littered a table beneath pipes used for watering, while a few scraggly tomato vines crawled up their cages. Two shovels had been propped near the door. She grabbed the closest and began running again, out of the greenhouse, around the house, past the ferns still damp from an earlier rain, and the cobwebs stretched lacelike from one tree to another.

Surely there was nothing under the smooth stone.

Of course she was imagining that her son's body might be buried beneath the soft loam of the garden.

She tried to tell herself there was no way her boy had been buried there.

Tears burned in her eyes as she made her way to the stone and forced the blade of her shovel beneath the rock's edge. In the thin moonlight, she read her son's name, etched into the smooth marble.

"Oh, sweetie," she whispered, her breath fogging, her heart aching, dread crawling slowly up her spine. The night was cold, only the watery illumination from the security lamp mounted near the garage adding to the frail moonlight.

Wedging the blade deeper, she pushed hard on the shovel's handle and felt the stone move. "Come on, come on," she said under her breath as her muscles strained and the rock moved. She didn't know what she would find, what she expected; she only knew what she feared.

But there was probably nothing but wet earth, gravel, and insects underneath this stone. Still, she couldn't stop her furtive and insane mission. As she worked, the wind picked up and the smell of coming rain was heavy in the air.

"There's nothing here," she told herself as she slid the stone aside and began to dig. She forced the shovel into the soft, damp earth and stepped hard on the shoulder, driving the cutting edge even deeper.

With force, she flung the loosened earth aside, then plowed the blade into the ground again. More loam was cast aside. Her fingers tightened over the handle and shaft as she caught a rhythm, forcing the blade deep only to cast the loosened earth aside.

Stop! Now! Put it all back before anyone sees you and sends you back to St. Brendan's.

Again she plunged the shovel into the ever-widening hole she was creating. Sweat began to collect between her shoulder blades and around her neck. Her hands, unused to this kind of work, cramped, but she continued to dig.

Frantically.

In a fevered pitch.

Compelled to find what lay beneath the stone, she plunged her shovel into the soft earth over and over again.

There's nothing here. It's futile and if anyone sees you . . .

The hole deepened and widened, the pile of dirt beside her growing with each shovelful. Mouth dry, muscles beginning to protest, her dread mounting, she kept on.

"Hey!" A male voice stopped her cold. She glanced up and saw a dark figure approaching, and her hands flexed over the handle. "Ava? What're you doing?" Dern's voice. She relaxed a little as he stepped out of the shadows and into the soft, filtered light of the moon.

"Digging."

"I see that. For what?" he asked, and she felt suddenly ridiculous shoveling dirt in the middle of the night.

"I don't know," she admitted, barely able to voice her fears as Dern and the dog at his heels drew closer. "Maybe . . . maybe my son."

"What?" He grabbed the shovel's shaft and stopped her from another thrust into the soft ground. "Ava, what're you thinking?"

Swallowing hard, trying to get a grip, she shoved the dirty fingers of her free hand through her hair. "I just know that there's something strange going on here."

"Here? As in the garden?"

"As in on the whole damned island!" Glaring up at him, she refused to let go of the shovel.

"And you think that something, maybe your son's body, is buried here?"

She heard the skepticism in his voice. "I don't know. Just a feeling." She yanked on the shovel, but he wouldn't let go.

"Ava . . . I don't think . . ."

"What? You don't think what? That Noah's here? That I'll find anything at all?" she demanded. "Maybe you think I'm flat-out crazy, too."

"I was going to say I don't think this is a good idea."

She grappled for the shovel. "Then leave me the hell alone!"

Still he held tight, and she met his night-darkened gaze as thick clouds began obscuring the stars. "Let go, Dern," she ordered, and saw a tightening of his jaw. "This is my thing. It has nothing to do with you."

"Oh, for the love of Christ!" He yanked the shovel from her hand. Without another word, he began to shovel dirt, big scoops from the hole onto the ground beside it.

"Stop. I'm serious. You don't have to do this."

He kept at it. She felt the first drops of rain against the back of her neck as another scoop of dark earth was flung to the side. "Tell me when I'm deep enough," he ordered.

He shoved the blade deep into the dirt again, deftly tossing scoops. Working rhythmically, he deepened the hole, and as the mound of discarded earth grew, so did Ava's realization that maybe she'd been wrong. She'd let her wild imagination get the better of her once again. She'd fallen victim to her own desperation, to—

Clang!

The blade of the shovel hit something that sounded like metal.

"Hell," he whispered, and her heart stilled. All her fears solidified, and for a second she heard nothing save the ever-constant rush of the sea.

Clang!

Again metal scraped metal, and Dern looked up, his gaze finding hers in the darkness. "Maybe we'd better stop."

Steeling herself, she shook her head vehemently and trained her eyes on the dark pit. "I have to know." Her heart was thundering in her ears, her palms sweating, denial pulsing through her brain.

"Sure?"

She was nodding, but all the while her inner voice was screaming, *No, no, no!* She didn't know how she could live with herself if she found her son's body, if she would finally be forced to give up all hope of seeing him again.

Jaw set hard, Dern went on working. In the hole, a metal box, the size of a child's casket, began to emerge. *Oh, God, please no . . . please don't let Noah be inside!* Heart clamoring, she barely heard the crunch of footsteps on gravel.

"We've got company," Dern said as raindrops began to pepper the ground in earnest. Ava barely noticed. Her gaze was riveted on the dirt-crusted box as he lifted it with some force and slid it onto the ground in front of the bench.

"What's going on here?" Jacob's voice rang down the hillside, but Ava hardly heard him or the deep growl from Rover's throat. All of her attention was focused on the box.

"It's not empty," Dern said. "Possibly twenty-five, maybe thirty pounds." Warning her.

"What the hell is that?" Jacob appeared in the clearing and, using his iPhone, shined a light on the scratched, filthy metal box. "Oh . . . shit." His cocky attitude drained away as he put the pieces together. "That was buried under the marker?"

"Yes." Ava's voice was the barest of whispers, and she felt as weak as she ever had. Her legs were shaking. But she had to know. Had to! Bile crawled up her throat. "Open it."

"You're sure?" Dern asked again.

"Yes!" *No, oh, God, no!*

"Fuck!" Jacob, the sharp beam of his iPhone light still trained on the box, backed up slowly. His face had washed of all color, the hand holding the phone shaking madly. "I . . . I don't know what the hell this is, but I don't like it."

"Open it," Ava said again, a dull roar resounding in her ears as the storm gathered force.

Dern bent down near the box, trying to force off the lid. "It's locked. I'll need to get a knife or a crowbar."

"I don't think so." With cold certainty, she pulled the key from her jeans, crouched beside the small coffin, and, throat as dry as sand, slid the key into the lock.

A perfect fit.

Oh, God. Oh, dear God . . .

"Jesus Christ," Jacob whispered, the beam off his cell phone wavering, "you're not going to—"

Click.

The lock sprang.

"Ava." Dern's hand clasped over hers. Strong. Calloused.

Using all her strength, Ava yanked the lid open. Jacob's light played upon the interior.

There, lying faceup, eyes open wide, the pale light shivering over it, was a small, lifeless body.

Chapter 28

"Holy shit!" Jacob dropped his phone and scrambled backward, startling the dog. Already nervous, Rover let out a worried growl.

Horrified, Ava bit back a scream and stared at the lifeless form in the makeshift casket. The tiny body was dressed in Noah's red sweatshirt, his tiny faded jeans, his . . .

Bile shot up her throat as nausea overwhelmed her. Reflexively, she leaned over and lost the contents of her stomach even as her mind screamed that the body in the casket wasn't her son. The thing inside the "casket" wasn't even really a cadaver; something was off about it. She knew that at a gut level, but she was still freaked.

"It's a doll." Dern's voice was surprisingly calm, underscored with an anger that showed the tension of his jaw. His gaze centered on Jacob. "Bring that light over here."

Too late. Ava was already scooping up the iPhone and training its little beam into the coffin, where, lying on a folded blanket, there lay a large, ancient, porcelain-faced rag doll. Its once-perfect complexion was now destroyed by chips and cracks. An ear had broken off, and one eye stared fixedly upward, while the second eye's lid was at half-mast. The doll's hair had been chopped off and stuck up in sharp little ragged tufts, only slightly visible near the edge of the sweatshirt's hood.

Clearly, the doll had been altered to resemble Noah, a sick prank.

Her heart squeezed painfully and she trembled inside. Thank God the body was not that of her son, that there was still hope Noah was alive, that she'd see him again. But this—Who would do this awful thing? Who hated her so much as to go to so much trouble to cruelly torment her? She bit her lip to keep from crying.

"Ever seen this before?" Dern asked.

Ava shook her head. "No." She had to force her voice to work. "But . . . but the clothes. They belong to my son."

Dern stared at the effigy.

"The sweatshirt," she whispered. "I recognize it."

"Dude, this is *so* fucked up!" Jacob stumbled even farther backward, as if he were afraid the rag doll might spring to life.

For once Ava agreed with her cousin.

"You think someone dressed a doll like your boy, then buried it here," Dern said carefully.

"Yes. Absolutely. It's a girl doll, at least it was originally, and then someone cut the hair to make it look like a boy, like my son." Ava felt a chill in the deepest part of her soul. "Then they left the key for the casket where I could find it, to toy with me and taunt me, testing me to see how long it would take me to figure out where the lock was." Slowly, her despair was giving way to anger. Who would do such a thing? *Who?* "Someone hates me so much they want me to suffer the worst kind of pain a mother can endure."

"But you might never have found this box, never figured out that you had to dig it up." Rain was coming down harder now, and Dern wiped the drops from his face with his sleeve.

"They would make sure I'd find it. I'm sure if I hadn't wondered about it tonight, whoever buried this casket," she said,
kicking at the metal box, "would just leave me more and more
clues, getting off on my frustration, thinking I was stupid and
all the while luring me in the right direction."

"Who?" Jacob asked on a gulp.

Anyone in my family. Again her stomach roiled as she considered the long list of her relatives. A lot of them might resent
her, even talk behind her back or feel some sort of satisfaction
that she was mentally unstable, that she was no longer the take-
charge, my-way-or-the-highway woman she'd once been. But
this intense vitriolic loathing . . . this was something else altogether.

Turning, trying to get hold of her nerves, Ava looked back at
the huge house looming above them on the hill. Dark for the
most part, her gaze was drawn to the windows where lights
were blazing, glowing squares of illumination. The kitchen and
dining area were visible, and on the second floor, an eerie bluish
light trembled in Jewel-Anne's suite of rooms where she was
watching television or staring at a computer monitor in the
dark.

The curtain over Jewel-Anne's window moved slightly.

As if someone were watching and had ducked backward, like
a turtle's head retreating into its shell. "Jewel-Anne," Ava
whispered, because in that split second, her suspect list was
quickly honed to one, twisted individual, the woman who refused to grow up, who was determined to ever play the victim,
the cousin who blamed her for Kelvin's death and her own injuries. "Bitch," Ava muttered under her breath as, with new
conviction, she hauled the horrid doll out of its box and started
marching up the hill.

"Where're you going?" Dern demanded.

"The house," she snapped, and increased her pace. *Jewel-
Anne. It has to be Jewel-Anne with her damned dolls. Who*

else? Racing through the rain, her fingers tight around the doll's soft shoulder, Ava ran to the house. The altered rag doll was the size of a six-month-old baby, not a toddler, and the clothes it was dressed in were too large, but the point had been made. It was a twisted representation of Noah.

By Jewel-Anne!

Behind her, Dern was closing fast, his footsteps slapping the soft ground, but she didn't slow, didn't so much as glance over her shoulder. Now she was of singular purpose. Up the porch steps she flew and through the kitchen, her shoes resounding on the tile floor, Virginia's black cat, Mr. T, frantically scrambling out of the way.

At the main staircase, Dern was right on her heels. "You don't know that Jewel-Anne is behind this."

"Like hell!" Fury burned through her as she hurried up the runner. She knew who the culprit was but didn't understand why her cousin would resort to such emotional cruelty. "Let me handle this!" she said as she made her way along the upper gallery to the wing of Jewel-Anne's suite. Ava didn't bother knocking, just burst through the unlocked door.

"Hey!" Jewel-Anne said. "Wha—" Earbuds plugged in, sitting at her computer, she glanced up sharply. "What do you think you're do— Oh, dear God, what is *that?*" Her myopic gaze was fastened to the doll dangling from Ava's hand.

"What do you think?" Ava tossed the wet rag doll at Jewel-Anne.

Recoiling in horror, Jewel-Anne let out a howl as the dirty thing slid to the floor. "Ava! Oh, God!" Jewel-Anne cried, cringing away.

"You really don't know?"

"What are you talking about?!" She was shaking her head violently.

Ava grabbed the thin wire and ripped the tiny headphones from Jewel-Anne's ears. "You *know!*"

"What're you doing?" Jewel-Anne gasped.

"Getting your full attention!"

"Ava," Dern warned from the doorway, but her hand shot up, palm out to silence him as she glared down at Jewel-Anne.

Her cousin's revulsion was nearly palpable. "Where the hell did you get *that*?" Jewel-Anne demanded, one finger jabbing the air in the direction of the limp doll.

"Buried in a coffin in the garden! Right under the stone with Noah's name etched on it. Where you meant for me to find it!"

Jewel-Anne stared at Ava, her skin white as chalk, her eyes round behind her glasses. "A coffin? Buried? What? Are you out of your mind?"

"You tell me! Who else would do it? Plant a doll under the stone with Noah's name. You're always wheeling yourself out there, visiting the spot. I always wondered what your fascination was. Now I know."

"No . . . no, I was just paying my respects."

"Like hell!"

"Ava, listen to you. You're raving, out of your frickin' mind! I've *never* seen that"—again she pointed toward the doll that had slithered to the floor and now was twisted, its head lolling to one side at the foot of Jewel-Anne's cast-iron bed, one of its legs hidden under the frilly, little-girl bed skirt—"*thing* before in my life!"

"Take a closer look," Ava suggested, dragging the doll from the floor to hold it in front of her cousin's face, so that its chipped porcelain nose was nearly touching Jewel-Anne's. "Its hair has been chopped off to make it look like a boy."

"You're freaking me out!" If possible, Jewel-Anne shrank even farther into her wheelchair.

"Good! You need to be!"

"Stop." Dern, no longer content to stand in the doorway, strode into the room.

"She did this!" Ava glared at him.

"How?" Jewel-Anne asked. "How in God's name could I dig a hole and stuff a . . . what did you call it? A coffin, that's what you said, right? A coffin? How the hell could I stuff a coffin into a hole in the ground, then cover it up so that no one noticed, so that it looked perfect? I can't even move the stone!"

She appeared so childlike, so self-righteous, so certain that Ava was making it all up, that Ava felt a shiver of doubt.

But it had to have been Jewel-Anne. Had to have! Who else? Footsteps sounded in the hallway a few seconds before Demetria appeared. "What's going on here?" she demanded.

"Jewel-Anne's been gaslighting me." Ava held the doll up for the nurse to see. "With this."

"Gaslighting?" Demetria repeated.

"She thinks I'm doing things to make her *think* she's crazy. Manipulating her somehow," Jewel-Anne clarified. She'd regained some of her composure, and twin, red spots of anger flushed her cheeks.

Dern gazed at them, his face a mask, taking it all in but not offering judgment.

"Let's start with Noah's wet shoes," Ava said. "Then there was the key left in my pocket that just so happened to open the casket. And a doll—*this* doll." She shook the rag doll so hard its head rolled back and forth.

Jewel-Anne's mouth was quivering. "Don't blame your stupid paranoia on me. You're the one who's insane, Ava. You probably did this all yourself! That's probably why you tried to kill yourself! It's . . . it's your guilt coming to the surface."

"Don't turn this around on me."

"It's what everyone thinks, including the police! You're the reason Kelvin took the boat out, the reason he died and I'm in this damned wheelchair. You were the last one to see Noah alive. And now you're the last person to visit Cheryl Reynolds before she was murdered. It's a pattern. This . . . this 'discovery' of yours is probably a setup. How convenient that *you* found Noah's shoes in his room when everyone else saw them in your closet. And as for that stupid key"—she flapped a hand to dismiss it—"you could have planted it in your pocket and maybe even forgot you did. *And* if I was trying to trick you, why would I use a doll that isn't mine? I've never seen that monstrosity before in my life, but of course the doll would be a big red arrow pointed right at me. Why would I do that?"

"Because you thought you could trick me," Ava answered, but already some of Jewel-Anne's logic was starting to take hold.

"You're just tricking yourself!"

"That's—"

"Insane! I know. But there's a chance you don't even know what you're doing, Ava. You probably believe all this . . . this stuff you're saying because you don't remember. Like those people with split personalities . . . What's it called now? Not schizophrenia, but . . ." She glanced up at Demetria. "Help me out here."

"Dissociative identity disorder," the nurse supplied.

Ava stared at Demetria, then back at Jewel-Anne. "I did *not* do this!"

"No?" Jewel-Anne demanded, and sat up straighter, even wheeling her chair a little closer as she turned her accusative gaze up at her. "How would you know?"

The doll fell from Ava's hand. It slumped into an ugly pool, the half-open eye seeming to stare up at Ava in accusation. She could almost hear it talking: *You did this, you fruit cake. You did it to yourself.* And then the hideous laugh, as if the doll and everyone in the suite were in on a cruel, terrifying joke. It was all Ava could do not to clap her hands over her ears and run out of this wing that spanned one side of the house. To where? No place was safe. To whom? She could trust no one. She glanced over at Dern, whose expression was hard and set.

As if taking a cue from Ava, he said, "I think we should all dial this back. No accusations."

Ava said, "*Someone* dressed that doll up like my son, stuffed it into a box that looks like a coffin, and then waited, teasing me, pushing me, urging me to find it."

"Why?" Demetria asked.

"To push me over the edge," she said with conviction.

Jewel-Anne, her face contorted in disgust, said, "I don't think you need any help in that department!"

"Okay, that's enough!" Dern picked up the doll with one hand and grabbed Ava's arm with the other. Jewel-Anne's eyes narrowed on her with fury and something else. Wasn't there just the tiniest trace of satisfaction, of an unspoken victory, in her cousin's gaze, too?

"Are you all right?" Demetria was asking of her charge as Dern shepherded Ava out of Jewel-Anne's suite.

"What do you think you're doing?" she demanded, trying to shake him off once they were in the hall.

"Saving your hide."

"From what?"

He propelled her down the hallway to the corner where her room was situated, the door ajar, a light glowing from her bed-side lamp.

"I don't know what the hell's going on here," he said as he stepped across the threshold, dragging her with him and kicking the door shut behind them, "but I'm damned sure whatever it is, you have to remain cool."

Emotions raw and bleeding, Ava yanked the doll from his hands and shook it in front of his face. "How can I remain cool when this, whatever the hell it is, is happening?"

"I don't know." He lifted a hand, showing his own frustration. "But if you really think someone is trying to get you committed again, you have to stop acting crazy."

"I'm not acting anything!"

"What do you think would happen if Dr. McPherson or someone else saw you and some other psychiatrist was called in to evaluate you?"

"I'm not crazy, Dern!" she said, inching her face up to his, staring him down eyeball-to-eyeball. "You were there. You saw the damned coffin."

"I didn't see who put it in the ground, but I'd be hard pressed to believe it was someone confined to a wheelchair," he shot back. "So, if not her, then who's the accomplice? Her brother? Jacob acts like an ass, but from his reaction, I think he was as freaked out as anyone. So, who else? Who are you going to finger? Who else would care?"

"Any of them," she said, and he let that sink in, as if he, too, were running through a list of suspects, all of them being related to her.

"I know it's disturbing—"

"Disturbing?"

He gave a short nod, his mouth tight. "Until we figure out what's really going on here, who's doing this to you and why, you're going to have to somehow maintain control."

"Control," she repeated through her teeth.

The fingers surrounding her upper arm tightened. "Control." His eyes, already dark brown, seemed to deepen. "I'm serious, Ava."

She let out her breath slowly and mentally counted to ten as she tried to gather her frayed emotions. At least he was on her side.

How do you know? He could be playing you, too. Taking advantage of your crippled mental state. In cahoots with someone else. He does just seem to show up whenever you're in a crisis, doesn't he? Why is that? Is he a hero? Or an opportunist? Or worse? You just don't know, Ava. You cannot trust him!

Despite the arguments burning through her brain, she felt compelled to have faith in him. There was no one else she could even remotely trust, not even her husband. "Do you believe that someone's trying to get me committed again?" she finally asked.

"Something's off. I don't know what." Then, almost to himself, he asked, "Why would anyone want to put you in a mental hospital?"

"I don't know."

Lines etched across his forehead as he gave it thought. "Then that's what you need to figure out. I'll help you." He offered her the ghost of a smile, and the hand on her arm seemed less like a shackle and more like a connection to another human being, and dear God she needed that.

Though she knew she was being foolish, she leaned against him for support. Closing her eyes, she nearly sighed with relief. How long had it been since she'd really let down her guard, trusted someone else? Beneath his shirt, she heard the beating of his heart, steady and strong, just like she needed to be. Distantly, she was vaguely aware of the sound of a boat's engine, faint but growing louder.

Dropping the doll, Dern folded her into his arms. "We'll figure this out," he promised, and ridiculously she felt a new spate of tears burn the back of her eyes.

"God, I hope."

Outside, the dog gave up a gruff bark, and the wind rushed through the bare branches of the trees.

But inside, in her room, Austin Dern smelled of autumn, rain, and earth with an underlying maleness that she found comforting. Reliable. Steady. If she thought of it, she knew little about this man, but she didn't care. She buried her face in his shoulder, wanting to wrap her arms around his neck, to feel the brush of his warm lips over hers. She remembered the dream, the passionate lovemaking, and should have felt embarrassment. Instead, she experienced longing.

It was foolish, she knew, and dangerous, thinking she could trust a stranger, a man of whom she knew so very little. Yet her family, the people she had known all of her life, seemed to be the unknowns, the ones against her—the enemy. She knew that sounded so paranoid. No wonder everyone thought she was out of her mind.

The truth was simple: She was losing touch with reality, was having trouble distinguishing between fact and fiction. A new drip of fear, icy and cold, slid down her back. There was a chance Jewel-Anne was right.

Could it be that she was so emotionally distressed, so insane, that she was gaslighting herself?

A door opened and closed. The front door. Dern stiffened. "Someone's here," he said, and for a split second she thought he might kiss the top of her head as he released her.

Footsteps pounded up the stairs as Dern stepped away from her.

A quick, insistent rap, then the bedroom door was flung open.

Wyatt stood on the other side, in the hallway, water running from his raincoat. His hair was wet and plastered to his head, his face red, as if raw from the wind, his mouth a line of displeasure. "What's going on here?" he demanded, and his features, already drawn into concern, darkened with a quiet rage. "Dern?" Wyatt said, his lips barely moving. "What the hell are you doing with my wife?"

Chapter 29

Ava wasn't about to be bullied by her husband. "Mr. Dern helped me, even when he thought I was nuts to be digging in the garden."

"Digging in the garden," he repeated tautly. "And you ended up in the bedroom."

"He was trying to talk me down. I was pretty hot, making a lot of accusations at Jewel-Anne, and he tried to defuse the situation."

"It's not his fight." Wyatt shot the rancher a look.

"You know, I've had a pretty rough night," Ava said wearily. She didn't have the energy for another go-around with Wyatt.

Some of his agitation evaporated. "I heard. Jacob called. He told me about the box with the doll in it."

"Wait a second! Did you say '*the box with the doll in it*'?" she repeated. She bent down and grabbed the rag doll to hold it in front of Wyatt's face. "*This* is what we dug up." She shook the doll, causing its good eye to open and close rapidly, its arms and legs wiggling as if in some macabre dance.

"Jesus!" Wyatt actually took a step back. His eyes were fixed on the effigy, and repulsion contorted his face.

"It's supposed to look like Noah!" Ava's voice rose, and she realized that she was starting to sound as if she were raving again. Maybe she was. Who cared?

Wyatt's gaze shifted to Dern, then settled on his wife again. A bit of the self-righteous starch in his spine seemed to evaporate, though he was still wary. "Fine," he finally said, folding his arms over his chest. "Why don't you tell me exactly what happened?"

"I had an epiphany, I guess you'd call it. I've been seeing Jewel-Anne alone in the garden . . ." She told both Wyatt and Dern what had just transpired. "I had to know," she defended herself, rubbing her arms and feeling the weight of both Dern's and Wyatt's gazes upon her. "Jewel-Anne's behind all this, Wyatt. I know it," Ava finished. "She's intent on making my life a living hell. I think it's because of Kelvin. She blames me for her handicap and thinks I'm responsible for my brother's death. And she's using Noah as a way to really get to me."

"I can't believe she'd do that," Wyatt said, but his words lacked conviction. His raincoat was dripping on the floor, and as if he recognized it for the first time, he shed himself of the wet garment and tossed it over his arm.

"Someone is," Dern said.

Wyatt's lips thinned. To Ava, he said, "All right. I believe someone's messing with you." He hitched his chin toward the doll, lines of concentration appearing between his eyebrows. "I don't think it's Jewel-Anne. For one thing, it's a physical impossibility."

"Unless she had an accomplice," Ava suggested.

Wyatt looked up quickly, his gaze centering on Dern, to see if he was on board with this. "So now it's a conspiracy?"

"Maybe." Ava held her ground. Dern didn't say anything, and they both kept their gazes on Wyatt as he tried to wrap his brain around her theory.

"Even if Jewel-Anne was behind this," Wyatt said slowly, "even if she had some sort of secret agenda—not that I believe it for a second—if she blamed you and was out to get you, why would anyone else go along with her?"

"I don't know," she admitted, trying to piece it together herself. Frustrated that she was so close to understanding but still at a loss, she threw up her hands. "It could be that she's in cahoots with Jacob. He's against everything. Or maybe with her father? Uncle Crispin was never happy that he lost his share of Neptune's Gate. He took all the blame for Lester Reece escaping from Sea Cliff, and then the hospital closed on his watch and he was forced to sell his share of the estate. That couldn't have sat well with him."

"So Uncle Crispin, along with Jewel-Anne, buried a doll dressed in Noah's clothes in our yard?"

Even to her own ears, the theory sounded lame. Far-fetched. As if she were grasping at straws.

"I don't know *why*, Wyatt, but *some*one did it. And if not Crispin, then someone else who is in league with Jewel-Anne."

"Ava," he said in a despairing voice, and from the corner of her eye, she saw Dern's lips tighten. "Don't make this worse than it is."

"I don't think I can," she said angrily.

"You agree?" he threw out at Dern.

The ranch hand lifted a shoulder. "I do think someone's deliberately terrorizing your wife." It seemed hard for him to get out those words, and he took a deep breath, then exhaled. "Look, maybe I should go. You two work this out."

And then he left, the sound of his boot heels softened by the runner on the stairs.

Wyatt closed the door and they were alone, husband and wife. "I don't know what to say," he admitted.

"How about 'Now I get it, Ava' or, 'Wow, you were right—

someone is out to get you!' Or even, 'I'm glad that it wasn't Noah's body in that tiny coffin, so, come on, let's go find him.'"

He stared at her. As if she were a stranger rather than the woman he'd chosen years before as his bride. How long ago that seemed. Anger warred with distrust on his face. "Okay." He pushed his wet hair from his forehead. "Let's do just that. Find our son." Her heart lifted for a second as he said, "But first let's clear something up. Tell me you're not in love with Austin Dern."

"What?" She almost laughed. "No!" she declared quickly. "I barely know the man." That much was true enough. Her husband arched a wary brow. "I'm married to you, Wyatt."

"But you were going to divorce me."

She nodded slowly, the piece of that time in her life not completely clear.

"I was wondering where we stood on that?"

"I wish I knew," she said honestly.

"I heard you fired Evelyn."

"She quit," Ava corrected. "Referred me to another doctor."

"She felt forced. Ethically. Because of your ridiculous accusations."

"She told you this?"

"She called me. As I was the one who hired her, she thought it was only fair. She's downstairs now."

"You brought her here?" Ava asked in surprise.

"Yes."

"But—"

Betrayal burned through her, but before she could speak, Wyatt went on: "When Jacob called me and told me what you were doing, digging up the garden like a maniac, I phoned Evelyn—er, Dr. McPherson—and convinced her to come out here so that she could talk with you."

"I don't want to talk to her."

"Not even after this?" he said, and picked up the doll dressed to look like their son. It dangled limply from his fingers. "God, I feel like *I* need therapy now."

"Then go talk to her yourself." Ava was sick of being pushed around, sick of this sham of a marriage, and sick to death of being toyed with. "And take that"—she pointed at the doll with its weird eye—"with you!"

"Ava—"

"Don't placate me, Wyatt. Don't."

All tenderness she'd seen in him, any sign of the love they'd once shared, disappeared.

"This is a mistake, Ava," her husband warned as he walked to the door and yanked it open.

"Probably. But it's not the first, Wyatt, and I'm pretty sure it won't be the last."

"You know, Ava, this doesn't have to be so difficult."

"Doesn't it?" She met his gaze levelly, despite the roil of emotions tearing through her, and when he left, she walked to the door and locked it behind him.

Snyder balanced the pizza box in one hand, unlocked his apartment door with the other, and swore when his cell phone, tucked deep into his pocket, began to ring.

Once inside his unit, he slid the wide box onto the kitchen counter and saw his partner's name flash on the screen of his cell phone. "You're making a habit of this," he said as he answered. "People are gonna get the wrong idea."

Lyons laughed, that deep chortle that he kind of liked. "I just wanted to give you a heads-up."

"On what?" He'd left the station a few hours before, took a detour to the gym, then stopped at Captain Awesome's Bar, two blocks down, where he downed two beers while waiting for his pizza.

"Probably nothing, but Biggs called me. You know, he's related to some of the people who live out on the island."

"Yeah." Snyder flipped open the top of the box, saw the tangy pieces of pepperoni and sausage swimming in mozzarella cheese and tomato sauce. "Biggs is like an ex-brother-in-law of the cook or something, so he's still considered the uncle of Virginia Zanders's kids."

"Well, she called to relate some bizarre story about a mannequin being buried in a plot at the house, a doll of some kind that was dressed up to look like the missing kid."

"What?"

"There's no crime and no one expects us to go out there," she went on, "but it's one more strange thing happening out on Weirdo Island."

Snyder didn't like it. "So what was it? A prank? The remains of some freaky ritual?"

"Don't know, but according to Biggs, the mother of the kid did the digging and discovered the mannequin in a makeshift coffin. She went off on her cousin, the one in the wheelchair, who freaked and claimed she didn't do whatever it was Ava Garrison accused her of. Again, no crime. Bunch of freaks out there, if you ask me. More than one off a rocker or two."

Snyder agreed, his pizza momentarily forgotten. "You think this is somehow connected to Cheryl Reynolds's homicide?"

"Don't see how, but it could be connected to the missing kid's case."

"Biggs want someone to check it out?"

"Not yet, but who knows?"

They both were frustrated with their boss, a sheriff with far too little practical experience and a lot of name recognition who kept getting reelected. Biggs's main attribute was that he hired the right people and knew how to glad-hand. And he'd been lucky. Aside from Lester Reece's escape from Sea Cliff, there hadn't been a lot of violent crime in the area.

Unfortunately, it looked like all that was about to change.

"Anything new on the Reynolds's homicide?" she asked.

"Since I last saw you? No."

Snyder felt the clock ticking. They were waiting for the autopsy report, a few callbacks from friends and family, and insurance information. It looked like Cheryl might have died without a will, and she only had enough life insurance, it seemed, to bury her. Aside from the house and its sizeable mortgage, she didn't have much, less than five thousand in savings.

Worth killing for? Maybe . . . He'd seen victims offed for a lot less. He hung up and picked up a slice of pizza, watching as the cheese strings lengthened. Yeah, this was a heart attack in the making.

Tonight, he didn't much care.

Ava heard the voices again. Soft. In the outer hallway.

She blinked her eyes open and slid from the bed. Her head was pounding, as if she'd drunk far too much wine, though she hadn't had a drop.

Her bare feet hit the floor and she was dizzy for a second, as if she were drunk.

Holding on to the bedpost, she steadied herself until she was thinking clearly again. She knew she'd been dreaming, could feel the remnants hiding in the corners of her mind but couldn't gather the images.

Now, though, she blinked awake, realizing she was alone. Her fight with Wyatt had assured her that they wouldn't share the same bed. That pretense was long over. It had been since their child's death.

Tiptoeing across the room in her nightgown, she hardly dared breathe as the sounds filtered through the door.

No baby crying tonight.

No soft sobs whispering, *Mama*.

Tonight the voices were adult, and she was nearly certain Wyatt's was one of them. The other was that of a woman, but the dialogue was off-kilter, out of sync, almost as if there were two separate conversations going at once, both filtering up the main staircase, perhaps from different areas on the floor below.

She glanced at the clock by the bed; the red numbers glowed that it was midnight, and, as if on cue, she heard the dulcet tones of her great-grandfather's clock striking off the hours.

Bong!

"It won't be long now," a woman said with a smile in her voice.

Bong!

". . . odd that, don't know what to think of it." The woman again? No, *another* woman.

". . . remember what she used to be like?" This person was speaking over the first and second.

"Wish I could help, but it's hopeless." A *third* woman? Dr. McPherson? This late?

Bong!

"You've done the best you can." Male. Wyatt. He must've been talking to the psychologist. Who else?

". . . only a matter of time . . ." This from the second woman's voice, the one she couldn't quite place.

Bong!

Each time the clock struck, her head pounded a little and the conversations became garbled, all mixed up. She cracked open the door and, seeing no one in the darkened hallway, stepped out of her room.

The air here was colder, causing goose bumps to rise.

Bong!

She nearly gasped, as the clock was so much louder in the hallway that rimmed the staircase.

". . . have to be careful . . . she's getting suspicious." A whispered voice barely audible over the resonate strikes of the clock—the third woman? Or a person speaking so softly it was impossible to figure out his or her gender.

"Just be careful." Wyatt again?

Click! A lock sprang. *Creeeeeak.* The front door opened.

Biting her lip, her hand on the railing, Ava hurried down to the first floor to the living area of the house.

Bong!

She nearly tripped as the clock struck again and the front door closed with a thud. In the foyer, a single lamp glowed, but the cool air, laced with the scent of rain, still lingered.

The foyer was empty, the clock finishing its loud message, and Ava stepped to the narrow windows flanking the door. Through the glass, she was certain she saw two figures escaping. A tall man—Wyatt, she thought—with his hand on the small of a smaller figure's back. He was with a woman, probably Evelyn McPherson, and they were heading to the dock.

Despite both of their denials, it was obvious they were romantically involved. And they'd been discussing Ava. God this was so screwed up!

". . . almost off the rails," a woman's voice whispered through the empty foyer, and Ava's heart turned to ice. The second conversation. Of course. But where was the speaker? The house was dark aside from a few strategically placed night-lights that gave enough illumination so that she could see shapes and doorways. But with the clock resonating, counting off the hours, she couldn't distinguish the location of the conversation.

Bong!

That *had* to be the final strike of the clock, she thought. But the voices had stilled as well, almost as if it had been planned for the conversation to be disguised by the noise.

Slowly she crept toward the den. Telling herself that this was *her* house and she had every right to be in whatever room she chose, regardless of the time of day or night, she was still nervous, her heart beating rapidly, her nerves strung tight. Despite the earlier murmur of the conversation, she now felt as if she were alone, the only person up at this hour.

And yet . . .

Palms sweating, she slipped through the half-open door of her husband's retreat. The voices had come from around this area . . . right? She took two steps and saw a shadow, a flit of movement near the bookcase.

Her heart nearly stopped.

With a growl, something leaped out at her and she gasped, stepping backward as she recognized Mr. T. The cat, twice his usual size, hissed viciously, then scurried through the open door.

Ava sagged against the corner of the desk.

It was just Virginia's cat, nothing more.

Except that Mr. T isn't capable of sounding like someone whispering and creating a conversation. Nor could he cry like a baby . . .

In the distance, she heard a boat's engine roar to life. So Wyatt and Dr. McPherson were gone. *Good riddance*, she thought, then heard the first muffled baby's cry. *Oh, no!*

"*Mama,*" the tiny voice whispered, and her insides turned to mush.

"Baby?" Her answer was involuntary. Of course Noah wasn't in the house. She knew that, but there was something . . .

After rounding Wyatt's desk, she tried several doors and rummaged until she found a flashlight. Then, rather than turn on any lights in the house, she used the handheld light's yellowish beam to walk up the stairs to the second floor and to Noah's room. She hesitated at the door, then opened it quickly, and, her heart pounding, she shined the light in the nursery where the slats of his crib looked like bars on a jail cell, and his toys, shadowy in the dim light, looked hideous and grotesque

rather than fluffy and soft. A striped tiger's eyes glowed with
an evil vigor, and Noah's favorite toy dinosaur appeared more
like a gargoyle showing vicious teeth and snarling snout.

*Get over yourself. They're just toys, for crying out loud. Toys
you didn't have the heart to give away . . .*

"*Maaaamaaa . . .*" Her blood curdled in her veins, and she
nearly dropped the flashlight as her son's cry whispered through
the room.

Chapter 30

"Mama, Mama, Mama!" His voice broken by sobs, Noah called for her. Ava's heart wrenched. Where was the sound coming from? *Where?* Frantically, she shined her light around the nursery, then hit the switch for the overhead light and the room was suddenly awash with illumination. *Noah . . . oh, baby, where are you?*

"Think," she ordered herself. There had to be a way for his little, innocent voice to project from this room to the den below and whisper through the hallways so that she could hear his cries from her own room.

Searching the ceiling and floorboards, even along the walls, she found nothing out of place. But somewhere . . . somehow, someone was piping in a baby's cries. She was certain of it. No matter what everyone else thought about Jewel-Anne, Ava was certain that she was behind this whole gaslighting thing.

With no evidence of anything awry in the nursery, she switched off the lights and walked into the hallway again. If not here, then where? The crying had stopped for now, so she couldn't follow the sound, but she doubted she would find

anything if she searched either this floor or the one below.
There were too many people who cleaned, repaired, or just lived
in the first stories of the house. Which left the basement, and
she cringed at the thought of returning to that cobweb-riddled
cellar, or the third story, once occupied by servants and now
considered an attic, used only for storage.

"No way," she thought aloud. The elevator didn't run to the
third story, and the access from this floor had been blocked
forever, the door locked securely.

Unless someone had a key. Or climbed up from the doorway off the pantry on the main floor.

Figuring she was about to follow another dead end, she
found her way to the main staircase, hurried down, and slipped
across the foyer and through the kitchen. Around the pantry,
she walked to the old staircase that no one used, as it was as old
as the house and needed to be replaced.

Tonight, though, Ava decided to mount the rickety stairs
rather than face the basement again. She flipped on the light
switch, but one of the bulbs was burned out, so the path up to
the second story was dim. At the second floor, she ran her
flashlight's beam around the door that was locked from the
outer hallway near one of the spare bedrooms. There was a flip
switch on this side, similar to a dead bolt, and it worked easily,
as if it had been recently oiled.

Odd.

And disturbing.

Sweeping the beam of the light over the stairs, she saw that
the dust on each step was uneven and disturbed, that someone
had used them recently.

She stared up the curving staircase and wondered if someone
was still in the unused rooms. No better time to find out than
right now. As quietly as she could, she hurried up the remainder of the flight, the beam of her flashlight catching in cobwebs
and showing evidence of mice.

At a final curve, she found another door.

And it was locked, of course. *Great. Now what?* She tried the handle, but it wouldn't move, and the hinges were on the inside, so removing them was out of the question. But there had to be a way.

When she was a kid, her grandmother had employed a full staff, and not only a governess but also two maids had lived in these quarters. The door, as she remembered it, had never been locked, and the only other access was the fire escape located on the back side of the house or . . . She looked around a curve, where the stairs narrowed noticeably and wound upward, to the roof. Carefully, she worked her way up the old stairs and saw that here, the dust hadn't been disturbed, and the cobwebs were thicker as she made her way to the final door that led to the roof and the widow's walk, upon which no one had trod for years.

Of course it was locked.

She pushed her shoulder hard against the door, but it wouldn't budge.

Stymied, she ran her light around the casing, hoping to find a key tucked on the top of the door. No such luck. But someone had to get up there, on the roof, in case repairs needed to be made. Someone had to have a key. Same with the third floor. If there was a problem with water leaks or pests or whatever, someone in the house needed access. At one time, she'd had a key ring that held the keys to every room in the house, every outer doorway, even the outbuildings, but she hadn't seen those keys since returning from St. Brendan's. In fact, when she had used the car, Wyatt had given her his car key.

She'd asked about hers, and he'd smiled and said, *"Of course you can have them when you're better."*

At the time she'd been so fragile she hadn't cared, but now things had changed. Convinced she wouldn't find a hidden key anywhere on the staircase, she made her way back to Wyatt's den and began the search. Some of the drawers in his desk were locked, and after rifling through the drawers and cubbies that were open, she found nothing that would help, not even a letter opener.

She was nervous, beginning to sweat at the thought that she'd be caught snooping through his office. How long had it been since he'd boated across the bay? Was he coming back tonight? Would he find her? There had to be an easier way.

Think, Ava, think! This is your house. You've lived here most of your life. You know its secrets. There can't be just one set of keys. What if one got lost? Someone—a caretaker—had to have access to all the floors, to the damned roof—

The keys in the back hallway!

Hadn't she seen them there recently?

Down the stairs she raced, nearly tripping as she made her way to the first floor and the small closet wedged between the pantry and the staircase. Inside, she shined her flashlight over a few tools, old canning jars, and there, on a hook protruding from a beam, were several key rings. They were marked: for the boathouse, the sheds, the stable and barns, and the house. She plucked the ring down and was about to leave the closet when her flashlight caught the glint of metal deep within one of the cubbyholes. She reached inside and found a separate key ring that, upon closer inspection, didn't match those she'd discovered earlier. There was a brass plate with the initials CC etched into it, and she thought they were her father, Connell Church's. They must've been his when he died, she thought, and didn't have time to think about it any further. For now, she had to get upstairs again and hope that one of the keys on the house ring would spring the lock to the third floor. She wasn't certain that Wyatt would return tonight, but if he did, Ava didn't want him to know what she'd been doing. She did take the time to rummage through the tools, however, and came up with a screwdriver in case she had to jimmy something open.

Then, up the stairs she flew, to the third floor where she tried every key on the ring, each unable to slide into the lock. Frowning, sensing time ticking by, she selected each key once, more carefully this time.

Nope. None of them opened the door to the old servants' quarters.

Shining her light over the lock again, she finally understood. The lock had been replaced at one point. Its metal plate was shiny and appeared newer than those on the doors of the lower levels. Obviously it had been changed. But when? And by whom?

A new anxiety crawled through her.

It's just a changed lock, she reminded herself. *Not necessarily part of a conspiracy, nor the embodiment of evil.* And yet she knew in her heart that something important was hidden on the third level.

Frustrated, she looked around herself. Now what? Here, in the darkened staircase, when she was so certain the evidence she needed to prove that she'd been gaslighted lay just on the other side of the door, she was stymied. She stood on the steps, the cold air in the stairwell chilling the sweat that had collected on her skin, the house still save for the creaking timbers of the old mansion settling and the wind whistling far away.

Shining her light up the narrow stairs leading to the widow's walk, she wondered if she could unlock its small door. Why not try? From there, she could take the fire escape down to the third floor. She followed the curving stairs, and as she reached the top, she examined the lock closely, seeing it was the same vintage as most of the others in the house. Trying several keys, she heard a satisfying *click* with the fourth key as the lock sprang.

She tried to open the door, but it was stuck fast, swollen shut. "You bastard," she muttered at the old panels, and threw her weight into it. Once, twice, three times only to get nowhere. Panting, placing her flashlight and the keys on the steps, she grabbed the handle with both hands, turned, and tried again. Finally, the old wood gave, splintering around the cylinder, the door flying open. Rain immediately lashed inside. Her flashlight rolled down the stairs behind her, thumping loudly, its beam swinging wildly over the dirty walls and ceiling before she was able to retrieve it. Cursing the fact that she hadn't bothered with slippers, she grabbed her flashlight, walked onto the flat part of the roof, and as the wind tore at her hair, stared out to sea.

The water was dark, whitecaps forming, the surf roaring. The sound reminded her of the fateful boat trip that led to Kelvin's death. The wild ocean, the bobbing boat, the ultimate doom. The memory, as cold as winter rain, was stark. Painful. Jewel-Anne blamed her for that fateful voyage and now, thinking about it, she wondered why she'd insisted they go out.

Had it been her idea?

Or someone else's?

Why, when she was pregnant, would she risk a journey on a choppy ocean when she'd suffered so many miscarriages? True, it was later in the pregnancy, but still . . . something didn't feel right about it.

Don't think about it. Not now. Move. Before Wyatt returns and you have to explain yourself!

Heart in her throat, she edged across the wet roof to the side, where the ladder for the fire escape was visible. Fir needles and years of sludge slid between her toes, but at least the walk seemed solid. She probably could go down to the second floor and climb up, through one of the guest rooms, but it was so close to Jewel-Anne's bedroom that she didn't want to risk it. No, it was better to go down from the top.

Wind buffeting her as it screamed across the bay, she found the ladder's handholds and swung a leg over. The rain was pummeling her now, and she realized if anyone saw her, she'd be thrown back into a psychiatric ward so fast her head would spin. If she made it.

On the first rung, her foot slid a little, so she gripped with her bare feet as best she could, slid the screwdriver into her mouth, and descended slowly. In one hand, she still held the flashlight as well as the railing; in the other, she held on tight to the wet, slimy handholds.

Her heart was pounding with fear, but she didn't look down, just eased from one rung to the next, slowly descending, making certain her grip was secure on a ladder that was far from stable and groaned against her weight.

What if the attic is empty? Devoid of anything but furniture draped in old sheets and spiders scuttling to dark corners? What then?

She closed her mind to the nagging thoughts and slowly descended. One foot slipped and she gasped, nearly dropping the screwdriver and losing her flashlight.

But she caught herself, and as rain poured from the sky, she reached the window of the third floor and the tiny landing that creaked and wobbled with her weight.

You ARE insane, her mind taunted, but she went to work. Crouched on the landing, the flashlight wedged between her teeth, she trained its frail light to the windowsill where she tried to open the old window. Expecting it to be locked tight, she was amazed that it gave way easily, rattling upward with only a little pressure and no need of the screwdriver.

Finally, a break! Carefully, she pulled down on the inner shade and released it slowly so that it rolled upward without snapping before she slipped inside. The room smelled musty, as if no one had been inside for years.

Dear God, what if she'd been wrong? What if this was just used as a storage area? Ava's heart sank as she closed the window and blind behind her. Carefully, she walked through the maze of rooms tucked under the eaves. There were beds covered in sheeting, draped lamps and chairs, everything covered and eerily forgotten. In the closet-sized bathroom, there was a stained toilet and sink. The small kitchen had cabinets and chipped laminate that looked like something straight out of the 1940s, its appliances long removed.

"No one up here but the ghosts," she muttered under her breath as she shined her light on the door to the stairs with its newer dead bolt. What the devil was that all about?

"Mommy . . . Mommy!" Noah's voice echoed from the rafters, and Ava bit back a scream and stumbled back against an old record player in what had been a dining area. She dropped the screwdriver, then stepped on it as she scrambled to pick it up.

Her son was *not* up here! He couldn't be.

And then the broken crying resonated through the rooms again.

What was this? Not her baby. She knew better now.

Swallowing back her fear, she walked again through the apartment as it went silent again, and she wondered if someone below could hear her footsteps.

But nothing was disturbed. Everything seemed as if someone had shut the door on this floor a decade earlier and never returned.

The silence was crushing.

No more cries.

Only the keen of the wind.

All she could see were draped pieces of furniture. Slowly at first, then more quickly, she started throwing off the sheeting, exposing forgotten kitchen chairs, an ancient chaise used by her grandmother, televisions from the eighties, pictures of long-dead relatives, and an easy chair that had been her father's favorite. One by one, she flung the sheets off, then stopped suddenly.

She thought she heard the sound of a boat's engine over the rush of the wind. *Wyatt!*

She had to work faster.

Smarter.

The baby's cries had sounded in Noah's bedroom on the second floor and Wyatt's office on the first, so if the sound traveled down some shaft, then it made sense that it would start from the room directly above, or below; although, so far, she'd discounted the basement. Now she walked down the short hallway to the bedrooms, found the one she thought was in the right area, and stepped inside.

The floor wasn't as dusty in here it seemed, but the room was furnished sparsely, with two twin bed frames without mattresses pushed to opposite walls, on either side of a window. She pulled open the window shade and peered outside, spying the upper branches of the same tree that could be seen from Wyatt's office and the nursery.

This had to be the room.

But it was empty.

She shined her flashlight all along the floorboards, then opened the closet. Empty, aside from some luggage, an old trunk, a few dusty suitcases, and a hatbox on the shelf.

She pulled out the hatbox and found nothing but a pink pillbox hat reminiscent of Jackie Kennedy and the early sixties and a few faded but dressy "hostess" aprons, one with the price tag still on it, all circa 1960.

Heart sinking, the sound of the boat's engine growing louder, she felt as if she'd failed. But she'd heard her son's voice. Loud. From this damned attic—she was certain of it.

She glanced down at the suitcases in the closet. Two red Samsonite bags with plastic handgrips and a smaller roller bag.

She stared at them, feeling the hairs on her arm lift. She had no idea when roller bags came into fashion, but certainly a lot later than the 1960s. It was out of place. Hardly daring to breathe, she carefully unzipped the bag and, pulling up the top, she found what she was looking for: a small digital player and some kind of wireless connection.

"You bitch," she said between clenched teeth, because she was certain Jewel-Anne was behind this.

But how could she set it up? She's in a wheelchair.

Ava's first thought was to rip the damned roller bag from the closet and drag it down to Jewel-Anne's room, throw it onto her cousin's frilly bed, and lift the top, then demand answers.

But she wouldn't get any.

Jewel-Anne would just deny it. Everyone would insinuate Ava had somehow rigged the equipment up herself. No, that wouldn't do. Somehow, she had to beat Jewel-Anne, and whoever else was behind this, at their own game.

As the drone of the boat's engine slowed, indicating it was being docked, she set the suitcase back in its spot, closed the closet door, and quickly and carefully threw back the dust covers she'd torn off the furniture. The rooms weren't quite as they had been when she'd entered, and the dust had surely been disturbed, but she couldn't worry about little details.

Heart drumming, she glanced around. The screwdriver! She stumbled and groped till she found it; then she turned off the flashlight, let herself out the back window, and climbed back up the fire escape. She only prayed that Wyatt, or whoever had docked the boat, wouldn't see her. With surprising agility, she scaled the ladder, her feet slipping only once. Hauling herself over the rail, she scurried across the widow's walk to the door at the top of the stairs.

The rain was still lashing, but she ignored it as she forced open the door, then reentered the uppermost hallway, grabbed the keys, and locked the door behind her. Her nightgown was dripping on the stairs, but there was nothing she could do about it, so she raced downward, past the third floor, and paused at the second. If she could let herself out here, take the chance that whoever was behind this wouldn't notice the dead bolt had been turned . . .

She had to do it. It was too much of a risk to run down to the first floor and chance running into whoever was returning.

It's Wyatt; of course it's Wyatt. Who else would take the psychiatrist back to Anchorville?

Weird, though—why wouldn't he stay the night?

To keep up pretenses, of course!

Taking a chance, she let herself out of the stairwell and stepped onto the carpet of the second floor, just as she heard the front door creak open.

Damn! How could she explain herself, the fact that she was drenched? If only she could trust her husband, confide in him, but she was certain he was part of those who were against her.

Why? If he's in love with another woman, why not just divorce me?

But he had been against the divorce before—she remembered that much—and though she knew not a shred of love still connected them, and he was involved with someone else, he refused to give up.

Because of the money. He wants control of this estate and everything you've inherited or made.

That thought had crossed her mind before, but she'd always dismissed it. Wyatt was wealthy in his own right, had a great job, made more than enough money. He didn't want hers. And if he did, why not just kill her and be done with it? She knew the answer to that. Wyatt wasn't a murderer. It wasn't in his blood.

Then why am I so scared? My heart is racing, my hands are sweating, and I'm hardly daring to breathe for fear that I'll be caught.

Because deep in her soul, she believed he wanted her committed, was looking for a way to send her back to St. Brendan's, or worse.

She heard him walk into the den and knew that this was her chance. While he was still settling into his chair, turning on his computer and the lights, she had to dash up the stairs and hope that he didn't notice.

Easing along the hallway, she sneaked a peek over the railing to the foyer and then, seeing the lights go on in the den, she ran, on her tiptoes, soft and light. *Quick, quick, quick! Don't trip!*

He cleared his throat and she nearly missed a step but continued around the corner. The door to her room was open, but she didn't dare close it for fear he would hear the noise. In the dark, she opened her drawer, found a new set of pajamas in the bureau, then slipped into the bathroom where she quickly changed and towel-dried her hair. Thinking he might have heard her rustling around, she kicked her nightgown into the corner of the room and flushed the toilet.

She stepped into her room and gasped.

She wasn't alone.

A man stood in the doorway, the light from the hall spilling his looming silhouette into stark relief.

"What's going on, Ava?" Trent asked just as she recognized her cousin.

Ava almost sank to the floor with relief that she didn't have to explain herself to her husband.

"I just went to the bathroom."

"From the hallway?" he asked. "I saw you in the corridor."
Busted!

"Oh . . . well, I did go to Noah's room," she said, thinking quickly. "Please don't tell anyone, but I thought I heard him again, and I just went to the nursery before I realized . . . that it couldn't be. It must've been all part of a dream. A . . . nightmare."

He eyed her nightgown and wet hair

"What're you doing up so late?" she asked, trying to deflect the conversation.

"Just got back from across the bay. Wyatt asked me to take Eve, er, Evelyn home."

"Why didn't he do it himself?"

Trent lifted a shoulder. "Beats me."

"Where is he now?"

"Again, I don't know, but you should." He glanced pointedly at the rumpled bed. "Wyatt sleeping in another room?"

She didn't answer and he inclined his head, taking her silence as an answer. "I think I'll turn in." He gave the door frame a couple of pats. "See you in the morning."

"Yeah."

"And, Ava?"

"Hmmm?" Suddenly bone-tired, she was already walking to the bed.

"The next time you go climbing up to the widow's walk in the middle of the night in a friggin' monsoon, you might take an umbrella."

"Wha—"

Her heart sank as she realized she'd already been caught in one lie and would have to come up with another.

"I saw you, cousin. On the roof." Lines of concern bracketed his mouth. "What the hell were you doing up there?"

"I couldn't sleep," she lied easily. "I was thinking of my son and my brother. Kelvin never even got to meet his nephew, and so I went up to the widow's walk because that's the best place to view the spot where the *Bloody Mary* went down."

"So why lie to me about it?"

Was he actually hurt?

"And admit to doing one more crazy thing?"

He sighed, looking back toward the hall and running a hand around the back of his neck. "Going up there in the rain in the middle of the night, in a rager like the one tonight? It really isn't sane, Ava. It's dangerous. Like chasing after an image of your son and ending up in the bay."

"Please, Trent. Don't tell anyone."

He hesitated and she felt his indecision, his faith in her sliding away.

"Please."

He let out his breath in a rush as from downstairs, the grandfather clock bonged once. One o'clock. "I won't say anything, but you have to promise me you'll get help. If not with Eve, then someone else. This isn't right, Ava," he said, shaking his head.

"I'm not crazy. I'm really not." She couldn't help the feeling of disappointment deep in her chest or the slight sound of accusation in her tone.

"You need help, Ava," he retorted. Then, shaking his head, he added, "Maybe we all do. But go to bed, would ya? And stay there till morning, this time. It's late."

"I will," she promised, and as he shut the door, she realized she'd lost the trust of one of the few people she'd considered an ally. Trent would never believe her again.

Now she was completely on her own.

Chapter 31

The trouble with lies is that they continue to grow and grow and not always in a straight line. Sometimes they twisted, like a writhing snake; other times they split as if they were a forked tree; other times they splintered, flying in all directions, shards of the lie cutting deep and showing up where least expected. If you were going to be a liar, and a good one, you had to be at the top of your game, always remembering to whom you said what, which was difficult. Since a lie wasn't based in reality, there was no sound basis on which it stood, no solid rock; instead it was based on shifting quicksand ready to drag you down and bury you with your inconsistencies.

Fortunately for Ava, lying hadn't been a problem. She'd always been a straight shooter.

Until now.

"Get used to it," she muttered, her cell phone to her ear as she stood at her window watching the clouds shift across the bay, waiting for Tanya to pick up. After her discoveries last night, Ava needed an accomplice, someone she could trust—and the people in that category were dwindling fast.

She heard Tanya's muffled voice as she spoke to someone nearby, then more clearly, "Okay, I checked my schedule and I really can't get out of here until after three unless I can do some serious appointment shuffling. I've got Gloria Byers coming in at one for a cut and color, and it always takes a couple of hours, minimum. After that, I'm good. Russ has kid duty tonight. He's picking them up after school, trying to play the part of 'good dad' again, I guess. It makes me nervous, but there's nothing I can do about it, so I've got the evening off."

Ava glanced at the clock on the bedside table. It was nearly ten already. "I'd like to leave by noon, but see what you can do and call me back."

"Will do. You know, sometimes it's just a bitch being a single mother." She hung up, her frustration still sizzling over the wireless connection, and Ava tried to figure out what she would do if she didn't have Tanya as her "cover." Without a friend with her, it would be almost impossible to avoid suspicion about her trip to Seattle for the equipment she needed.

She gritted her teeth, already worried about buying the microphones and video cameras. Wyatt would be able to see the bank statement if she used a credit or debit card, and she didn't want him becoming suspicious.

She'd always had her own, separate checking account, credit cards, and savings. She'd managed her investment account and created her own financial independence only to lose it upon her admission into the hospital. Since that time, however, whenever she'd brought up the need for her "own" money, Wyatt had assured her that they'd "work things out" once she was "better."

Him having total control over her finances would have to stop. Directly after this subversive trip into Seattle.

As she was reaching for her sweater, her phone vibrated in her pocket and she saw Tanya's number flash on the screen.

"Okay, it's a go," Tanya said cheerfully. "I managed to

switch everything around. Turns out good ol' Gloria needed to reschedule anyway. Looks like I can get out of here at eleven."

"Perfect. I'm on my way! Can we use your car?"

"You bet. As long as you buy me lunch. And I'm not talkin' about a hot dog and a soda at the ferry landing. Uh-uh. I'm talking *serious,* over-the-top Seattle lunch complete with an expensive glass of wine and a view of the harbor. Treat me like the GD princess I'm supposed to be."

"You drive a hard bargain."

"Always."

Ava laughed for the first time that day. "It's a deal."

Thank God for Tanya!

The Reynolds case was going nowhere fast, and Snyder was bugged as he sat at his computer, a cup of coffee long forgotten on his desk. He didn't hear the phones ringing nor see the two deputies saunter past his desk on their way to the back of the building. He was too engrossed in his work and was reading the autopsy report on Cheryl Reynolds for the third time.

Not that there were any big surprises in the document, but he'd hoped he'd missed something important in the first two passes. According to the ME, Cheryl Reynolds had died because both her jugular vein and carotid artery had been sliced open, after she'd been nearly strangled to death.

So the killer had to be someone strong enough to crush her larynx before slitting her throat from one ear to the other. Brutal son of a bitch . . . and he probably knew her. The attack seemed personal, as if the person wanted to make a point rather than just kill the woman.

He switched the screen and stared, once more, at the list of trace evidence found at the scene. Nothing that would help. Nothing out of place, except for a single black hair, that, for all he knew, could belong to one of the cats or even another of Cheryl's clients who'd stepped into the laundry room. Nothing stolen, it seemed, and no one even trying to mask the crime as a robbery gone bad.

Again, he thought the attack was pointed and personal.

There were no eyewitness reports of someone lurking about, no neighbor spying a stranger or anyone suspicious on the premises. The tenants upstairs, possibly smoking dope from the scent in their apartment, hadn't heard a thing.

Typical.

Why, he wondered, would a woman who had lived in Anchorville peacefully for decades, with no known enemies, suddenly be the victim of such a vicious, pointed attack?

Random?

It just didn't feel like it.

The last known person to see Reynolds alive was Ava Garrison, but her story had seemed to hold water; her statement and timeline about seeing the hypnotist was spot-on and gelled with other witnesses' accounts who'd helped offer up an alibi for her. But Cheryl Reynolds's time of death had happened soon, if not immediately, after the Garrison woman had left. And she was far from mentally stable, had even tried to kill herself.

Maybe that counted for something; maybe it didn't.

Other than her one suicide attempt, there was no history of violence surrounding her. She had been rumored to be a hard-nosed businesswoman once, a bitch by some standards, but that was before she'd had a son and then lost her only child.

He grimaced. Too bad, that.

She'd never given up on the kid, and after she'd shown up at his office a few days earlier, Snyder had pulled the file and reviewed it. There had been no leads in the case from the get-go and none since. The kid had vanished, and when no ransom note had appeared, when no kidnappers had contacted the Garrisons, his theory had changed. Snyder's private opinion, a theory he couldn't prove, was that there had been some bad accident, where the kid had died and whoever had killed him had dumped the body—stashing it somewhere before dropping it in the open sea.

The mother? Unlikely.

Then again, she had issues.

Frustrated, he drummed his fingers on his desk while he rolled over all the evidence in his mind.

So lost in thought was he that he didn't notice Biggs stroll into his cubicle. Only when the sheriff cleared his throat did Snyder look up and find the ponderous man filling the little extra space around his desk.

Biggs's reading glasses were pushed onto the top of his head, and he was chewing gum with a vengeance. "Anything new on the Reynolds case?"

"Just goin' over the autopsy and evidence reports, but no, nothing."

Biggs scowled. Chewed harder. "The press is all over the PIO, and I'd like her to be able to give them something positive to work with."

It figured. "As soon as I have something that won't compromise the case, I'll call Natalie." Snyder thought about the petite, wiry public information officer and didn't envy her that job.

"The sooner the better. I can't have an unsolved homicide on my watch." He shook his head, the glasses shifting enough that he pulled them from his graying crew cut, folded the bows, and stuffed the readers into a shirt pocket. "And I'm sick to the back teeth of my ex-sister-in-law calling me about all that shit that goes on out on the island. Buried dolls and all that." He made a disgusted snort. "Virginia, she doesn't know what *ex* means." Frowning, he said, "I suppose there's still nothing on Lester Reece, right? I'd love to give the press something to feed on."

"No recent sightings, no, sir."

Biggs's eyes narrowed a bit, as if he thought Snyder might be putting him on. "He's never shown up anywhere, you know."

"Could have drowned. Been washed out to sea. Eaten by sharks or orcas." Snyder lifted his shoulder. "It's been a long while."

"Nonetheless."

"We're always keeping an eye out for him."

"Good," Biggs grunted, then shifted and winced. "Goddamned knee. Hurts like a mother sometimes." Rumor had it that his doctor had suggested knee replacement surgery. That same rumor said Biggs, ever bullheaded, had told the doc just where to shove that idea. Now, still chewing furiously, Biggs headed stiffly toward the back of the office building where the kitchen and restrooms were located.

Snyder turned back to his work and barely looked up when he heard Lyons approach.

"Get the pumped-up 'we've got to catch this sum-bitch and nail his hide' speech?"

"Yep." He glanced up at her. "You got something?"

"I found her computer notes. Plan to check 'em."

"Aren't those confidential?"

Morgan looked toward the ceiling and shook her head. "Not unless you're a physician. Or a lawyer. Which she was neither. I just hope to all that's holy, and unholy, that something in there helps us catch a killer."

From the watering trough where he was repairing a leaky faucet, Dern surreptitiously watched Ava leave. Twisting a wrench on the pipe, tightening the new stem washer over the spindle, he was finally satisfied that there would be no more leakage as he saw Ava hurry along the street. He would've thought it odd she didn't take the car but figured it was because of the limited ferry schedule, and, he knew Wyatt did keep two vehicles garaged on the other side of the bay.

As she disappeared onto the marina, he replaced the faucet's handle, managing to resist the urge to follow her. Just. That part, the leaving her alone, was getting tougher and went against all of his ridiculous, primitive yearnings.

Setting his jaw, he jogged back to the stable where he'd shut off the main valve for the outside water. He opened the valve, then returned to the trough where he checked the flow of water pouring from the faucet, then turned the spigot off and checked his work, confirming that no water was seeping out. The new washer was holding. "Good enough," he said to himself, and felt one of the horses approaching. Looking over his shoulder, he spied Jasper, who snorted softly, shooting twin jets of hot breath from his nostrils.

"Want to help?" Dern asked. "Or maybe a drink, eh?"

He filled the large cement basin that looked as if it had been around for over fifty years, and the horse moved forward, put his head over the trough, and snorted again, sending the fresh water rippling away.

"You know the old saying about leading a horse to water?" Dern asked, and patted the gelding's broad forehead as he glanced out to the bay and watched a boat head across the steely waters toward Anchorville. "So," he said to the horse, "how about you and me take a ride?"

Still wondering where Ava was going, he snapped a lead onto Jasper's halter, then led the gelding to the stable where he saddled up before heading out again. It didn't matter that Ava had left the island; Dern considered it a good sign that she was getting off this damned rock, but it seemed wherever she went, trouble followed.

And more often than not, trouble's partner was danger.

Isn't that hypocritical considering your own agenda?

He stared at the boat speeding across the bay and felt an overwhelming urge to take off after it. "Idiot," he told himself, and fought back the temptation. He couldn't tip his hand. Not yet. If he constantly showed up every time Ava was somewhere off the island, and she caught sight of him, she'd become suspicious and he couldn't have that. She wouldn't buy the whole coincidence explanation. She wasn't *that* crazy. In fact, he suspected, she wasn't crazy at all. But someone on this island was. The buried doll was proof enough of that.

He glanced at the garden as he swung into the saddle. Who the hell had decided burying a likeness of a missing child was a good idea? Or a bad joke?

Yeah, things were certainly not on the up-and-up here at Neptune's Gate, but then, he surmised, they never had been. The old mansion built into the sides of the hill held secrets, some much darker than others.

Today, he needed to take advantage of the fact that no one was looking over his shoulder. He needed a few hours alone, without anyone's prying eyes watching him. The sands of time were slipping by far too quickly, and he had to work fast. He couldn't be derailed from his mission. Not even by Ava Garrison.

Lord knew she was a major distraction.

"Come on," he urged the horse, who broke into a smooth lope. Up through the woods he'd ride, only veering south once he was assured no one could see him.

Then he'd sneak into his final destination: the abandoned walls of Sea Cliff.

"So what's all this cloak-and-dagger stuff?" Tanya asked Ava as they walked along the hilly sidewalks of Seattle. Tanya was dressed in a fur-lined coat and boots with four-inch heels. As they strode along the steep incline, she tried and failed to keep an umbrella from turning inside out in the wind that blew in off of Elliott Bay. "I mean, what's with the spy cameras and recording devices? Don't tell me . . . you're going to become a PI. Good! I'll have you take pictures or videos of Russell when he's got the kids."

"I don't think I'd make a very good private detective," she admitted with a laugh. During the drive to the city, Ava had kept mum about her mission. Only now, after they'd gone to an electronics store and, using Tanya's credit card to avoid any link to Ava, had purchased the items she thought she needed was she ready to explain, if only a little. She owed her friend that much.

"Then why all the James Bond equipment?" Tanya pressed.

"I'm just trying to turn the tables on whoever is gaslighting me." They sidestepped a man walking a schnauzer in the opposite direction, then waited for a light so they could cross the street to the waterfront restaurant Tanya had chosen for their late lunch.

"You think it has anything to do with Cheryl's murder?" Tanya asked nervously. She hadn't been silent about her belief that Ava's visit to the hypnotist had something to do with Cheryl's death.

"I don't see how." Which was true, but still it bothered her. A lot. Not only had Cheryl's life been taken brutally, but, Ava, too, worried that there might be a connection.

"Well, it's weird and scary—no, make that terrifying—and it makes me paranoid!"

"Join the club."

The light changed and they waited a beat for a maniac driving a Volkswagen bug to zip through the intersection on a red. "Idiot!" Tanya yelled as the driver of a Ford Escape laid on his horn as the escaping yellow beetle careened around a corner.

Once Tanya and Ava were no longer in jeopardy, they quickly crossed the broad street to the waterfront where the air smelled of the ocean and seagulls cawed and wheeled in the gray skies overhead. Ferries chugged across the choppy water, sending up frothy wakes, and in the distance, through a thin layer of fog, the sweeping Olympic Mountains were visible.

As one, they walked to Pier 57, then slipped through the swinging doors of a bistro located over the water and known for its fresh seafood. There were only a few patrons inside, as the lunch crowd had thinned and dinner seating was hours away.

Once seated in a booth near a window with a view of Puget Sound, they ordered drinks and a crab and artichoke dip appetizer that they shared, then individual specials of fish stew and Dungeness crab cakes.

"Okay," Tanya said, once her pomegranate martini was delivered, "so spill. What's with the high-tech spy gizmos?" She sipped her drink and eyed her friend from across the table.

Drawing a fortifying breath, Ava unloaded about the night before and how she'd broken into the third floor only to discover the recording device. For once, Tanya didn't interrupt; she just listened as she sipped her drink and nibbled on the dip and crusty sourdough bread.

"Something's very rotten on that island," she finally said once Ava had finished. "But Jewel-Anne? Let's face it, even if she could climb the stairs, which she can't, is she really that tech savvy to set up some kind of elaborate system?"

"She could have had help. Her brother, Jacob, is a computer genius. Still in school, but he's already been contacted by several software companies here, in the Seattle area and Silicon Valley." She tried her soup and found it hot and tangy, weaving the flavors of tomato, garlic, and fennel to complement the halibut, mussels, shrimp, and bass.

"But why?" Tanya asked. "Why go to all this trouble?"

"I don't know. Maybe because I own Neptune's Gate."

"Mmmm. Money. The age-old culprit."

"Maybe."

"But then what about Noah? You think they had something to do with his kidnapping?"

Her heart grew heavy again, the fear that she'd never see her son again sometimes so dense she felt as if she couldn't draw a breath, couldn't force her lungs to work. "I don't know." She ignored her glass of Chardonnay and suddenly found the soup unappealing, too. "I don't know how."

Picking at her crab cakes, Tanya said, "You know that gossip runs fast and hot through Anchorville, and one of the hotbeds, of course, is my salon."

"Of course."

"So I heard there was a body found buried in the garden at Neptune's Gate?" She was buttering a piece of bread but stopped long enough to skewer Ava with her gaze. "Is that what you mean by 'gaslighting'?"

"Not a body. A doll. I'm sorry I didn't mention it earlier," Ava explained, and then, deciding she had to confide in someone completely, told Tanya everything that had happened on the island. She didn't care if her friend thought she was nuts; she laid it all out, from seeing her son's image on the dock to finding his wet shoes in the nursery, to her believing that her husband was having an affair with her psychologist.

When she was finished, she felt better. Unburdened. Tanya had barely taken a bite. "Wow," she finally said, "I think I'm going to start calling you Alice. You've definitely been down the rabbit hole."

"Several times."

They finished their entrées, and when dessert was offered, Ava passed, opting for an espresso, but Tanya ordered a Northwest apple and cranberry cobbler with a huge scoop of vanilla ice cream and two spoons. Ava grudgingly took several bites as she sipped her dark coffee.

She'd just finished signing the credit card receipt for the bill when Tanya said, "So on the way back to Anchorville, you can tell me all about Austin Dern."

"And why would I do that?"

"Oh, I don't know, maybe because you fancy yourself in love with him?"

Ava was shocked. "Is that what it sounded like?" The last thing she needed, the very last, was any complication in her love life, and Dern was definitely a complication.

"You didn't mention him much, but when you did, you actually blushed," Tanya said, jabbing her spoon at her friend. "Don't deny it. I'm an expert at these things. I'm a beautician, remember? I've listened to women's life stories for years, and it always involves a man, or more often than not, men."

"I don't even know the man, not really, and besides, since you can't seem to remember, I'm married."

"Not much, you're not. Where're your rings? If I remember right, you had something like a two-carat diamond and a wedding band."

Good question, Ava thought. She hadn't thought about that. "I think maybe they're in a safe somewhere, or a safe-deposit box." She looked down at her naked left hand and rubbed her fingers self-consciously.

"You really don't remember, do you?"

"I guess not."

"You threw them into the bay."

"*What?*" Ava gasped.

"I was there." Tanya casually took another bite of ice cream laced with berries.

"But I would never—"

"Sure you would. Because you caught Wyatt cheating, and it wasn't the first time."

"No, I mean, I don't believe that . . ." But her voice trailed off, and some of the sharp little pieces of the past started fitting together, bit by bit. "With who?"

"Does it matter? In my book, cheating is cheating. No matter who the other half of the equation might be."

Ava's insides twisted and she felt sick. There was truth to this. Some truth.

"Come on, Ava, you have more than holes in your memory. You have giant abysses that span months, maybe even years." Tanya set down her spoon and pushed the rest of the melting dessert aside. "Look, I haven't said anything because I didn't want to make you worse. But I've seen you struggling, trying to remember, and now things are getting really, really weird. You need to get out. While you still can." Tanya was serious now.

"You think I'm in danger?"

"Well . . . yeah. Maybe. Probably. Look what happened to Cheryl."

"That's something else."

"Is it?" Tanya's eyebrows drew together, and lines of worry creased her forehead. "The timing . . . it all seems like it goes together. You know it, too."

She did. The fears that she'd tried so desperately to fight loomed ever stronger. "No. That's leaping to conclusions. And really, if anyone wanted me dead, I would be."

Tanya wasn't buying it. "It's not that easy to kill someone and make it look like an accident these days. Nuh-uh. Too much forensic evidence and they always look to the family first. I think they're hoping you freak yourself out to the point where you do it yourself."

"No."

Tanya reached across the table and clasped one of Ava's arms. Rotating it so that her wrist was partially exposed, parts of scar tissue visible, she said, "I've known you a lot of years, Ava, and until Noah went missing, you were the last person I would have believed capable of trying to commit suicide. The very last. You were the sanest person I knew. So what happened that night?"

Ava swallowed hard. "I don't know," she whispered. "I can't remember." But there were murky images, like pictures that had been overexposed, the edges in shadow. She did recall the bathtub with its foaming bubbles, the warm, comforting water around her naked body, and in an out-of-body experience, she had seen the bloom of blood sliding into the water, staining the frothy bubbles a pale, deadly pink. The razor was on the side of the tub . . . so easy to reach . . . to slide against her white, veined skin . . .

Now as she thought about it, her heart was pounding, a metallic taste rising in her throat.

"Think, Ava. It's important," Tanya pleaded from somewhere in the distance. It was as if she were suddenly in an icy cave on the shore where the thunder of the waves crashed against the rocks and the wind in the cavern rushed so loudly she couldn't think.

"Was anyone else in the room with you?" Tanya's voice. Far, far away . . .

Shaking her head, willing the cloudy memories to clear, she forced the images of that night into her brain. In her mind's eye, she saw herself, arms and legs seemingly detached from her body, the mirror over the sink foggy with steam from the hot water, the lights dimmed and candles burning, red wax running like the thin trickle of her own blood.

Was there someone with her? No . . .

"Who found you? Wyatt, right?" Tanya's thin voice again.

Everything blended together, spinning in some great vortex, clouds swirling, but she was there, in the tub, feeling lightheaded.

"Ava? Are you okay?"

Was that Tanya, now, here in the restaurant, or someone on the other side of the bathroom door, knocking frantically, trying to break in?

"Who found you?"

She blinked. Realized who she was with. Found herself clutching the edges of the table. Focused on Tanya, who was rising out of her chair as if she expected Ava to faint.

"I . . . I don't remember, no . . . not Wyatt. Not first." That was right, wasn't it? Yes. She remembered her cousin's distorted, horrified face. "It was Jewel-Anne. She was freaking out, screaming and crying and . . ." The image started slipping away again, and she grabbed hold of it, certain that she'd seen the girl in the wheelchair, calling for help, yelling and screaming that Ava was dead. And then there had been lights, flashing against the windows, reflecting in the raindrops.

As she'd been lifted from the tub, she'd heard Wyatt's comforting voice, asking that she please be covered as paramedics tended to her. In the farthest reaches of her consciousness, she recalled the bumpy ride across the water to the hospital. . . .

It was all wrapped in delusions and dreams, a fog created by her own despondency and the pills she'd taken before stepping into the warm, soothing water, enough to make her relax.

As it was, she'd barely escaped with her life, had passed out in the rescue boat, hadn't awoken until days later.

Now she swallowed hard, the memory causing goose bumps to rise on her flesh as she mentally returned to the nearly empty restaurant and her best friend. "I lied," she said, and cleared her throat. "I do remember. Just not all of it."

"You didn't try to kill yourself, did you?"

"No," she said, now more certain than ever.

"So who did?"

"That I still don't know," she admitted, the possibilities running through her mind, "but I intend to find out."

"Be careful, Ava," Tanya advised, looking scared. "Be real careful."

Chapter 32

Dern felt the first drops of rain as he tied his horse to a sagging limb of a pine tree near the old asylum. Sea Cliff was showing its age. The cracked concrete, rusting pipes, and moss growing over old gardens were evidence enough of its disuse and emptiness, and the wind sweeping in, smelling of salt water, couldn't quite hide the odor of abandonment.

From one of the rooftops a crow cawed, ruffling his feathers as he looked down at the empty yard, and above the roar of the sea, a chain rattled against one of the unused flagpoles.

All in all, it was a lonely, eerie place that probably should be torn down, Dern thought as he made his way inside. He knew his way around, had learned it by trial and error, having visited the empty mental hospital three times previously. Each time he'd visited, he'd explored a section of the asylum for an hour or so before returning to his studio over the stable and hoping no one had seen him leave, usually by horseback, with an excuse ready should anyone ask of his whereabouts. He'd already mentioned riding the fence line, and today his excuse would be he thought he'd seen someone up in the woods and he wanted to check out if someone was camping on the property or needed assistance. He could use these simple lies to avoid too many lifted eyebrows or clouds of suspicion to gather.

So far, no one had noticed him missing, so he hadn't been forced to lie.

For the time being, he needed to keep his fascination with the institution a secret, and so far, he thought he'd accomplished that much.

Now, at one of the rusted side gates of the complex, he retrieved a pick from his set of slim jims, worked the old lock, and let himself inside. A gravel path choked with weeds wound through what had once been the gardens that separated several buildings on the premises. He passed a section of row houses that had been accommodations for some of the staff. Two of the houses had been remodeled, the common wall between them taken down to allow for one larger home; the rest looked as if they hadn't been touched since Eisenhower was in office. Across a dying hedgerow, he skirted the long clinic building that had been used for outpatient appointments.

Though the entire enclosure was fenced and gated, there were interior security walls as well, and the primary facility, the hospital itself and center of the complex, had its own set of locks, gates, and surrounding fences.

Aside from the fact that there were no towers at the corners of the fences, and no razor wire glinting over the tops of the concrete walls, this area resembled a prison.

"All very civilized," he said under his breath, then picked the lock of the main gate and slipped inside the heart of Sea Cliff. A portico with a sagging roof stretched over the entrance, where a bank of windows and wide double doors greeted visitors.

This lock was a little more stubborn, but eventually it unlatched as well. He pushed some cobwebs aside as he stepped inside, to a place where time and humanity had seemed to have been forgotten. He walked into what had been the reception area of the hospital.

It was empty aside from a broken desk resting against one wall, collecting dust. Through the reception area, he entered into a large office, that of the hospital administrator, the last of whom had been Crispin Church, Ava's uncle. The file cabinets were empty, of course, and the credenza with a broken leg covered what had once been the heat ducts.

He'd been in here before and found nothing on this floor. Nor had he discovered anything of significance in the row houses or clinic buildings that he'd searched. That left the upper floors of the main hospital with its mazes of hallways, nurses' stations, abandoned group rooms, and empty wards.

The elevators didn't work, so he took the stairs, his boots ringing against the concrete steps. The stairwell was dark, the wire glass windows opaque to begin with and now covered in grime. The asylum bordered on creepy, but Dern wasn't one to be easily freaked. If so, he would have lost it when digging up the tiny coffin. Now, *that* had been unnerving. It was a wonder Ava was holding on to her sanity.

The second floor's layout was nearly identical to the first, the only difference being that the reception area below had been relegated to a kitchen and dining area on this floor. There was slightly more furniture in the rooms. A bed with a stained mattress stood in the middle of one patient room, and the frames of two others littered another, larger room nearby. A chair, circa 1972, had been pushed up against a window, forgotten, its stuffing exploding out of scratched faux leather, a frothy cascade of batting.

Nothing of interest.

He climbed the stairs to the third and top floor of the building. It appeared much the same as the others except for the water stains seeping in from the ceiling. Again, here was the common area and nurses' station, but this time he felt a prickle of apprehension as he made his way down one hallway and stopped at the corner room, only distinguishable from the others because of its two windows.

Was the dust in this room disturbed slightly? For a moment he thought he saw the print of a shoe, but it was just a trick of light.

The space was empty, its famous inhabitant leaving not a trace of himself behind.

"Where the hell are you, Reece?" Dern asked, his question echoing off the crackled walls and scratched tile floors. The man was a ghost, haunting this island and the town of Anchorville, leaving behind him an almost tangible legacy. As much of a monster as Lester Reece had been while alive and visible, since the mystery of his whereabouts had never been solved, he'd become a legend, part of the mystique of this part of the world. The old coots in the bar hadn't been mistaken. Like D. B. Cooper, who'd jumped out of a hijacked plane in the sixties with two hundred thousand dollars and two parachutes, Lester Reece had his share of admirers, those fascinated by criminals who had escaped justice and couldn't be proven to be dead or alive. People liked to believe myths and think that someone could get away with murder or money. Lester Reece had gotten away with both. The money he'd stolen had never turned up, nor had his body, but his myth lived on.

And Dern was out to prove the bastard dead, or nail his pathetic hide to the wall once and for all.

Standing at one window, he looked through the murky glass streaked with dirt, the outer sill covered in bird droppings, the interior walls showing black spots where someone had put out a cigarette or two . . . or three. Recently?

He felt a niggle of anticipation, and if he tried hard, he thought he could smell the faint scent of cigarette smoke . . . but that was probably just his imagination working overtime.

He couldn't tell if the black marks were from recent smokes

or from cigarettes that had been extinguished years before. "Hell," he muttered, and peered out the dirty window. From this vantage point, he observed a span of restless water that stretched to the far, rocky, tree-lined shore of the mainland. Reece's escape route, or so it was presumed by those who believed him alive.

Maybe.

Maybe not.

A glint of light caught his attention, and he moved his gaze to the north, along the edge of the island. There, through the trees, barely visible, was a patch of illumination. "What the devil?" he whispered, and craned his neck to take a second look. Sure enough, through a chasm in the hillside, a space where the trees were particularly thin, he caught a glimpse of the backside of Ava Garrison's home.

Not that it meant anything.

And yet he had the uneasy feeling that he'd just stumbled upon something important, a connection between Lester Reece and Ava Garrison's huge house, or more precisely someone who lived there.

Slow down. You're leaping to conclusions.

From here, he was able to see portions of the widow's walk. Cut into the roofline were windows on the third floor, probably to the servants' quarters, which, to his knowledge, were unused. The illuminated window was one floor lower and faintly visible. It was obviously the back of the house, and even in the gray daylight, a lamp was burning.

How many times, Dern wondered, had Lester Reece stood in this very spot and looked out the window to the back of Neptune's Gate?

Maybe never.

Or, more likely, he thought, his mind darkening with the revelation, every damned day.

*   *   *

"This is never going to work!" Tanya squinted through the windshield, her hands holding the wheel of her Chevy Trail-Blazer in a death grip. It wasn't quite six, the night had settled in, and a thick mist forced Tanya to turn on the windshield wipers. Leaves fell, dancing and swirling, caught in the head-light's glare as the SUV's tires hummed over the two-lane road that cut through the forests and gloom.

Truth be told, Ava, too, was feeling nervous, as it was more than possible that she could get caught with spy cameras and the like. But she had to try.

All the way home, the closer they'd gotten to Anchorville, the more worried and quiet Tanya had become. What had seemed a lark earlier in the day had become a worrisome real-ity as, in her beat-up Chevy, the two women had ferried across Puget Sound, then driven through the port towns and north coast of the Olympic Peninsula, heading ever closer to Anchorville.

As a Seattle station played a mix of soft and hard rock, Tanya slid a glance into the backseat at the large bags they'd brought with them. Ava's cover was a girls' day out, which supposedly included a shopping spree in downtown Seattle, a massage at a local spa, and lunch on the waterfront. They had done all of those things, and she had the shopping bags to prove it, but tucked deep in a Nordstrom bag were the devices she'd picked up at a small electronics store not far from the University of Washington. She'd hidden all of the equipment in shoe boxes and a new purse she'd purchased and hoped to high heaven that she could make it inside the house without anyone wanting to see what she'd bought or asking too many questions.

An accomplished liar she wasn't.

But she was learning.

"Seriously, what're you going to do with all this stuff?" Tanya asked, motioning to the sacks in the backseat.

"Set it up."

"Do you know how?"

"No, but it comes with directions, and the guy told us it was simple enough that a ten-year-old could handle it." The "guy" was a geek at the high-tech store who looked like he could set up a computer system for NASA.

"I'm talking about *you*," Tanya reminded.

"Your faith in me is underwhelming."

Nervously, Tanya stretched her hands over the steering wheel and slowed for a turn. "All this bothers me. I don't like it," she said.

"Me neither."

"Oh, damn!" A raccoon waddled across the narrow, two-lane road, and she swerved slightly to avoid hitting it.

Anchorville was less than two miles away, and Ava could feel her anxiety ratcheting up.

Wyatt had called while she'd been shopping in Seattle; she'd seen his name on the phone's small screen but couldn't pick up in the electronics store.

Now she called him back, and he picked up before the second ring.

"Hey," he said.

"I just noticed that you called earlier," she lied. "Sorry."

"I was just checking in."

"Tanya kidnapped me," she said, keeping her voice light. "Lunch, shopping, a spa treatment, you know, the works."

"You had a good time?" he asked while Tanya fiddled with the knob of the car's defroster and pretended not to eavesdrop.

"A really good time."

"So where are you?" he asked.

"A few miles out of Anchorville."

"You know you missed the last ferry."

"I can probably catch a ride with Butch or one of the other

guys who ferry to the island. I should be home in less than an hour."

"No. Just wait at the coffee shop. I'll pick you up."

Her stomach sank at the thought of juggling packages and hiding what was inside them on the boat with Wyatt at the helm. "Thanks, but really, I'm sure someone will be available. If not, I'll call—"

"I'm on my way," he cut in.

"Seriously, Wyatt, you don't have to . . ." She caught Tanya's worried glance.

"It's not a problem. I'll see you soon!" He hung up before she could protest any further.

"I knew it!" Tanya said, giving up on the heater. "He's suspicious!"

"He's *always* suspicious." Ava dropped her phone into her purse and leaned back in the seat while trying to convince herself she could pull this off.

Twin beams from the headlights of an oncoming car washed over the interior, illuminating Tanya's concerned face for a split second. "You could always stay with me."

"Thanks." Ava touched her friend on the shoulder. "But that would just raise more suspicions. Don't worry. I'll be fine."

The lie stretched between them.

"I'm a mother," Tanya said. "You know that worrying is second nature." Her SUV rounded a final corner, and the lights of Anchorville came into view.

As they passed the blue and white WELCOME TO ANCHOR-VILLE sign, Ava told herself that she could get through this, that the worst that could happen was someone finding out and either calling her paranoid or trying to commit her. She'd suffered through worse.

But her confidence was eroding.

It didn't help when Tanya said, "There's a reason Cheryl was killed, Ava. I have no idea what it is, but I'd bet my tips for a month that it has something to do with you." Ava opened her mouth to argue, but Tanya wasn't finished. "Don't even say it, okay?" She slid her friend a don't-bullshit-me look. "This is all too weird. I mean, I'm nervous as all get-out ever since I found out that Cheryl was killed. *Killed*. I check and recheck the locks on my doors at night. I test every window latch, and I still think I hear noises—someone—in the basement."

"But why are *you* afraid?"

"I don't know! That's what I'm saying. It doesn't make sense. Guilt by association, I guess. Like Cheryl." She waited at a blinking red light for a pickup heading out of town to roll past, then turned down the hill to the road that ran past the marina.

"You mean by association with me?" Ava asked. "You think I was the target?"

"I don't know what to think." She nosed her TrailBlazer into a nearly empty parking lot across the street from the waterfront. "But to tell you the truth, I'm just glad Russ has got the kids tonight. Jesus, did you ever think I'd say that?"

"No."

"Just goes to show how freaked out I am." Shoving the gearshift into park, she let the SUV idle. "You have to be careful, Ava. Promise me."

"I will."

"You could just go to the police, you know."

She thought of Detectives Snyder and Lyons, then the sheriff. "Not yet. Not until I have some proof," she said, opening the car door. A gust of cold, damp air swept inside. "Thanks for everything, Tanya."

"NBD."

Ava laughed. "You're wrong. It is a big deal. A very big deal."

With a dismissive shrug, Tanya said, "Fine, then. Thank me by saying hi to Trent for me."

"I still owe you, but okay. Will do."

Some things never changed. Tanya, it seemed, had never lost the soft spot in her heart for Trent.

Grabbing her bags from the backseat, Ava waved good-bye, then walked down the asphalt path to the marina. Her stomach clenched with each footstep. Somehow she had to get through the next few hours with Wyatt and pretend to enjoy spending time with him when all she wanted to do was get back to the island and set up the recording equipment. She'd lock herself in the bathroom, run the shower, and connect all the pieces of her spy equipment so that all she had to do once everyone in the house was asleep was place the camera and recorder in the attic. Motion activated, it would only record when someone came into the bedroom and checked his or her equipment. "*Spy vs. Spy,*" she whispered, thinking of the old comic strip and cartoon show she'd seen as a child. "Two can play at this game."

But first she had to deal with her husband.

On the waterfront, lights were strung near the entrance to the marina. She passed the open market, where the smell of fish was overpowering, and she saw Lizzy helping to scoop out a mound of shrimp for a couple who were perusing the glass display case.

Three doors down, she entered the coffee shop where the scent of brewing coffee was strong and rows of brightly colored Christmas gifts for the coffee connoisseur were displayed near a case of coffee cakes, doughnuts, and croissants. She ordered a pumpkin latte she really didn't want, then sat at a tall table near the window, her bags at her feet.

Sipping the latte, she set her elbows on the top of the bistro table and stared out the window toward the waterfront, dreading the boat ride with her husband.

Earlier, Tanya had mentioned that Wyatt had cheated on her, though her friend couldn't, or wouldn't, supply the names of whoever had supposedly been romantically involved with him. Now, as she tasted the spicy foam over her hot drink and stared out the window to the inky waters of the bay, she tried to recall who it could be and when it had happened.

Did it matter?

Of course it does. You need to remember everything. Good. Bad. Ugly. True. False. Whatever. Think, Ava. Concentrate. Everything's locked away, deep inside of you, but you can find it if you look hard enough. Just think!

Her head pounded and her stomach was in knots. Just a few more hours and she would be able to set her plan in motion. Her cell jangled.

Instinctively, she reached into her purse, her fingers grazing the ring of keys she'd stashed there. With all the excitement of the day, she'd forgotten them, but now she pulled them out of the bag, dropped them, clattering, onto the table, then withdrew her phone.

Wyatt again.

"Hey," she answered, ignoring the tightness in her chest as she fingered the old set of keys.

"I'm about there, but wait for me. We can have dinner in Anchorville and then head back."

Oh, Lord. She glanced down at the packages she wanted desperately to stash in her closet. "Virginia isn't expecting us?"

"Doesn't matter. We'll call."

Whatever you do, don't make him more suspicious than he already is.

"Okay. I'm already at the coffee shop. I'll wait for you." Her own words circled back at her and slapped her in the face. *"I'll wait for you."* When had she uttered those before? Her skin crawled and she stared out the window, catching sight of her watery, worried reflection in the glass, a ghost of the woman she'd once been.

Again, she wondered about Wyatt's lover, the woman with whom he'd had the affair. Her head began to pound painfully as she dug into her mind, piecing the past together, forcing the sharp-edged pieces into a pattern she could understand.

Suddenly, the door to that part of her memory flew open.

And all the sordid little details of that time in her life came rushing back to haunt her.

Chapter 33

The memory was so vivid, almost as if she'd turned back the clock a couple of years, to an autumn when the first frost had already covered the yellowed grass and all the leaves of the maple trees near the house had blazed orange and yellow, as if they'd been on fire.

Noah was as busy as ever, getting into things, opening doors, climbing the stairs, insisting upon playing peekaboo and hide-and-seek.

That evening, Ava had been on the phone as she'd carried Noah into the house. He'd been overjoyed with the pumpkins growing in the garden and had pointed repeatedly at a squirrel that had scolded them from the higher branches of a fir tree.

". . . I just won't be able to make it home for dinner tonight," Wyatt was telling her as she set Noah on the floor and, holding the phone against her ear, tried in vain to unzip her son's coat before he took off at a dead run through the foyer. "It's all right," she'd said. "Noah and I will grab something to eat and then I'll get him ready for bed. He's tired, but I'll wait for you."

"Don't bother. It's going to be late. I might not make it back until morning. I'll probably just crash here."

"At the office."

"Yeah, I'll sleep on the couch. I've got an extra suit and there's a shower in the executive bathroom."

"But—"

"Give Noah a hug for me." He clicked off, and in that moment, the truth hit her with a blinding force. He was with another woman. He was lying. She'd stared down at the phone in her hand, numb, as she put two and two together, all the times lately he'd called to postpone a plan or work late or . . .

"Mommy! Catch me!"

She looked up sharply, saw her son on the landing, and her heart galumphed. For a split second, she thought he was going to jump. Instead he kept scrambling up the stairs, obviously hoping she'd give chase.

Pushing thoughts of Wyatt and whomever he was with out of her mind, she ran after Noah, catching him up as he giggled in delight. She'd then managed to get through the next few hours. During dinner, while alone, Noah in his high chair next to her, she thought she'd caught pitying glances from Virginia but chalked it up to her overactive imagination. No one knew about the affair, for God's sake; she'd just learned of it.

Still . . .

The clock had seemed to move at half its regular rate as she bathed Noah, read him a story, and put him to bed. Afterward, she'd closeted herself in the bedroom she shared with her husband and stared at the digital clock as it slowly counted off the minutes.

That night had been the longest of her life. Her mind had raced. Questions had burned through her brain, and she hated not knowing, imagining her husband in bed with another woman. The sex—was it wild? Intense? Had words of love been spoken, maybe even a joke at her expense as she'd been the trusting little wife? It had made her crazy, and after drifting off for a few hours, she'd awakened gritty-eyed but determined not to play the pathetic victim.

At first, for a week or so, he'd denied her accusations. None of this was a surprise.

Finally, in the middle of a huge fight in the living room, several weeks later, he'd thrown up his hands in surrender and given up with his denials and excuses.

Furious, his face twisted in anger that wasn't the least bit tinged with guilt, Wyatt had finally admitted to having been "half in love" with another woman. Despite her suspicions, hearing it from his own lips had been like a mule kick to the stomach, and she'd realized then that deep down, she'd hoped she was wrong.

"Okay, okay, I was involved with someone at the office," he declared. "There! Are you happy now?"

"Of course I'm not happy," she'd said, tears hot in her eyes, her chin thrust forward. She would not break down, though, not shed one more tear of grief for a marriage that had probably been long dead. "What's her name?"

"It doesn't matter."

"Like hell!" It galled her that he would protect this other woman, this stranger who dared insert herself into another woman's marriage!

"She's already gone, okay? Couldn't take the guilt. It ruined her marriage, too, so she left the firm and took a job across the country." One of his fists balled in frustration, and Ava wondered if he would raise it to her, threaten her.

"Who is she, Wyatt?" Ava had pressed, unable to let it go.

"Why the fuck do you care?" He stormed out of the room and into the foyer, where he'd grabbed his coat and briefcase and walked out the door. With a window-rattling thud, it slammed behind him. Through the window, she watched as he marched down the hill to the boathouse, his coattails billowing behind him.

"Bastard," she'd muttered, then reminded herself that he was the father of her only child. Noah, it seemed, would be raised in a family that was splintered, something she'd hoped to avoid.

Wyatt had already moved out of their bedroom, and after this fight, she knew he would stay away. As it was, in the next few months, he'd spend more time off the island than on.

He'd sworn the affair was over. "It's history, okay? Forget it," he'd advised a month or so later.

Ava hadn't believed him, but she did contact a friend who worked in Wyatt's office, and Norm, a junior partner in the firm, confirmed the story. "I thought about telling you," Norm admitted over the phone, "but I was between a rock and a hard spot with you two. Truthfully, I didn't see what good it would do to let you know what was going on. It would've just hurt everyone."

"So you let him dupe me," Ava had charged.

"I did it to protect you, Ava. It wasn't about Beth, but hey, it doesn't matter now. It's over."

"Of course it matters!" she'd said, angry tears streaming from her eyes. She'd hung up and felt miserable all over again. Torn between rage and pain, she had to know more, to dig until every little bit of dirt was turned over, until all of her curiosity was satisfied and she could move forward again.

Norm had said the woman's first name. Beth. A slipup? Or purposely said? Didn't matter. It was a start. Obsessed, Ava hired a private detective who within three days had confirmed that a Bethany A. Wells had moved from Seattle to Boston less than two months earlier. A divorce with the woman's husband was pending. And in the past few weeks, according to the PI, Wyatt hadn't been in contact with her. The affair had ended when she'd moved.

It hadn't mattered; the ending of the affair was too little, too late in Ava's opinion. Infidelity was infidelity. She'd started divorce proceedings against Wyatt and then . . . and then . . . Oh, God, Noah had been taken from them, and everything else, including her husband's betrayal, had seemed unimportant as she had lost her grip with reality.

Now that same cold feeling of utter abandonment returned as she thought of Wyatt's latest fling. What was it her mother had always said? "Once a cheater, always a cheater."

Though he denied his current affair, she knew in her heart that he'd found someone else to be "half in love with." This time, though, she wasn't devastated. This time she was relieved. Evelyn McPherson could have him.

She dropped her phone into her purse and looked out the window again. Sure enough, she saw the running lights of a boat crossing the bay, growing closer. Her guts twisted as she took another sip of the latte. Somehow, she'd get through the meal, she told herself as she started to return the keys to her purse, then stopped, one of the keys catching her attention. It was different from the others, not a house key but a car key. Turning it over in her fingers, she saw that it was meant for a Mercedes.

Her father had always driven Fords, her mother a variety of domestic cars, her grandmother only Cadillacs. The only member of the family who'd ever owned a Mercedes had been Uncle Crispin. *This* was his set of keys, then. Huh. The Mercedes was long gone; he'd sold it just after losing his job at the hospital. . . .

Oh, crap!

The ring of keys had to be to all the locks at Sea Cliff! Her uncle had left them at the house? Along with a set for the car he'd sold ages ago?

A forgotten set, or more likely a lost set.

Ava straightened, feeling she was on to something now. And her memory was starting to return. Good. Through the window, she watched her husband dock the boat, and she stuffed the keys into a hidden pocket of her purse. Then she finished her latte and met Wyatt at the door of the coffee shop.

His hair was windblown, his face ruddy, his smile seemingly sincere as he brushed a kiss across her cheek. Somehow she managed to force a smile as he motioned to her two large shopping bags. "Wow. Looks like you cleaned out the store," he joked. "Let me carry these."

He reached for the sacks, and it was all she could do to let go and whisper, "Thanks," while silently praying that he not try to peer inside.

"What'd you get?"

"Lots of things—shoes, a purse, a couple of pairs of jeans . . ." God, it was difficult making small talk.

They walked through a cool mist to a fish house located on the waterfront, a couple of blocks from the marina.

Once they'd been seated in a corner booth, near a hissing gas fireplace, a waiter took their drink orders, then left menus and a basket of warm bread. A few other couples were scattered at nearby tables and booths, the conversation and clink of silverware audible.

Wyatt, ever attentive, again asked Ava about her day while she felt her damned bags nearly glowed in bright neon: *spy equipment inside!*

"It was nice to get out of the house," she said once they'd ordered. That much wasn't a lie. "The weather was great, so we didn't get wet dashing from store to store."

"Downtown?"

"Mmm." She nodded, reaching for her water glass just so she didn't have to look into his eyes as she repeated the story she'd created earlier in the day. "Tanya's great at bargain hunting, so she knew just where to go. And, oh, they were having a major sale at Nordstrom. Tanya was in heaven."

"How is Tanya, by the way?" The waiter brought Wyatt a glass of wine and Ava the club soda she'd ordered to keep up the pretense that she was still taking her prescribed meds and thus avoiding alcohol.

"Crazy as ever." To hide her case of nerves, Ava unwrapped the bread and buttered a slice. "She talked nonstop about her kids and remodeling the shop, which she hopes to do next year.

I got the blow-by-blow of dance recitals and soccer matches for Bella and Brent—cute kids, of course."

Somehow she ate the slice of bread and nattered on about nothing and finally asked, "What about you?" just as the waiter returned with their meals, steak and prawns for Wyatt and a salmon pasta salad that Ava had ordered and couldn't imagine forcing down.

"I've been away from the house most of the day," he said. "I'll be out early tomorrow. Into the office and then depositions for the next couple of days."

"Anything interesting?" She wanted to keep the conversation focused on him.

"Nothing I can talk about," he said between bites of steak, and their small talk dwindled. Ava picked at her salad, forcing down bites as Wyatt dug in with the same gusto he'd had for as long as she'd known him. The silence stretched thin as they ate. The couple at the next table finished and left, and eventually, he'd had his fill and pushed his plate aside. "I think we should talk."

"About?" Every one of her muscles grew taut. Her heart began to drum. Where was this going? Was he planning to bring up her fights with Jewel-Anne again? Or something even worse?

"Us."

Her heart was really pounding now. "What about us?"

"There is none. We aren't us any longer." He looked down at his hands before meeting her eyes. "You feel it, too, Ava. I know you do."

She didn't respond. Didn't know how to handle this kind of honesty from him.

"We're barely civil to each other. Neither one of us trusts the other. We don't make time for the other person." His face tightened with frustration. "Oh, hell, I'm as much to blame as you are."

"So . . . what're you saying?" she asked. "You want to start over? Split up?"

"I want you to get well, Ava. I know you haven't been taking your medication, and now you're trying to get rid of Dr. McPherson under some ridiculous pretense that she and I are involved."

Oh, God, she wasn't ready for this. Not when she was about to finally set her own plan in motion.

"You want to have this discussion now? Here?"

"I just want to clear the air. First of all, I'm not having a damned affair with your psychologist or anyone else! That's all in your mind. And you keep coming up with wild scenarios in which you see Noah when you and I both know he's gone. Forever."

She gasped. "I thought you said we'd find him. . . ."

He leaned closer over the table and lowered his voice. "I just want you to get better and I don't think you can unless you go back to St. Brendan's."

"*What?*" He wanted to commit her again?

"Look, if you don't want to go there, we'll find another hospital in Seattle or San Francisco or, oh, hell, I don't care where!" He stared at her as if he'd never seen her before. "You're sick, Ava. You need help."

So there it was. His cards, all out on the table. "Why do you want me to leave so much?"

"I just told you."

"You might not believe this, Wyatt, but I am getting better. I'm starting to remember. Everything. Bit by bit. And it's not because of medications that make me feel like a zombie or a shrink who thinks she's in love with you."

"I said I'm not—"

"Stop! Just stop, okay?" she insisted, her temper snapping. "I said I'm starting to remember!" She watched as his eyes narrowed a bit. She knew she should control her tongue, but she couldn't. Not now. Not when she was starting to feel like her old self again. "One of the things that I recall a little too vividly is that this affair isn't your first, Wyatt."

He remained calm. Didn't argue. But the tic near one eye gave his emotions away.

"I thought the reason I'd started divorce proceedings before was because I couldn't get my life on track after Noah disappeared, but it was more, wasn't it? You were having an affair with someone . . . someone in your office. Just before we lost our son and then everything went to hell."

"That was over a long time ago. I came clean about being involved with a woman in the office."

"Beth Wells. I remember." If he was surprised, he hid it admirably. "So I recognize the signs. It's happening again, Wyatt. You're right. We've lost that emotional connection we once had, but it's been gone a long, long time."

"Have you ever, for one minute, considered that we've drifted apart because of you? Your obsession about Noah pulled you away from me, not the other way around."

"Not true."

His jaw clenched hard, the tic working double time. "The only way you're ever going to get well is if you go back to a hospital. I fought the idea. Hoped that you could, with a doctor's help, come back to me. But that's not happening. I made a mistake by letting you come home, and as your guardian, I'm going to see that you go somewhere and get the treatment you need. I've already talked to Dr. McPherson about it, and she agrees that you need more help than she can give."

Ava was on her feet, knocking a butter knife to the floor, toppling the rest of her drink. "My guardian? Seriously. I don't need you or anyone else to decide my fate," she gritted out. "You can't send me anywhere, Wyatt. I'll petition the court. I'll . . . I'll prove that I'm sane, that I can take care of myself!"

"Can you? What if Dern hadn't fished you out of the bay?

What if he hadn't shown up when you were riding on the ridge?"

"Who told you that?" she demanded.

"Who do you think I asked to keep an eye on you?"

"*What?*" A new sense of betrayal burned through her. She couldn't believe it. She'd started to trust Dern, to think of him as one of the few people at the house who was her ally! He was working with Wyatt? "You hired Austin Dern to spy on me?"

He glanced up at her as he fished in his pants for his wallet. "That surprises you?" An amused smile played upon his lips, and he looked suddenly cruel as he recognized how shattered she was. "Oh, no, it's more than that, isn't it?" he tossed out, his voice filled with sarcasm. "You have the nerve to play the victim, to accuse me of screwing around on you when you think you're in love with a man you barely know—"

"I'm not—"

"Oh, come on. It's obvious to everyone."

Don't believe him. It was just a lucky guess.

But true?

Wyatt must've read the emotion on her face. "So tell me, Ava, how sane is that? Fantasizing about the ranch hand? Coupled with everything else you've done lately, you've got some twisted, convoluted paranoia that everyone you've known for years is out to get you, but you can fall in love and trust a stranger?" His face was bland, the tic disappearing as the enormity of what he was saying sunk in. He'd planned this all along. Every last little detail, even hiring Austin Dern.

"You bastard." She scooped up her bags and started out of the restaurant.

"Wait! Ava!" He was fumbling with his credit cards while trying to catch the waiter's attention.

Shouldering open the glass doors, she tried to grab hold of the strings of her rapidly fraying grip on reality as the brittle-cold night slapped her in the face. The thought that Wyatt planned to have her committed was devastating, but she should have expected it. Damn it all to hell! She'd never find Noah if she was locked away, forced on medication, under complete observation. Even if she convinced the psychiatrists on staff that she was sane, it would take weeks . . . oh, God, oh, God, oh, God.

Don't let it happen! Pull yourself together! You can do this, Ava. You have to. Your son needs you! Half running along the sidewalk, panic chasing her down, she headed for the marina.

She nearly ran into a teenager skateboarding in the opposite direction. In a thick jacket and watch cap, he was texting and smoking. "Hey! Watch it! Shit!" His cigarette fell from his lips, and adeptly he picked it up. He cruised by, one shoulder connecting with hers.

"Oh!" Her feet slid on the slick sidewalk and she fell. *Bam!* Her left knee cracked hard on the concrete.

Pain jarred up her leg and she lost her grip on one of the sacks. It skidded toward the street.

The teenager rounded a corner, didn't even look over his shoulder.

"Ava!" Wyatt's voice.

She wasn't going to listen to him a second longer. Their sham of a marriage was over, and they both knew it. Struggling to get upright, she grabbed hold of a parking meter and pulled herself to her feet, then yanked up her bag. The handle snapped off and the sack with all its contents hit the wet ground hard.

Damn. The camera was inside. All of this plotting, the effort, the lies, and now . . .

Angry at herself, she picked up the bag and held it tight to her body, the other sack swinging from her fingers as she started walking again.

"Ava! Wait up!" Wyatt yelled from somewhere behind her. She ignored him. This day had turned into a disaster of epic proportions. "Hey," he said as he caught up with her at the marina. "I'm sorry."

"Get away from me."

"I shouldn't have gotten so angry." He reached for the crook of her elbow, but she yanked her arm away, juggling the broken bag and feeling a dull ache in the knee that had hit the sidewalk.

"I said I'm sorry," he repeated, sounding injured.

"I heard you."

"I'm trying to apologize here!"

When he touched her again, she whirled on him and said slowly, in very distinct words, "I want a divorce. Not someday. Not in the future. Now. I'm calling a lawyer in the morning." Fury consumed her. "Don't bother coming back to the island."

"Ava . . ."

His patronizing tone was the last straw. She strode past him toward the bay where the black expanse of water stretched into the frigid night. Murky and roiling, the waters were as uncertain and cold as her own future. She shuddered involuntarily because she sensed, just beneath the dark surface, the truth was rising, fangs sharpened, jaws open.

But at least now she knew where she stood with her husband.

Chapter 34

Boot heels sinking in the soggy yard, Dern walked around the perimeter of the behemoth of a house. The dog was with him, sniffing tree trunks and lifting his leg but never wandering off far.

During the day, Neptune's Gate was inviting, its architecture reminiscent of an earlier era of sailing ships and horses and the dawn of electricity and indoor plumbing. But at night, it loomed dark and foreboding, like one of those sinister-appearing castles in an old vampire movie. No amount of outdoor lighting could soften the sharp angles and ominous appearance of the place.

He was certain that the window he'd viewed from Lester Reece's room at Sea Cliff was part of Jewel-Anne's suite. Unsure of the configuration of her rooms, he figured he'd find a way inside and take note of her bedroom view. As for the widow's walk and third-story windows tucked under the eaves, he'd create some maintenance excuse to work his way upstairs so that he could check the sight line to Sea Cliff.

It's nothing, he told himself again, and once more, as he walked toward the gardening shed, he couldn't convince himself.

"You're grasping at straws," he told himself, wondering if he was making some kind of connection that just didn't exist. Lester Reece was in the wind, had been for years, and yet Dern was determined to overturn every slimy rock on this island to be certain.

Walking around the corner to the front of the mansion, he glanced up at one of the windows to Ava's bedroom. She was gone. Out for the day, so his bodyguard duties were over until she returned.

Originally, Ava's husband had hired Dern as a ranch hand with maintenance duties, and then, once he'd agreed, there had been Wyatt's request to "keep an eye on" Garrison's wife. Wyatt had mentioned he was concerned for her safety and while he wanted to let her have a little freedom, he needed another set of eyes to make certain she didn't "hurt herself."

Dern, needing a job on the island, had instantly agreed, and then, before he'd even met the woman, she'd taken a flying leap into the bay. No wonder the husband was concerned. Dern had taken his duty seriously and had believed Ava Church Garrison was a bona fide nut job, willing to do anything, even hurt herself, in her obsessive need to find her kid. With his duties on the estate expanded to a kind of quasi-bodyguard, he'd had free rein to continue on his own personal quest: finding Lester Reece.

The trouble was that he'd begun to believe that the only person who wasn't losing all their marbles on this island was Ava. Everyone else—from that computer nerd with the bad attitude who lived in the basement, Jacob, to the do-nothing cousin Ian, who seemed to just hang around—didn't seem to be completely together. Even Trent had blown onto the island and seemed to have no immediate plans to leave. Didn't anyone have a job?

And the nutcases just kept on coming. Jewel-Anne with her dolls and Elvis obsession had her own set of issues, and everyone on the staff was a few steps away from normal. Virginia was an opinionated bitch, related to the useless sheriff somehow; Khloe and her husband, Simon, the cryptic ghost of a gardener, were on again, off again and neither one gave him the time of day; Graciela, he suspected, had a secret life, though he hadn't checked yet; and then there was Demetria, the sullen nurse who kept to herself when she wasn't taking care of her charge. Except for Graciela, they, like Dern, all lived at the estate. Not exactly a happy lot, he decided.

So finish your business and get the hell out. Why are you hanging around, still fantasizing about a woman who everyone else thinks is a toehold away from a complete and utter mental breakdown?

Because he didn't believe it.

With his knowledge of her past through records and articles on the Internet, and glimpses past the frail shell-shocked person she'd become to the hard-edged woman lurking beneath the surface, he thought there was a chance Ava would come around.

She's still married.

And that was why he had to wrap this up fast. He had a phone call to make, a report to give, so he turned his collar to the damp night, the dog at his heels, and started for his apartment.

Wyatt had taken off a few hours ago to retrieve his wife.

Soon the happy couple would return, Dern thought sarcastically, and told himself he had no claim to that woman. No claim whatsoever.

Now, if he could just convince himself it were true.

Wyatt caught up with Ava at the dock.

"Hey . . . look . . . I'm sorry," he said, and this time when he touched her shoulder, she held her ground and didn't draw away.

"You don't get to do that," she whispered. "Attack hard, then apologize like everything's okay."

"I just don't know what to do," he said, and for the first time that night, she actually believed him. "You're slipping away, not trusting me, going to all lengths to avoid me and even fantasizing about another man. You do crazy things and then fire your therapist after accusing her of having an affair with me."

"She quit."

He turned her shoulders so that she had to face him, to look into his eyes, illuminated only by the streetlamps and the bulbs strung over the marina. "Don't you love me anymore?"

"I don't *know* you anymore."

Deep brackets appeared at the corners of his mouth. "I could say the same. I would do anything to see you get better," he said, and something inside her wanted to break, to still believe in him even though she knew better.

"I hired Dern as a ranch hand, yeah," Wyatt admitted, "but I asked him to look out for you, that's all."

She doubted that.

"And you're right. I do like Evelyn McPherson. A lot. I think she's done wonders for you. But that's as far as it goes." The wind blowing in off the sea ruffled his hair and chilled Ava to the bone. "And I did have an affair a long time ago, but it's over and I thought, I mean, I hoped, we were past that." He dropped his hands. "I just want my wife back. Is that too much to ask?"

"It's not enough," she said carefully. "You need to want your son back, too."

His head snapped up. "That goes without saying, Ava." Then a spark of accusation in his eyes again and his spine stiffened slightly.

She wasn't going to back down.

"Come on, let's go home. Let me take those." He reached for the bags.

"I can handle them," she said tautly, then, unwilling to have him even speculate for an instant that she had something to hide, she reluctantly handed him the larger, plastic sack and kept the one with the broken handle. Hugging that bag close to her chest, she said, "Fine. Let's go."

Heart in her throat, she continued onto the dock and even allowed him to help her into the boat. It rocked a little, and the sharp pain in her knee reminded her of her fall. Looking across the water, she wondered nervously how easy would it be for there to be an accident that took her life?

He could say she jumped into the water. His wife was just crazy enough to do something so bizarre and risky; she'd proved that often enough before. Or, he could say it was an accident. They'd hit choppy water and she'd fallen overboard, never to be seen again. Ava, like her brother, Kelvin, would die in the frigid salt water, the result of a tragic chance event. Her mind raced with scenarios in which she never made it to Neptune's Gate.

When Wyatt stepped into the boat after her, she nearly bolted. Being alone with him on the boat was insane!

Don't make him mad. Just play it cool . . .

Her mind flashed back to the night Kelvin died, to the pain and the freezing waters that surrounded her, the fear that had enveloped her when she thought she might drown.

Panic seized her now.

Get out. Get out!

Wyatt set the unbroken bag onto one of the boat's seats and it slid to the deck, its contents spilling onto the oiled teak. She jumped, ready to hide everything quickly, to force the contents into the sack, but he saw his mistake and reached forward.

"What's this?" he asked, and her heart froze. She was certain he'd found the spy equipment and now had more evidence of her paranoia. "A new purse?"

She tried not to sound nervous. "I told you." *Play nice, play nice! Don't let him get more suspicious than he already is.*

"It's big."

"Thought it might hold my laptop." She held her breath as he looked it over, studying the bag.

Don't peek inside. For God's sake, Wyatt, don't peer into the zippered area and find the camera and recorder.

"It might," he said, dropping the purse into its shopping bag and looking up at her. "So . . . we're good now?"

Not even close. But she had to play this right. "No," she said cautiously, "we're not good, but maybe better." She cast him a glance and feigned worry. "Maybe getting everything out, is . . . a step in the right direction."

"So you're not throwing me out?"

She forced a smile that felt like a grimace. "Undecided."

"At least not tonight?" He gave her a long look.

She nodded jerkily and tried not to feel sick inside. She was a hypocrite, pure and simple. *But you have to pretend, to play the part of the wife wanting to repair this broken marriage so that you can find the truth, prove that you're not insane. . . .*

"Fair enough. Oh, and, Ava?" he asked, his voice a little sharper.

Here it comes! He did *see the spy equipment! Oh, sweet Jesus, you're doomed!* "Yes?"

"Put this on." He grabbed a life vest from under one of the seats and handed the flotation device to her. "You know what they say: You can never be too careful."

"So we've got ourselves a witness who's seen Lester Reece," Lyons said as she and Snyder walked toward the station house. They'd had a quick dinner and were on their way back to the office.

"I don't call Wolfgang Brandt a credible witness."

"If you ask me, Brandt's just one rung lower on the whopper-teller ladder than some of the others who have 'seen'—and I use the term loosely—Reece over the years." Wolfgang Brandt was around thirty-five and had been in and out of trouble with the police for years. "Deputies talked to Brandt, then went out to the old hunting lodge where he'd claimed he'd seen Reece. No one was there. No evidence of anyone but hunters and maybe some teenagers who'd broken in and had a few beers a while back. Big surprise. You're new here. You'll get used to the Reece sightings soon enough. Besides, what does Lester Reece have to do with our case?"

"Why do you have to be so damned negative?"

She was unwrapping a scarf before going to work on the buttons of her jacket as they walked through the reception area. It took a code to get through these days, and a camera was filming their every move. He wondered about that. With all the phone cams and computer cameras and all, why hadn't anyone seen or photographed anything unusual at Cheryl Reynolds's home? The trouble was, her place of business was in a part of Anchorville that was zoned residential; the store cams and traffic cams were located a few blocks closer to the waterfront and the heart of town.

"Brandt's not the only one who saw him. I heard a couple of the deputies talking. One of them—Gorski, I think—plays poker with a group of guys, one of them being Butch Johansen, who claimed, after a few beers, that he ferried a guy who looked a helluva lot like Reece out to Church Island recently."

"Lots of stories about guys who look like Reece, but they never pan out. Case in point the hunting lodge. Besides, Reece is ancient history."

"Is he? Doesn't seem like the sheriff thinks so."

Inside his cubicle, Snyder removed his jacket and sidearm while Lyons motioned toward the restrooms in the back of the building; then, boots clicking, she headed off.

The Reynolds case was getting to him. The only homicide in years and just not enough evidence to put it together. Taking a seat at his desk, he checked his e-mail and found a note with an attachment from the lab. A couple of clicks of his mouse and he was looking at an analysis report of the hair discovered in Cheryl Reynolds's laundry room.

By the time Lyons returned, with a cup of coffee for him and some decaf herbal tea that smelled like old lady's perfume, he'd printed out the report and handed it to her. "Thanks," he said, taking his cup. "Looks like the mystery of the black hair is solved."

"Synthetic?" she asked, her eyebrows drawing together as she stood near the desk, leaning a hip against it and reading the report. "Someone was wearing a wig? The killer?"

"Maybe. Maybe not." He clicked to a file with pictures taken of the crime scene. "Look here, on the bookcase of her office." He pointed at the screen. Lyons bent down for a better peek, and he tried not to notice that her breasts nearly brushed the desktop. Again he clicked his mouse, enlarging the photograph on the shelf in question—it was of Cheryl, dressed as a cat, with all of her cats close by. Along with a leopard-print costume, fake tail, ears, painted-on nose and whiskers, she was wearing a long black wig.

"Anyone find the wig on the premises?" Lyons asked, sipping her tea while her gaze stayed fastened to the screen.

"Let's see . . ." More clicks and he found a list of the contents of the area around the crime scene. "Nope, don't see it."

"Halloween was just a few weeks ago."

"Only if the picture was from this year. It could have been taken a decade ago."

She shook her head. "The cats in the picture? All the same as she has now. A couple of them are young, recent additions if the neighbor is right, so it's from this year."

"So where the hell is the wig?"

Lyons smiled and it was one of those slow, I've-got-a-secret smiles he found attractive. "With the killer." She was dunking her tea bag as she nodded, happy with herself.

"Or in the bay."

"With Lester Reece?" As she squeezed the tea bag between her fingers and tossed it into the trash, she added, "There could be a chance that when his remains finally float to the surface, his skeleton will be dressed in drag, like a sexy, if emaciated, kitty cat."

"Huh," he grunted. The truth was that the black hair found at the scene was damned near a dead end. Trouble was, it was the only clue they had.

Bam!

The boat slammed hard against the wake of a speedboat flying in the opposite direction.

"Shit!" Wyatt stood at the helm, steering into the darkness, the few lights of Monroe visible ahead. "Idiot! I should report that guy!"

Ava barely heard, nor was she aware of the icy wind that blew against her cheeks and tangled her hair. Even her shopping bags were forgotten as the boat shimmied a little and she was thrown back in time to another trip across the water, to the late afternoon when Kelvin had died. This was a memory she didn't want to review again, but she seemed destined to replay it over and over.

Her flesh actually pimpled at the thought of the approaching twilight and the raw fear of those moments. In her mind's eye, she saw the tragedy unfold all over again.

The wind had been fierce, the waves wild at the sudden squall. Ava remembered the sheer terror of the outing, how she'd prayed they'd make it safely back to shore, how her fears had centered on the baby . . .

Pregnant, Ava was almost at term and . . . No. She frowned. That wasn't right. Noah had come early and . . .

Something pricked at the edges of her brain, something cruel and sharp, the edge of a lie. Her gut twisted almost painfully as she tried to recall what it was, but like a moray eel lying deep among the rocks of the ocean, it poked its head out only to retract again, teasing but not coming clear.

"What is it?" she asked, thinking so hard a headache formed. It was something to do with the baby, the pregnancy, and . . . and . . . an idea formed and she discarded it quickly. No, that couldn't be right.

And yet.

She thought back to the first trimester. No morning sickness.

And the second. When had she learned she was carrying a boy? Why couldn't she remember visiting the gynecologist, having the ultrasound, seeing Noah as he grew inside her . . . ?

"Oh God." A cold certainty began to envelope her and she started hyperventilating.

Why didn't she remember much about the hospital and his birth? Why were there no pictures of the delivery?

Because it was traumatic. Taken after the wreck. Kelvin had already been pronounced dead, the doctors were working on Jewel-Anne, so your impending labor was cause for concern. No time for cameras or flowers or balloons or . . . anything.

She swallowed hard and her lungs could hardly take a breath as the wind screamed past, seeming to mock her and her inability to face the truth that now came screaming back at her. Images of that night flashed like a harsh kaleidoscope behind her eyes. Bits and pieces, shattered into odd shapes—the wreckage, the rescue, the hospital, the news of Kelvin's death, the fear that Jewel-Anne might not make it. And the baby. In the hospital, he'd been screaming and squalling, a red little bundle without much hair, his little fists raised . . .

"He needs to be fed," she'd said, her voice echoing through her mind. "Please . . . he needs to be fed."

"We'll take care of him," the nurse had said, and her heart had ached as they took him from her.

Why? Did they take him away to clean him off?

To measure and weigh him?
To check his vital signs . . .

More images surfaced and they fought with the truth as she knew it.

Wyatt slowed the engine and, using the remote, raised the seaward door of the boathouse. An interior light switched on, and Ava, struck to her very soul, counted her heartbeats. Wyatt docked the boat, tied it up, and helped her onto the skirt around the boat slip. *No!* she thought wildly. *No, no, no!* She had to be wrong!

"I'll get these for you," he offered as if from somewhere far away, and she didn't launch the tiniest of protests as he carried the shopping bags up the walkway and into the house.

She was too stunned with her revelation, lost in her own world, trying desperately to discount what she was remembering as she followed him up the stairs.

"Are you okay?" he asked as they reached her room. He deposited her shopping bags onto the floor near the closet. "You've gotten quiet."

"J-just tired," she lied.

His eyebrows beetled in concern. "You look like you've seen a ghost."

"It's been a long day. That's all." Hearing how short she sounded, she added, "I just need some downtime."

"Okay." This time he didn't bother pressing a kiss to her cheek.

As he closed the door, she kicked off her boots as quickly as possible, then tore off her clothes, tossing her jacket, long sweater, and leggings into a pile on her bed. Next her bra and panties before she flew into the bathroom to stand in front of the full-length mirror, her body completely naked, her soul now stripped bare. Her skin was in good shape, and though she was thin, her muscles were smooth and strong, a few ribs more pronounced than they should be. Her breasts were still firm and high, the nipples dark, and her hips were as slim and tight as they had been when she'd run in college.

So where were the stretch marks on her breasts or stomach? She turned and looked over her shoulder, checking the tightness of her buttocks.

Nothing in her build suggested "mother." But she could be just one of those lucky women who hadn't gained a lot of weight in pregnancy and whose skin had enough elasticity to avoid stretch marks. She didn't remember nursing, so her breasts could have maintained their shape.

Or not.

The body in the mirror's reflection did not look like the body of a woman who had carried a baby to term.

With a sick feeling, she stormed into her bedroom, threw on an old pair of pajamas, and hurried downstairs to the den where Wyatt, still in his business suit, had already settled behind the desk.

"I thought you were tired," he said, looking up from his computer screen.

"I was. Am. But . . . oh . . ." There was no easy way around this. "Where are the pictures of my pregnancy?" she demanded, distantly hearing the sound of the elevator clunking as it stopped.

"What?" He actually looked surprised. "The pictures?"

"I want to see them."

"Why now?" he asked as the hum of Jewel-Anne's wheelchair grew louder.

"I need to see what I looked like," Ava said, her heart nearly breaking, the truth causing her damned voice to crack. "I need to prove to myself that I really was pregnant."

Chapter 35

Wyatt jumped up and started around the desk. "Of course you were pregnant!"

"Then show me," Ava said. "Prove it!"

"Oh, for the love of God—"

"I'm not kidding, Wyatt. They should be here on the computer, shots that were never printed and framed. We had a digital camera then. There have to be dozens of pictures that were uploaded."

"I don't think you wanted to be photographed much. Because of all the miscarriages, you were kind of superstitious about it."

"But there has to be something," she insisted. "During the holidays or at a family barbecue, a group shot where I'm trying to either hide or display my baby bump."

"I don't think so."

"Let me see." Rounding the desk, she stubbed her toe, swore under her breath, and swung the computer monitor toward her as she worked the keyboard. "Most of our pictures are in here, except for those we printed out, right?" She looked up at the bookcase where family portraits were posted, and sure enough, there she was with Kelvin, a few weeks before the accident. The picture was taken at the marina, sailboat masts rising above them, and only showed them from the chest up. They were laughing and she, at least facially, didn't have an ounce of extra fat on her.

"Wait a second," Wyatt said just as Jewel-Anne rolled into the room.

"Let her look," Jewel-Anne said, and there was something in her tone that was a warning.

"Okay. Four years ago . . . ," Ava murmured. Wyatt had reluctantly given up his chair and she sat down, taking over the keyboard, pulling up the family picture files. She sifted through dozens of shots of various family members, and in any picture that showed her, her back was turned or it was a head shot. There were none that showed her pregnancy.

Wyatt asked, "Why are you obsessing about this now?"

Ava didn't answer, just kept looking. Her fingers flew over the keys, and she scrolled through file after file, finding nothing until . . .

Noah!

All at once, pictures of her son dominated the files. Hundreds of shots documenting him returning from the hospital, sitting up for the first time, then crawling and walking. There were videos as well; she'd watched them hundreds of times in the past two years, keeping his image alive. Her insides turned to jelly. Something here was wrong . . . very wrong. But Noah was real. The pictures and videos proved what her memory insisted. She sank deeper into the chair.

"I don't think I . . ." She swallowed hard, then forged on. "Did we adopt Noah?" Her brain was thundering. "Is that what happened?"

He didn't answer. Looked away. And that was an answer in itself.

The silence in the room stretched to the breaking point. She heard the pounding of her own heartbeat in her ears and wished she could take the words back. Dear God, was it true? Was she not Noah's mother?

"Tell her," Jewel-Anne urged, and Ava whipped around, her gaze zeroing in on her cousin. There was just the hint of malice in her eyes.

Ava's world seemed to collapse. "*You* knew?" she charged. Then to Wyatt, "Tell me what?" Bracing herself on the desk, she tried to keep the pounding in her head at bay. Now, after wanting to know the truth for so damned long, she was afraid of it. Her gaze strayed to the computer where hundreds of pictures of Noah were saved. *Her* baby. *Her* son.

Jewel-Anne couldn't stand it. "Of course you're not his mother!"

"Shut up!" Wyatt snarled.

Rather than pin Jewel-Anne with her gaze, Ava turned accusing eyes on her husband. "What is this, Wyatt?"

He seemed to struggle with some inner battle, then gave it up. "You *are* Noah's mother, of course you are. But . . ." His jaw worked. "You didn't give birth to him. It was a private adoption."

Ava didn't move. Couldn't breathe. Her heart was drumming, denial burning through her veins, though she sensed she was finally hearing the truth, or at least part of it. "You were five or six months along and had surprisingly barely begun to show. Then you lost the baby.."

Her heart cracked . . . pain swept through her.

"It wasn't the first miscarriage, of course, but this one, a boy, was the closest to term," he said quietly, his eyes dark. "You took it so hard. You just lost reality. Adoption seemed like the right choice. I knew of a pregnant teenager. She was looking for a private adoption through our firm," he said quietly. "The timing was perfect. She gave birth right after the boating accident. You were still recovering and we decided not to tell anyone that the baby was adopted."

"And no one questioned it?" Ava was shaking her head. Though bits and pieces of his story struck a chord, the pieces were disjointed, not connecting in her brain, like flotsam and jetsam strung out in dark, shadowy water. "The staff . . ."

"Were all paid well."

"And no one broke their silence?" No, that couldn't be. Pointing a finger at Jewel-Anne, Ava said in disbelief, "*She* knew and didn't tell anyone?"

"I can keep a secret if I have to," Jewel-Anne shot back, tossing her head primly.

"Why would you *have* to?"

"Because it was the best for everyone. Especially *you*," Jewel-Anne snapped. Absently she stroked the head of her doll, and Ava couldn't help but remember the effigy she'd dug up in its tiny little casket. Jewel-Anne had to have been behind that somehow.

"I don't think you'd do anything for my benefit," she said slowly.

"But then you don't really know me at all, do you?" her cousin tossed out, a smirk twisting the corners of her mouth again.

Wyatt said, "No one has said anything. Yes, Jewel-Anne knew, and so did Khloe and her mother. Virginia's loyal and Khloe is one of your best friends. She and Simon were split at the time. I doubt that he even knows. As for Demetria, she was hired later, after Jewel-Anne came back to the island. Graciela wasn't on staff at the time, though she had been earlier, and the ranch hand who was working then knew how to keep his mouth shut."

"But everyone else . . . ," Ava whispered.

"None of the rest of the family knows. Not even Ian. They weren't here then and have never questioned that Noah was our son, our own flesh and blood."

"I don't believe this," Ava whispered, though part of it rang true. She sensed, deep in her heart, that Noah hadn't been born from her body, that there was another woman who had given him life . . . a faceless woman who had given up her son. "You shouldn't have lied to me," she told her husband in a shaking voice.

"Ava, you were so messed up." Wyatt walked to the bookshelf, looked at a picture of the three of them taken when Noah was barely one. The happy little family—all of it a damned lie.

He touched the picture frame, then said, "You made yourself believe that Noah was our flesh and blood, and any other suggestion would throw you into a frenzy, a panic attack. I talked to you in the hospital, but at the mere mention of the word *adoption*, you freaked out."

She remembered so little of her stay at St. Brendan's. "So the staff there, at the hospital—they know?" There had to be some way to check out this story.

"Just Dr. McPherson and that's patient–doctor privilege."

"Who is the mother?"

"It doesn't matter."

"Of course it does!" she said, jumping up from the desk chair. "She's the one! Don't you see? The birth mother, she's the one who stole our baby!"

"Don't be irrational!"

"Irrational? I just discovered the baby I thought I'd borne was adopted and you're calling me irrational?" Her mind was scrambled, images of the past burning through it, each and every one at odds with the truth. "What about the baby's father? I mean, the biological father?"

"Out of the picture."

She was shaking her head, trying desperately to sort every-thing out. "He signed off his parental rights?"

"Never even knew he had a kid."

"Then he could be behind it!" Frantic, Ava looked from Wyatt to Jewel-Anne. Her cousin's smirk had fallen away. Now she appeared as shell-shocked as Ava. "Have you tried to track these people down? Do the police know?" she demanded. "We should call Snyder right now!" She was already reaching for the house phone on the desk, but Wyatt grabbed her wrist.

"Don't, Ava," he warned.

"Why not?"

"It won't do any good."

The receiver still grasped in her hand, she felt a sudden pre-monition. "You know what happened to our son," she charged, breathing hard, staring Wyatt down. His face was only inches from hers, his features hard and set, the darkness in his soul re-flected in his eyes.

"The birth mother and father of our son are dead."

She shrank away from him. "Dead?" This was too much to take in all at once. "How?"

"Motorcycle accident."

"Both of them? Together? And he didn't know about the baby?"

"They'd split up for a while." He released her hand, and she put the phone back in its cradle. "Then got back together. I don't know if she ever told him about Noah; if so, nothing came of it before they were killed, riding the bike down the Oregon coast. As I understand it, he was driving and tried to pass one of those motor homes hauling a car and didn't see the oncoming car. He skidded out trying to avoid it."

She felt sick to her stomach. "Oh my God."

Don't take this at face value. It could all be a convenient lie! He's lied to you for years.

Jewel-Anne was silent. She seemed subdued, maybe non-plussed, and the joy she'd gotten from taunting Ava had totally seeped away as one hand idly touched the shiny dark hair of her doll.

"What are their names?" Ava asked.

"Ava, don't do this. Let it go," Wyatt said.

"I want the names of my child's birth mother and father," she insisted, anger flaring that he'd kept this secret so long. "Who were they? Who were they, Wyatt? Who were the birth parents of *our* son?"

He glared at her for a full five seconds and time seemed to stretch forever. Only after the clock in the hallway chimed the half hour did he say, "Tracey. Tracey Johnson and Charles Yates."

Jewel-Anne drew a breath. Obviously this was new information to her as well.

Something inside of Ava cracked. Hearing the names made the faceless people who had created her son so much more real. "Clients of yours?"

"An associate's."

"You should have told me, Wyatt." She skirted around him and headed out the door, squeezing past Jewel-Anne and her wheelchair. "You should have had enough faith in me to tell me the truth about our son!"

"Ava!" he yelled.

She ran. Instead of footsteps following her, she heard a frustrated, "Son of a bitch," that chased her as she flew up the stairs, her dull head swarming with questions, her heart twisting with the pain of her new discoveries. It was as if she lived in a House of Horrors where nothing was what it seemed.

Everything Wyatt had told her about Noah and the fact that he was adopted swirled around in her head. Tracey Johnson? Charles Yates? Had she ever heard the names before?

Wait, Ava. Don't fall for this! Wyatt lies!!

In her room, she yanked her computer from its case, and even though her husband probably had some tracking device attached to it so he could see every Web site she visited, she Googled the names he'd given her along with the words *motorcycle accident* and *Oregon*.

It took some sifting, as she wasn't an expert surfing the Internet, at least not as quick as she'd once been, but eventually she found a few hits. Sure enough, there had been a horrendous motorcycle accident three years earlier, about the time Noah had been one. Both Charles Yates, twenty-six, and his twenty-one-year-old fiancée, Tracey Johnson, had died as the result of their severe injuries.

"No," she whispered, but she searched for their obituaries and finally found them. The obits listed their hometown, where they'd graduated from high school, that Tracey was a student at a community college and hoped to become a nurse. Yates worked for a small trucking company.

Real people.

With next of kin who were listed as well.

Her hands were shaking over the keys. She had to see these people. She had to try and discern any resemblance to her son.

It took a while, but she was able to locate pictures of the victims. Staring at the flat images, she wondered if Noah had Tracey's pointed chin or Charles's curly hair. Possible? Yes. Proof? No.

She needed more than Wyatt's word and a confirming accident report and obit to trust that she had truly found her son's birth parents.

No, no, no! her mind screamed, and yet there was truth in Wyatt's confession. Should she believe that he was only protecting her, that he'd worried the truth would send her spiraling back into a complete mental breakdown?

She shook her head.

In the obituary, Tracey's parents, Zed and Maria Johnson, were listed as living in Bellevue, a city east of Seattle. She started looking for the proverbial needle in a haystack. *You can do this,* she told herself, though the task was daunting.

Using several search engines on the Internet and the phone book listings, again via her computer, she narrowed things down to Z Johnsons in the greater Bellevue/Seattle area. Of course, the phone number could be unlisted, the parents split up, or they could have moved. Half a dozen reasons to abandon her search flew through her brain and she dismissed them all.

"Nothing ventured, nothing gained," she said aloud just as she heard a knock on her door. "Yes?" she said, expecting Wyatt to poke his head into the room.

Instead of her husband's voice, Ava heard Khloe's. "Hey, Ava, are you okay?"

She sounded worried, but Ava wasn't even sure of her friendship any longer. Theirs had been a rocky relationship, ever since Kelvin's death. After closing her laptop, Ava climbed off her bed and tucked the shopping bags onto the highest shelf of her closet. There was just no reason to invite questions, not even from Khloe.

Cracking the door, she said, "I'm fine."

"Jewel-Anne told me what happened. I walked into the kitchen to grab my reading glasses and there she was, looking like she'd seen a ghost. I made the mistake of asking her what was wrong." Khloe, glasses still curled in her fist, hesitated, then added, "Look, Ava, I don't know what to say. Did I know about Noah being adopted? Yes. Did I want to say something to you once you'd forgotten? You bet. But . . . you were so . . . volatile. So distrusting. So . . . well, out of it. I was scared that you might relapse even further."

"So you were never going to say anything?"

"We wanted you to know. It was just a matter of when." She sighed and glanced down the hall. "Mom and I discussed it often enough, but we needed you to be able to deal with the news so that you wouldn't flip out and . . . you know, hurt yourself again."

Again.

Self-consciously, Ava tugged at her sleeves to hide her scars.

Little lines of worry burrowed between Khloe's eyebrows as her eyes met Ava's again. She shrugged, seeming suddenly embarrassed. "I just thought I should tell you I'm sorry. About . . . about everything."

"Me too," Ava agreed, and felt a lump forming in her throat. Why was it when someone showed her the least bit of kindness she was suddenly near tears?

"I, um, I was a real bitch when Kelvin died," Khloe whispered, glancing at the floor a second. "I blamed you."

"Everyone did."

"I know, but it wasn't your fault," she whispered, emotional herself. Clearing her throat, she added, "I can't speak for anyone else, but for me, I was so caught up in needing to blame someone, anyone for his death, that I really didn't consider that you lost a brother, too."

"So why didn't anyone notice I wasn't pregnant?"

Khloe shook her head. "You'd gained so little weight I guess and no one saw you much. Even me. We'd go months . . ." She lifted a shoulder. That bothered Ava. A lot.

"I guess I never really did the math." Her face showed lines of strain. "Let's face it—I really didn't care. I was too deep into my own misery at losing Kelvin. Maybe we all were, but I just wanted you to know that I'm sorry. Though I don't wish your brother dead, if he were still alive, I might not have met the love of my life." She brightened a little and Ava let it slide. Khloe and Simon's marriage had never been stable, but everyone, it seemed, lived in his or her own fantasy around here.

"You want to come down and bury our sorrows in chocolate cake? Mom made a three-layered one for Simon's birthday."

Her eyebrows lifted a bit and Ava was reminded of Khloe as a child, the oldest of six kids, the girl who had, years before, done anything on a dare, was always up for the next party, and had been Ava's best friend.

All before Kelvin's death, of course.

"Fudge icing," she said, hoping to lure Ava.

Ava glanced down the stairs. "Thanks, but I had a big dinner."

"And a big fight," Khloe said.

"Yes."

"I thought you might want to talk."

"Not now, but I'll take you up on the cake."

Khloe brightened. "Good."

Together they walked downstairs and Khloe found a packet of instant decaf coffee. Heated in the microwave, it was tasteless, but it didn't matter. They split a piece of the gooey-rich cake that was large enough to feed half of Anchorville.

All the while, she was aware of the seconds being ticked off, time she could be using to locate relatives of Noah's birth parents or getting familiar with her new microcamera and recorder. Again, she was cautious, trying not to rouse any more suspicion than she already had, so she forced herself to dally over the last bites, even pressing the tines of her fork into the crumbs as if she couldn't give up a final taste of the dark chocolate.

It was all a sham, of course, and even though reconnecting with Khloe felt good, she just didn't have time for it right now. After sipping the last dregs from her coffee cup, she yawned and stretched her arms over her head as if she were bone tired. Another fake-out. Inside, she was jazzed. Ready to set her plan into motion.

Wyatt walked in on them just as she was shoving her chair back to its spot at the table. Ava didn't know what to say to him, but Khloe did: "Pretty big lie," she pointed out, and when he looked up sharply, she added, "Jewel-Anne told me what happened."

He said, "I guess the secret's out."

"It should never have been a secret," Ava retorted.

He nodded, but Ava didn't believe he really felt contrition. Besides, his reactions were all wrong. While Ava felt as if she could jump out of her skin, anxious to look into a new lead in her son's disappearance, Wyatt hadn't even bothered trying to find the birth grandparents. What was wrong with him? Why wasn't he chasing them down? And why all the damned secrecy?

Because he knows. He knows that Noah's not coming back.

Her heart shattered, but somehow she managed to carry her cup to the sink and rinse it out. Her fingers shook, but hopefully no one noticed as she placed the mug into the dishwasher, said her good nights, then hurried up the stairs.

As she reached the second floor, she heard the soft sound of Jewel-Anne's electric wheelchair retreating down the hallway. For a fleeting second, Ava wondered if Khloe had purposely come to distract her so that Jewel-Anne could snoop inside her room. . . .

Stop it! Those two women don't even like each other! It was nothing! Forget it, and get on with what you need to do.

Inside the bedroom, she saw nothing out of place, no telltale wheelchair tracks on the carpeting around her bed, nothing moved that she could tell. She yanked her computer down from the top shelf and fired it up. Quickly, she retrieved her previous search and then, taking her cell phone into the bathroom, she made the first call to one of three Z Johnsons listed in the phone book.

Nervously she waited. The phone was answered by an automated voice that told her the phone number was no longer in service. The second wasn't answered, not even by a machine, but on the third, a woman answered, her voice groggy with sleep. "Hello?"

"Mrs. Johnson?"

"Yes."

Here goes nothing. "My name is Ava Garrison, and I'm sorry to bother you, but I was hoping you could tell me something about Tracey."

Silence.

Ava plunged on. "I believe she was your daughter."

"Who is this again?" the woman asked. "Why are you calling me?"

"I know this is hard, but I had a son who was adopted, and I think Tracey was his birth mother."

"What! No!" *Click!* The phone went dead.

"Damn it." She dialed again and this time a man answered.

Before she could say a word, he said, "Leave us alone. I don't know what you want, but let our daughter rest in peace."

"Please, please don't hang up. My son is missing, has been for two years, and I just found out that Tracey might have been his birth mother. Can you please help me?"

A pause and then a long sigh. "I'm sorry, lady, but this is too painful for us."

"I understand," she said desperately, "and I'm sorry, but I've lost my son, too. I'm trying desperately to find him. If you could please help me. My name is Ava Church Garrison, and I adopted my son about four years ago." She gave the man the date of Noah's birth and her phone number. "I'm trying to find him. You've lost a child. You know what I'm going through. Please, can't you help me?"

There was a long pause, and then muffled conversation as if he were talking to someone else. Holding her breath, Ava waited, counting her heartbeats. Finally he said, "All we know is that Tracey got herself into trouble, and she told us about it, but she went away, gave the baby up. We don't know anything else. So, please, don't call back. If you do, we'll have to call the police." Another hesitation, then, "Good luck."

Click!

The phone went dead again and she knew if she dialed back, she'd get nowhere. Was the threat empty? Did the Johnsons know where Noah was, or was the connection no more than another dead end?

Chapter 36

Reversing their usual roles, Snyder, having braved the cold, blustery day, had walked back to the station from a coffee kiosk a couple of blocks off the waterfront. Once in the surprisingly quiet office, he fumbled through security and made his way into Lyons's cubicle, where he set a coffee drink on her desk. It was one of those frothy, sweet things he hated and that she seemed to consume without so much as a thought to the exorbitant cost or high calorie count. He'd even remembered the straw, which he found extraneous.

She was leaning forward, elbows on the neat surface of her desk, her eyebrows pulled together in concentration as she listened to whatever was coming through the headset covering her ears. An older-model tape recorder complete with cassettes sat on her desk. Nearby, wedged between her computer monitor and a small terrarium packed with succulent plants—those weird alien-looking things his grandmother cultivated—was a perfect stack of tiny cartridges.

"Wow." She clicked off the recorder, ripped off the earphones, and picked up her drink. "Thanks." After taking a sip, she made a grateful humming noise. "Eggnog?"

" 'Tis the season."

"Almost. Mmm." Another sip. "So what got into you?"

"I'm just that guy," he said, and she laughed, nearly choking on the latte. "And I figured you might need a break. You've been at this most of the day."

"Any news on Cheryl Reynolds's wig?"

He shook his head. "Still MIA. What've you got?"

"Interesting stuff," she said, and tapped a finger on one of the short stacks of cassettes, all marked in Cheryl Reynolds's distinctive hand. Leaning back in her chair, she waved him into the office and he, with his plain coffee, dropped into one of the side chairs. "I'm still missing the latest tapes from Ava Garrison, which bothers me."

"Me too."

"We'll keep looking, but in the meantime, I've got these."

"And they are of . . . ?"

"Jewel-Anne Church."

"Did you know that when her father, Crispin, was the warden—I mean, administrator—of Sea Cliff that the family lived on the premises for a while?"

"Of the hospital?"

Lyons nodded, holding her cup and staring thoughtfully at the recorder. "It seems they'd lived up in the big house, but there was some kind of rift with his brother, who ended up dying not long after. Connell, the brother, is the father of Ava and Kelvin. Ava's brother died in that boating accident a few years back. The rest of the tribe was fathered by Crispin, compliments of two wives, Regina, now deceased, and Piper, the younger one who's the mother of his youngest two children, a boy named Jacob and then Jewel-Anne."

"The cripple?"

"The PC term is *handicapped*."

He lifted a shoulder.

"I got all this information from doing a little research, and

Jewel-Anne confirmed it in these tapes." Lyons picked one up. "From what I can piece together, the two brothers had a falling-out, and then Crispin gave all his pieces of Neptune's Gate to his kids. Subsequently they all sold out to their cousin Ava. Except Jewel-Anne. She won't budge."

"And because of the sessions with Cheryl you know why?" he guessed.

"Maybe." She was concentrating again, chewing on the straw protruding from her drink. "But here's the deal. The family was living in two of the row houses at Sea Cliff right before Crispin Church was fired and Sea Cliff closed."

"So?"

"So, it turns out Jewel-Anne had contact with some of the patients."

"Inmates," he said.

"Call them whatever. A lot of them weren't dangerous, just had mental issues."

"Off their collective rockers."

She scowled at him. "The point is, one of the patients held a particular fascination for Jewel-Anne."

He saw it coming then . . . and waited.

Lyons offered up a cat-who-ate-the-canary smile and played with her straw, moving it up and down in her drink. "It seems Daddy's little girl fancied herself in love with the most notorious of all of Sea Cliff's patients: our good buddy, the missing Lester Reece."

"You've been spying on me!" Ava charged as she strode to the stable the next day and found Dern brushing Cayenne's sorrel coat until it gleamed. Pale, wintry sunlight was filtering through the windows, and the tufts of red hair glinted as it caught in the light. The stable was warm, filled with the scents of horses, hay, and dust, though Ava, who'd spent most of the night installing her new spy equipment, barely noticed.

"Excuse me?" From Cayenne's stall, Dern glanced her way but kept moving the currycomb over the mare's broad back.

Several horses in nearby stalls lifted their heads, ears pricked forward as she passed their mangers, and Rover, lying near a feed bin, thumped his tail.

All in all, the interior of the long building was serene, until the firestorm that was Ava arrived.

"You've been spying on me, reporting back to Wyatt, telling him where I've been! I accused you once of being my body-guard and you scoffed at the idea."

"Because I'm not." Staying within the confines of the box stall, he rubbed Cayenne gently with a towel. The mare switched her tail and snorted a bit, but put up with his grooming.

"Dern, I *know*. Wyatt admitted it."

"Did he?"

"Yes!" God, the man was frustrating. In a whole different way than her husband.

"About time." Then to the horse, "There ya go, girl, all gussied up."

He exited the stall and latched the gate behind him.

"I don't like you spying on me and running back and reporting to Wyatt," Ava told him coldly.

"That's what I'm doing?" He was singularly unconcerned.

"He claims so."

"And you trust him?"

"He knew that I'd been up on the ridge, and the only other person who knew was you, Dern. You're just another of his minions, aren't you?"

"I told him about the ridge because I figured someone else might figure it out, and I wanted him to trust me."

"What a crock of BS that is!"

One side of his mouth lifted in a crooked smile that had no right being so coolly sexy. Damn the man with his beard-darkened square jaw and intense eyes. In the half-light of the stable, the blades of his face in shadow, he was too rugged and handsome for his own good. "Not a crock."

"Then tell me why," she demanded.

"Because I was told to." Folding his arms over his chest, stretching the shoulder seams of his suede jacket, he suggested, "Why don't you take a deep breath and start from the beginning."

Wound up and running on very little sleep, Ava could feel her ire rising. "Last night, Wyatt and I got into another one of our fights. In the middle of it, Wyatt told me how he asked you to keep an eye on me. Like I'm five or something!"

"He did ask me." Dern was nodding as if agreeing with himself in a silent argument. "I told you that."

"And you didn't think you should warn me that my husband had his spies out?" she demanded. Dern was the one person she thought she could trust on the island, the only damned one.

"Now, that would've defeated the purpose, wouldn't it?"

"Purpose?"

Leveling his gaze at her, he said, "So that I could pick and choose whatever I wanted to tell him."

"Wait a sec—"

He lifted a hand. "Hear me out. You're right. I wasn't going to tell you because I knew it would only get you all upset again, and the way I figure it, you need a friend right now."

"And you're it?" she said sarcastically.

"I'm on your side."

"*My* side?" She hooked a thumb at her chest. "Not by ratting me out, you're not."

"Look, I didn't volunteer for the job, and it wasn't part of our original deal, but I agreed because I needed the work."

"You could have told me. I can keep a secret."

"Can you?" Everything in his expression conveyed doubt.

"Well, so can I. For example, I haven't ratted you out about your forays up to the widow's walk in the middle of the night."

She couldn't believe it! He knew about that?

"You've been up there twice as far as I know."

"No, I wasn't anywhere near—"

"Like hell, Ava." Quick as a snake striking, he reached out and grabbed her arm, his fingers strong and hard through her sweater and jacket. "I saw you, followed you, but decided if you were going to pull some crazy stunt like climbing on the damned fire escape, there wasn't much I could do about it. I didn't think it would hold both of our weight, and by the time I saw you and your flashlight, it would've been too late for me to do anything about it, so I just waited. What the hell's wrong with you?" The fingers around her arm tightened. "You have some kind of death wish?"

"Of course not!"

"Then what were you doing?"

"I can't talk about it."

His lips curved down and he studied her face. Though he didn't say a word, an unspoken threat hung between them.

"You're going to tell Wyatt."

"Not if you explain."

"I knew it."

"Tell me."

"I can't trust you."

"Sure you can."

"You just said you're working for my husband."

"What I said was, I pick and choose what I tell him." His eyes searched the contours of her face, and she felt light-headed, her heart trip-hammering.

Don't trust him. You can't! He's playing you. Just like everyone else on this damned island!

He inched his face closer, and she knew in an instant that he intended to kiss her. *No!* Her heart was already clamoring, her breath catching in her throat. *Oh, God!* Closer still, the hand on her arm drew her near, and though her feet were planted solidly, her upper body came forward.

"This is a mistake," he said, his breath warm against her face.

"I know. I can't . . ." But as the words escaped, his mouth suddenly molded over hers. He yanked her close, strong arms surrounding her, lips hot, hard, and sensuous.

Don't, Ava. Don't do this. Getting involved with Austin Dern is insanity!

Turning off the voice in her head, she let go, winding her arms around his neck, pressing her anxious mouth to his, hearing him groan in his own protest. Her blood ran hot through her veins, racing to the beat of her erratic heart. Her head swam with denial and desire, and every part of her was electrified, wanting . . . needing . . . finding solace and joy in the touch of this man. He found the buttons on her coat, and she slid her hands beneath his jacket, feeling rock-hard muscles under his shirt.

Something deep inside of her broke, something hot and molten, and the arguments in her mind faded into the darkest corners of the stable. Her knees went weak and her mind filled with searing images of glistening, sinewy muscles, of hard, naked buttocks and firm pectoral muscles. She imagined him above her, parting her legs, thrusting into her as she clung to him and pressed her lips and teeth into the side of his neck. . . .

As if he saw the window into her fantasy, he lifted his head and swore under his breath, then released her and stepped away. Gazed at her through smoldering eyes from a fire that hadn't quite been extinguished. "This is wrong."

"I know." Shame washed up the back of her neck. "I'm sorry."

"Don't be." He grabbed her hand and held it tight, so hard it was nearly painful. "My fault." As if he realized he'd squeezed too hard, he let go. "It won't happen again."

"It takes two, Dern," she said, her voice husky. "I was into it. You're not the one who's married."

"That has nothing to do with it."

"It has everything in the world to do with it."

She turned and began walking toward the door when his voice stopped her. "I don't know what the hell you were doing up on the roof, but stop it, will ya? You could get killed."

Looking over her shoulder, she asked, "You won't tell?"

"Not if you take me with you next time. If you're gonna die, I may as well die with you."

"That's crazy."

"Crazy's normal around here," he said, and she half laughed as she left, even though, deep in her heart, she knew that she would be a fool to trust him.

Fact was, she couldn't trust anyone, and as she walked back to the house, she crossed her fingers that he would keep his mouth shut about what he'd seen last night, like Trent had promised. Hopefully no one else was aware what she'd been up to. She didn't need anyone foiling the trap she planned to set tonight.

She waited until after two before heading to the attic again.

The installation of the camera and recorder were as easy as the salesman had insisted. After putting the wireless spy equipment together in her bathroom, Ava had watched the clock until the middle of the night. Sweating bullets in the fear that someone would see her, she'd first taken the risk of shutting down the main switch for all of the electricity to the house, as the computer salesman had suggested, so that whoever had set their recorder in the attic might have to reset it due to the electrical interruption. She'd waited a full five minutes, thinking someone would wake up to the too-quiet house without the rumble of the furnace or the hum of the refrigerator or one of the beeps from electronic equipment that had been suddenly disconnected.

Her heart had been pounding so loudly, she'd thought the whole world could hear it, but when no one came thundering up the back stairs, she'd let out her breath and quietly placed the camera in a darkened corner of the back staircase. Then, assured she still was the only person awake, she'd climbed up to the widow's walk and down to the third floor again. In the old servants' quarters, she'd installed two other tiny cameras, including one in the closet where she'd found the recording device that gave off recorded cries of Noah calling for her.

She'd been a nervous wreck setting up the spy cameras, and twice she'd thought she'd heard someone creeping around on the lower level. She'd frozen, waiting and sweating before determining that the noises were just the result of the old house creaking and groaning as it settled around her.

Fortunately, she hadn't been caught while the power was down, and hopefully the interruption in the electricity and blinking digital clocks would be attributed to the weather. Now she prayed her new equipment would do its job. With the system's motion detector, the camera would only video if there was activity on the staircase, and it would send the video and audio images to a small receiver Ava kept inside her purse. She could check the information as often as she wanted, replaying it on her computer. The worst part was hiding the packaging. She flattened the boxes and slid them between the mattress and box springs of a bed in an unused guest room and stashed the packing material in a box that held Christmas ornaments, again in the spare room. Hopefully no one would notice them before she'd collected the evidence she needed and finally had proof that she wasn't going insane, that someone was really trying to gaslight her.

It had taken her nearly two hours to fall asleep after she'd returned to her bedroom to wait, but so far this morning, no one besides Dern had mentioned the fact that they'd heard someone up last night; nor had anyone commented on the fact that she looked tired as hell, which she hoped could be explained by the fight with Wyatt that Jewel-Anne had no doubt told everyone she'd witnessed.

Good enough for her cover.

For now.

Now it was after ten. Graciela was vacuuming in the hallway outside the bedroom door, and she barely looked up as Ava walked back inside, turned on her computer, and checked the cameras. They had shown no activity. Finally she accessed her bank accounts.

Both Tanya and Dern had suggested she look to the money to find out who would want to make her feel as if she were going out of her mind, and she had, but all her funds appeared to be intact. She couldn't remember finite details, of course, but essentially there weren't holes in the bank balances, and though the stock and real estate markets fluctuated, her assets were as she remembered them.

With her memory returning day by day, she was more likely to discover discrepancies, but so far there was nothing out of the norm. At least nothing she could see at first glance. She'd dig deeper, of course, and talk to her broker and banker, but first she wanted to make a call to a private investigator.

It was time to find out everything she could about Tracey Johnson and Charles Yates, and the search would include all of their remaining relatives. With all the things she was starting to remember, the names of Noah's birth parents rang not one single bell. So, if she couldn't make the search herself without raising suspicion, she would hire someone.

Tanya, never trusting her ex, had used a guy . . .

Ava didn't waste time. She picked up her phone, called her

friend, and got the name of a PI in Seattle. "He's good," Tanya told her, "but not cheap."

"The truth never is," Ava had replied. Within fifteen minutes, she'd worked her way through a mousy-voiced secretary to the man himself and secured the services of one A. B. "Abe" Crenshaw.

Now, maybe, she'd find out the truth.

Chapter 37

Dern was a distraction.

One Ava didn't need, but there it was. She'd avoided him in the two days since confronting him in the stable, but she hadn't forgotten the man, his betrayal or that damned kiss. It had seemed to linger on her lips for hours, and ever since then, when she should have been thinking about everything *but* Austin Dern, he was always on her mind, maybe not front and center, but certainly on the sidelines, his image ready to play havoc with what she wanted to do at the slightest opportunity.

So far, she hadn't heard from Abe Crenshaw, and for the first two nights, her camera caught nothing, nor, thankfully, did she awaken to Noah's cries. Wyatt had come and gone several times, and the air between them had been strained, like the calm before a storm, the electric feel of oncoming doom rolling in off the sea. They didn't discuss the adoption further. Ava didn't want to, and Wyatt obviously didn't, either.

Then on the third night, lightning struck.

Wyatt and she, barely civil, had eaten dinner together in the dining room and though Virginia's chicken and rice casserole was delicious, one of her favorites, the bites had stuck in her throat. Across from her, Wyatt had barely met her eyes and the conversation that had bounced around them covered everything from Trent planning to leave on Saturday to Jacob being "pissed as hell" at one of his professors, and Ian saying he might just take off for a few days to go with his brother back to the mainland. Everyone seemed restless, except for Jewel-Anne, who picked at her food and complained of a stomachache.

After the meal, Jewel-Anne had Demetria whisk her up to her room while the twins talked about going into Anchorville to one of the bars. Jacob seemed torn, almost going with his half siblings, but then, after he received a text message, he mumbled something about having to get to the mainland to help a friend with a failing wireless system.

After they all dispersed to separate areas of the house, Ava was alone with Wyatt. She braced herself when he pushed his plate aside, but all he said was, "I talked with Dr. McPherson today."

"Okay," she said cautiously.

"I reinstated her as your doctor. It took some doing, but I convinced her she was the best choice."

"She and I agreed—"

"I don't care what you agreed," he cut her off coldly. "For the love of God, Ava, I'm trying to help you."

"We already had this argument!"

"And you said you didn't want to go back to the hospital. This is the alternative."

"I don't *need* to go to a hospital. I've said that before, too. And I'm not dealing with Dr. McPherson again, Wyatt."

"I thought you might say that, so I called St. Brendan's. It turns out they have a room with a view of the—"

"Pay attention to what I'm saying! I'm *not* going back there. *Ever!*"

"That's why I hired Evelyn," he said with maddening circular logic.

"I don't know why you think you have to control me, but it's over. I already called an attorney—and not one in your firm—to start proceedings to remove you as my guardian. So it's over." She strode out of the room and felt the anger radiating off of her in waves. It was impossible to hold on to her patience when he was forever trying to control her. Though she'd told him a lie—she hadn't actually talked to an attorney yet—she did have a list of names, and as soon as she found out who was gaslighting her, she planned to take all of her evidence to the most prestigious lawyer in the state and regain control of her life.

And she was going to divorce Wyatt, the son of a bitch. It was as simple as that. She'd married for life and had meant every word of the "for better or worse" part of the vows, but she was pretty sure the worse part didn't include adultery and God only knew what else.

As she climbed the stairs, she heard his phone ring, then a short one-sided conversation. A few minutes later, she watched him leave. Head bent against the storm that was coming in off the ocean, he headed to the boathouse. Ian, Trent, and Jacob left in his wake.

As the first drops of rain drizzled down the bedroom panes, she saw the boathouse lights go on, heard the rev of the boat's engine, and saw them all leave. Her husband was heading to the mainland without a word to her, and all she could feel was relief. "Good riddance," she said. Turning, she spied her medication all laid out for her, little pills next to a cup of water. She was about to throw them down the toilet when she realized that, for all she knew, her room could be surveilled, tiny hidden cameras mounted in hidden corners.

What makes you think that you're the only one with a cam-

era? Just because you didn't find any evidence of this bedroom being bugged while you were in the attic, how do you know?

She snapped on the television in her room, but found that she had trouble maintaining interest, even when the "breaking story" was that another person had reported a Lester Reece sighting. The screen filled with the last known picture of Reece while, off camera, a reporter reminded the viewers of his crimes and how he'd escaped from Sea Cliff. Reece was a handsome enough man, kind of rugged and athletic-looking, with thick dark hair and intelligence lurking beneath his eyes. "Charming" some of his neighbors had called him. "Quiet. Kept to himself." And now, Anchorville's most famous criminal.

The legend of Lester Reece wouldn't die, Ava decided, and was about to turn off the television when a slim African American woman in her early forties appeared on the screen. She was identified by a reporter as the public information officer for the sheriff's department. The reporter then proceeded to ask the woman about the Cheryl Reynolds homicide.

Ava sat on the edge of her bed and watched as the policewoman basically dodged questions. No, there were no new leads, but the police were doing everything in their power to bring the person responsible for the crime to justice. The public was urged to come forward with any information, should they have it, while a picture of Cheryl filled the screen.

Sadness crept into Ava's heart. She'd liked Cheryl. Considered her a friend. Had confided in her. To think that someone had so brutally slain her, possibly only minutes after Ava had left, made her shudder. Who would do such a thing? And why?

A number for the sheriff's office was flashed upon the screen before the station cut away to a commercial for a local car dealership. Ava snapped the television off and grabbed a mystery novel that had been sitting on her bedside stand for weeks. Propped against pillows stacked to cushion her headboard, she tried to read, but after starting the same page over four times, she tossed the paperback aside. Nervous energy propelling her, she wandered the hallways of the house for a while, hearing Elvis crooning from Jewel-Anne's wing and no other sound in the rest of the house.

The door to Noah's room was ajar and she walked inside, past the crib with its sea creature mobile to the dresser where the jars of ointment and cream sat. "Sweetheart, where are you?" she said aloud. Even though she'd hired the private detective, she'd searched the Internet herself, looking for any shred of evidence linking her son to the couple who had died in the motorcycle accident on the snakelike section of Highway 101 just south of Oregon's Cannon Beach. She'd wanted to drive to the site, but it was over two hundred miles away. She'd tried talking to the Johnsons again, but they hadn't answered when she'd phoned, no doubt recognizing her number on their caller ID.

After touching a soft worn, stuffed beaver that had been Noah's favorite, she walked to the back guest room that afforded a clear view of the stable and Dern's apartment. She kept the room dark and opened the blinds, her eyes searching the darkness.

Dern had seen her on the widow's walk, which was odd. What was he doing up in the middle of the night? Checking on the livestock? Letting the dog out? Just restless? Or had he been spying on her? No, no . . . of course not.

She witnessed the door to his studio open, then saw a man hurry away, a tough, rugged-looking individual who . . . For a second she thought she was seeing Lester Reece, but of course that was a ridiculous notion, brought on by the recent coverage of Reece on the television. Squinting, she realized the man hurrying down the outside stairs was Austin Dern.

Of course.

What had she been thinking?

And looking at him now, she felt her pulse quicken a bit, her blood heat stupidly. As he made his way into the stable below his tiny unit, she felt the urge to track him down, to find out more about him, to talk to him and . . .

Don't even go there. You had your kiss and your fantasy. Enough. Stay away from him. For now.

Stepping away from the window, she let the blind fall back and made her way to her room, where she forced thoughts of Dern and Noah and Wyatt aside. Picking up the damned mystery novel again, she kicked off her shoes, slid between the covers, and forced herself to read.

She'd deal with Wyatt and her freak show of a life in the morning.

Some things never change, Evelyn McPherson thought as she considered her pathetic love life. It had been a bad day—no, make that a bad week—she decided as she unlocked the door of her home: one side of a duplex, a small place she'd bought when she'd decided to put down roots in Anchorville after Sea Cliff closed. The building, with its two cozy ground-floor units, had seemed a good investment at the time, but now she wasn't so sure. The second half of her home was vacant, a FOR RENT sign in the window and an ad placed on Craigslist. Her last tenant had moved out three months earlier, after stiffing her for two months' rent and trashing the place. It was finally back to the condition where it had been before Jerry the Party Dude moved in. She should have known the second she read the bumper stickers on his souped-up pickup.

Tonight, she didn't care. Sighing, she tossed her keys into a dish on a table near the door, dropped her laptop and purse onto that same table, and then unwound her scarf. The unit was cold, the old furnace spotty at best, and she fiddled with the thermostat in the hall until she heard it kick on. Currently the temperature was hovering at sixty-five. "A few more degrees wouldn't kill ya," she muttered, then walked into the kitchen to heat up some tea . . . no, forget that. Tonight she would uncork the bottle of Chardonnay she'd opened two nights earlier and left in the refrigerator. After taking off her coat, she scrounged around for some crackers and a little cheese—smoked Edam, all she found loitering in the refrigerator—and called it good.

After all, what did one have for dinner when one had not only been fired, but had also been accused of having an affair with the patient's husband? True, technically she'd offered to quit seeing Ava, but then Wyatt had stepped in. Though it had happened days before, it was as fresh today as when it happened.

God, she'd screwed up her life.

Because Ava Garrison's charges weren't too far from the truth. More than once, Evelyn had caught herself thinking what life would be like married to Wyatt. Handsome and well built, he was a lawyer who could be as charming as he was attractive. He also maintained offices here in Anchorville as well as in Seattle, and he had a beautiful, historic home with a knockout view of the bay and sea.

And a wife!

A woman struggling to remember what happened to her child.

Who just happens to be your patient.

"Shit," she muttered as she looked around her tidy living room with its modern furniture, all picture-perfect, as if it had come out of a showroom window. Two matching overstuffed chairs, a long low, sofa, and a couple of glass lamps that winked warmly. A gas fireplace that could be clicked on with the flip of a switch finished the room. Across the wide mantel, opaque glass jars coordinated with scented candles, just the way she'd seen in a store in Seattle. There were pictures on the mantel as well. All of herself. Either alone or with a couple of girlfriends from college, where she'd known Trent Church. "Go Ducks!" she said sadly, repeating the cheer that was forever yelled on campus or written on banners or sent via e-mail and Facebook to anyone connected with the U of O.

Man, this was turning into a pity party of royal order! Clearing her throat, she poured a glass and told herself she wasn't half in love with Ava's husband, but that was a lie. And it wasn't one-sided.

She knew that Wyatt felt it, too, that little hum of electricity whenever they were together. He did seem to light up a little when she was around and was always trying to get her into a quiet spot so they could talk without interruption.

About his wife!

She took a long swallow. The cold wine slid down easily, still tasting divine, and she thought she might just polish off the bottle. Hey, why not? If she got a little tipsy, who cared?

"Right, who the hell cares?" *No one, Evelyn. You're going to live your life alone. No husband, no children, no large house overlooking the sea.* She took another sip, and then a third before refilling her glass. This was supposed to be a celebration; she'd been released from dealing with one of the most difficult patients of her practice.

She should be thrilled. But she wasn't.

She closed her eyes for a second.

Click!

A soft noise caught her attention. Something out of place. Coming from the bedroom. She stopped, straining to listen, but the noise, if there had been one, didn't repeat.

Your imagination.

Maybe just water dripping?

Nothing to worry about.

Yet, she was a little unnerved, probably due to being called out and fired by her patient and also, let's face it, because there had been a murder in this small town; the first one Evelyn had ever heard about. Well, other than those committed by Lester Reece.

She didn't want to go there, to think of the sadistic killer who, she knew from counseling him at Sea Cliff, could charm the panties off the most devoted nun. The man had something . . . dark, dangerous, and deadly—a bad combination, and one from which she hadn't been immune.

Now, alone in her kitchen, thinking of the men who'd been a part of her life and the mistakes made, every last one of them, she felt the heat of embarrassment rush up her neck.

Had she been a colossal fool over Wyatt? Had she misread the signs? Hadn't his touches on her sleeve or back lingered a little too long?

She'd thought so.

Hadn't his stopping by her home and her office under the guise of being concerned for his wife been just an excuse to see her again?

"Idiot," she muttered, and started cutting the small brick of cheese.

When had her female radar gone so haywire?

Oh, come on, your radar was always messed up. Remember Chad Stanton in high school? That ended when you found him with your best friend, Carlie, and then there was the string of guys in college. Not one turned out to be the love of your life. Especially not Trent Church—you had a thing for him, didn't you? She winced as she recalled getting drunk and throwing herself at him. They'd ended up in bed and he'd slipped out in the middle of the night. She'd woken up with a headache and a flower, near her bed, a rose he'd picked from a scraggly bush near her apartment's front door, but he'd left no note, and there had been no phone call from him in the ensuing days. In fact, the next time she'd seen him, he'd been friendly enough, as before, as if *nothing* had happened, and when she'd pressed him to talk about it, he'd said, "It really wasn't that big of a deal, was it? I mean, we enjoyed ourselves, but that was it."

She'd wanted to drop through the lush grass of the quad. Somehow they'd remained friends, and she'd attended that fateful Christmas party with him, the one from which Noah Garrison, Wyatt's son, had gone missing, but Trent and Evelyn never ended up in bed, or a relationship, again.

And grad school was no better, she chastised herself. *Remember the professor, only six years older than you? And then, oh, God, then Sea Cliff . . .*

She closed her eyes at that. Didn't want to think that she was even remotely attracted to one of the patients, especially a dangerous, convicted killer. But it was true, she thought with a grimace; the wrong men had always held a fascination for her, men who were either distant, unavailable, or dangerous, and there were all kinds of reasons for that. She was a mess when it came to love and sex.

So she was lucky she'd gotten fired before she did something stupid! She'd been on the brink of—

Ouch!

Needle-sharp pain burned at the tip of her index finger, where, distracted, she'd nicked herself with the knife while slicing the damned cheese.

"Stupid, stupid, stupid," she whispered, then stuck the throbbing finger into her mouth and walked through the master bedroom where she snapped on the switch and a bedside lamp turned on. The temperature in this part of the condo had seemed to drop another five degrees, but she couldn't bother with the heat now. She made a beeline to her bathroom where she kept all of her first-aid supplies. She was certain she had a tube of Neosporin in the medicine cabinet.

Her injured finger still in her mouth, she didn't bother flipping on the overhead, just let the light from the bedroom spill into the room as she opened the medicine cabinet.

There was enough illumination that she could see—and there it was, the small tube kept right near her box of Band-Aids. Closing the cabinet, she saw a face, shadowy and dark in the mirror.

Dropping the tube, she started to scream, just as strong hands caught her from behind, fingers digging deep into her throat, forcing her Adam's apple backward, cutting off her air. She flailed frantically, wildly, striking backward, her hands glancing off her attacker's head and body. She tried to kick but missed.

The world turned blacker.

Her lungs felt as if they would burst.

She felt the heat build in her head, and her hands scrabbled and clawed at the gloved hands surrounding her neck, cutting off her air. *Oh, God, she was going to die! This monster was trying to kill her.* Frantically, she struggled, knocking over bottles and cans on the counter.

Crash! A glass candle smashed against the tiles of the floor.

Why? she silently cried, and desperately wished she had a weapon—a knife or a towel bar or a lamp or *anything*! The fire in her lungs became unbearable.

She couldn't die like this!

Not single, with no children! This wasn't how it was supposed to happen! In the darkened room she struggled, but more slowly, her reactions slowing, the world spinning.

In the mirror, her gaze met that of her attacker. She saw the cold, hard hatred in soulless eyes . . . eyes she recognized, despite the pathetic disguise of a long, black wig.

Why? she asked herself again, just as the tightness on her throat lessened and she drew in a minuscule amount of air. Light-headed, she couldn't fight, tried and failed to stand and nearly toppled against the counter. In the mirror, she saw her assailant withdraw a knife from a jacket pocket.

She stumbled, tried to get away.

Too late!

Sharp and gleaming, the blade flashed in the mirror.

Quickly.

Across her throat.

She gasped.

Tried to scream.

Watched in horror as the spray of her own blood spattered the mirror crimson, red drops drizzling down the glass to obscure the malevolent smile of her killer.

Chapter 38

Fully clothed and still lying atop her bed, Ava awoke with a start. Her heart jolted, a spurt of adrenaline rushing into her blood. Something had woken her. Something out of the ordinary, something that wasn't right.

Then it came again. A sound as plaintive and heart-wrenching as any she had ever known. "Mama . . . Maaamaaa!" and then the sad, frightened sobs of her son echoing down the hallways.

"Son of a bitch," she whispered between clenched teeth.

She threw back the covers and, in stocking feet, crept to the window. Half expecting to see her son on the dock, she stared outside to only darkness and the whitecaps, frothy and visible on the water. But no Noah. That image of him in his little sweatshirt on the dock was of her own making, the product of a desperate, broken mind, aided by the hallucinogens in her medication.

Evelyn McPherson had insisted she continue the use of the drugs and her own physician had agreed. "Bitch," she muttered as Noah's voice rang through the hallway. Couldn't anyone else hear him? Why only her?

Outside the room, in the corridor, his voice whispered to her, and she realized for the first time it wasn't that loud, that only someone in the rooms nearby would hear the soft, frightened cries of her child.

She started toward Noah's room.

From the first floor, the grandfather clock bonged loudly, causing her to jump as it chimed the half hour. And then the cries stopped. Abruptly. The house again growing quiet. Seemingly empty.

But someone was up.

Someone had to be!

Before she went banging on doors, making wild accusations, Ava returned to her room, found the receiver for her equipment in her purse, jammed the connection into her computer, and as her heart counted off the seconds of her life, she saw an image appear on the screen.

Big as life, in black and white, Ava witnessed her "handicapped" cousin Jewel-Anne pull herself out of her wheelchair and, using her arms while dragging her feet and moving awkwardly, haul herself up the rickety stairs. She disappeared from view for a while, then appeared again later, on the screen from a different camera, the one in the room with the hatbox. Using handholds in the closet, hooks used to hang clothes in bygone years, Jewel-Anne hauled herself to her feet, retrieved the box and equipment inside, and then, humming Elvis's "Suspicious Minds," reset her machine.

"You're right, you bitch," Ava said to the screen where Jewel-Anne was caught replacing the suitcase from the sixties with the equipment inside. "You are definitely caught in a trap!"

She didn't waste a second, just e-mailed the video to herself and Tanya for safekeeping, then saved it onto a small jump drive. There was a damned glitch in her computer and it took her several minutes to get the information "Sent". Then, fury propelling her, she grabbed the drive with its new information and marched down the hallway to the suite of rooms where her cousin resided.

Why was Jewel-Anne so hell-bent on torturing her? What had she ever done to her cousin for her to so cruelly twist her heart, make her think she was going out of her mind?

Had there been enough time for Jewel-Anne to return to her suite? She was pretty sure, but at this point, she didn't much care. If she caught Ava at her door, so be it. They could have it out in the hallway.

Angrily, she pounded on the thick door to Jewel-Anne's suite. *Bam! Bam! Bam!* "Jewel-Anne," Ava yelled through the panels. "I want to talk to you."

"Go away," a groggy voice responded.

So she was there. Ava pounded even harder.

"It's nearly three in the morning!" Jewel-Anne complained.

"Open up, Jewel-Anne, or I'm breaking in." Ava tried the door, found it unlocked, and stepped into the little-girl apartment. Larger than her brother's room in the basement, Jewel-Anne's suite had her bed, desk, and sitting area along with a private bath, retrofitted for someone in a wheelchair.

"Why?" Ava said, her fury mounting as she glared at her cousin lying in the bed, surrounded by those weird glass-eyed dolls, all in pajamas, cuddled up around her. "Why did you do it?"

"Do what?" Jewel-Anne blinked and yawned, as if she'd been dead asleep. Her hair, caught into a thick braid, was slightly mussed around her face. She was wearing her nightgown, but her glasses were neatly in place and the computer on her desk was just shutting down, making all the appropriate clicks and noises, indicating someone had just pressed the key to close down its programs.

Ava crossed the room, then hit the button on the keyboard to bring it back to life.

"What're you doing?" Jewel-Anne pushed herself upright, knocking a red-haired doll with freckles onto the floor where it collided with her stupid bunny slippers. "Now look what you've made me do!" She picked up the doll quickly, tucking it under the covers next to the others. "It's the middle of the night, for God's sake. I was asleep and—"

"I'm tired of your lies," Ava bit out. "You weren't asleep."

"Of course I was! How dare you accuse me of . . . of . . . lying. I don't lie. Ever."

"Yeah?" Barely able to keep her composure, Ava glanced at the computer screen, which was glowing again, the system going through its machinations as the CPU came back on.

"Get away from my things," Jewel-Anne was scrambling out of the bed now, pulling her wheelchair closer to the edge of the mattress, frantic to stop Ava.

"Not yet."

"I mean it, Ava, get out!"

"Not until you tell me why you tried to make me think I was going crazy."

"Leave my things alone!" When Ava showed no signs of ceasing and desisting, Jewel-Anne, who'd hauled herself into the wheelchair, scooped up her cell phone from her nightstand and warned, "I'm calling Demetria and Wyatt!"

"Good. I think they'll be interested in this, too."

"In what?" Jewel-Anne asked. For the first time, there was a bit of trepidation in her voice.

"Just watch."

"What the hell are you doing?" she asked as Ava jammed her flash drive into one of the USB ports. "Stop it! Get away from my things! You're trespassing and . . ." Her voice trailed off and her skin turned the color of death as images appeared on the screen, and there, in clear black and white, was Jewel-Anne hauling herself upstairs and then resetting the camera in the closet. "This . . . this is a mistake. You . . . you created this!" Jewel-Anne cried.

"I just took your lead."

"I don't know what you're talking about."

"Yeah, let's get Demetria and Wyatt and everyone in the house in here so that they can see *I'm* not the one who's crazy!"

The range of emotions that crossed Jewel-Anne's face went from horror to resentment to fury. She jutted out her chin and her lip curled in disgust. "Get out of my room! Now!"

"Or what?" Ava found the desk chair and sat down. "Why, Jewel?" she asked, her voice low. "Why in God's name did you go to all this trouble to make me think I was going insane?" She was shaking now, her anger pulsing through her veins.

"It wasn't much of a push!" Jewel-Anne cried.

"But there has to be a reason."

Jewel-Anne actually winced.

"What is it? Tell me. I intend to show this little video to everyone here, so you may as well tell me now. What reason did you have for terrorizing me, for letting me think my little boy was haunting me, crying out for me. Do you have any idea how that tore me up inside?"

"Yes!" she nearly shouted. Her little-girl features twisted with a hatred so intense, Ava recoiled a bit. Hard eyes bored into hers. "I do know," she snarled. There was a sudden gleam in her eye that suggested she would relish showing how she'd duped Ava, pulled one over on her successful cousin.

"You know, for a woman who's supposed to be smart, with a near-genius IQ, you sure are dense," she said.

Ava was shaking her head and feeling, again, as if she were standing in quicksand, slowly but surely being sucked under.

"I guess it's time you knew the whole truth." Jewel-Anne's malicious smirk stretched wide, an ugly curve across her face. "You can't even remember who the birth mother of your child is, can you?"

Ava felt like the room was receding, like she was at the end of a long corridor. She lifted a hand to ward off what was coming, but it was a useless gesture.

"That's right, Ava. Wyatt's story about . . . who? Charles

Yates and Tracey Johnson?" She gave a brittle laugh. "News to me, too. That cock-and-bull story was made up just to confuse you." She was nearly rabid now, her eyes glowing with the truth, her need to rub it in overpowering. Her voice rose, carrying into the hallway and reverberating in Ava's brain. "I'm Noah's mother, you stupid bitch! I was the one who carried him. I was the one who felt that he was ripping me up inside that night on the boat! Noah was *my* son, Ava, and you couldn't even acknowledge that simple, but oh-too-important fact: Noah was *my* son. Not yours. *Mine!*"

"No . . ." She wouldn't believe it. Couldn't. But the truth was bared, no longer hidden in a web of lies. Was it possible her son, her beautiful son, was really Jewel's?

Shaking her head and backing up, she had to deny it. "No!"

"The truth, Ava. Truth."

Oh, God, she remembered. She remembered! Jewel-Anne had been pregnant, too, at the same time as Ava, never divulging the father of her child, acting as if she were some modern-day Madonna . . . Oh, Lord, this was all so, so twisted. So painful. So wrong. Her insides wrenched and she thought she might throw up as she remembered losing her child and, in her grief, willing to do anything to replace him.

"Noah was my baby!" Jewel-Anne crowed again loudly.

"Was?" Ava repeated, hearing the past tense for the first time. No, oh, no. Noah couldn't be dead. He *couldn't* be. Like a zombie, Ava felt dead inside, denial rippling through her, and yet she advanced upon her cousin, towering over her. "What the hell did you do to my son?"

"I don't know what happened to him."

"You little faker!" Ava clasped her hands over her cousin's shoulders and yanked her to her feet.

Jewel-Anne shrieked in horror. "Let go of me!"

"Tell me where he is!" Angrily, Ava shook her cousin. Jewel-Anne's head bounced around like one of her eerie dolls.

"I don't know!"

"Liar! You've been lying the whole time. For two damned years. Gaslighting me! Making me think that I saw my son, that I heard him crying for me!"

"Let go of me!"

For an answer, she dragged Jewel-Anne into the hallway. The smaller woman wriggled and writhed, flailed with her hands, her legs moving wildly, uncontrolled.

"Ava, what're you doing? Don't!" Jewel-Anne cried as Ava pulled her toward the stairs. "No! Oh, God!"

"Where is my son?"

"I don't know," Jewel-Anne insisted, her eyes round, panic showing as they reached the top of the staircase. "Really, Ava, I don't! Stop this!" She was blubbering now.

Ava pushed her cousin against the rail, bending her back over it as Jewel-Anne clung to her. "Why did you set up the recording?" she demanded. "Why did you let me think Noah was here in the house? Why did you try to make me go insane?"

Fear rounded Jewel-Anne's eyes. "Ava, please—"

"*Why?*"

"Because you got it all!" Jewel-Anne blurted, frantic. "The house, the estate, the looks, the athleticism. Everything. You and Kelvin, you inherited everything. I tried to buy you out, but *oh, no,* you wouldn't even think about it. I'm a part of this family, too. I am! My father owned half of this place, and you should have found it in your heart to let me buy back some of the parts you bought from my stupid brothers and sister! But you never would. *Never!*" She was crying now, tears drizzling down her cheeks, her fingers digging into Ava's shoulders as she was bowed over the rail. "And then . . . and then you *took* my *son.* Wyatt worked a deal and it was all for *you. You!*"

"Ava!" Wyatt's voice boomed from somewhere nearby. He'd returned and was bearing down on them. "What the hell are you doing? Stop!"

A door opened and footsteps pounded in the hallway. "Jewel-Anne!" Demetria yelled. "Oh, sweet Jesus!"

Ava wanted to hurt Jewel-Anne like her cousin had hurt her. She wanted to strangle the truth from her, wanted to squeeze the breath from her lying throat. But the world began to swim a bit as she recalled pieces from the past, her son's birth, her own miscarriage . . . Jewel-Anne was telling the truth. Noah was hers, not Ava's.

Ava's knees buckled and Jewel-Anne screamed as they started to pitch over the rail together. Ava hung on hard. "You sold Noah?" she accused.

Nodding frantically, Jewel-Anne sobbed as she clung to her cousin for dear life, her fingers clawing at Ava, digging into her flesh as the terror set in. "Yes," she admitted, gasping. "I sold my son!" She was sobbing pitifully now, as if her heart were breaking into a thousand painful shards. "But," she cried, starting to hiccup, "I'm not the only one to blame. You played a part in this, too!" she accused as the damned clock began to chime from below. "I did sell my baby, but damn it, Ava, you bought him!"

Chapter 39

"You bought him. You bought him. You bought him . . ."

Reeling, Ava felt as if she'd been kicked in the gut.

The accusation that she'd actually purchased her child echoed in her brain as the floor a story beneath suddenly seemed to swirl seductively. *Jewel-Anne sold Noah, but* you *bought him.* You *and Wyatt. You* were a part of this hideous lie. You bought your own son and covered up the truth! You're no better than Jewel-Anne!

"Where is he?" Ava demanded hoarsely. Leaning over her cousin, she pressed her weight into the younger woman. She wondered if they would fall . . . if it would matter.

Jewel-Anne screamed in sheer horror.

"Stop!" Wyatt ordered. He was running barefoot, his hair mussed, wearing only pajama bottoms. Upon them now, he yanked at Ava's arm. "Christ, Ava. Don't do this!"

Again Jewel-Anne screamed, and this time Ava snapped back to reality. She recognized the horror of the situation just as Wyatt jerked her away from the railing, pulling both Jewel-Anne and her to safety.

Ava started shaking uncontrollably. She could have easily lost her balance and pitched over the railing, killing them both. In her mind's eye, she saw her broken body as well as her cousin's, their arms and legs sprawled at impossible angles, their heads twisted on broken necks, her blood seeping into Jewel-Anne's on the polished tile floor.

"Oh . . . dear . . . God . . ."

Jewel-Anne was crumpled in a heap on the floor of the balcony. Tears streamed down her chalky face. Scooting away from Ava, she glared up at her and spat, "You really are a freak show!" She could scarcely catch her breath as she pointed an accusing finger up at Ava. "You need to be locked up! Forever! You can't go around assaulting people. I'm . . . I'm pressing charges! And don't think I won't! Assault or intent to kill or whatever!" Her face contorted with her hatred. "You should have died, you know. That night on the boat? It should have been you! Not Kelvin! You hear me? You!" Her finger jabbed the air as she sobbed wildly. "You should have died with your baby!"

Ava staggered back at the vitriol coming out of her cousin.

Slowly, eyes focused on Ava, Jewel-Anne used the bars of the stair rail to pull herself to her feet. When Wyatt tried to step in, Jewel-Anne, red-faced, sweating, tears and snot running down her face, turned her fury on him, too. "Leave me alone!" she yelled at him, but her gaze was fixed on Ava. "Next time you try to commit suicide, give me a call. I'll be glad to help."

"That's enough!" Wyatt said sharply, but Jewel-Anne sneered up at him.

"You're no better," she charged, holding the rail with one hand and swiping at her face with the sleeve of her free arm. "The only reason you stick around is because of the money!" She looked from Wyatt to Ava. "You're right—he's having an affair. I heard him on the phone."

"Shut up, Jewel!" Wyatt warned as Demetria, pushing Jewel-Anne's wheelchair, reached them.

"Everyone just calm down," Demetria ordered, grabbing Jewel-Anne and helping her into her chair.

But Ava wasn't finished. "Who is he?" she demanded of her cousin. "Noah's father. What's his name?"

Jewel-Anne clamped her jaw shut.

"I can't believe you were involved with anyone . . ."

"Of course you can't," Jewel-Anne said, sniffing loudly. "It's incomprehensible to you that anyone would want me, isn't it?"

"Who?" she asked Wyatt.

"She's never said."

"And you didn't ask?"

"Of course he asked, but I'll never tell!" Jewel-Anne's smug superiority was beginning to manifest itself again. She smoothed her braid and said, "And you'll never know."

Ava turned to her husband and said in a dead voice, "It was Jewel-Anne. She's the one who's been gaslighting me. She recorded a baby crying and piped it into my room. I have proof: Her equipment is in the attic, and I caught her on video restarting it. That's what I bought in Seattle, spy equipment. So I could flush her out!" Wyatt and Demetria stared at her as if she were stark, raving mad. "Look on Jewel-Anne's laptop if you don't believe me. On her desk. I downloaded the film onto a jump drive and played it for her. It's still there. She's been try-ing to make me look like I'm a lunatic."

"You *are* a lunatic. I don't have to help you," Jewel-Anne rebuffed, then to Wyatt, "She set me up. Through some kind of trick photography or Photoshop magic, or whatever. Anyone can mess with computer graphics these days, you know. Ava showed me video that's *supposed* to be me climbing up the back staircase. Oh, yeah. Like I could do that." Even staring upward, Jewel-Anne managed to somehow look down her nose at Ava.

Wyatt turned to Ava. "I never heard the crying," he said carefully, as if he were inclined to believe Jewel-Anne!

"It was somehow piped into my room and the nursery. And Jewel-Anne, she even said she heard it, just . . . just to throw me off track. For God's sake, look on her computer! The images that I caught on tape, the *unaltered film,* is still there!" Giving herself a quick mental shake, Ava pulled herself together as much as she could, then stormed after Jewel-Anne and the nursemaid to her cousin's room. Wyatt was on her heels, and though Jewel-Anne tried to shut down her computer, Wyatt stopped her from reaching the keyboard, and while she protested mightily, he watched the screen where Jewel-Anne was pulling herself upstairs.

"So you can walk," he stated flatly, his gaze fastened to the image on the monitor. "And you did this thing? You tried to make Ava appear paranoid."

"She is paranoid!" Jewel-Anne insisted. "And I *cannot* walk. Just . . . kind of balance myself."

Demetria, her gaze glued to the computer, said softly, "We're working on balance and strength, hopefully movement, with the physical therapist. But I had no idea . . ." She cocked her head toward her charge. "Jewel-Anne?"

There was no denying the tape. Trapped, Jewel-Anne glared hotly at Ava. "Okay. Yes!" she snapped, then climbed back into the bed with her bevy of scary-looking dolls.

"Why?" Wyatt demanded.

Ava said, "She blames me for Kelvin's death and for not selling her the house and for her accident and for her having to give up the baby and everything. All of her misery, it's my fault."

"It is!" Jewel-Anne insisted, as if she truly believed her lies. "You've never understood how much I hurt inside. You act like I'm invisible."

Wyatt whispered, "Jesus."

"And you!" Jewel-Anne snarled at Wyatt as she yanked up

the fluffy pink covers. "You were the one who wanted to keep the big lie going, weren't you? Let her think that she gave birth to Noah! So don't go all judgmental on me!"

"You're deluded," Ava said.

Jewel-Anne snorted a bitter little laugh. "Look who's talking!"

"You left Noah's wet shoes for me to find," Ava charged. "You put that sick doll in its casket." Fury burned through her veins. "You planted the key to that casket in my pocket and kept taunting me, wheeling out to Noah's memory marker in the garden, trying to get me to figure out that something was buried there!"

"No, I—" Jewel-Anne started.

"You need to leave my house," Ava cut her off, quaking inside.

"It's my house, too!"

"We'll buy you out," Wyatt said suddenly.

"*I'll* buy you out," Ava corrected. Wyatt wasn't an innocent in all of this; Jewel-Anne was right about that.

Jewel-Anne shook her head violently, then arranged the dolls around her. "I will never sell."

"Then I'll find another way," Ava warned.

"You can't," Jewel-Anne said, certain she had the upper hand.

"Don't push me," Ava gritted.

Wyatt's hand clamped over her arm, drawing her back. "I think that's enough," he said quietly.

She shook him off. "We're not done here," Ava insisted.

"How could she possibly dig a grave?" Wyatt asked.

"She had help," Ava said. "She had to have had an accomplice." Ava turned to her cousin. "Jacob. His reaction to digging up the doll was just an act."

Jewel-Anne rolled wide eyes toward Demetria and said in a little-girl voice, "I'm really tired."

"Fine! If you won't tell the truth, I know someone who

will!" Ava had come this far; she wasn't going to stop now. She started for the door.

"Wait!" Wyatt called. "Ava, what do you think you're doing?"

"Going to talk to Jacob!"

"But it's —"

"Three in the morning. Yes." He was right on her heels, but she didn't care. As she'd said, her husband was a part of this, too, probably more than she could even imagine. And he wasn't alone. Everyone who knew that Noah had been adopted was involved, all part of the ever-widening conspiracy against her. Not just Jacob. Members of the staff. Maybe Ian and Trent, even Zinnia in California could be a part of this. And where was Noah? Did any one of them know? Could he be hidden away somewhere?

Stop it! Pull yourself together! One thing at a time.

"You need to wait until you calm down," Wyatt ordered as she dashed through the kitchen and out the back door to the porch. Just a step behind, he caught her elbow and propelled her backward, spinning her to face him. "Slow down, Ava. You can't go off half-cocked, accusing people in the middle of the night."

She couldn't believe that she'd ever been in love with him. A damp wind rustled through the branches of the fir trees, chasing across the yard, smelling of earth and sea, causing her skin to prickle with the cold. "You should be demanding to know about your son. Our son. Why didn't you tell me, Wyatt? Why?"

"Because Dr. McPherson thought it best if you worked it out on your own. She was certain your nightmares have as much to do with the child you lost as with Noah. Deep down in your subconscious, you knew about the miscarriage, and you couldn't face it. You transferred it to your worries about Noah."

"What kind of psychobabble is that?" She jerked her arm

away from him and heard an owl hoot, as if in warning. "Thanks for the Psych 101 lesson, but I'm going to find my son!"

With that, she took off again, down the steps at a dead run. Mr. T, hiding near the stairs, hissed and slunk under the house while she hit the walkway and found the winding path leading to the exterior steps of Jacob's studio. Down she hurried, then banged noisily on the door. "Jacob!" she yelled, ignoring Wyatt as he caught up with her. But then he grabbed her wrist before she could pound any further.

"Stop it!" he ordered.

"Let go of me!" she yelled back.

A muffled, "What the fuck?" came from inside the apartment.

Ava said, "Jacob, open up!"

"Is there a fire or something?" He yanked open the door. His hair was mussed, his eyes red, and he was wearing only boxer shorts that showed off massively hairy legs. The scent of marijuana lingered in the air, and the entire studio was a cluttered mess of dirty clothes, empty pizza boxes, and glowing computer screens. His bed was mussed, the covers spilling onto the floor.

"What do you know about the recording equipment on the third floor?" Ava demanded.

"The what?" He scratched the stubble on his chin. "Are you fuckin' nuts?" He staggered back inside and Ava and Wyatt followed.

With an effort, Ava held on to her temper as she related the discovery of Jewel-Anne's attempts at terrorizing her.

"No shit!" was Jacob's response, sitting on the edge of the bed.

"You helped her," Ava accused.

He shook his head. "Uh-uh. No way."

"She couldn't have done it herself," Ava insisted. Wyatt seemed to want to say something but remained silent.

Jacob answered, "Well, yeah, you got that right. I don't see how. Hell, it's amazing she could even do what you say you caught on camera." He seemed genuinely astounded and almost envious.

Ava declared, "You had to have helped her. You're the techie around here."

"I didn't know anything about it." He held up both hands and looked at Wyatt. "Seriously, man."

Ava couldn't believe it, but he seemed sincere. Either he was putting on an Oscar-worthy performance or he really wasn't involved.

Wyatt said, "Come on, Ava, we'll sort this all out in the morning."

She turned on him. "Including how you made up fake names for the biological parents of our child? I called them, you know, put them through the hell of reliving their daughter's death! What were they, clients of the firm?"

He didn't respond but she could tell she'd hit the mark. The Johnsons must have come in for some legal advice, and that's how Wyatt had learned about their daughter's plight.

"Jewel-Anne's right," Jacob said to Wyatt. He hooked a thumb at Ava, "She *is* fuckin' nuts."

Ava lifted her arms in disbelief, then left her cousin in his pigsty of a room Outside, the darkness surrounded her with the breath of November rattling the trees. Could she have been so wrong about Jacob being involved? If not Jewel-Anne's brother, then who? To Ava's mind, there was no doubt that she'd had an accomplice. All she had to do was flush him out.

Or her. It could be a woman.

Wyatt was a couple of paces behind her. Feeling suffocated even being around him, she picked up her speed and jogged back to the house and the relative safety of her room.

Lyons hit him with the news the minute Snyder walked into his cubicle the next morning. "Guess what?" she asked, and was once again wearing a smile that caused her eyes to sparkle mischievously, like a child who could barely hold in a secret.

"What?"

"Guess who was pregnant during her sessions with the hypnotist?"

"Jewel-Anne Church?"

"Mmm-hmm."

"Really?" he said, sitting down as she nodded, leaning against the frame of his cubicle. Her cell phone was in one hand, a small cassette in the other.

"Heard it on this little gem right here."

"Who's the baby's daddy?"

"Unknown."

"And where's the baby?"

"Also unknown. Yet. I still have three more sessions to listen to, but I'll keep you informed."

"Do that," he suggested, then added, "You know, I don't know what this has to do with the case."

"Neither do I. But I have a feeling there's something."

"Maybe you just like eavesdropping."

"You have a better idea?"

He shrugged.

"Didn't think so," she said as his desk phone jangled. He picked up as she walked down the hall toward her own cubicle. He didn't watch her leave, told himself he didn't care what her butt looked like in the slim gray skirt she was wearing. Didn't care at all.

For Ava, the next day was hellish. Jewel-Anne, playing the victim in all of this drama, spent most of her day in her room. Jacob, before and after he went to the mainland for school, threw her dark looks. Virginia kept muttering under her breath, "What goes around, comes around," and Ian didn't even try to hide the fact that he was so nervous he'd started

smoking again. Trent, Ian, and Wyatt had all left early, right
after breakfast; Ava had again watched them boat across the
bay, much as they had the day before. Graciela had played
dumb, doing her work almost mute, and whenever Ava crossed
paths with Demetria, Jewel-Anne's nurse sent her daggerlike
glares meant to cut deep.

Oh, save me. Ava wasn't taking on *that* guilt. She had enough
to deal with as it was.

Khloe, often her champion, followed her upstairs to her bedroom after breakfast and said, "Couldn't you have found a better way to confront Jewel-Anne? You can't go threatening a
girl in a wheelchair and almost throwing her over a second-
story balcony."

Ava had picked up her laptop, but now she set it back down.
She'd started doing her preliminary search for an attorney, one
that wasn't associated with her husband, a lawyer who could
help her become her own person again, break the guardianship
and perhaps help her with divorce proceedings. She wanted to
get back to her search, but not while Khloe was there.

"Just play it cool, okay?" Khloe advised.

"Jewel-Anne's Noah's mother and has been silently lording
it over me for years. I don't know how cool I can be."

"You're not helping your case by assaulting a handicapped
girl."

"I know, and Wyatt wants to send me back to St. Brendan's.
I certainly didn't help matters."

Khloe froze. "What?"

"He and Dr. McPherson think it would be best for me."

"Didn't you fire her?"

"Yes, well, technically I think she quit. It doesn't matter.
Wyatt rehired her. He can do that as my guardian."

"You should fight that. The guardianship, I mean."

"I am. I just have to find an attorney." She scooped up the
laptop again and sat down in a chair. "I thought catching Jewel-

Anne on tape would vindicate me, that everyone would see that she was behind all my paranoia, but even that seems to have backfired."

"It's all too weird," Khloe said. "I don't even remember Jewel-Anne dating. Ever. So if she's Noah's mother, I mean like really his mother, who's the father?"

"She wouldn't say, and I've been wracking my brain and coming up empty." Ava snorted. "Maybe there's not enough gray matter up there to wrack."

Khloe smothered a laugh. The truth was, Ava was just about out of ideas. She'd been trying to remember anyone Jewel-Anne could have slept with sometime over four years ago. She'd considered people who lived in Monroe: a male physical therapist, her own husband . . . maybe even Kelvin, though at the time he'd been engaged to Khloe, and Ava couldn't imagine him cheating on Khloe for a fling with his first cousin. Would he really? Didn't sound like Kelvin.

Khloe's cell phone rang. Pulling it from her jeans pocket, she made a face. "Simon." Rolling her large eyes, she whispered, "He's been in one of his moods ever since his birthday. A real bear."

"Why don't you just leave him?"

"It's not that easy," she said as the phone rang a second time. "Ava, what if you found Noah and the news was just . . . awful?" Khloe posed.

"Noah's alive. I just know it."

"Okay, I'm just saying you should prepare yourself. Even if he is alive, you may never find him and you could end up looking for him, never knowing what happened to him, for the rest of your life. Is that what you want to do?"

"If I have to," she said.

Khloe's phone rang a third time and she turned to the door and said, "Guess I'd better answer it."

For a few seconds after she left, Ava sat silently. Then she set down the laptop and climbed onto her bed. Khloe's words had sunk deep. Her throat grew hot and swollen as she considered a life of not knowing what happened to her boy.

There was a chance Khloe and everyone else was right. What if the truth was worse than not knowing? Immediately, she scratched that thought. No. Nothing was worse than not knowing.

She glanced at the nightstand. Another day's worth of medication was set out for her already. Someone—Khloe? Graciela? Wyatt?—had made certain it was ready. And the pills were seductive; they could take the edge off, help cocoon her from the pain.

"Damn it," she whispered, and pulled her legs up as she lowered her cheek to her knees and let the tears run. She sobbed softly as she thought of Noah and the so obvious truth that she might never see him again. It broke her heart to think of him forever missing.

Again she glanced at the pills.

Her fists curled. She wouldn't give up.

Never!

Climbing out of the bed, she again put on the ludicrous act of swallowing the pills before flushing them away. She had to start at the beginning. If Jewel-Anne was Noah's mother, who the hell was his father? Could this mystery man be Jewel-Anne's accomplice?

Ava set her jaw. She had to find out who Jewel-Anne's secret lover was. Maybe that man was the key to finding Noah.

Chapter 40

"Son of a bitch!" Snyder slammed down his phone and reached for his shoulder holster in one move. Ten seconds later, he was shrugging into his jacket and making his way to Lyons's desk. He found her, headphones in place, furrows marring her forehead.

As he closed the distance, she held up a finger to keep him from speaking. "Just a sec." She said it a little louder than she should have. "Jesus, Joseph, and Mary!" She punched the cassette button and replayed a section one more time. As she listened, the look of confusion on her face gave way to one of surprise and dawning comprehension. Shutting down the recorder, she yanked off her headphones. "We just found out the name of Jewel-Anne's baby's daddy. Give it a guess."

"We can play twenty questions in the car. Right now we need to investigate a possible homicide, and I used the term *possible* lightly. The first responder has no doubt."

"What? Who?"

"Evelyn McPherson."

"The psychologist?"

"Yeah."

"To Ava Garrison?" Lyons gave him a long look, which he ignored.

"One and the same. Found at her house. The neighbor noticed a change in routine and called; then when no one answered, she investigated and saw McPherson's car in the garage. She tried the bell several times. When no one answered, she called the city cops."

Kicking her chair back, Lyons climbed to her feet and reached for her coat, scarf, and sidearm. "What a co-ink-i-dink, as they say. Any other details?"

"Not yet."

She flashed him a determined smile as she unlocked her desk drawer and retrieved her purse. "Let's go get some. I'll drive."

Together they walked through the building to the back parking lot where they dashed through the spitting rain to Lyons's car. Once inside, she fired up the engine and hit the defroster.

He rattled off Evelyn McPherson's address and snapped his seat belt into place. "Okay," he said as Lyons slipped the car into gear. "I'll bite. Who knocked up Jewel-Anne Church?"

She slid him a glance out of the corner of her eye. "None other than the hero of Anchorville's very own favorite ghost story."

He stared at his partner as if she'd lost her mind. "Lester Reece?"

"Yessirree." She flipped on the wipers and gunned it out of the lot, taking a corner fast enough to make the tires screech. "The timing's right, if you figure it out. Jewel-Anne and her family were living on the hospital grounds. She'd met Reece and could have been fascinated. From what I understand, lots of women were."

Snyder said, "You're thinking she got involved with him, got pregnant, and then helped him escape."

Lyons responded, "From what I've read on the case, there's always been speculation that someone helped him, but the focus has always been on his nurse. But what if it was Jewel-Anne? She's certainly smart enough."

"That's a pretty big leap," he said, glancing out the window to the naked, wet trees lining the street, but as he thought about it over the crackle of the police band radio and the hum of the car's tires on wet pavement, he thought it might just be a possibility.

She said thoughtfully, "You know, his name just keeps coming up."

"And?"

"People keep saying they see him, and all of a sudden we have two women who are killed very similarly to how ol' Lester took care of his victims."

Snyder didn't like it, even though it made a certain amount of sense.

"I know it would be easier for you to think Reece is dead, his body rotting in the ocean, but there's a chance he's not." She slid him another look. "This, Evelyn McPherson, could be his work." When he didn't respond, she added, "I'm just sayin'. Y'know? We need to keep our minds open."

"Okay."

The drive took less than fifteen minutes through rain-washed streets that glistened under the pale light of the street-lamps. As the cruiser rounded the corner to the block where Evelyn McPherson resided, they were greeted by county and city vehicles huddled around the duplex with their lights flashing, strobing the nearby houses. A cluster of neighbors had collected on the sidewalk one house down, and a couple of officers were just finishing stringing yellow crime scene tape around the perimeter of the yard.

"Already a circus," Snyder muttered under his breath as

Lyons pulled into a parking spot across the street from McPherson's residence.

"Bound to get worse." She cut the engine and pocketed her keys, then climbed out. They both avoided puddles as they walked through the rain to the front door.

"Careful," the officer signing people into the scene warned as they each slipped covers over their shoes. "Crime scene guys aren't here yet."

"We won't disturb anything," Snyder assured him.

After signing the logbook, they walked carefully inside. It was always disconcerting stepping into a murdered person's home, and Snyder had never really felt comfortable sifting through the personal effects of a life cut so violently short; it seemed like an extra violation of privacy even though he knew he was the victim's advocate. Today, he carefully stepped through McPherson's house, where a single half-drunk glass of wine and a plate of sliced cheese sat on the kitchen counter. The knife she'd used to cut the cheese had been left near the remains of a wedge.

"Snack for one," he observed.

"Maybe dinner." When he arched a brow, she said, "I'm a single woman. I recognize a meal when I see one."

"If you say so."

The living room was untouched, extremely tidy, everything in its place, like a staged room out of one of those decorating magazines. No struggle here.

They made their way into the bedroom and adjoining bath. Evelyn McPherson, fully dressed in slacks and an expensive-looking sweater, lay on the floor, staring sightlessly upward, her eyes already becoming opaque, the deep slit beneath her chin dark red and gaping, blood pooled beneath her and splattered around the small room.

Here's where the struggle had taken place.

And it had been violent.

The shower curtain had been thrown open, smeared dirt showing where someone had stood in the tub, waiting. Blood had sprayed on the walls, mirror, sink, and counter, some running down the cabinetry in red streaks to pool on each drawer. Bottles and jars of makeup and cleansers were scattered on the floor, glass broken on the tiles, lipstick tubes red from having rolled through the blood.

"Not much of a question of homicide," Lyons said, her jaw tight as she surveyed the scene.

"Nope." Such a waste, he thought, not stepping into the room where Evelyn McPherson had breathed her last.

"Look familiar?" he asked his partner.

She was nodding, as if reading his thoughts. "Looks like the Reynolds scene. Victim two of the same killer." She glanced up at him. "Both of whom were close to Ava Garrison."

"And possibly a lot of other people."

"Possibly," she allowed, but they were both thinking along the same lines. The obvious connection between the two victims was a one-time mental patient who was obsessed with finding her missing son, a boy who most people assumed had wandered out of the house, down to the dock, and into the water where he'd drowned and been swept out to sea as his parents reveled at their Christmas party. Snyder figured Ava Garrison's obsession with finding her son was all about guilt, though, hell, he wasn't a psychologist and the one she'd been seeing was now very dead.

"Sick bastard." He started to step away, then stopped. "What the hell is that?" he asked, pointing to the bathtub. Rivulets of drying blood smudged the polished surface and a single black hair lay across the rim.

"Oh, shit," Lyons said, leaning down to get a closer look. "That's our connection to the two crimes." She glanced up at him. "Kinda makes you wonder if Ava Garrison walked off with Cheryl Reynolds's Halloween costume."

"You think she could do this?" He motioned to the bloody, lifeless body of Evelyn McPherson.

"I'm thinking whoever took the wig also took the tapes of Ms. Garrison's sessions with the hypnotist. Who would want them other than the woman herself?"

Snyder felt a niggle of anticipation fire his blood. "If your theory's right, then all of the missing tapes are with the killer."

"Or already destroyed."

She straightened and crossed the master bedroom to a desk in a corner that was empty except for a spot for a laptop docking station. She pointed to the obviously empty spot. "We need to find this computer."

"And check her office."

"You read my mind."

They looked around for a little while longer and found no murder weapon, unless the murderer had used one of the kitchen knives and either left with it or cleaned it and put it back where he'd found it. Snyder wasn't betting on that. Also missing was the laptop computer that fit into the docking station on McPherson's desk, her purse, and her cell phone. None of those items had appeared in her car, which was parked in the attached garage. The house showed no sign of forced entry, either; all the doors were locked and windows latched.

The neighboring unit was clean as well, locked up tight but vacant. Snyder assumed she'd either let the intruder in, or he'd found a key or open door and locked it later . . . Odd. Ten to one, the killer had her personal items, including her computer. They could only hope that McPherson had another one in her office or a backup disk somewhere, and once they got back to the office, they'd start checking her cell phone records and Internet accounts, her e-mail and social media contacts, and try to figure out who was the last one to see her alive.

They talked a little with the forensic guys when they showed up, then with the neighbor who had called the city police, but learned no more than what the first responding officer had reported.

They left deputies in charge and headed to Dr. McPherson's office just as the first van from a local television station was parking at the end of the street.

"You know we're going to end up heading to the island to talk to Ava Garrison," Lyons said as oncoming headlights illuminated her face.

"Yeah."

"It makes you wonder, doesn't it?" she added, almost to herself. "What's so damned important that two women are slashed to ribbons?"

"It's personal," Snyder said as he looked out the passenger side window, thinking about the violent way the women had been killed. In Cheryl Reynolds's case, she'd nearly been strangled to death, but the killer had taken the time to finish the job with a knife that had a serrated, nine-inch blade. He was willing to bet a year's vacation pay that once the autopsy on Evelyn McPherson was complete, they'd discover the exact same MO.

And the killer still had the murder weapon.

Seated at his kitchen table, Dern took a swig straight from his bottle of Jack. The TV was on, turned low, an old Clint Eastwood movie playing, not that he cared.

From the rag rug near the woodstove, the dog cocked his head, his dark eyes focused hard on Dern. "It's waaay after five, Buddy, so no judging," Dern said, but he capped the bottle anyway. It had been a long day after a crazy night. He'd heard the ruckus when Ava had flown down the stairs to the nerd's apartment and nearly beat down the door with her bare fist after, from what he'd discerned since, nearly killing her crippled cousin. Not that Jewel-Anne hadn't deserved it, from what he could tell by comments made by Ian earlier in the day.

"It's a goddamned house of horrors," Ian had confided while

smoking near the greenhouse where Dern had been looking for another shovel. "Ava's gone totally around the bend and Jewel-Anne . . . well, she's been messed up for years. I guess having to give up a baby and losing the use of your legs can do that, but wow. She's been terrorizing Ava ever since Ava got back from the hospital." He relayed the events of the night as he'd heard them, though both he and Trent, after knocking down "a few drinks" in Anchorville, had slept through all the commotion. That, in and of itself, was incredible, Dern thought, but didn't say so.

Drawing hard on his Camel filter tip, Ian had tossed the butt into the wet grass where it had sizzled. "And it's contagious, you know? The other day, I swear to God, as I was driving the boat back from Anchorville, I thought *I* saw Lester Reece, right here on the island, up at the point, kind of in the fog and staring down at the boathouse."

He reached into his pocket for his pack of smokes and shook out a fresh cigarette even though the last was still smoldering in the lawn. "Crazy, right? Now I've caught Ava's fuckin' paranoia!" Fumbling in his pockets, he found his lighter and jabbed his cigarette into his mouth. "No way Lester Reece could still be alive, much less be on this damned rock, right?" he asked, the filter tip bobbing as he clicked his lighter several times before a tiny flame appeared and he was able to light up. Sucking hard enough to inhale every iota of nicotine from his cigarette, he paused, letting the smoke fill his lungs before exhaling. "I blinked and he was gone, just like that." Ian snapped his fingers. "Probably a goddamned hallucination, but that's it. I'm getting the hell out."

"And do what?" Dern spied the shovel through the dirty panes of the greenhouse.

"Don't know. But I've got friends in Portland. I could crash with them for a while." He'd seemed freaked out at the time, but then the entire household of Neptune's Gate had been on pins and needles. "All I know is, I'm soooo outta here." Then he'd walked around the house, leaving Dern to grab the shovel and head back to the stable and his apartment.

Thinking about everything now, Dern reluctantly found his untraceable cell phone and made the call he'd been dreading for hours.

Reba picked up on the second ring. "Hello?"

"Hey." He smiled at the sound of her voice. "How're you doing?"

"I've been better."

"Any more phone calls?"

"No." He imagined her shaking her head, her forehead wrinkling. "Have you found him?" she asked.

"Not yet," he admitted, "but he's here, on the island. I can feel it. I just can't prove it . . . yet." He didn't add that he'd thought he'd caught a glimpse of the bastard, but like smoke, Reece had disappeared before Dern could reach the spot where he'd seen him. He'd been riding near Sea Cliff. Dern had a feeling Reece was holed up in the old asylum, but there were just too many places to hide for Dern to find him or even where he was camping out. The trouble was that Reece knew the place like the back of his hand. Once Dern had proof that Reece was there, he would call the police. He just wouldn't tell his mother until after the fact.

"Don't hurt him," she begged, and Dern knew he'd have to lie. Again. Well, hell, he was getting good at it. Had years of practice.

"I'll do my best."

"Promise me, Austin. You have to bring Lester in alive. He has to be safe."

"If I can."

"Promise me!" she insisted, her voice rising, and he thought of her in her wheelchair, staring out the window, her fingers gripping the arms. "If I could, I'd be there with you, but I can't, so you have to do this for me. For us. Our family." Her voice broke, but he knew she was dry-eyed. She'd learned not to cry years before.

"I promise, Mom," he finally said, though he was certain they both knew he might not deliver.

"Don't get the police involved. They'll . . . they'll shoot to kill and you know it."

She was referring to his own stint as a cop. It had been short-lived, but he knew the police, too, wanted to catch Reece and bring him to justice. "I know they'll do their best."

"Oh, Austin. Don't let them—"

"I'll try to bring him in alive. Get him safe."

"Thank God." She sounded so relieved and his heart twisted a bit. "Just go find your brother."

He hung up with that same hollowness in his soul he felt whenever he talked to her. She was dying, prematurely, but living on borrowed time according to all the doctors.

He knew it.

She knew it.

Reece knew it, too. That's why he'd surfaced again, taken the chance and contacted a mother he'd barely known, a woman who had let a rich, if abusive, father take away her firstborn. Lester had been a wild boy of four when she started a new life with a new man who wasn't much better than the first, but a man who gave her a second son whom she'd named Austin, for the town to which she'd fled.

Lester Reece had then grown up privileged and educated, but he had suffered at the hands of his father and a series of stepmothers who were more than a little responsible for his criminal ways, at least according to his defense team at his trial.

Dern, on the other hand, had been raised in a relatively stable, if poor household with his other siblings. His old man, a ranch hand who had taught his boy his trade before taking off when Dern was ten, had been a hard-drinking, hardworking man who seemed to like horses better than people.

To this day, Dern never knew what happened to him.

When his mother, a few years later, had taken up with a new man, a stepfather Dern didn't care to know, he'd moved out. It wasn't until much later, when he was doing his time in the service overseas, that he'd learned the truth. Reba, facing her first serious health scare, had written him, finally explaining about her first short marriage and the child she hadn't seen in over a quarter of a century, a man who was accused of killing his ex-wife and her friend, a man who was dangerous.

She'd felt guilt for abandoning him, but Dern had thought Lester Reece was best left alone. He didn't need to meet this half brother who had a tendency to cut up women.

Then Reece had been caught, tried, and sent to the mental hospital. Good riddance, Dern had thought.

Until the son of a bitch escaped and pulled the best damned disappearing act in recent history. And now his dying mother wanted to know that he was safe and not hurting anyone else.

So that was Dern's mission.

He looked at the dog again, frowned, and opened his bottle of Jack once more. With one finger pointing at the dog, he took a long pull, felt the whiskey warm his throat, then said, "We've still got our deal, right? No judgments."

Rover thumped his damned tail just as Dern heard the sound of footsteps on the stairs leading to his apartment. The dog gave off a soft, and much-too-late warning bark.

He glanced at the clock. It was after ten-thirty. Odd time for a visit. Who knew what was coming? Quickly, he pocketed his phone. When he opened the door, Ava Garrison stood on the landing at the top of the stairs.

His gut tightened as she turned those incredible gray eyes up at him. Shit, what was she doing here?

"I saw that your light was still on, that you were still up and . . ." She shrugged. "I'd like to talk to you." Then, as if realizing she could be interrupting something, added, "If you're not busy."

"Come on in." He pushed the door open a little wider so she could enter and see that he was entirely alone, only the muted TV and the shepherd for company. "Can I buy you a drink?"

Stepping inside, she glanced at the small plank table in the kitchen and the open bottle of whiskey. Without a second's hesitation, she nodded. "You know what? I could use one."

Chapter 41

"... and so that's what happened last night," Ava admitted, staring into her small glass of whiskey where a couple of ice cubes were slowly melting. She'd decided she had to tell Dern her side of the story because she was certain he'd heard about her fight with Jewel-Anne the night before in bits and pieces from members of the staff, and she wanted him to hear her version. "I got angry and pushed it too far, but I couldn't take the lies and the gaslighting another minute."

"Don't blame you." Dern was straddling his chair, arms resting over the back, his drink for the most part untouched. Without interrupting, he'd listened to her tale as she'd explained about Jewel-Anne's complicity in terrorizing Ava, the recording that was wired to play a little boy's frightened screams, and the fact that Jewel-Anne claimed to be Noah's birth mother.

"That was something I didn't remember at all. There's just a big blank hole there. I was pregnant, though not as far along as Jewel-Anne was ... and with Kelvin's death and Jewel-Anne's paralysis ..."

"But she can walk. She's not paralyzed."

"She can stand, and she's working with a PT. On the camera, I saw her moving but not walking exactly. More like hauling herself along with her upper body." Ava felt a twinge of guilt at that, at the fact that she'd let her pent-up rage control her actions. "I know she's been through a lot, but man . . ."

Dern reached across the table and took her hand. "So have you," he said, his strong fingers tightening, as if to reinforce his words. "She tried to ruin your life by manipulating you, making you think you were losing your mind, teasing you with terrified recordings of a child you thought was your son."

Her heart warmed at his words. Could she trust him? Who knew? But at least for the moment, he seemed sincere and that alone brought a lump to her throat, made her feel closer to a man she barely knew. "Thanks," she said.

Again his strong fingers tightened, and for just the tiniest of seconds, his thumb ran over the inside of hers.

She glanced up, caught him staring at her, and in that instant she once again imagined making love to him. She pulled her hand away quickly and cleared her throat. "Anyway, I thought I'd better give you my version, though after our last fight—"

"We didn't just fight." His gaze found hers again, and she remembered all too vividly what it had felt like to kiss him and feel his rock-hard body against her own.

"We didn't." Feeling suddenly awkward, she picked up her glass and swirled the contents, sending the ice cubes swaying in the amber liquid. "But I think I accused you of being part of a conspiracy or something."

He smiled slightly, a crooked grin buried deep in his beard shadow. "Or something."

"So . . . I've decided it's not such a bad thing to have someone looking out for me."

The grin widened. "Let me guess: You could have used

someone on your side last night. The bodyguard you thought was a pain in the backside."

She finally smiled back and hated the warmth she felt with him, here, in the small apartment, the dog basking by the woodstove, an open bottle of whiskey between them. How had that happened? It was almost as surreal as the rest of her life.

As if he felt it, too, an intimacy that was far too seductive, he broke eye contact. "How's Jewel-Anne?"

"I don't know. She's been hiding in her room most of the day. Came out for lunch and to throw me a few dirty looks, took her dinner in her room, and has holed up there. I guess . . . I guess I should feel sorry for scaring the crap out of her, but I don't, not after what she did to me."

"What happens now?"

"Same as before. I keep looking for my son," she said, and took a final swig from her glass and stood.

"Anything else?"

"Yeah, I think I'm cleaning house. If I can find a way to get Jewel-Anne and her siblings out of Neptune's Gate, I'm going to do it."

"What about the staff?"

"Don't know yet."

"So, then, it'll be just you and Wyatt?" he said, kicking back his own chair and walking her to the door. "Marital bliss."

"You were married once, right?" she asked him.

"For a short time. I think I told you."

"Then you know sometimes there's not a whole lot of 'bliss' involved." Her memory suddenly kicked in and she recalled her separation from Wyatt, that he'd lived in Anchorville for a while. But after her hospitalization, he'd been back, sleeping in another room while they "figured things out."

"My marriage has been dead for a long time, Dern. Unfortunately, I was the last one to realize it."

Before she did anything stupid like brush a kiss across his cheek and invite more trouble, she slipped outside, into the cold November night. No moon was visible, the rain was lashing, and the big house was dark for the most part, but a light shone from Jewel-Anne's room and Ava decided it was time to have another talk with her cousin. She wouldn't let things get out of hand like they had the night before, but she was certain that the key to Noah's whereabouts was his father, and she needed to know who he was.

And the only person who could answer that question was Jewel-Anne.

Be calm, Ava told herself. *Make her think she has the upper hand. Play into her vanity, make her think you are too slow to figure it out and she won't be able to keep herself from teasing you with bits of information, allowing her to feel superior. Whatever you do, don't get violent . . . just play her as she's trying to play you.*

She headed through the back door and walked across the darkened kitchen. The house was silent aside from the hum of the refrigerator and the drip of a leaking faucet. As she passed the sink, she stopped briefly to tighten the handle and then walked through the foyer to the stairs. Faintly, from the wing housing Jewel-Anne's suite, she heard the sound of music, some old Elvis tune, of course, about fools rushing into love.

The song was getting louder as she approached Jewel-Anne's bedroom and that gave Ava pause. Since when did her cousin blast music? And especially in the middle of the night. Jewel-Anne was usually plugged into her headphones.

Weird. But then what wasn't when it came to Jewel-Anne?

She rapped on the door and waited

Nothing.

Maybe her cousin just couldn't hear over Elvis's warbling.

"Jewel-Anne? Can I come in?" She pounded again, more loudly.

Again, no response.

Twisting the doorknob, she pushed open the door and stepped into the younger woman's inner sanctum of pink, ruffles, and dolls. "Jewel?" she called. She wasn't in her bed, nor the sitting area. Her computer was glowing on her desk, her iPod plugged into it and playing through the laptop's speakers. Her wheelchair was empty, abandoned near her walk-in closet.

Ava felt a first shiver of dread. "Jewel?" She snapped off the iPod and the room went silent. "Are you okay?" Snapping on the light for the closet, a huge room large enough for her wheelchair to turn around, the shelves and hooks all retrofitted for a short person.

Empty.

Which left the bathroom. Ava tapped on the door. "Hey, Jewel. It's me. Ava. I want to apologize and maybe we can talk?"

Bracing herself for a snotty "Go away!" she lingered at the door.

No sound emitted.

This wouldn't go well, she knew, but she tried the door anyway and stepped inside. "I don't mean to bother you, but I just want to . . ." The words died in her throat as she took in the scene in front of her.

Jewel-Anne, wearing a black wig and completely dressed, was lying in the tub. Her long throat had been slit ear to ear, a red smile of blood draining down her front. Tucked next to her were two dolls, each staring upward, their plastic necks cut, their heads nearly severed, the gashes colored a dripping, dark red.

They both had straight black hair.

The scream that erupted from Ava's throat shattered the still night air. Shaking, disbelieving, a moment later she forced herself to take Jewel-Anne's pulse, but of course there was none; her flesh wasn't even warm. "Oh, Jesus, oh, Jesus, oh . . ." Ava backed out of the room, stumbling against the wheelchair as she scrambled to get out. "Help!! Call 911!!!" she cried before realizing she had her own cell phone and scrabbled in the pocket of her sweater for the damned thing. "Help!" She punched in the numbers and was connected with an operator.

"Nine-one-one, what's your—"

"Send help! There's been a murder! On Church Island!"

"Ma'am, can I get your name?"

"I'm Ava Garrison and we need help. My cousin Jewel-Anne Church, she's been killed! Oh, God, please just send someone to Neptune's Gate on the island!" She rattled off the address as footsteps sounded in the hallway and Demetria, groggy and frightened, stumbled into the room.

"What happened?" she demanded, flying past Ava and toward the bathroom. She let out an ear-piercing scream that sent Ava's insides quivering. Then the whole house came alive and Ava, in shock, leaned heavily against the wall of Jewel-Anne's suite. Wyatt, in pajama bottoms and nothing else, ran into the room. He checked the bathroom, then backed out. In a raw voice, he asked, "Dear God, Ava, what have you done?"

The call came in at twelve fifty-seven, according to the glaring readout of his digital bedside clock. Snyder had been deep in the middle of a damned good dream about his days as a high school football star when it was interrupted by the shrill ring of his cell phone and Sheriff Joe Biggs telling him about a possible homicide on Church Island. The victim: Jewel-Anne Church, birth mother of the missing child, lover of Lester Reece, and handicapped woman who lived at Neptune's Gate. Biggs told him that two officers had been dispatched and were at the house, securing it and rounding up witnesses.

He collected Lyons, who, even roused from bed, managed to look fresh as a goddamned daisy. Her hair was clipped away from her face and she was just wearing jeans, boots, and a heavy jacket, but to Snyder, she was too damned attractive for her own good. She'd brought a small case that he knew carried her tablet computer.

"Can you believe this?" she asked, her eyes luminous as they drove to the marina where the sheriff department's craft would ferry them out to the island. It was raining hard, the wipers working double time.

"None of it."

"Biggs has ordered dogs and a manhunt of the entire island. At dawn."

"What?"

"He's covering his bases. Too many sightings of Lester Reece for him to keep ignoring them."

"He called you, too? Personally."

"Seems to have a major stake in what goes on out there."

"So you told him that Reece is the biological father of the missing boy?"

"Well, I said *possibly*—no, more like *probably*." She fiddled with the heater, trying to warm the interior of his old Dodge.

This was getting out of hand fast. "How'd Biggs get word? Dispatch usually doesn't call the sheriff."

"No. He said it was someone from the island, an ex-in-law."

Heat started blasting from the vents, just as they reached the waterfront. A launch was waiting, idling at the dock, a deputy at its helm.

"The cook," Snyder said.

"Yeah, and this cook said that there was a big ruckus the night before, that Ava Garrison nearly killed her cousin by almost tossing her over the second-story balcony. Jewel-Anne Church."

"And she's the victim?"

Lyons nodded. "Looks like it."

"Guess we've got suspect number one," Snyder said, feeling tired.

"Except things are never as easy as that." She was already unsnapping her seat belt.

"Nope, they never are," he said as he rammed the car into park. Climbing out, he was hit by a blast of icy wind blowing off the Pacific. "Showtime."

"Let's get to it." Flipping up the hood of her jacket and carrying her tablet computer in its case, Lyons was already hurrying toward the dock.

Snyder had to run to catch up to her, and as he did, his cell phone rang. The message was a simple confirmation that Evelyn McPherson's next of kin had been notified. The press was already getting the information, and therefore the people isolated on Church Island would hear the news of the psychologist's death.

If nothing else, at least he'd get to see their reactions, which could be helpful, as now three women connected to Ava Garrison had been killed, and nearly everyone else she dealt with lived on that friggin' island.

"Move it, Snyder!" Lyons was already in the boat.

Stashing his cell in his jacket, he climbed in after her. "Next of kin for McPherson's been notified," he told her.

"Good. Let's see what the Island People have to say about that."

Within half an hour, over choppy water, whitecaps frothing around them, dark clouds obscuring the stars, they pulled up just past Monroe at the private dock of Neptune's Gate. The wind was screaming in off the sea, rain lashing as they made their way, with the deputy, to the front steps.

"Like something out of a horror flick," Lyons said, eyeing the huge mansion built before the turn of the *last* century. "Big, creepy house, the middle of the night, a weird family of misfits. And a murder. It's got all the elements."

A female deputy manned the front door, keeping a log of anyone who came in and went out. She explained that her partner was keeping all of the witnesses in a family room/den off the kitchen and that the victim was upstairs, untouched, found by Ava Garrison, the woman who owned the place.

And who allegedly had nearly killed the victim the night before, Snyder thought.

He and Lyons walked through a massive open foyer. He remembered the impressive staircase that wound upward to a second-floor gallery that opened to the bedrooms.

"Dillard has everyone in the family room," the deputy said. "We haven't interviewed them individually, but the long and the short of it is that the owner, Ava Garrison, had been visiting the ranch hand who lives over the stable on the property." The deputy checked her notes and read from them. "She'd seen lights on in the victim's room and went up to talk to her. This was around midnight. She heard the clock. She knocked on the door, no one responded, and after several tries to get the victim to answer, walked inside and found the victim in the bathtub. Already deceased." She told them the location of Jewel-Anne Church's set of rooms.

"Let's take a look." Lyons was already heading up the stairs. Snyder was a step behind. They found the open door to the victim's room, which was decorated straight out of Sleeping Beauty's castle in Disneyland. Pink and lavender, canopied bed, and white, feminine furniture. "My dream room when I was nine," Lyons muttered before opening the door to the bathroom and exposing the garish scene within. The victim lay in the tub, fully clothed, flanked by two dolls with eyes that opened and shut. Antiques, these days. All three had their throats slashed, and the dolls' necks had been painted with something to simulate blood.

"Nail polish," Lyons said. "How bizarre." She snapped pictures on her iPad.

"Yeah and check out the wig."

Lyons stopped taking pictures long enough to look over her shoulder at him. "You think it's a match?"

He grimaced, not liking where his thoughts were taking him. "I'd bet my badge on it."

Chapter 42

Ava suffered through it all. Confined to the first floor, in close contact with the members of her family and the staff as they waited in the large room off the kitchen, Ava thought she would go out of her mind. Dern was included in the roundup of everyone who lived at Neptune's Gate, but she kept her distance from him, didn't want to give anyone any inkling to her feelings. Besides, she was upset. Beyond upset.

Who? she wondered over and over again. Who would kill Jewel-Anne? Could the killer be in this room even now? Her skin crawled at the possibilities, and when she remembered her cousin, all the blood, the hideous dolls, she cringed inside.

And they blamed her. She felt it in the looks cast in her direction.

Her head was pounding, her heart heavy, her stomach on the verge of losing whatever was in it, and she couldn't avoid the silent accusations in Jacob's and Demetria's eyes. Though she turned her back to the family and stared out the window at the darkness beyond, she felt them watching her, felt the weight of their gazes. They all thought she was responsible.

But someone knew the truth.

Someone had to.

Because someone was guilty as sin; she just didn't know who the culprit was.

Raindrops drizzled down the glass in crooked lines, and the leaves of the rhododendrons, visible in the thin light from inside, shivered with the wind. Still it seemed safer outside in the elements.

Never had this large room seemed so small. It had always been a comforting, family place with its gas fire and oversized furniture, a spot where one could read a book, watch the television, or just hang out. Sadly, Ava remembered curling up with Noah and reading a favorite story aloud. Even Jewel-Anne, with her clicking needles and ever-present dolls and earphones, had spent time here.

Now the sanctuary was a prison. Crammed into the room, everyone was nervous, barely talking, and Ava imagined they were all going through their own surreal thoughts. Jacob and Demetria, closest to Jewel-Anne, appeared shell-shocked. Khloe, Simon, and Virginia huddled in one corner, whispering among themselves. Ian and Trent took up residence near the fireplace, Ian nervously jangling the keys in his pocket, the fire hissing as flames licked the logs.

Standing stiffly near the doorway was Wyatt; his face was the color of ash and his arms were crossed over his chest, almost defiantly, as he remained tight-lipped. It was obvious that he stood as far from his wife as he could, on the opposite side of the room, oceans of dark emotions and unspoken accusations separating them. No more did he pretend to be the attentive husband; it was almost as if his belief that she killed Jewel-Anne was the final blow to an already shattered marriage and he was now resigned to its failure.

Not that Ava cared. She continued to stare outside, looking past her own ghostly reflection on the glass to the inky night beyond. Let Wyatt think whatever he damned well pleased.

Dern stood at the other window. Leaning one shoulder against its frame, he also stared outside to the darkness and probably wished he, too, could be anywhere else but in this tense, uncomfortable room.

Never once did she meet his eyes.

Graciela was missing, but she wasn't due to arrive for work until morning. Noisily the two detectives returned to the first floor and made their way into the den. As Ava turned to face them, she tried to remain calm and hang on to her wits.

Snyder said, "We're going to need to talk to each of you, alone. One of the deputies will stay with the rest of you while we interview individuals. You'll all be asked to make a statement. I'll talk to some of you in the den, and Detective Lyons will talk to the others, again, one at a time, in the dining room." He rubbed the back of his neck, as if trying to figure out how to break some more bad news. Ian quit his key jangling. The group in the corner stopped whispering.

Ava's stomach tightened. There was something in his attitude that made Ava's muscles tense. Dear God, what now?

"Before we start with the interviews, I think you should know that there's been another homicide, very much like this one."

"What?" Trent stared at the detective. "*Another* one? Besides Jewel-Anne, you mean?"

"Besides Cheryl Reynolds," Wyatt interjected.

"Besides Ms. Reynolds," Snyder clarified, and Ava stood stock still, disbelieving.

Please, not someone else close to me . . . oh, please.

"It looks like we have another victim who may have been the target of the same killer."

He paused to take a breath, and everyone in the room stared at him. Waiting. Nervous.

"Evelyn McPherson was also murdered."

"What?" Ava gasped. "No!" One hand flew to her mouth and her knees nearly gave way. *Dr. McPherson?* The woman she was certain was having an affair with her husband? "There has to be some mistake!" Shaking her head, she conjured up Evelyn's face, her sad smile, her knowing eyes . . .

"That's not possible!" Wyatt said, his face draining of all color. "Evelyn's fine!"

Trent took a step toward Snyder. "I can't believe that anyone would do anything to Eve. . . ." But the serious expression on both detectives' faces stopped him short, seemed to convince him. "Jesus. Why?"

Everyone in the room was stricken, all in various stages of denial. Two murders? Of people who spent so much time here? It just didn't make any sense. . . .

"When?" Ava whispered. "Where?"

"At home, sometime yesterday, probably last night. Still waiting to find out."

"There's been nothing in the news!" Wyatt still wasn't accepting it.

"Her body was discovered only today."

Jacob's eyes narrowed on the cops. "What the fuck is going on here?"

"That's what we're here to do, to sort it all out."

"Well, fuckin' do it!" Jacob said, reaching for his jacket as if he were planning to leave.

Lyons raised a hand. "Settle down!" she ordered. "We know this is a shock, but we ask that you all just try to stay calm."

"How the fuck can we do that?" Jacob threw at her. "You just told us two people we know have been murdered. My sister and the shrink. Shit! Calm down, my ass!"

Lyons wasn't having any of Jacob's histrionics. "You know, we could make you all come to the station, so if I were you, I'd just take a chill pill." Her eyes were zeroed in on Jacob, but her words were for everyone in the room.

No one else argued. They were all too stunned, and Jacob, sufficiently schooled, dropped back onto the couch again. "Fuckin' sideshow," he said, but his voice was barely audible.

Lyons didn't rise to the bait, and Snyder took over. "Listen," he said, "I'm sorry, I realize you all knew her, so this is tough. We know that. But in light of what happened to Jewel-Anne, I thought you should know." Clearing his throat, he paused a beat, then added, "We discovered her body earlier this evening, and we think she'd been dead for nearly twenty-four hours at that time. We're still waiting for an official time and cause of death. Her family's been notified, so now at least we can let the public know, and I'm sure the press will be all over it, as they've already been calling the station."

"That will happen here, too," Ian said, horrified. "Reporters everywhere."

"I'm afraid so, yes," Snyder said, and Lyons nodded her agreement.

Wyatt muttered, "Great," under his breath.

"This is too creepy." Khloe shuddered. "Cheryl Reynolds, Evelyn, and now . . . now Jewel-Anne."

"I know. We'll get through it." Simon placed an arm around his wife's shoulders, as if to comfort her, but the gesture seemed awkward. Stiff. All for show. Ava couldn't help but wonder if he, so secretive, could have had anything to do with the murders. A fleeting, stupid idea. Why would Simon go to all the trouble?

"So, in our interviews," Snyder was saying, "we'll be discussing what you know about Jewel-Anne's homicide, but we'll also need to ask you when was the last time you had any contact with Dr. McPherson."

The temperature in the room seemed to drop ten degrees as Ava processed what was going on.

Three women.

Three homicides.

And the police thought they were linked.

Because the victims all knew you! You're the link, Ava. That's what the police think.

Ava swallowed hard. Her head was thundering, visions of Jewel-Anne appearing in her mind. She imagined how Cheryl and Evelyn had died. Had they been wearing wigs? Positioned by treasured items . . . Cheryl with the cats. Jewel-Anne with her dolls. Ava had no idea what Evelyn considered valuable, if anything, but she told herself to stop thinking about it. Yes, she'd known each of these women and they'd known her, probably more intimately than any of the others in the room had. Cheryl because of the hypnosis and shared confidences, Evelyn through psychological sessions, and Jewel-Anne by observation and proximity.

Again Ava's stomach felt as if it might empty.

Heart heavy, she realized she wasn't just the link between the victims but she was also probably a prime suspect. With her history of mental problems, her own violence toward herself, it would be an easy leap to think of her as capable of murder. In her mind's eye, she saw the evidence stacking up against her. They really couldn't think that—

"Mrs. Garrison?" Detective Snyder said, bringing her back to the here and now.

Her stomach nearly dropped to the floor. She wasn't ready for this but realized the interview was inevitable. She had to give a statement, no matter how difficult it might be. With all eyes trained on her, Ava somehow managed to force her legs to work and follow Snyder into the den, even though she knew deep in her heart the interview wouldn't go well.

From the corner of the room near one of the windows, Dern had observed the spectacle unfold and had decided to hold his tongue, at least for the time being. Of course, he had a lot to say but thought it might be smarter to confide in one of the cops once they were alone.

Not so, Ava's husband. Typical.

"I'm an attorney," Garrison stated, finally acting a little concerned for his wife as Ava was being ushered into the den office for her questioning. The two cops exchanged glances. "I don't want my wife to be interviewed without legal counsel."

Dern wasn't buying Garrison's act, not for a minute. He had the feeling that Garrison would throw Ava to the wolves if it would pad his wallet in some way. The guy seemed to have snake oil in his blood. Also, as Dern saw it, Ava could hold her own; she didn't need any help from Wyatt. The fact of the matter was, Dern flat-out didn't like the guy, didn't trust him, and wondered what the hell Ava had seen in him in the first place.

"Ava, you don't have to talk to them," Wyatt said softly, as if he cared.

Snyder shepherded Ava away, pausing for a second to give Wyatt an almost bemused glance. "You wanna sit in?" He cocked his shiny head toward the den. "If your wife doesn't mind, it's okay with me."

"I'll be fine," Ava said.

"Are you sure?" Wyatt rounded an edge of the couch where Jacob, pouting silently, sat in the corner of the cushions.

As if she knew that allowing Wyatt into the interview was a mistake, Ava said firmly, "I think I can handle this."

"Good. That's settled, then," Snyder said. "We're just taking a statement here. No one's charging your wife or you or anyone else here with anything."

"But she's been ill," Wyatt told the detective, then, more softly, as he touched her shoulder, "It hasn't been that long since you were released from St. Brendan's, honey."

She shrank away from his touch. "Don't worry about it. I've got nothing to hide."

"But—"

"Let's go," she said to the detective, cutting off any more arguments as she left the room.

"She's going to blow it!" Wyatt worried aloud, pacing.

"Have a little faith," Dern suggested. Ava had a lot more grit than anyone gave her credit for.

"She's fragile," Wyatt said. "She could snap like that!" He snapped his own fingers to emphasize his point.

Dern lifted a shoulder. "I don't think you give her enough credit."

"You're not paid to think," Wyatt said before stopping short as the sound of his own words echoed in the room. He was suddenly aware of the eyes of everyone else waiting to be interviewed watching him. "I'm sorry. I'm just upset."

Sure. It's not that you're an egomaniacal prick. But Dern let it slide. There was no reason to antagonize Garrison any further or give the cops anything more to think about.

Besides, Dern had a couple of his own bombshells to drop.

"So after spending a little over an hour in Austin Dern's apartment, you were just going up to your cousin's room to talk to her, find out the name of the father of her child, the one you adopted but didn't remember?" Snyder asked. Seated in Wyatt's executive chair, he was taking notes on a small spiral-bound pad, even though a small recording device had been placed on the top of the desk.

Ava sat on the opposite side of the desk, nervously propped on the edge of her grandmother's favorite chair. "That's right." Ava had told him everything she could remember about the night before. "I admit it, I was furious and determined to find out who was the father of my son. I thought she was lying to me and probably knew where Noah was, so I went up to Jewel-Anne's room. I knocked, called through the door, and when she didn't answer, I let myself in and . . . and . . ." The grotesque memory of Jewel-Anne in the bathtub with the dolls and all that blood assailed her. "And I found her." Shuddering at the memory, she knew how bad it sounded. She'd been angry with her cousin, again, not long after nearly throwing her over the railing.

Snyder had been scribbling, but his hand stopped writing

and he looked up at her. "You have no idea who could be Noah's biological father?" His eyebrows raised a fraction.

"No," she admitted. Looking at him, seeing his face remain much too bland, she felt a little buzz on her spine, a warning. "You do?" Her heart began beating crazily at the thought that this man had information about Noah.

The detective nodded. "We have reason to believe that your cousin might have been sexually involved with one of the patients at Sea Cliff."

"A patient . . . ?" she repeated, hearing her own heartbeat in her ears as an image came to mind.

"Lester Reece."

A little squeak of protest escaped her lips. The murderer? *He* was perfect little Noah's father? "No!" *No! No! NO!* "That can't be right. There must be some kind of mix-up, because there's no way that a serial killer could be . . . No!" She didn't realize she was shaking her head.

"You didn't know this was a possibility?" Snyder asked.

"Of course not! How could . . . ?" She thought of Jewel-Anne with her smug little I've-got-a-secret smile. But . . . but *Lester Reece*? "I don't believe it."

"She and her family lived at Sea Cliff. Her father was the head administrator."

"I know that!" she nearly screamed as her mind raced. Was it possible? No . . . oh, no!

"She spent time with the patients. Worked there, didn't she? As an aide of some kind."

Ava's heart grew cold. Yes . . . she remembered Jewel-Anne talking about some of her chores at the hospital, how she'd gotten to know some of the patients. Still she couldn't, *wouldn't* believe this nonsense. Her voice was hard to find and she had to clear her throat. "Uncle Crispin would never allow anything like this to happen." But Jewel-Anne had always been sneaky and rebellious and stubborn, even devious. For the love of

St. Peter, could it be true? Though she wanted to deny, deny, deny it. How could she?

"You'd never considered the possibility?"

"No," she finally whispered, and swallowed back the bile that rose in her throat and reminded herself that she could face anything—she just had to find her son. No matter what. Closing her eyes, hearing her heart drum denial in her ears, she took several deep breaths before opening her eyes again.

"Why? Why do you think he's the . . . ?" She couldn't even get the word over her tongue. Barely able to hold on to the shreds of her composure, she listened mutely as Detective Snyder explained further about the connection between Reece and Jewel-Anne. The police had connected the dots; they were confirming with others, including Piper and Crispin, who had been informed of their daughter's violent death and were headed to Neptune's Gate, a place Crispin had tried to avoid.

Ava listened to the detective's theory, and though she wanted like hell not to believe it, the idea that Jewel-Anne had rebelled and fallen for Reece made a peculiar kind of sense. After all, *someone* had fathered Noah.

Ava answered all of the detective's questions as best she could despite the fact that the headache building at the base of her skull had her head pounding. Denial was still a roar in her brain, as loud and bitter as a keening wind that carried with it a sharp little shard of truth. "You have to find him," she told Snyder, suddenly desperate to face the monster. "Lester Reece. You have to find him!"

"We don't even know if he's alive."

"But he has to be," she insisted. "Don't you see? He's the one who kidnapped Noah!" Her voice was rising now, her desperation palpable. It all made sense. He'd come back for his boy! Even now he could have Noah locked away on the island!

"Of course . . . however, right now, though, we're in the middle of a murder investigation," he reminded her.

"But the killer? Couldn't it be Lester Reece? He's done it before and you think he's on the island."

"You think he killed the others?"

"I . . . I don't know . . ." It didn't make sense, but then what about murder did?

"You found Jewel-Anne's body. You think Lester Reece would take the trouble to place dolls around your cousin? Slice and paint 'em up?"

Ava shook her head in mute bafflement. "I don't know. Maybe?"

"I heard that you found another doll," he added carefully. "In a casket. Buried by the victim, kind of a way to get back at you."

She gazed at him, aware of the dominoes starting to fall, the list of events and her own actions that made her look guilty. Standing, leaning across the desk, she said clearly and precisely, just so he got it, "I didn't kill Jewel-Anne, Detective. Nor anyone else. I'm just trying to find my boy and I'll swear to that on his life!"

Chapter 43

Feeling like a caged animal in the den with the rest of the Church family, Dern managed to hang on to his patience, but it took more than a little effort. Outside, the night was thick, impenetrable, while inside the house, a pall had settled over the residents.

More cops arrived, along with the medical examiner and the crime scene people. Even J. T. Biggs, the sheriff himself, in full uniform, showed up in the early morning hours, though he spent more time outside the house organizing the search party than inside.

While the staff and occupants of the house were called in for interviews one by one, the technicians and investigators began collecting evidence. Everyone was questioned, even Graciela, who arrived for work several hours into the interviews and was escorted into the den. Doe-eyed, she, too, waited to tell everything she knew about Jewel-Anne's death, which she'd only heard about when Khloe had texted her earlier.

When it came to his turn, right after Wyatt Garrison, Dern was led into the dining room, offered coffee, which he declined, and was pointed to a chair on the opposite side of the table from Detective Lyons. She was typing on a tablet computer, her coffee forgotten, not so much as a lipstick stain on the rim of the cup.

The interview was quick. "Just tell me what happened last night," she instructed. Obviously the police already knew about the altercation between Jewel-Anne and Ava that had occurred the night before the murder. What they didn't know was where Lester Reece was hiding or that Austin Dern just happened to be his half brother. Dern decided to lay all his cards on the table. First with the cops; next with Ava. He figured he owed her that much. So, after explaining about the night before and answering a few subsequent questions to his statement, he said, "You know, there's another wrinkle here."

"Is there? And what's that?" Lyons asked as she typed on her keypad.

"I'm Lester Reece's half brother."

Her reaction was swift. She looked up sharply, her fingers quit moving, and her gaze focused hard on him.

"Is that right?" she asked.

He nodded.

"You know," she said, her eyes narrowing a little, as if she really thought he might try to con her, "I haven't seen any record of Reece having a sibling."

"Then your records aren't complete." Dern was ready for the argument, had figured no one would believe him, and he didn't really give a damn one way or the other; he just wanted to say it. "Here's the short and the long of it: Reece and I have the same mother." She glanced at her iPad. Probably checking out his facts as he gave them to her. "My mother is Reba Melinda Corliss Reece Dern McDaniels. The marriage to Reece was short. She lives in Texas. Moved around a lot. El Paso, Houston, a couple of smaller towns. She's now living in a town called Bad Luck. Kind of appropriate."

Her eyebrows lifted a bit as her gaze moved from the small screen to his face. "So many names. Your mother was a serial marrier?"

"You could say that." He tried not to be rankled, to let it slide, but he'd always had a soft spot when it came to Reba.

Lyons's eyebrows puckered together, and Dern could almost see the wheels turning in her mind. She clicked a pen as she thought. "I don't know how we could have missed this."

"Me, neither. But I'm just telling you straight up," he said.

"Okay, go on." Finally he'd caught her interest. She leaned back in her chair.

"Well, here's the good news," he said cautiously. "I think I can lead you to Reece."

"Seriously?" Again the skeptic.

"Yep."

Her smile said she didn't believe him for a second, but she quit clicking her damned pen. "Okay, Dern, I'll bite. That's the good news? So what's the bad?"

Dern said, "He ain't gonna like it."

"So I should have told you sooner, I guess," Dern admitted after telling Ava that he was Lester Reece's half brother.

"I don't guess," she said angrily. "I *know*!" Ava couldn't believe what she was hearing, but Dern seemed dead serious as he broke the news to her in the kitchen, less than an hour after he'd finished his interviews. He'd spoken for a long time with Lyons and then spent another hour or so in the dining room talking to both cops after Lyons called Snyder in. Ava had guessed whatever he'd told them was important, but she hadn't expected this—that Dern was Lester Reece's damned half brother. Dear God, was everyone related to the maniac? First Noah and now Dern.

Not everyone—just the people you care about!

Ava had witnessed Lyons, obviously agitated, summon Snyder and sequester him for a while; then each detective had left the dining room and made a couple of calls, one at a time, while leaving the other to keep the interview going. Even J. T. Biggs had deigned to come up from the stable area where he was amassing the search party and had closeted himself in the dining room with the others.

Whatever Dern had told them, it had an impact.

At the time, she'd wondered, Was he a suspect? Had he told them Ava had been hell-bent on getting Jewel-Anne off the island? Or was it something else?

Ava and everyone else in the house had seen Biggs join the detectives, but no one had been able to guess why.

"What the fuck is all *that* about?" Jacob had asked as his cell phone jangled. "Oh, great. Mom and Dad have touched down in Seattle. This is just getting better and better."

Ian had groaned and went looking for a cigarette break, which was finally allowed, and Trent, seeming to have aged five years in as many hours, walked into the kitchen for a cup of coffee while Virginia, Khloe, and Simon waited to talk to the cops.

Ava hadn't said anything but had wondered what Dern had told Lyons to get the detective so riled up.

Now she knew.

But she was having a lot of trouble digesting the information.

"I don't believe you," Ava said, the odor of stale coffee lingering in the kitchen.

"Why would I lie?"

"God knows."

"I swear to you."

"Great. Go ahead. Swear till you're blue in the face." She was tired, cranky, still shocked at having found Jewel-Anne so gruesomely killed and sick at the thought of Lester Reece being her son's father . . . now *this*? After everything else?

"Ava," he said, reaching for her, but she stepped away. "I'm telling you the truth, and trust me, I don't like it any better than you do."

The honesty on his face got to her. And there were other reasons to believe him as well, even though she wanted desperately to deny the obvious. Hadn't she always thought he reminded her of someone? Hadn't she once imagined she'd viewed Lester Reece in the rising mist, only to look again and discover she was staring at Austin Dern?

"Just listen," he said, and as they stood near the sink, he explained about him and Reece having the same mother and her being married several times, but it was too much for her to take in after sleepless nights and the shock of Jewel-Anne's and Evelyn McPherson's murders. Tired to the bone, she listened but couldn't help but wonder what other secrets this man had kept from her. Why had she trusted him, fancied herself falling in love with this stranger, this man who had no more substance than the fog rolling in from the Pacific?

Because you're an idiot. A damned romantic fool. That's why.

"So . . . why didn't you tell me you were related to Reece earlier?" she asked, hurt and more than a little pissed. "Why let me go on believing that you were someone you weren't?"

"The timing wasn't right."

"Oh. Great!" she said sarcastically. "Tell me, when was the timing ever going to be right?"

"Don't know."

"Maybe never?"

"Didn't turn out that way, did it?"

More good news, she thought, anger sharpening her disappointment that he hadn't confided in her before. "So . . . let me get this straight. And help me out if I get this wrong, okay?" she said as she tried to make sense of what he'd told her. "You're saying that you're . . . you're Noah's biological uncle?"

"I don't know. That isn't a leap I can make. You don't really know if Noah is his son." Leaning his hip against the counter, Dern rubbed the worn tile with one finger. "The truth is, I really don't know Reece. At all. Don't even know that much about him. He was raised by his father, who I never met. I'd barely even heard of the guy. My mother didn't discuss him and preferred no one knew that she'd ever been involved with him. Believe me, Ava, I had no idea Lester Reece had a kid. I've never heard that. It's just what the cops have conjectured, right? The only person who really knows is Jewel-Anne."

"But—"

"So far it's all just speculation."

"Isn't everything?" She stared at the faucet where a drop of water was forming on the spigot. "God, I'm sick of this . . . the second-guessing and not knowing and . . . all of it. Every damned thing!"

"I know." His gaze found hers and her throat tightened. She thought he might reach for her, but he was smart enough to give her some space. Besides, though they were alone in the kitchen, the house was crawling with people.

As everyone milled around, the cops still collecting evidence or talking to each other or on phones, her family being questioned, she was still trying to understand how this—her life, her son's disappearance—all fit together. And it didn't. For God's sake, how could it? Austin Dern was the half brother of one of the most heinous murderers in the state. Not to mention uncle to her son. Really? And he just happened to be hired by her husband on the QT. No way was it all coincidence. "Is that why you took this job?" she asked. "Because of Reece?" She noticed the water still dripping from the faucet and she cranked hard on the handle.

"One of the reasons. I had a suspicion that he was back on the island."

"Why? I mean, he escaped from Sea Cliff. Why would he come back?"

"He could have run out of options. Maybe he felt safer here

and thought the cops would never come back here since it was combed years before. It might be that he was drawn back because of Jewel-Anne or something else. Who knows. But the island is isolated. Has deep forests where anyone could get lost. It's surrounded by ocean. Not all that inhabited. He could have some freedom without fear of too many people seeing him."

"But he would be trapped here."

"He's trapped in his own damned skin."

"Yeah, but anyone here who did see him would recognize him. He could get lost in a city, a big city far away. No one in Boston or Miami would know or probably even care about him."

Dern was nodding, as if he'd already considered her arguments. "Reece could have changed his appearance. It's been a while, but you're right—the few sightings that there were caught my attention. And the local rumors about him. Was he like Bigfoot, or was he really here? Thought I'd find out for myself. That's one of the reasons I came here, took the job."

"The island's been searched before."

"As I said, a long time ago. I figured he probably left for a while. Who knows? But for some reason he came back, felt safe here at the very place where it all started: Sea Cliff."

"He *escaped* from Sea Cliff. I'd think it would be the last place on Earth he'd want to be," she said, keeping her voice low as Virginia seemed to hover near the door either to eavesdrop or just keep an eye on the area of the house she considered her domain.

"Exactly. That's what any sane person *would* think. He could have figured he was going to use it to his advantage."

"Pretty far-fetched."

"Or not. I've been up to the hospital a couple of times. Broke in and poked around. I've found evidence that someone's been hanging out there, but I haven't explored all the buildings; there are a few places locked so tight, I wasn't able to break in." He frowned, the edge of his jaw sharpening. "Yet."

Her head was pounding with bad news followed by worse.

She hadn't yet come to grips with the fact that Jewel-Anne and Dr. McPherson had been killed by the same homicidal maniac who had murdered Cheryl Reynolds, and now Dern's announcement that he was related to the guy who could have killed them? "I can't deal with this right now." She started to walk away, but he grabbed the crook of her elbow.

"You don't have a choice, Ava," he whispered, turning her to him, his nose nearly touching hers, his gaze so intense she felt as if he could see into her soul. "There are people here who think you killed your cousin as well as two other women."

Her insides turned to ice at the thought that not only her family, but also the police might try to make a case against her, a strong case.

Dern was the one person who believed in her. Yes, he'd lied, but who on this damned island hadn't?

"I think Reece is behind the murders. He just can't help himself. It's an obsession with him. Who knows if he's killed others while he was off the island—like you said, in other big cities— but these three women, so close together, they have to be his work."

Snyder's earlier question flitted through her mind. *"You think Lester Reece would take the trouble to place dolls around your cousin? Slice and paint 'em up?"* She said, "You know, he might not be the killer."

"There's that chance, yes. But if we can flush Reece out, we can find out. Maybe end all this insanity."

That she believed. And she was tired of sitting around, letting the cops try and prove she was behind the deaths of three women. "Okay," she said, feeling a little sizzle of electricity through her blood that she could actually do something. "Let's find him. I'm in!"

"Wait a second."

"I'm coming with you."

Dern shook his head. "No."

"What do you mean no?" She wasn't going to be deterred. "You've convinced me that Lester Reece might be on the island, so let's go find him." She pressed her face even closer to his. "Killer or not, he's the only person who might have an idea where Noah is!"

"You don't know that," Dern said slowly.

"I don't care! Reece is the only hope I have right now." That thought was depressing; she couldn't pin all her hopes on the known killer. Frustrated, she glanced out the window at the bevy of police vehicles that had been ferried to the island, all gathered near the gates of the estate, headlights on, though dawn was finally approaching. An armed posse, with Joe Biggs as their leader. *Oh, Jesus.* "They'll kill Reece," she said with sudden clarity. "They'll kill him." Grabbing hold of Dern's shirt, her fingers curled into the worn fabric. "And if they do, I'll never know what happened to Noah. Don't you see?" Desperation cracked her voice. "He'll be lost to me! I *have* to go!"

"Oh, honey . . ." Sighing, Dern folded her into his arms and held her tight. She heard the beating of his heart, felt his breath in her hair, felt weak against his strength. "Listen," he said softly, "just hang tough. The police are only letting me go because I think I know where we can find him and because I was once a cop. Still in the reserves. I know what I'm doing. I won't get in the way and I won't be a liability."

"And I would? This is my son we're talking about, Dern! My baby."

"And we'll get him back. If we can."

Tears threatened her eyes. She was so close to maybe learning something finally, locating the boy who'd been missing for so long. Her heart was cracking, but she couldn't break down. Wouldn't. She hated to admit it, but Dern was right. The police would never let her join them. No matter how she begged. But there was something she could do to help. Slowly she gathered her strength and made a long-overdue decision. Extricating herself from his embrace, she walked rapidly to the foyer and returned with her purse.

"What's going on?"

"I think I might be able to help." She fished inside her bag for a second, dug into a zippered pocket, then withdrew the set of keys she'd found earlier. She slapped the ring into his palm. "I found these the other day. I'm pretty sure they're a master set of the keys to Sea Cliff. They belonged to my uncle and probably open every door."

"How do you have them?"

"Long story. We don't have time now. Let's just say I found them."

"Found them?" His eyes flickered with a dozen questions, but one side of his mouth lifted into that crooked smile she found so sexy. "Okay." He seemed about to ask another question, then changed his mind and closed his fist around the key ring. "Thanks."

"Just keep Reece alive so I can find Noah."

"I'll do my best."

"Do better than that, okay?"

His eyes flashed. Then, impulsively, he grabbed her again, pulled her close, his body fitting snugly against hers. She gasped as he kissed her. Long. Hard. His lips hot. Her breath caught in her throat as the kiss deepened, an unspoken promise. She closed her eyes and her mind to everything around them, and for a few glorious seconds, while his fingers tangled in her hair and his hips pressed hard to hers, she was lost in him and swept away from the pain of what was real.

Forbidden pleasures sprang to her mind, and for just a heartbeat she imagined what it would be like to love this man, to be with him.

But she couldn't.

Not now . . .

Not ever.

As if he felt the shift in her emotions, he lifted his head, swore under his breath. "Damn it all to hell." His gaze held hers for an instant; then, as swiftly as he'd caught her, he let her go. Took a quick step back. Rammed stiff fingers through his hair in frustration. "I should say I'm sorry, but I'm not," he whispered, and she felt the heat of the moment still burning on her cheeks.

"Me neither."

This was insanity! With everything else going on, she couldn't let herself be distracted for even a moment. She looked away, putting some emotional distance between them just as a stern-faced deputy entered the room.

"I heard you're with us," he said. African American and taller than Dern by four inches, the deputy was built more like an NFL linebacker than a typical cop. His nametag read DEP-UTY BENNETT RAMSEY and his expression said more loudly than words he wasn't about to take any crap from anyone. "It's time."

"I'm coming, too," Ava insisted, and glanced out the window. Dawn was approaching, the sky lightening to a gloomy gray, rain still falling from the leaden sky.

"I was told to bring only Dern," Ramsey said firmly.

"But I know the island better than anyone! I could help. Really!" Frantically, she argued her point. "I've lived here most of my life and there's a chance Reece knows where my son is!"

"Just Dern." There was a glint of compassion in his eyes, but he stood firm.

"No, really, I have to come with you," she insisted, frantic. The thought that she would be left behind and that somehow she would lose her chance to find Noah panicked her. If Reece was cornered and fought back, or some cop got trigger-happy . . . "Please!"

The deputy's impenetrable expression cracked a little. "I'll talk to the commanding officer. That's the best I can do, ma'am," Ramsey said, relenting a little.

"Mrs. Garrison?" Detective Snyder walked into the kitchen.

With him was someone from the crime scene team. "Can I have a word?"

"I was just going to go with them." Ava motioned toward Deputy Ramsey and Dern.

"It's important." His face was impassive, but there was something in Snyder's stance, something a little more aggressive than before that made her take notice.

Dern, too, sensed it. As Ramsey shepherded him toward the back door, he held up a hand. "Just a sec."

"I only need to speak to Mrs. Garrison," Snyder insisted.

Ramsey had already opened the doors, the screen screeching as he pushed it out of the way, cold air sweeping through the kitchen. "If you're going with us, you'd better come along," he told Dern. "The sheriff doesn't like to be kept waiting."

Ava took a step toward the back door, but Dern gave a quick, short shake of his head, warning her off. "I'll find him," he promised as he grabbed a jacket off the back of a hook mounted near the porch. "If Reece has Noah or knows where he is, I'll find him."

"But—"

"Ava. Please. Trust me." And then, before she could launch into any arguments, he was gone, through the door, the screen slapping resonantly behind him.

Ava felt a part of her leave with him.

She held tight to his promise, but she knew it could be empty. What happened in the showdown with Reece, if there was one, would be out of Dern's control. And even though he hadn't uttered the damning words, Ava realized Dern, like most everyone else, believed Noah was dead.

Through the window, she watched as the two men jogged toward the stable where officers, some on horses, some with dogs, others in four-wheel-drive vehicles, had gathered. Headlights glowed in the gloom while officers in rain gear, weapons visible, stood in small clusters. A few smoked, two were on cell phones, and another held three dogs on leashes.

Was it possible? After all this time, would they actually find Lester Reece on the island?

Ramsey and Dern joined the group and it looked as if quick introductions were made.

Her throat was thick, her nerves stretched to the breaking point as she thought not only might she never see her son again, but also that Dern, too, could be lost to her. Once he located Reece and brought him to justice, he would have no reason to stick around.

"Mrs. Garrison?" Snyder again. His voice a little sharper. "Would you come with me, please?"

"Of . . . of course."

"Upstairs."

She steeled herself at the thought that she might have to view Jewel-Anne's body again. So far, she hadn't witnessed anyone carrying a body bag down the stairs, so she assumed Jewel-Anne's corpse was being checked over. The thought made her shudder.

"This way," Snyder said as she turned at the top of the steps to head toward the wing her cousin had occupied. Instead, he led her to her own bedroom.

Why?

Then she knew. She was the primary suspect, the person who had found the body, the family member with a very sharp ax to grind. Her heart beat a little faster.

The room was disheveled, black fingerprint powder on all the surfaces, the bed pulled apart, bedding removed, the box springs and mattress separated, the mattress standing on its side near one wall.

"What's going on here?" she asked, heart drumming. Whatever it was, it wasn't good.

"We wanted to ask you about this." Snyder pointed to her bed where a reddish brown stain was visible on the box springs. Seven or eight inches long, an inch wide . . .

Dear God, what . . . ?

Her gaze moved to the mattress propped on its side, and of course it, too, held a similar stain. Obviously an object had been pushed between the two. Her pulse jumped. "What?" she murmured, a new panic surging through her blood as she got it. The stain had to be dried blood, and it was formed into the distinctive shape of a long-bladed knife. Her stomach convulsed. "God in heaven," she whispered, and glanced back at Snyder, who was holding a plastic bag.

Inside the bag was the missing knife. Its serrated blade was sharp and deadly, smeared with blood.

Jewel-Anne's blood!

Her knees threatened to buckle, and she had to steady herself by leaning against her dresser. Obviously the cops thought this was the weapon used to slice Jewel-Anne's throat. Her stomach roiled, nausea bubbling up at the thought of the ugly blade carving into her cousin's flesh. She ran into the bathroom and heaved over the toilet. Once. Twice. Her stomach cramped and tears burned in her eyes as images of her handicapped cousin being attacked tore through her mind. She retched again, her stomach empty, only foul bile spewing into the toilet bowl. Had Jewel-Anne known her attacker? Obviously the killer understood about her attachment to the stupid dolls. But who . . . ? She felt time passing as she clutched the rim of the toilet, saw beads of sweat drip from her nose into the murky water.

"Mrs. Garrison?" Snyder again. Sounding as if he were miles away when he was standing in the doorway.

Finally, her stomach calmed. After flushing the toilet, she paused at the sink, rinsed her mouth, and caught her reflection in the mirror. Ashen. Hair a mess. Eyes haunted.

Too bad.

She wasn't guilty!

Her legs still shaky, she made her way into the bedroom and saw that Snyder's serious partner had joined him.

"Sorry." Ava focused on the bag he was still holding, the

bloody knife visible through the plastic. "That"—she pointed to the bag—"it's not mine. That knife . . . I don't know how it got here, in my room."

Lyons was obviously skeptical. "We have a few more questions for you, Mrs. Garrison. But they might be better answered at the station."

What? No! "Wait. I . . . I can't leave. Not now. The search party is out looking for Lester Reece and my son . . ." Her voice trailed off as she realized no one was asking her permission. They actually thought she might have killed Jewel-Anne and probably the other women as well. It was all ridiculous. Why would she do such a horrid thing? Commit such gruesome, malicious murders?

Because they think you're nuts. Homicidal. Probably suicidal as well and any other -idal there is.

Remember, Cheryl Reynolds and Evelyn McPherson knew all of your secrets. Didn't you accuse good old Doc McPherson of having an affair with your husband? Didn't you try to fire her? Yeah, that's right, you did. Everyone knew how you felt about her. Weren't you the last one to see Cheryl Reynolds alive? Maybe you said something you regretted . . . hmmm? And then there's that sticky little matter of nearly tossing your dear cousin over the railing the night before. Everyone here at Neptune's Gate knows how you despised her, how deep the rift between you ran, and then you found out she was Noah's biological mother. You snapped, Ava. That's what they all think. You lost it and became a murderous beast. And now they have the knife, the murder weapon. Face it, Ava, you're screwed. Whoever did this was pretty clever and made sure that you would be the first and maybe only suspect.

Lester Reece, Schmester Reece, the cops and everyone else will think it's you.

Again her stomach convulsed and she nearly dry heaved thinking how she'd been set up. Her breath was coming in short little breaths and fear crawled up her spine. This, the officers taking her to the station on the mainland, was just one more step in someone's elaborate plan to destroy her.

Who?

Why?

"I . . ." She was going to deny everything, to spill her inner thoughts, to tell them that someone was manipulating everything that was happening to her, but she realized if she started arguing now, she would appear as paranoid as everyone claimed her to be. Both officers were staring at her, and even the tech, carefully sifting through the drawers, looked over her shoulder at her. *Be cool! They're all looking at you under a microscope, waiting for you to make a mistake!* "I . . ." Clearing her throat, she met Snyder's gaze. "I'll get my coat."

Chapter 44

The search party reached the abandoned asylum just as the wind kicked up, driving the rain and whipping the ocean far below the rocky outcrop for which Sea Cliff had been named. On horseback, on foot with dogs, in four-wheel-drive vehicles and even helicopters, and with several sheriff's department boats positioned in the bay should Reece decide to take a dive into the freezing tide, the cops surrounded the hospital.

"This time, he ain't gettin' away. Not on my watch!" Biggs had announced as the wind nearly tore his hat from his head and the surf pounded the shore. The group had gathered outside the walls of Sea Cliff where the sheriff intended to stay while the search party fanned out inside the complex. The sheriff's department wasn't alone. There were also troops from the Washington State Patrol and the Homicide Investigative Tracking System, over a dozen officers and Dern, all chasing the ghost of one man.

The sheriff had originally ordered that Dern was to stand down and wait on the outside, but since he'd come up with the theory of Reece's location, knew the hospital, had found evidence of someone living within the walls, and had somehow come into possession of the "keys to the castle" as Biggs had called them, he was allowed inside. It didn't hurt that he had been a cop and was still in the reserves.

"Just don't get in the way," Biggs had grumbled, his face red and raw with the cold, his jacket straining around his girth. "We got this."

Dern held his tongue. If indeed Biggs's team really did "get this," then it had been a long time coming and not without Dern's help. And, Dern suspected, if things went bad, the press would be all over this story, and he would be the fall guy.

This was Biggs's show.

Denied his service weapon, Dern was given a protective vest and jacket that identified him as a cop, along with instructions to stay in the rear, as a deputy unlocked the gates and the search party broke into two groups. One started with the residences and outbuildings, the other, of which Dern was a part, began at the hospital.

"I heard you were Reece's brother," a female cop said as they approached the front entrance.

"Half. Never knew him."

"Still." She glanced up at him. "It sucks."

Dern didn't comment, and with four other armed cops, they searched the abandoned building. No one said a word as they passed through unused corridors and restrooms where rust was evident and spiders collected in the dark crevices. Up the stairs and down empty hallways and through individual rooms to the floor where Reece had been a resident, the room with a direct view of Neptune's Gate.

No Reece, of course.

That would have been too damned easy.

They searched the roof.

Empty, the roofing material spotty, a few vents broken, a single smokestack knifing the dismal sky.

But no Reece.

That left the basement.

"If he was here, he probably already took off," grumbled one of the male deputies, a burly guy with no neck.

"Damned wild-goose chase," another said. He was short and wiry, with a ruddy complexion and small, suspicious eyes.

Burly snorted. "Biggs is going to shit little green apples if we don't find him."

"Shut up!" one of the women officers hissed.

Everyone quieted. Using high-powered flashlights, they searched the subterranean hallways. Narrow, dark, and labyrinthine, the tunnels connected all sections of the complex. In some areas, the concrete had cracked and water had puddled. Other areas were bone-dry and covered with dust that clogged Dern's nostrils. The scratch of tiny nails indicated they weren't alone, that rats or mice or God knew what else were keeping residence in the cobwebby bowels of the old institution, but they found no footprints or other evidence that a human being had walked these twisted corridors any time recently.

Nonetheless, the search was nerve-wracking and Dern's pulse was elevated, his eyes straining, his muscles tight, and he wished to heaven that he'd been allowed his service pistol.

They reached a room Dern hadn't been able to break into, and the female deputy, using Crispin Church's keys, opened the door. It swung open noiselessly, and the minute they stepped into the large mechanical room, the temperature and smell of the area warned them that things had changed.

Dern noticed Burly draw his weapon from its holster, though he assumed the cop had enough brains not to fire the Glock if at all possible. Ricocheting bullets were far more dangerous than the killer.

The beams of their flashlights illuminated the area where huge heat ducts rose to the ceiling and heavy water pipes climbed up the wall. Electrical junction boxes were visible near huge waste bins, and several disabled furnaces stood next to what once had been an active incinerator, its iron doors black, the smokestack rising upward.

The place was quiet, not a sound as they fanned out, weapons drawn, nerves strung tight. Dern's ears strained, but he heard nothing other than the other cops as they moved through the area and his own galloping heartbeat.

Carefully he stepped around a furnace. There, blocked by the huge firebox, was the heart of a camp, presumably Reece's. *Got you, you son of a bitch!* He motioned to one of the deputies, who shined her light over the filth of a dirty sleeping bag, camp stove, clothes, and garbage scattered in one corner. A couple of pails, one with clean water, one fouled with waste.

But no Reece.

They combed the area.

"He's gone." A male cop sounded disgusted. "In the wind."

"Looks recent," another one said, shaking his head.

Dern touched the camp stove. "Still warm."

"Where the hell could he go?" Another cop shined his flashlight over the walls. "Looks like only one way out of here."

"Heat vents," another said.

"They go straight up. He couldn't climb up sheet metal, and they're not big enough. Reece is over six feet."

"Shit!"

Dern eyed the cavernlike room, looking up at the ceiling until finally his gaze landed on the incinerator. They'd already looked inside, of course, but something about it bothered him. The big firebox seemed out of place. And there were a few ashes on the outside floor. He opened the door again, but the bin was empty. Shining his flashlight upward, he noticed the interior ladder, used probably for cleaning the chimney.

"He's on the roof!" Dern was already running for the exit.

"Hey!" Burly shouted after him. "We already checked up there."

"I know, but he heard us and waited, then climbed into the

incinerator and used the ladder. He's on the friggin' roof!"
Rather than wait for the ensuing discussion, Dern flew up the
stairs. He heard boots clattering behind him, even a curse or
two, but he kept running, taking the steps two at a time and
hoping that at least a couple of the cops climbed the incinerator
ladder.

"He'll be trapped up there!" someone behind him said as
Dern reached the first floor.

"Unless he decides to take a flying leap!"

"Oh, Christ! Well, he wouldn't survive. It would serve the
bastard right and save the state a whole lotta money!"

Taking the steps two at a time, Dern flew by the second
floor, passed the third, and reached the roof access. It was
locked. Probably by Reece, from the other side. "Bastard!" he
muttered.

Grabbing both handrails of the stairs, he swung his body
and, using momentum and all the strength he could muster,
kicked the door with his feet.

BAM!

Frame shattering, the door flew open, banging loudly as a
rush of wind whistled down the stairwell. Hearing the thunder
of footsteps from the group of cops behind him, Dern scrambled to his feet and flung himself onto the roof. Once again he
wished he had his pistol as he walked slowly around the stairwell to the perimeter of the building, his eyes searching as he
fought the screaming wind and heavy rain.

"What the fuck?" someone behind him said.

Dern turned to see the disgust on Burly's face.

"He's not here! He's flown the damned coop, I tell ya." The
deputy was already reaching for his phone to call the sheriff
with the bad news. Dern turned and looked at Sea Cliff. From
here, the widow's walk of Neptune's Gate was visible, and in
his mind's eye, he saw Ava, climbing down the damned fire escape.

Just like this damned place!

It all clicked. He'd spied the ladder on the south side of the island earlier. Now he raced across the soggy roof to the edge of the building where twin handles looped over the ledge to connect with the railing of the fire escape. Cautiously he peered over the edge.

Two floors down, clinging to the rusted railings for his life, his body battered by the gale-force winds buffeting the island, was Lester Friggin' Reece. Sensing Dern, he looked upward for a frantic second.

"Hello, Brother," Dern said, though the desperate man far below, staring up in panic, couldn't hear him over the thunder of the surf and the scream of the wind.

Over his shoulder, Dern yelled, "Hey! Over here!"

Reece started scrambling downward.

Burly, lumbering over, two other deputies on his heels, shined the beam of his light down the dirty exterior walls and caught the killer's face looking up again. Terror registered in Reece's eyes. "You'd better be scared, you sum bitch," Burly said. "We got your skinny ass now!"

He started to radio to the cops on the ground just as Dern climbed onto the fire escape. "Stop! What the hell do you think you're doing?" Burly demanded. "Hey!"

Dern didn't listen to any lame-ass "this is police business" excuses as he lowered himself quickly on the slick rungs. He remembered Ava on the fire escape, how she'd climbed to a lower floor, and he wasn't going to take the chance with Reece. What if the guy had an escape route, one the police would have trouble finding? He could slide inside through a window, take a back staircase, disappear again, or he might just take a chance on jumping.

Either way, Dern was on his heels.

"For the love of Christ!" he heard Burly say over the rumble of the ocean, and he felt the ladder shimmy a bit. He figured the big cop was giving chase, but he didn't look up, just kept his eyes on Reece as he hurried rung by rung down the rusting ladder.

Reece squirreled down the escape. He was agile and quick, and the group of cops that Dern had expected to appear on the ground below once Burly had radioed them hadn't arrived when Reece, at the end of the ladder, jumped to the ground.

"Shit!" Above him, Burly had witnessed Reece's escape.

Dern hurried, hoping the damned cops and dogs would appear on that bit of lawn, but as he reached the first floor, no officer appeared and Reece took off down a slippery, weed-choked trail that forked. One path led to the fence and a gate that opened to the front of the building; the second fork angled toward the bay.

Reece, damn him, headed for the open sea.

"Great!" Dern grumbled, and using his hands and gravity, kicked his feet free and slid down the final rungs before dropping to the ground. He landed hard, his ankle twisting, but he was on his feet in a second, chasing the madman who was his brother. He couldn't lose him now—not after all this time and his promises to Ava and his mother—and he wouldn't let the cops shoot first and ask questions later. Faster and faster he raced, cold air burning through his lungs, his eyes trained on Reece's head as they flew along the slick, weed-choked path that wound through rocks and patches of beach grass. Behind him, he heard shouts. The police finally arriving.

Where the hell were the dogs?

Dern expected the dogs to gallop past him, fast on the scent of their quarry, but so far, nothing. Probably locked on the other side of the fence or some other snafu.

Don't worry about the damned dogs. Just get this sucker!

Reece, as slippery as the wet rocks of the headland, knew this area better than anyone. "You're not getting away, you bastard," Dern said, his eyes trained on the man he was chasing and silently cursing the sheriff for not allowing him a gun. At each dip and turn in the path, Reece disappeared for a second, and Dern feared that he would veer off, slither away in the beach grass, find a hidden cove, or take to the ocean.

"Police! Stop!" he heard from behind, and prayed that they wouldn't shoot. His jacket identified him, but it wasn't safe and he wanted Reece alive.

On he ran, boots sliding in the mud, his damned ankle beginning to throb. Still, he was slowly closing the gap. Reece was fifteen feet ahead of him, but slowing. Soon it was ten feet, then five.

He could hear the rasp of his brother's breath as he slowed.

"Reece! Give it up!" he yelled, and his half brother looked furtively over his shoulder, his eyes wild. He muttered something unintelligible, dug into the pocket of his jeans, and kept running toward the damned ocean. Did he think he could swim away? Get lost in the sea before he drowned or hypothermia took him?

No effin' way!

Police were shouting. A warning shot fired.

But Reece didn't break stride. Only feet from the surging ocean's edge, he looked about to dive in.

Gathering all his strength, Dern launched himself.

Reece spun.

A knife was in his hand. With a ghoulish smile twisting his narrow face, he actually grinned. "Come on, dick face, just come the hell on!" he said as Dern landed on him and the skinny man drove his blade into Dern's chest. The air rushed out of Dern's lungs as together they toppled into the sand. Reece tried to squirm away and sliced at Dern again and again, thrusting his knife hard. "Die, you fucker! Die!"

Dern wrestled with the maniac, using all the tactics he'd learned on the force, but his half brother was slippery and hopped up on adrenaline, fighting for his life, his deadly blade ever in Dern's view.

As one, they rolled toward the ocean, the rain pounding down, the sound of footsteps heavy, the voices of men shouting audible over the rush of the ocean.

Dern twisted and writhed, grabbing at the man's arms and finally using his legs to turn Reece facedown while trying to avoid the deadly slash of the maniac's blade.

An icy spray of sea foam splashed over them as they wrestled. Dern sputtered, salt water filling his nose and mouth. Slowly but surely, Dern forced Reece's hand backward, farther and farther, until the older man was writhing in pain, still trying to strike. Another wave pummeled them.

Reece squealed like a stuck pig, sputtering, coughing, and spitting sand and salt water.

Dern gave another little twist. This time he felt sinews pop.

Howling in agony, Reece dropped the knife.

"I should kill you, you miserable piece of shit!" Dern said.

"We've got him!" Burly yelled.

Dern didn't budge. He straddled the prisoner, not letting him go, feeling the arctic chill after another wave struck hard. Finally, four other cops arrived, weapons trained on Reece.

"I said, we've got him," Burly repeated into his phone as he shoved Dern aside and cuffed the subdued, coughing prisoner.

"You sure do," Dern said, freezing, with sand and salt water sticking to his skin, his hair plastered to his head, the flak jacket that had saved his life from Reece's rabid knife thrusts hard against him. Shivering, he stared at the monster who had killed so many, a maniac with the same blood as Dern's running through his veins.

Once he was cuffed and hauled to his feet, Reece, still spitting sand, zeroed in on Dern. His filthy jeans and jacket were two sizes too big and his once-blond hair, now wet and stringing to his shoulders, showed hints of gray. Dark eyes squinted a bit as if some memory tugged at his brain. "Who the fuck are you?"

Dern didn't respond, wouldn't give the prick the satisfaction. Because this pathetic homicidal maniac, no matter what, was no brother to him. If Reece figured out who Dern was, fine. Surely he'd learn it from the cops, but Dern wouldn't give the psycho the satisfaction of an answer.

"I said, who the hell are you?" Reece yelled, nearly frothing for the truth.

Burly snorted. "I think he is your worst nightmare, Reece. But then, that's what you are to the rest of us."

Dern, limping slightly, followed the officers and their prisoner up the trail to the hospital where Biggs and a bevy of other cops were waiting. All eyes followed the prisoner, and Dern could feel the sense of relief, even elation rippling through the sodden group. The dogs whined, a few cops told jokes, still others were on phones or smoking or texting.

Once he was shackled, the prisoner was prodded toward a waiting car. Biggs was already beaming. The most reviled man in Washington State history had been captured on his watch, and no doubt, the big man was already considering how to make political hay out of it. Not that it mattered. The man would be behind bars and his reign of terror cut short. Reba could rest easy.

Dern found his way to the sheriff and pushed his way past a few of the cops who were discussing their next move.

"Just a sec," Biggs said to one of his deputies, cutting him off as he turned to Dern. Rain dripped off the brim of his hat, but he was grinning from ear to ear, obviously feeling as if he'd pulled off the collar of the century. "You need something?"

"Yeah. To talk to Reece."

The sheriff laughed. "You and a million others."

Standing in the pouring rain, nose to nose with Biggs, his ankle throbbing, his flesh nearly frozen, Dern wasn't in the mood for jokes. "I need to speak with him. Without me, you wouldn't have made this arrest. I led you here. Brought him down. I want to talk to him."

"I realize you were integral in Reece's capture, but I can't—"

"Sure you can, Sheriff." He'd almost suggested Biggs grow a pair but bit his tongue. However, he must've conveyed the message telepathically because Biggs snorted and seemed to have second thoughts. "Tell ya what. I'll see what I can do. In the meantime, have the paramedics look at your ankle."

"Screw my ankle! I need to talk to him now!"

Biggs's smile fell away. "No way, son. Lots more important folks are standin' in line. You had your chance out there when you were playing lone cowboy and gettin' in the way of the officers."

"*I* found him."

"Yeah, yeah, I know," Biggs conceded, then added, "Look, you might get a chance later, at the sheriff's office. But the feds will be there, so I can't make any damned promises. That's it. Take it or leave it." And then he was off. Without so much as a "thanks."

Bastard!

Seething, Dern ignored his throbbing ankle and decided he'd "take it" as he watched the vehicle carrying a cuffed and shackled Reece drive off. The prisoner would be driven back to the marina in Monroe, then shuttled by boat to the mainland.

"This way!" Burly said, coming up behind Dern and patting him on the back. "I'll give ya a ride to the ER. See that you get your ankle tended to."

"Just take me to the station."

"But—"

"Let's not argue, okay? It's my damned ankle."

"Do it, Orvin," the female officer ordered, revealing Burly's real name. "Least we can do."

"Oh, fuck. Biggs won't be happy."

"He never is," the woman cop said, then motioned to a vehicle and said to Dern, "Well, what're you waiting for? Get in!"

With Orvin settling behind the wheel of a county-issued Jeep and Connie, the woman deputy with whom he had spoken earlier riding shotgun, Dern was offered the backseat, a towel, and a blanket. He climbed inside and they, along with a convoy of other vehicles, headed to Monroe where the ferry was commandeered into making several trips to the mainland. Spirits were up, the officers regaling each other with their take on the capture as they waited to be ferried to the mainland.

Seated in the Jeep, waiting for the next ferry, Dern found his cell phone in his jacket pocket. Waterlogged and covered in sand, it wouldn't so much as power up.

"Great."

"It might dry out," Connie said, spying Dern's attempts to use the thing. "In the meantime, you can use mine."

"You got Ava Church's number?"

"Nah." She shook her head. "But I'm sure we can find it once we get back to the station."

"Never mind."

Ava was probably still at the sheriff's office, and he'd try to connect with her there. At least at the station, with Reece collared, Ava was safe. Surprisingly, he felt a sense of relief. Hopefully now she could find some peace. No more hallucinations about her boy, and no more jumping into the bay or climbing on the damned roof in the middle of the night. With Jewel-Anne's gaslighting plot exposed and over and Reece in custody, Ava could finally get on with her life.

What the hell do you care? She's still married to that prick. Right?

And that was a problem, a big problem. Whether he would ever admit it or not, he was in love with her. He stared out the foggy window of the Jeep and silently cursed himself as a dozen kinds of fool. Ava was married, had a history of mental problems, was obsessed with a kid who was probably dead, had once tried to commit suicide, believed in conspiracies, flirted with paranoia, and had a razor-sharp tongue when her temper exploded, which it did often enough.

Not exactly the poster girl for a love interest.

"Hey, here we go." Connie pointed at a ferry chugging across the bay. "Won't be long now."

She was wrong. It took another hour and a half for their vehicle to arrive in Anchorville, where the news of Reece's capture had raced like wildfire through the shops, restaurants, and offices. At the marina, a crowd had gathered, swapping stories, trying to get information from the police as the ferry docked and the government-issued vehicles wound their way up the narrow streets to the station house.

Despite the storm that was unleashing its fury on the area, the eager press was waiting. News vans, reporters, cameras, and satellite equipment was being set up near the steps of the offices of the sheriff's department. A crowd of looky-loos had already collected and was growing, people bundled in rain jackets and hats, huddled under trees or in vehicles, hoping to catch a glimpse of the area's most notorious criminal.

It was kind of a sick media circus, Dern thought, though he felt not a drop of empathy for the man in custody. Nor did he sense any latent brotherly connection. Reece was a convicted killer. End of story. And the sooner Dern got through all the red tape and found out what he knew, the sooner they could lock the bastard up and throw away the key for all he cared.

Joe Biggs, on the other had, was eating up the drama. All smiles, he emerged from his vehicle, and rather than going in the back door, he made his way to the top of the short flight of steps. Beaming, he'd given the reporters a quick interview and proudly said "We finally got him!" into more than one outthrust microphone.

Despite the dismal weather, Sheriff Joe T. Biggs was definitely in his element. The crowd outside the station swelled. Dern, who had hurried into the building, had surveyed the production through rain-spattered windows. From a few quickly hurled questions, it seemed that most of the residents of Anchorville were disappointed that Reece hadn't holed himself up and come out, guns blazing. Yes, Reece was a criminal, a murderer, but he'd also become part of the local color of the community, hated and revered all in one breath. While a great percentage of the citizens of this small town would rest easier now that they've captured the madman who'd wreaked gruesome havoc a few years back, there would be a handful of locals who would hate to see the mystery solved and the legend destroyed.

Dern was just glad it was over but antsy that he couldn't see the man face-to-face. All he wanted was a few minutes alone with Reece, but Biggs announced that he was lucky to be allowed into the viewing room, able to watch the interrogation through a two-way mirror. It didn't matter that Dern had spearheaded the hunt, come up with the information leading to Reece's capture, was a reserve member of a police force, or even that he and Reece were related. Joe Biggs was standing firm. This was his department's moment.

"You're lucky I'm letting you get this close," he'd said to Dern before returning to confer with the public information officer, where he'd asked if the governor had called to congratulate him.

Disgusted, Dern now stood in the dark, peering through the two-way glass, and all the while Lester Reece, on the other side of the mirror, was being interviewed by a woman detective Dern didn't recognize. She'd introduced herself to Reece as Detective Kim. Not more than five-four, she was petite and tough-looking. With rimless glasses, short black hair, and a stubborn jaw that suggested she meant business, she started asking questions.

Reece was having none of it.

Though the cop was cool, Reece sat belligerently in his chair, arms wrapped around his chest, eyes glittering with hate.

"I'm telling you I didn't do it," he said for the fifth time. "I didn't kill any of those women. Hell, I didn't even know two of them! You're just trying to pin them on me cuz it's easier than finding the real killer!"

The detective was calm. Listening. Pretending to go along but persistent.

"You can ask me the same damned question a thousand times, and the answer isn't going to change. I didn't do any of 'em." He was getting agitated now, his yellow teeth visible, his bloodless lips curled in a snarl beneath his graying beard. He stared into the mirror as if he knew Dern was watching.

"What about Noah Church?"

"Who?"

"The boy who went missing from the island a couple of years ago."

"What about him?"

"You know what happened to the boy?"

"What? Are you fuckin' nuts? No, damn it! I had nothin' to do with that. Nothin'!" Reece was vehement.

"What do you know about him?" the detective asked calmly.

"I told you, nothin'!"

"Are you his biological father?"

"What?" Stunned, he was shaking his head violently, his long, wild hair shimmying with his denial. "Shit, no! What the fuck's goin' on here?"

"But you were involved with Jewel-Anne Church?"

"I *knew* her. Yeah, at the hospital. But I didn't *fuck* her. *Big* difference! Jesus H. Christ! You people are sick!"

"Why not?"

"What? Why didn't I get into her pants? Hell, I didn't want to, not there at the hospital. Her old man woulda killed me. Or worse." Then his expression changed and he looked slyly at the mirror. "But, you know, she wanted it. Wanted me to fuck her. Teased the hell out of me." He was nodding now, eyes bright. "She flashed me a couple of times, let me see her tits. Nice ones, by the way."

"But you didn't—"

"I said no, damn it! What do ya need? A DNA test? Then let's do it!" A muscle worked frantically beneath his beard. "I might be crazy, but I'm not that nuts!"

"Same diff."

"Listen, bitch," Reece said, his anger exploding as Dern and six others watched through the glass. "I did *not* kill those women, and I didn't fuck Jewel-Anne Church, and I'm sure as hell not that missing kid's daddy! You got that? Don't try to pin any of this on me."

"And don't you disrespect me. Got it?" She stared him down, then once the stiffness left Reece's shoulders, asked, "Do you know where he is?"

"Who? What? You mean the kid? No!"

"Any ideas?"

"Probably dead by now. Who knows? What the hell is this?" Spittle had collected in the corners of his mouth, and he wiped it away with the back of his hand.

Detective Kim didn't let up. "Tell me about Jewel-Anne Church, your relationship with her."

"I already told you, she came around when I was in the hospital. Fascinated by the killer-freak, I guess. I don't know. Anyway, she hinted that she'd let me do her, you know?" He was nodding, making an obscene gesture with his hands. "She even went so far as to help me escape; she'd found her daddy's keys, the ones he thought he'd lost." His eyes glittered. "One of the reasons he got fired, y'know. Losing his keys and not botherin' to change the fuckin' locks. She still has—had—'em."

"So she helped you escape and you went where?"

"Where do ya think? She got me off the island, gave me some cash, and I took off. Open water to Canada."

"Why'd you come back?" she asked.

He didn't answer.

"Come on, Reece, what is it? Things get too hot for you up north?" When the prisoner didn't respond, Kim said, "If I call the Canadian authorities, am I gonna find out that some other women died suspiciously? Had their throats slit?"

"No!" Reece slammed his fist onto the table, making the recorder jump. His face was mottled with an anger he couldn't quite suppress. He seemed on the verge of spilling his guts, battling an inner war. Just when Dern thought he would crack, Reece said, "I want a friggin' lawyer!" Then, glaring past the detective's shoulder, he stared at the mirror. "That's right, you bastards," he said to those hidden behind the glass. "You hear me? I know my rights, and I'm not saying anything more until you get me my lawyer. You remember him? C. Robert Cresswell? Get him!"

Everyone who knew anything about Reece recognized the name of the attorney who had helped Reece avoid prison by getting him committed to Sea Cliff instead.

Reece turned his attention back to the woman interrogating him and said, "So until Cresswell gets here, you all can sit tight. I'm not saying another fuckin' word."

Chapter 45

"We can't hold her any longer," Snyder said outside the interrogation room where he and Lyons had been questioning Ava Garrison. The station had become a madhouse with the capture of Lester Reece, the phone lines jangling, conversation buzzing, and more cops called into duty. The air seemed to crackle with electricity and excitement.

Through it all, he and Lyons had tried to break Ava Garrison's story.

They'd failed. Tripping her up had proved an impossible task as the woman who was supposed to be mentally fragile, a "basket case" in some references, had proven to be tough as nails. They'd learned little more than they already knew. Despite hours of grilling, she'd stuck to her guns. She didn't know how the knife had gotten into her room and had seemed shocked when confronted with it. Though they'd found one long strand of black hair from the wig that had been discovered on Jewel-Anne's head (and probably like the hairs found at the other two crime scenes), she'd sworn she'd never seen it before.

Even though she'd been the last one to see Cheryl Reynolds

alive, had accused Evelyn McPherson of having an affair with her husband, and had gotten into a physical altercation with her cousin the night before, the evidence they'd collected against her was still merely circumstantial.

Nothing solid connecting her to the crimes.

The knife that was probably the murder weapon that had been found in her room had no prints on it, and her alibis were still holding up. Snyder could only imagine what a field day any defense lawyer worth his salt would have if they ever went to trial. With so many people living in and around Neptune's Gate, any number of individuals could have planted the knife and the strand of hair from the wig. Whoever had killed Jewel-Anne Church wanted that link made; they'd left her wearing the fake hair so that the police would connect the dots.

And then there was her wild-ass story about Jewel-Anne gaslighting her, making her think she was going out of her mind. When pressed about the fight with her cousin, Ava had insisted Jewel-Anne and Lester Reece were the biological parents of her child (a fact she'd conveniently forgotten with her hospitalization) and that her crippled cousin, though confined to a wheelchair, had somehow set up an elaborate scheme to make her think she was hearing and seeing her missing son and thereby sending her into fits of paranoia.

Craziest shit he'd ever heard. But she claimed to have video proof. He'd see. Even videos could be altered though he doubted Ava Garrison would go to all that trouble. But, who knew?

And the thought of Lester Reece fathering a kid gave him chills.

"You don't think she did it?" Lyons asked, perturbed. Leaning one shoulder against the hallway wall, she looked as tired as he felt. It had been a long night that had bled into an even longer day.

"All I know is we can't hold her," Snyder answered.

"Sure we can. For a while."

"To what? Break her? Save her from killing someone else?"

"Yes!" Lyons said vehemently.

"She could ask for a lawyer."

"Let her."

Snyder rubbed his chin, felt a bit of stubble and wished the case was more clear-cut. Then again, he always did.

"Motive, opportunity, and means," she pointed out as an officer leading a prisoner in cuffs pushed past them, and the captive, a guy in jeans nearly falling off his skinny ass, a wet hoodie, and tattoos crawling up his neck slid an appreciative glance in Lyons's direction. She didn't seem to notice.

Snyder did.

But he ignored it and said, "The weapon has no fingerprints on it."

"But maybe some blood transfer? Could be that when the blood on the blade is analyzed, we'll come up with the DNA of the victim—or, I suspect victims—and the killer."

"That'll take time."

She snorted and dug in the purse hanging from her shoulder. "I say we arrest her. Shake her up."

"Not yet."

"Why? Because she's rich and can hire the best damned defense attorney around?" Lyons charged, frustrated. She located a rubber band and with the dexterity of years of practice began pulling her unruly hair into a ponytail.

"That's something to think about, yeah. But the main thing is, we just don't have enough to hold her."

Lyons rolled her eyes as she snapped her hair into place, a couple of curls already escaping. "I can't believe you're saying this. After busting our hump trying to find out who killed these women, you're going to let her walk. Hell, Snyder, I swear I have more balls than you sometimes!" And with that she marched off.

Ouch! His male ego stung a bit, but he couldn't give it much thought. He had too much to do, and he was so caught up in the case he almost didn't notice how Lyons's jeans hugged her buttocks as she stormed off. Or the way the newly formed ponytail bounced against her back with each of her quick strides.

Almost.

Like it or not, it was time to release Ava Garrison to the free world. Her husband was already here, making a fuss, demanding she speak with a criminal defense attorney. Freedom wasn't going to be much fun for her, he surmised, because the press was already going nuts. For the moment, they would concentrate on Lester Reece and his rich family and attorney. But the circle would widen quickly, like ripples in a pond when a stone skipped over the surface, and Ava Garrison would soon be of high interest. Her lost son was now rumored to be fathered by one of Washington State's most renowned criminals, and she was the woman at the center of an investigation where three local women had been brutally murdered, one of the victims supposedly the biological mother of Ava Church's missing son.

Oh, yeah, the fun had just started.

The way Snyder saw it, Ava Garrison would step out of the station a free woman and end up imprisoned on her island by the media.

He made his way to his cubicle and tried to ignore the general buzz of excitement in the hallways and offices of the station, wouldn't let the almost-giddy sense of accomplishment infect him.

Once at his desk, he grabbed his mouse and clicked on his computer. Within seconds, he was studying the crime scene photos of Jewel-Anne Church and scratching notes to himself.

The dolls bothered him a lot. Why go to all the trouble? No way would Lester Reece have done such a thing, nor Ava Church, but someone was making a point, probably about Jewel-Anne's fascination with dolls, which maybe stemmed from giving up her real baby? Who knew. He let that train of thought go and concentrated on another puzzle.

Why would the killer leave the wig if he planned on more homicides, more victims? Obviously parts of it were left purposefully at the previous crime scenes, so was leaving the wig some sort of message? With Jewel-Anne Church's death, was his work finished? Again he came back to the mutilated dolls. Were they payback for the doll that had been buried? Nothing was quite holding together.

Maybe Lester Reece could set the record straight. These current homicides weren't too far off from the murders that he'd committed years before. Only problem: the man, holed up under the old asylum all this time, didn't appear capable of killing anything more than a passing rat that might have haunted the old hospital.

Then again, he told himself, looks could be deceiving. And he did have a helluva fight with Austin Dern.

To get another perspective, Snyder decided to head down the hallway and listen in on the interview, see what old Lester had to say for himself.

It might just be interesting.

"Go on inside," Wyatt said as he cut the engine. "I'll put the boat away."

Good! Ava couldn't get out of the boat fast enough. The silent, nerve-wracking ride across the bay had been bad enough. Accusations had hung in the air, silently stretching thin over the whine of the boat's powerful engine, so Ava wasn't going to spend an extra second alone with her husband.

Outside the boathouse, with the cold night as a shroud around her, she stared at the house she'd once loved. Looming dark above the tidewaters, Neptune's Gate seemed more monstrosity than sanctuary. Never had it appeared less like her home.

A few lights glowed bright in the gloom, but they weren't enough to lift her spirits. There had been just too much tragedy and trauma in the last twenty-four hours. Two days ago, Jewel-Anne had been alive, tormenting her; now she would never see her cousin again, never be irritated by her humming wheelchair and catty remarks, never wish Jewel-Anne would find another artist to idolize—Michael Jackson, Katy Perry, Lady Gaga, anyone other than Elvis . . . not that it mattered any longer.

Walking toward the house, she rotated her neck, trying to loosen the stiffness that had settled in her muscles. She'd been up for what seemed days and had been interrogated at the sheriff's office for hours. Eventually they'd released her, and Wyatt, ever the doting if straying husband, had insisted upon ferrying her back to the island. During the voyage, he'd tried to make conversation, but she hadn't felt like yelling over the roar of the boat's engine, and truth to tell, she was sick of pretending at the marriage as well.

It was over.

They both knew it.

The rain that had been pelting earlier had subsided, leaving a soft mist that seemed to cling to the streetlamps and thicken the air. She looked toward the lights of Monroe. Only the market was still open at this hour, its neon beer sign glowing through the gathering fog. The island seemed a sad, lonely place tonight. Hands in her coat pockets, she walked past the dock where she'd jumped into the bay and wondered why she'd been so certain she'd seen her son standing on this very dock. How willing and broken had her mind been?

Her heart wrenched when she thought of Noah. From what she'd heard, most of it through Wyatt, Lester Reece had denied having taken the boy or knowing where he was. Was the killer telling the truth? Or had he done the unthinkable, and after all this time she'd have to face the horrid fact that her child was dead?

Her throat clogged.

She felt the sting of tears against her eyelids but refused to break down.

Once she was strong again, after about forty-eight hours of uninterrupted sleep, she'd rethink things. Until then, she was too worn out to even rein in her thoughts.

But first, the divorce. No matter how tired you are, tomorrow you'll get yourself out of bed and make that call to your attorney.

Rubbing the chill from her arms, she looked at the dock one last time and found it empty, stretching into the inky, roiling water. Tonight, and never again, would she see her son standing upon its edge.

Now, as she took the path to the house, she realized her life with her son was only a distant, fading memory. Again the tears threatened; again she pushed them back. "Please be with him wherever he is," she prayed, her breath fogging in the still night air, her heart in a million broken pieces.

Maybe it's time to leave the island. Start over.

She passed the garden where the marker for her son had been uprooted, the tiny casket discovered, and if possible, her soul tore a little more.

Could she actually let go of this house that had brought her so much heartache and pain? She'd be alone, because no matter what, she wasn't going to try again with Wyatt.

Walking through the front door, she shrugged out of her coat and tossed it onto the hall tree. The house smelled of old coffee, cold ashes, and dying flowers but was thankfully quiet. After being barraged by the detectives all day, she needed silence, time to quiet the pounding in her head, space to sleep and forget.

Other than the cat staring at her from the bench in the foyer, no one was around, and for that she was grateful. She heard Wyatt opening the back door. He had told her both Trent and Ian had left for the mainland earlier in the day, and Wyatt wasn't certain they would return. Demetria, beside herself at Jewel-Anne's death, had called one of her sisters, and now she was staying off the island for at least this night and probably only returning to gather her things. According to Wyatt, she planned to move permanently as soon as she secured new employment. Simon, Khloe, and Virginia were probably in their quarters and that left Dern. Would he stay on now that he'd located his half brother? Unlikely.

Ava climbed the stairs but hesitated at the second-story landing. Instead of walking directly to her room, she made her way along the gallery to the back guest room, where she peered out the window. Through the fog, she saw the outline of the stable, but no light was glowing from an upstairs window. Dern was probably still off the island.

Ridiculously, she felt more alone than she had.

She couldn't help remembering the feel of his arms around her. Or the kiss they'd shared. Had it been only twenty-four hours since she'd visited him? Only one day ago that Jewel-Anne had still been alive?

She left the room and saw the nursery door ajar. Her insides wilted, but she forced herself to walk along the open landing and take hold of the knob and pull the door shut. Someday she'd have to clean out the room; she couldn't forever hold it as a shrine.

But not tonight.

You can do this, Ava. You can. Somehow.

She started for her room again, and as she walked along the open balcony, she glanced downstairs, to the first floor. Past the foyer, she noticed a slice of light against the marble, lamp-light glowing from the den.

Wyatt was probably too wound up to sleep.

Good. No chance she would have to deal with him. Besides, she had the same problem. As exhausted as she was, she knew that sleep would be elusive, that her mind was bound to run in circles all night long. Already, images ranging from Jewel-Anne's corpse to the interrogation room with the cops to Austin Dern and what it would be like to make love to him had been with her. No doubt images of Noah would creep into her mind as well. Wyatt, too, was likely to pepper her thoughts, keeping her awake despite her sleep deprivation.

She cringed a little as she opened the door to her room. The last time she'd seen it, her bedroom had been chaos. However, when she poked her head inside, she felt as if she'd stepped back in time a few days. Someone—Graciela or Khloe or both—had cleaned the entire bedroom and put it back together. Of course, upon closer inspection, she noticed that the rug that had covered her floor was missing. Obviously a new mattress, from one of the guest rooms, no doubt, had been put in place of the one probably taken by the police, and new sheets and blankets had been put in place of the old.

The black powder was gone, and surreally, with the house returned to some kind of order, it was almost as if nothing had even happened, that three women hadn't been killed and an escaped mental patient captured. Life as she'd known it would continue.

On the nightstand, as always, were her pills laid out for her.

Oh, sure. As if she would actually take them.

Then, for a fleeting second, she actually considered it. *Why not? Let yourself go off to dreamland. You might not wake up for twenty-four hours. Wouldn't that be heaven?*

There's nothing more you can do tonight, and with Reece behind bars, everyone's safe. You can trust again . . . right?

"Right," she said aloud, and decided to just let go.

She reached for the pills, scooping them up and popping them into her mouth. Telling herself she needed water to wash them down, she walked to the bathroom. Then, as much out of habit as anything, she spit the capsules into the toilet and flushed. Who knew what the medication really was? Just because Reece was in custody and Jewel-Anne was dead didn't mean that Ava's life was back on track.

As if it ever was.

She opened the medicine cabinet and, digging around on the thin shelf, found an old bottle of over-the-counter sleeping aids with a pull date that had expired six months ago.

"Good enough," she said, and, watching her reflection in the medicine cabinet's mirror, took a double dose and leaned over to wash them down with water straight out of the tap. Soon, she hoped, she and the sandman would meet. Then tomorrow, once she was rested and clearheaded, she'd figure out what to do with the rest of her life.

She changed into an oversized T-shirt and while waiting for the sleeping pills to take effect, looked for her computer. It was missing . . . no doubt taken by the police, who had stripped her room of anything of remote interest.

"Perfect," she muttered. But she still had her cell phone, and she could connect to the Internet through it and check her e-mail. Groggily, she found the smartphone and saw an app she'd added just the other day, the one attached to her camera on the stairs so that she could view the steps and locked third-floor maid's quarters when she was away from her computer.

She wondered if the police had disabled that device as well, or had they, in their hurry to rush her to the station, transport Jewel-Anne's body, and find Lester Reece, neglected that part of the house?

What were the chances?

Nil. They're thorough. Then again . . .

Yawning, she clicked on the app, and sure enough, an image formed on the phone's small screen, a view of the third floor. She was about to turn it off when she noticed movement on the screen. "What?"

A niggle of fear slid down her spine.

Squinting, she caught a glimpse of it again, a shadow flitting into view.

Maybe a rodent had gotten inside or the cat or something bigger . . . ?

No! Someone was on the third floor! She nearly jumped out of her skin when a person came into the camera's eye, filling the screen. Ava froze, barely daring to breathe. Her skin crawled in warning. What was this? Jewel-Anne was dead, so who would be wandering around on the third floor? "Oh my God," she whispered as the image cleared and she recognized the person on the screen.

There, big as life, was Khloe Prescott.

Her caretaker.

Once her best friend.

Why would she be on the third floor?

Hadn't that been Jewel-Anne's territory, where she'd kept her nefarious secret recording device?

All along, you thought Jewel-Anne had an accomplice. It looks like Khloe, too, was in on the gaslighting, part of the plot to terrorize you.

Heartsick, Ava studied Khloe from her hidden camera. Clearly, Khloe was searching for something.

No, no, no, this is wrong. . . . There has to be some mistake! Khloe wouldn't have known anything about Jewel-Anne's plans. Couldn't have. No way would Khloe have been in cahoots with Ava's cousin.

And yet, it seemed that's exactly what had happened. Staring in disbelief, heart beating frantically, Ava watched as Khloe found the device in question, dragging it down from the closet shelf and then working feverishly to dismantle it. She pulled out the tape that had been recorded with some child's cries and ripped it to shreds.

Something was off here . . . very off, Ava thought, and fought the horrid idea that was forming in the back of her mind. And Khloe, who had been her friend for most of her life as well as Noah's nanny and later Ava's caretaker when she'd first been released from St. Brendan's, couldn't be involved in something as hideous as Jewel-Anne's deception.

Another thought, more chilling than the others, assailed her.

What if Lester Reece hadn't killed Jewel-Anne? What had the cop insinuated about the dolls with their slit throats? That Reece wouldn't have bothered? But Khloe had hated Jewel-Anne's obsession with her "babies" too . . . and then Ava understood that Jewel-Anne's need for the dolls was because she gave up her own child.

Dear God in heaven, was it possible that Khloe was somehow behind Jewel-Anne's murder? If so, had she tried to set Ava up as the prime suspect by planting the knife in her room? But Khloe had always been her friend, a close ally . . .

Not always!

Remember?

Her friendship with you was a long time ago. And the relationship had started crumbling in high school when you made the mistake of dating her boyfriend, Mel Lefever. Sure, they'd broken up, but less than a week later, you went out with him. Khloe had been hurt at the time, but that was just high school stuff. It all seemed forgiven, years before.

Maybe not. Was it possible Khloe still held a grudge? No way.

Then what about Kelvin? She was crazy in love with him when he died, and if she, like Jewel-Anne, blamed you for his death . . .

Ava's mind raced with the times Khloe had seemed distant

and dark, how she'd married Simon Prescott, a man with whom she'd rebounded and had a tumultuous, maybe even abusive relationship soon after Kelvin had died.

"Dear God," Ava whispered, trying to understand when nothing was making sense. Nothing! She was tired and her mind groggy, the sleeping medication starting to kick in. She fought it, had to stay awake, had to find out the truth.

She could confront her friend.

And how would that work out if Khloe is really a murderess?

"No way!"

The image on her computer blurred as a shadow covered the screen for an instant. Khloe looked up. Smiled. An almost naughty grin.

What?

Another person came into view. Tall. Broad-shouldered. Male.

The hairs on the back of Ava's neck stood on end.

Her heart nearly stopped.

It couldn't be! Couldn't! Her hand shook as she held the phone, staring at it in disbelief. The person entering the room was Wyatt.

What the hell was he doing in the attic? Still staring at the device in her hand, she edged to the door of her room, then poked her head out onto the landing overlooking the floor below. The light in the den was still glowing through the cracked door.

What was going on?

A dozen answers sprang into her head. Not one of them was good.

As she eased back into her room, she watched Khloe greet him with that slow and sexy smile. Ava could only see his profile, but he, damn him, returned Khloe's I've-got-a-secret smile with one of his own.

Really?

They were in league together?

She hadn't suspected, but then she'd been so certain he'd been involved with Evelyn McPherson.

On the screen, Wyatt closed the short distance between himself and Khloe, said something unintelligible, then, when she laughed, tossing her head back, he reached forward and caught the back of her neck with one hand. Khloe's eyes twinkled with a sensual, come-and-get-me fire.

Horrified, Ava watched as Wyatt dragged Khloe closer to him. She said something and he chuckled; then he kissed her. Long. Hard. As if he'd been waiting forever for just this moment.

Sick!

It wasn't Evelyn McPherson he was having an affair with, you idiot. It was Khloe! Oh, Jesus!

Had they . . . ? Her mind was reeling. Was it possible that they had actually killed Jewel-Anne and the others? No . . . of course not. That had to be Lester Reece. Had to!

Or not?

A cold panic was welling from deep within her. Of all the things she thought of her husband, not for a second had she ever considered him capable of murder.

But you didn't think he'd become involved with Khloe, now, did you? What do you really know about Wyatt . . . or Khloe? Only what they wanted you to.

Had they both been a part of Jewel-Anne's gaslighting scheme? Had something gone wrong and the cruel prank evolved into something more hideous than playing with Ava's mind?

She dropped the phone and had to let out her breath slowly. A million questions screamed through her mind, questions with no answers. She didn't want to believe these two lovers were involved in Jewel-Anne's murder, nor the other women's brutal deaths as well.

In her heart of hearts, she realized that Wyatt and Khloe had a hand in all of it. How deep they were involved she couldn't guess.

Think, Ava, think. You can't just stand here and digest this or puzzle it out. You have to do something.

However, she was a little sluggish, the pills she'd swallowed starting to work their sedative magic, despite the adrenaline coursing through her blood.

You have to confront them.

No. That wouldn't work. Retrieving the phone, she stared at the small screen and saw that they were still embracing, still kissing, really getting into it.

Get help. Find someone and then confront them.

Impossible! The house was empty. She'd felt it from the moment she'd stepped through the front door. No one was here.

Except Khloe and Wyatt.

Her insides turned to ice. Had Khloe gotten rid of everyone in the house? Then had Wyatt come to pick her up, playing the part of the devoted husband, to set her up?

She reached for the bedside phone, intending to dial 911 and try to locate Detective Snyder. Though he still considered her a suspect in the murders, he would be interested in this. They had a history.

She plucked the handheld from its base.

No dial tone.

No display on the screen.

No . . . anything.

Dread dripped down her spine.

It had to be a mistake.

She checked on the electrical connections, clicked the TALK button.

Nothing.

Oh, God!

They're isolating you!

This, tonight, is all part of their plot to make you appear insane.

Once more, she glanced at her smartphone's screen where the kiss was just ending. They smiled up at each other as if satisfied that their perfect plot was finally coming together.

Get out of the house! Take the boat. Get the hell off of the island! Now! While they're still in the attic, involved with each other. Go now! Think of Jewel-Anne. This might be your only chance to escape with your damned life.

But first . . . she punched out 911 on the cell before hanging up quickly. If Wyatt had really wanted to kill her, why hadn't he thrown her overboard on the way back from the mainland only an hour earlier? He could have claimed that she fell or jumped overboard, and with her history, no one would doubt him. No, no, no. She was confused. He didn't want to do her harm. That wasn't his mission.

Then what is?

You really can't afford to stick around and find out.

She found a pair of jeans and quickly slipped them on. With one eye on the small screen of her phone, she slid her arms through the sleeves of her jacket again. She'd sneak out of the house, get down to the boat, and . . .

And what? Run away like a coward? Let them get away with whatever it is they're doing? Tell the police that they were having an affair and destroying a simple recorder that played the sounds of a baby crying? You think they'll believe you? Or will the police, too, think you're paranoid or desperate or just plain crazy.

Take a deep breath, Ava. Then fight back! Beat them at their own game.

But she needed help. She couldn't do it alone. Clicking off the screen again, she dialed Dern and silently prayed that he would pick up, that his cell was turned on, that he wasn't out of range. She hadn't seen him since he'd joined the police in the search for Reece, though she'd overheard the buzz at the station indicating Dern had been instrumental in the fugitive's capture. Now, though, she had no idea where he was.

Her call went directly to voice mail. *Crap!* She didn't have time for long messages, but whispered, "This is Ava. Please come back to the island. ASAP! There's something happening here. Call me back!"

Despite her hammering heart, her blood was sluggish, her mind not quite as sharp as it should be. She checked her camera again.

Finally the long embrace had ended and something seemed to have changed. They were still standing close to each other, talking rapidly, but the sexy playfulness had disappeared, morphing into other emotions. Definitely, the mood had changed to something tenser, anger visible in their faces. Wyatt's jaw was rock hard and it seemed as if Khloe's eyes had darkened, her mouth twisting in a deep, seething fury. Obviously they were arguing.

About Jewel-Anne?

Or something else?

You, Ava. She's trying to get him to go along with killing you! Or maybe it's the other way around; maybe he's trying to convince Khloe to take your life.

Either way, it was time to leave.

Still staring at the screen, she headed out the door. She was at the top of the stairs when she saw things shift on the screen. Something was happening. The argument obviously escalating.

Oh, God. Ava stopped in her tracks and watched.

Khloe's stare was cold as ice.

Wyatt reached for her again, but Khloe stepped back, said something that stopped Wyatt in his tracks. His mouth rounded as if he were saying "No!" Then, quick as a snake striking, Khloe reached into her pocket and produced a knife.

What?! Ava gasped.

Wyatt held up a hand.

But with teeth bared, fury burning in her eyes, Khloe sprang.

The knife glinted. Wyatt feinted, trying to dodge the blow.

Too late.

Ava watched in horror as, with a look of primal victory, Khloe plunged the blade deep into Wyatt's chest.

Chapter 46

Reece wasn't the killer. If the cops didn't know it, Dern sure as hell did.

Which meant there was a killer still on the loose.

A killer who'd cruelly taken the lives of those close to Ava.

He found a ride back to the marina. A patrolling deputy dropped him off near the waterfront, and he hurried to find a ride to the island.

The station had been a madhouse, the press and different police agencies adding to the chaos, but out here, under the ethereal security lights, fog rolling in over the dark water stretching beyond the docked boats, the night was serene, at least to the naked eye.

But he felt it. A palpitating fear. An inner knowledge that evil reigned. Fortunately now he was finally dry, his clothes stiff from the briny water where he'd tackled Reece hours before. At the station, he'd made the call to Reba, heard her try not to break down after whispering, "Thank God," and finally, "Thank you, Austin." That part had gotten to him, and he'd hung up wondering why a sense of satisfaction was elusive.

Despite Reece's capture and the hours without sleep, Dern felt restless, his muscles sore, his mind keyed up. If Reece wasn't the killer, then who was? He'd been asking himself that same damned question for hours, even as he'd stood in the dark viewing room watching the maniac who was his brother deny, offer up bullshit and deny again and again. Insane? No way. Homicidal? Oh, yeah. But Reece had been adamant and believable about not "offing those bitches."

Which means the killer was still at large.

Someone had murdered three women in cold blood.

So far.

He jabbed his hands deep into the sandy pockets of his jacket, retrieved his phone, and tried to call Ava again, but his cell still wasn't working. When he'd learned she already left the station with her jerk of a husband, he'd tried calling the house on one of the sheriff's department lines but hadn't gotten through.

The fact that he couldn't connect with her bothered him a little. Well, actually, it bothered him a lot.

Not for a second did he believe Ava was the killer, though from what he'd overheard at the sheriff's office, the police were trying to mount a case against her.

Dern now believed Ava had been set up. Whoever had been in league with Jewel-Anne had turned on her and tried to make Ava appear to be not only paranoid, but also a killer.

He figured the killer had to be someone close to her, someone who could get on and off the island easily, someone who knew the ins and outs of Neptune's Gate.

He checked his cell phone again. Still not working, probably never would. Bad luck coupled with his own feeling that trouble was brewing.

Get over it; you'll be back on the island within the hour.

His boots rang on the damp boards of the marina, and the scent of briny water mingled with oil hung on the fog that had begun to roll in from the ocean. All of the boats were docked for the night, tied firmly in their berths, but he spied the *Holy Terror,* her captain sitting outside in the mist, the tip of his cigarette glowing red in the night. *Perfect.*

"I need a ride," Dern said to the owner. He'd met Butch Johansen a couple of times, thought the guy might be okay. "To Church Island."

"It'll cost ya." Johansen flipped the end of his cigarette into the night, its red tip arcing before dying an instant death in the inky water.

"Fine. Just make it quick." A sense of urgency drove him, and he couldn't help but worry that Ava was on the island, possibly with a killer on the loose.

"As quick as I can. Fog's comin' in." Despite his concerns, Johansen was already reaching for the ignition as Dern climbed aboard. As the engine fired and Johansen eased the *Holy Terror* out of the slip, Dern kept his gaze fastened to the murky night ahead. Though he couldn't see Church Island, it was out there. Somewhere. And Ava was probably there with that prick of a husband. That thought bothered him, too. He tried his phone again and though there was a glimmer of illumination on the screen, still nothing.

His worry increased.

"You got a cell phone?" Dern asked over the increasing roar of the engine.

"Radio."

"Seriously?" Who didn't have a cell these days?

"Got in a pissing match with the carrier. Guess who lost?" Johansen's gaze didn't move from the prow of the boat and the soupy night ahead.

Great. The wind was screaming past them as they cut through the fog, but they weren't going fast enough. "Can this tub go any faster?" he yelled, frustrated. It was dangerous, but Dern didn't care. A sense of urgency was driving him, fear for Ava.

"Yes, sir!" With that, Johansen hit the gas and the boat nearly flew across the water. As if they were outrunning the fog silently collecting over the black surface.

Still, for Dern, it wasn't fast enough.

No, oh, no . . . Ava stumbled backward as she stared in horror at the tiny screen in her hand. Khloe stood above Wyatt who was struggling, gasping for breath, a red stain blooming on his shirt.

"No . . . no . . ." She had to help him, save him, but the malevolent light in Khloe's eyes suggested she wasn't finished, and Ava remembered the garish slice across Jewel-Anne's throat. She needed a weapon. A gun, a knife, a baseball bat. *Any* damned thing. So she could fend off Khloe and help save Wyatt. If there was enough time. *Oh, please, God!*

She knew the police couldn't get to the island fast enough; saving Wyatt was up to her. Moving into the hallway, she dialed 911 again as precious seconds ticked away, seconds that could mean his life or death.

A raspy-voiced operator answered. "Nine-one-one, please state your emergency—"

Before the operator could ask any questions, Ava cut in. "Send help to Neptune's Gate on Church Island! Right away! My husband is being attacked! He . . . Oh, God, he might already be dead!"

"Ma'am? Calm down. Who are you and what is your emergency? An assault?"

"My name is Ava Church, and I'm watching someone try to kill my husband! Out here on the island. Send someone immediately!" She couldn't keep the panic from her voice. "She's got a knife and she's trying to kill him!"

"You're witnessing the attack?"

"On my phone! The camera on my phone!" she clarified,

hurrying down the stairs to the first floor. She was running out of time. With every second, Wyatt was bleeding out.

"Pardon me?"

"I have a camera set up! I can see what's happening." She was running now, barefoot across the foyer to the den, time her enemy. As she passed it, the grandfather clock began to strike loudly, each chime reverberating and counting off the seconds, the beats of Wyatt's heart—though, she realized, even now her husband could be dead.

Into the den she flew, forcing her tiring legs to keep running, her mind to stay focused, but she was clumsy from the drugs sliding into her bloodstream and she hit her hip on the corner of the desk, then stubbed her toe on a chair. "Ouch! Damn it!"

"Ma'am? Mrs. Church?"

The operator was still on the line. Ava said, "Just, please, listen! I'm telling you Khloe Prescott is stabbing my husband! For God's sake, send someone. Now!"

"You're watching this on your phone?" Skepticism.

"I told you, YES!!!!" Frustrated, she rattled off the address. "Get Detective Snyder or Detective Lyons. Please hurry!"

"If you'll please stay on the line, Ms. Church—"

"I can't!" she said, and clicked off and tried Dern again. Nothing. Quickly, she texted him:

Khloe stabbed Wyatt. In the attic. Send help!

After sending the text, she switched her phone to silent mode; she couldn't have it go off and alert anyone hiding in the shadows of her location.

Hurry, Ava, hurry!

Her mind screamed at her, but her body wasn't complying. All of her movements were sluggish, the sleeping pills taking effect. Still, she pushed onward. She was certain Wyatt kept a pistol locked in his desk; it had been a bone of contention between them when Noah was living in the house.

Of course the drawers were locked! "Come on, come on,"

she urged herself, and found the key he kept hidden, one she'd found years before. With fumbling fingers, afraid that Khloe would walk in on her at any second, Ava unlocked the drawer where Wyatt had always kept his gun and yanked the damned thing open.

Empty!

"Damn!"

Her heart sank. But she couldn't give up. She had to find the damned Ruger he was so proud of. Frantically, she searched the other drawers, flinging them open, tossing out the contents, searching wildly for the gun and coming up with nothing.

Khloe has it!

She's cut the phone lines and taken the gun.

Now what?

Don't waste any more time! Get a knife from the kitchen. Quickly! There are half a dozen in the magnetic rack above the stove.

Heart in her throat, Ava crept quietly toward the kitchen. Her stomach jumping, she expected to be attacked at every corner. Who else was in this horrid plot against her? Trent? Jacob? Ian? Were they even around? She'd felt that the house was empty, but obviously Khloe was around. What about Simon? Or Virginia? Did they have any clue that Khloe was a murderess?

Get a grip. Don't worry about the others. Just deal with Khloe and try to get to Wyatt. There still may be time! Hurry, Ava, move!

She reached the archway into the kitchen, but her movements were slowing, and she had to work hard to stay focused. At the threshold of the hallway, she stumbled slightly, her feet not working properly. *Come on, come on! You can do this.* Forcing herself, she eased through the darkness, only the palest of light from a far-off security lamp coming through a window and giving any illumination to the Stygian room.

A shadow passed by the window and she nearly screamed

before she saw that it was the black cat, hiding on the counter near the sink.

Her fingertips found the big gas stove, and she reached over the burners to the magnetic strips mounted on the wall tiles. Carefully, she ran her fingers over the knives. Feeling the sturdy handle of the butcher knife, she pulled it down and faced the yawning dark archway leading to the back stairs, then decided to take a smaller knife as well and slid it into her pocket. "Okay, bitch," she said softly, her tongue thick, and she stepped into sheer darkness. Up one step. Then the next. She couldn't risk the switch or a flashlight. She'd have to climb the stairs quietly, knife raised and—

Creeeeaaaakkk . . .

Far away, a door opened.

Oh, God!

Ava's heart nearly stopped.

She held her breath, not daring the slightest sound.

Footsteps came cautiously from the stairway above. Someone creeping, hoping not to step on a squeaky step.

Khloe.

Jesus, help me.

Slowly letting out her breath, she stepped backward, down the two steps she'd mounted, silently backing up as her heart thudded and beads of cold, nervous sweat collected on her forehead and palms. The knife in her hand felt as if it weighed a hundred pounds.

You can do this, Ava, you can. Think of Wyatt . . . He cheated on you, yes, maybe even was a part of the gaslighting, but he didn't deserve this . . . no way.

Throat dry, she hid in the darkness, just around the corner of the archway. Her heart was pounding, echoing in her head. Her eyelids were as heavy as they'd ever been in her life, and, back flattened to the wall, she was scared to death.

The footsteps were louder now.

Closer.

Help me.

Ears straining, eyes trying to see in the darkness, Ava waited, counting her heartbeats, ready to lunge. *Hold on for the right moment. Just take her by surprise, throw yourself at her, wrest her damned knife from her. Just disarm her. That's all you have to do. Oh, dear God . . .* Sweating in the cold room, she held her weapon with both hands.

Somewhere, far, far off in the distance, she heard the rumble of a boat's engine.

Her knees went weak. Thank God!

Dern. It had to be Austin Dern.

Hurry, oh, God, please hurry!

The footsteps creeping down the stairs stopped suddenly. As if Khloe, too, had heard the approaching boat. Then, movement again, the softer tread of shoes on the floor, coming closer only to stop somewhere in the middle of the kitchen.

"Ava?" Khloe said softly, and Ava wanted to fall through the floor. "I know you're down here."

What? No . . . oh, please no.

"Come out, come out, wherever you are."

Ava didn't move. Just held her knife aloft in the darkness. Every muscle in her body was tense. But she was tired . . . oh, so tired. . . . She had to fight to remain rigid, ready.

"Aaaavaaa," Khloe singsonged again. "Aaaaavaaa."

Sweat drizzled into Ava's eyes and palms, feeling slick against the knife's handle. "You saw it all on your little camera, didn't you?"

Ava swallowed hard. Didn't answer. The knife wobbled in her hands.

"Oh . . . I get it . . . you think you're going to get the drop on me, don't you?"

She was swaying, the knife so heavy, the drugs in her system dragging her down, not even her own adrenaline strong enough to counteract the sedative.

"Well, *friend,* it's never going to happen!"

It's now or never!

Wielding her butcher knife, Ava leaped forward.

At that moment, the world went white. Bright light burned her retinas. She only caught a glimpse of Khloe's surprised expression and the mega-flashlight in one of Khloe's hands.

In the other was the very blade that had plunged into Wyatt's chest.

The message came in late. After midnight. The 911 operator tracked Snyder down and gave him the news Ava Garrison had called in and claimed she was witnessing her husband being attacked by Khloe Prescott, that even now, Wyatt Garrison could be dead. Snyder listened to the tape twice. He didn't understand what was going on, couldn't begin to piece it together, but he didn't waste any time and coordinated with the pilot of the sheriff's department boat, then headed from the station to the marina. He'd been up for over twenty-four hours and was dog tired, but he shook it off as he left his bike in his office and took one of the department's cruisers. Lights on, sirens wailing, he roared down the streets toward the marina.

No doubt Lyons would be pissed that he hadn't called her, but he wasn't going to wait. He'd heard the sheer terror in Ava Garrison's voice on that tape and knew she was in trouble. Big trouble.

She was a suspect, yeah, but after spending most of the day interviewing her, he didn't believe she'd call for help if she didn't really need it.

The first response team was already on its way to the island, a Coast Guard cutter and helicopter dispatched. But Snyder intended to get to the island as well.

He drove through one yellow light and slowed for a red, but

the streets were empty and his lights were blazing, so he ran the light, taking the turns to the waterfront a little too fast, and screeched to a halt in the parking lot across from the marina in record time. Near the water, the fog was rolling in, thin wisps that promised to become a bank before dawn.

The boat was waiting.

Lyons, damn her, was already on board.

"So what the hell took you so long?" she asked, tossing him a life jacket and sending him a don't-ever-try-to-put-one-over-on-me-again grin.

"Go to hell." But he was glad to see her.

"Back atcha," she said, then to the captain, "Let's go!" and the boat took off, speeding across the inky water, cutting through the fog, heading for whatever.

"You goddamned bitch!" Khloe shrieked as Ava pounced on her, plunging her knife deep into Khloe's shoulder. The flashlight fell, crashing against the tile and rolling drunkenly away, its beam swirling crazily overhead.

Khloe, screaming, flailing with her free hand, tried to stab Ava over and over again as they hit the floor.

Crack! Ava's knee hit hard on the tiles, but she grabbed Khloe's wrist before she could be wounded.

In the weird light, Khloe's face was contorted in pain and hatred, her gaze drilling deep into her adversary. She'd missed with her blows but kicked hard, the toe of her boot connecting with Ava's shin.

Pain shimmied up her bone and she lost her grip.

Scooting away, she heard the slurping sound as Khloe yanked the knife from her shoulder and squealed again. The knife clattered to the floor. Frantically Ava scooted away, trying to stand, her bare feet slipping and smearing on warm, sticky blood.

"I should have killed you when I had the chance," Khloe snarled.

"So why didn't you?" Ava threw back at the woman who had once been her friend. *Keep her talking and keep her in your sight. . . . Don't be distracted for an instant.* "You had plenty of chances."

"It had to look like an accident, you idiot! Why do you think? That's a little harder than they make it look in the movies!"

"But the others. They weren't accidents." While she was talking, Ava was staring at the knife in Khloe's fingers and hoping that the police were on their way. Or Dern. Or anyone. She'd heard a boat approaching. Where the hell was it?

Khloe was advancing, trying to climb to her feet. *The knife. Where's your damned knife? She's hurt. You could get the drop on her, but you need the knife.* Desperately she searched the dark room, then remembered the knife in her pocket and the dozens in the drawers and racks in this room.

"They didn't have to be accidents," Khloe was explaining, seeming glad to tell Ava about her plans, how clever she'd been. "So the police would think you, the crazy woman, killed them."

"I had no reason." Carefully, keeping her gaze fixed on Khloe she slid her hand into her pocket.

"You hated them . . ."

"No! Not Cheryl!" she cried, thinking of the kind woman who had taken her in and quietly hypnotized her in the hopes of exorcising Ava's demons. Her fingers touched the tip of the knife in her pocket, but she had to keep Khloe talking, hope that she was distracted. "Why would I kill Cheryl?"

"Because she knew all your secrets. And when they finally find the tapes of your session that you hid in the floorboards of your closet, you'll be tied to the murders."

"What tapes . . . I never . . ."

Khloe's eyes glowed with her own warped sense of pride. "They'll find them," she assured Ava, and swayed a little on her feet. She was still bleeding, red drips streaking down her arm.

"You killed them all," she charged. "Why?"

"Shut up!" she yelled at Ava. "It doesn't matter. They knew too much. Had all, one way or another, learned about Wyatt and me. They . . . they had to go." She was breathing hard, dragging in breaths, her one arm limp, her eyes blazing. "Tell me, bitch, how does it feel to have lost the love of your life?"

"The what?" For a second, she thought of Dern.

"Your husband!" Khloe snarled as Ava kept sliding away from her. Ava's mind was racing. She wondered just how badly she'd wounded Khloe. The cut had been deep . . . but still Khloe kept coming, kept crossing the long room.

"Wyatt. We have to save him!" Her fingers curled over the hilt of the knife in her pocket.

"He's dead."

"No!"

"Oh, yeah. I made sure," Khloe said smugly. "I don't leave loose ends."

"But . . . you and he . . . why . . . Oh God," she whispered, sick to her stomach. Not that she loved him, not any longer, but to think that he'd given up his life at Khloe's hand . . . "How could you?" But then, how could this woman she'd counted as a friend become a savage, ruthless killer?

"What do you care?" Khloe said, and her lips twisted in a half smile. "He was just so fucking easy to seduce. I did it to get back at you, you know." Her grin, though a partial grimace, widened, and she seemed to enjoy stalking Ava, advancing slowly, stretching out her quarry's terror.

"Back at me for what?"

"Every damned thing! This house! The money! The fact that you were treated like a princess when I had all those brothers and sisters to take care of. How do you think I feel *working* for you? Having my mother and husband working for you?" Khloe threw up her hands, the knife wobbling, blood spraying.

Rage that had been building for years bubbled forth. "And then there's the men. First in high school, you weren't satisfied until you went out with *my* boyfriend."

"Mel? But that was years ago . . ." Ava couldn't believe Khloe's pure hatred. Her fingers tightened over the knife.

"And then Kelvin . . . just when I thought I had a chance to better myself . . . to taste a little of what you take for granted, by marrying your brother, you convince him to take the boat out."

"It was an accident."

"And you end up inheriting everything." Khloe's lip curled in disgust as she advanced. "So you see, Wyatt was a way to get back at you. Through him, I can get a part of this." She wobbled her knife at the interior of the kitchen, to indicate the house, the estate, all of Neptune's Gate.

"But you killed him!" This didn't make any sense. Still, Ava scooted away. She just had to keep this going until help arrived. Khloe seemed to want to gloat, to tell her all the little details. Because they both knew that Ava's chances of escape were small.

"Because the chickenshit backed out! Decided not to go through with it! In fact, the jerk said something about trying to patch things up with you. He liked being married to you, having it all. That's why divorce was out of the question. He'd rather you be alive and sequestered away in some loony bin so he could have control of everything."

"And you . . ."

"I had a better idea! I knew what Jewel-Anne was doing and just went along. If she made you crazy enough, you would kill yourself. When that didn't happen, I went to plan B."

"The murders. Setting me up to take the fall."

"See, you're not as dumb as you look."

Ava had to keep Khloe talking as she neared the far wall. She was close now. If she could only grab the door, swing it into Khloe's face, stab her in the gut, then take off, she might have a chance. *Where? Where will you go?*

The boathouse! If she had enough time. And the keys were in the ignition. Oh, God, if only . . . *Keep her talking. For God's sake, Ava, keep her distracted.* "What . . . what about Simon?"

"What about him?"

"He's your husband."

"Not for long. I've had one too many bruises from that sick son of a bitch. I'm divorcing his ass. He knows it. Won't fight me." She stopped for a second and blinked, as if to catch her escaping thoughts. Maybe Khloe was wounded worse than even she knew.

Again, Ava heard a boat's engine . . . or more than one. *Please, oh, please . . .*

Khloe took another step forward. "You know, this would have been so much easier if you had just drowned when you were supposed to. You know, when you thought you saw your damned kid. That would have been perfect!"

"Noah?" she whispered, her back connecting with the door casing.

"Of course Noah. Those pills we gave you were switched out. Hallucinogens. But you figured that out, didn't you?"

"This is unbelievable."

"Is it? You would do anything for that kid. We knew we could manipulate you with him."

"We?"

"Jewel-Anne and Wyatt and me. Who do you think? And the really perfect twist to the plan was that he wasn't even yours. Not really. How ironic was that? Not your damned kid."

"He was . . . is . . . mine!" She had to fight to get the words out, to stay awake.

"At least he was living with his real dad."

"Wait . . . what?"

"You really don't know?" Khloe asked, coming in for the kill. "Lester Reece isn't Noah's father. That was all a big lie. Just in case you found out."

"What?" Ava's head was spinning. She was still digesting the news that Reece was Jewel-Anne's lover and Noah's biological father. "Wyatt?"

Khloe grinned with malicious satisfaction.

"Wyatt and Jewel-Anne?" She thought she might be sick.

"Of course! Jesus, you're gullible. That's why Wyatt insisted she stay on the island here in the house!"

Stunned, Ava tried to put the pieces together. Nothing she was saying made sense, and Ava's mind was slowing down, the sedatives seeming determined to take hold. *Hold on to the little knife. Don't let go.*

"He had you and Jewel-Anne pregnant at the same damned time. How's that for twisted?"

Ava physically shrank at that thought. Wyatt and Jewel-Anne? "That's impossible."

"Impossible? It's the God's honest truth. Come on, Ava. Didn't you ever wonder where Jewel-Anne's arrogance came from? Why she always seemed so smug? She'd already broken up with Lester before Noah was conceived, not that anyone other than Jewel-Anne and Wyatt could figure it out."

"This is all mind games!" she said thickly. *Hold on to the knife. For just the right moment. Don't let go, Ava. Do NOT let go.*

"Can't face this truth, either, Ava? The reason Jewel-Anne felt superior was because she had something over you, the woman who had it all." Real emotion charged Khloe's words, hatred emanating from her. "Your perfect lawyer husband and a beautiful child, even if he wasn't yours."

"You're sick," Ava whispered, inching backward, struggling to stay awake. "And you helped her . . . it was you who buried the doll in the coffin. You killed her and sliced the necks of those dolls."

"As I said, she knew too much. Just like the others."

"I don't believe you," Ava said, though it was a lie.

"Think about the scars on your arm! How do you think you got those, huh? You really believe you tried to commit suicide?" she taunted as Ava's shoulder hit the wall. She'd run out of room, was now at the back door. "Don't you remember who helped you into the tub, who lathered you up, who gave you wine . . . with a little bit of something else?"

Ava blinked. Tried to think. Good Lord, her head was heavy . . . so heavy. Like it had been on that night. When Wyatt had helped lower her into the tub, adding the bubble bath, kissing her slick neck, and lifting the razor to her arm . . . the bubbles turning pink with her blood . . .

She thought she might be sick. *Wyatt? It had been Wyatt? He'd drugged her and slit her wrists in an attempt at a staged suicide?* Denial burned through her, but it quickly fled as she realized she'd been Wyatt Garrison's pawn and had made his life easier for a long time. He didn't dare divorce her—it would cost him too much and he was greedy enough to want it all. And if he killed her, it would look suspicious, but if she descended into madness and killed herself . . . he would be the perfect martyred husband. Ava actually retched.

"So now you finally get it, don't you?" Khloe sounded pleased, though her voice seemed weaker.

The knife! She started to pull it from her pocket, but the flashlight wagged in Khloe's hands. "Ah, ah, ah!" Khloe set the flashlight on the counter. "Don't even think about it. Of course you have another weapon. A backup. A knife? Pepper spray? Leave it." She sucked her breath in through her teeth as if suddenly in pain.

Good!

"And about that little boy you've been so worried about,

forget him. He died that night, Ava. Wandered off and drowned . . ."

"More lies!" Ava screamed, her insides shredding. Her fingers clamped tight around the knife.

"Face it, Ava, he's gone. And you've spent all that money, all that time, all your sanity searching for a kid who'll never come back. A kid fathered by your husband in an affair with your cousin."

Ava barely heard Khloe's explanation, her ranting, over the roar of denial thundering through her brain. Hearing that Noah was dead only furthered her despair. But now that she was unburdening herself, rubbing Ava's nose in how clever she was, Khloe couldn't stop. "Wyatt broke it off with Jewel-Anne after the accident, and she never let him forget that he owed her. She was such a bitch. But that was fine. It made it so easy for me to step in. At first Wyatt was comforting me, you know, with the loss of Kelvin, but things heated up quickly. As for Simon, he's just another pawn. To make Wyatt jealous so he'd *do* something, get off his ass and find a way to get rid of you! But then, it was obvious that he wasn't ever going to do anything." She laughed bitterly. "And you're such a moron, you never even suspected that Wyatt was with me and not that weak sniveling shrink!" She leaned against the counter, as if for support. "You know, Ava, you really do deserve to die! This is going to be fun."

As if suddenly tired of all the talk, she lunged.

A loud screech erupted.

Khloe took a misstep.

A dark shadow, hissing and spitting scuttled over the floor. The cat!

As Khloe tried to regain her footing, toppling forward, Ava yanked her knife from her pocket and pushed herself to her feet, trying to dodge the blow.

Too late. Khloe jabbed.

Pain exploded in Ava's arm. She stumbled backward.

"Stings like a bitch, doesn't it?" Khloe taunted, raising the knife once more.

"Tell me about it!" With all of her strength, Ava leaped at Khloe. She shoved her knife deep into Khloe's chest, and the other woman staggered backward. Spinning, Ava ran for the back door. She shouldered her way past the screen and raced as fast as her legs would carry her along the path to the dock.

Away from Khloe she ran.

Away from Neptune's Gate.

Away from the horrid knowledge that her son was dead.

Faster and faster she ran, forcing her legs to move, stumbling, her feet slipping on the wet gravel, the mist thick and wet against her skin.

Her thoughts were tumbling one after another, horrid, painful scenarios playing in her mind. Wyatt had tried to kill her, years before. He'd attempted to make it look as if she'd tried to commit suicide, and even now he was dead, lying in a pool of his own blood, but what really hurt, what caused the tears to flow from her eyes, was the suffocating truth that Noah was dead.

Dear God, why did he have to lose his precious little life?

Images of her son laughing, running, calling to her, flashed in her mind. "Mommy, you come, too! Mommy!" He had giggled before taking off, tiny legs moving fast as he'd looked over his shoulder to ensure that she was giving chase.

Sweet, sweet baby.

Oh, honey, Mama loves you . . . Mama . . .

Feeling the warmth of blood slide down her arm, she kept heading to the boathouse. If she could just start the damned thing . . . but as she ran, she noticed a light bobbing next to her . . .

The beam from Khloe's flashlight.

Uneven footsteps were clattering after her.

Run, run, run! She's injured. Worse than you. You can outrun her!

Casting a quick glance over her shoulder, Ava saw Khloe struggling, her face contorted in pain, blood running down one arm, a growing stain on her chest, the broken flashlight and knife in her free hand. Her eyes, focused on Ava, were black with loathing, her lips pulled back to bare her teeth. Propelling herself forward on pure hatred, she was relentless and her intent was clear: She was going to dispose of Ava as she had the others. No longer was she content to make it appear as if Ava had killed the other women. Now Khloe's determination was single-minded: Ava was going to die!

Down the hill and onto the dock Ava sprinted, frantically, awkwardly. Her bare feet slapped on the wet planks, her lungs drank in the briny air, and she felt a release as she ran, her fear dissipating.

The fog was thickening, getting soupy. Though she couldn't see across the bay, she heard the distinctive hum of boat engines coming closer, but suddenly she no longer cared about rescue.

The black water that stretched from the dock called to her, beckoned her, offered relief from the madness and pain that was her life. It would be so easy to jump. . . .

As if she sensed what was happening, Khloe yelled, "No, Ava, don't! Let me have the satisfaction—"

Too late. She forced her legs to race even faster, closer and closer to the deep, dark void. The planks beneath her feet stopped suddenly, but she didn't. At the end of the dock, she leaped high, flinging herself, body and soul, into the welcoming darkness.

Dern's cell phone flashed for a second and he saw Ava's text. **Khloe stabbed Wyatt. In the attic. Send help!**

What the hell? Khloe stabbed Wyatt? He tried to call her cell again, but his damned phone failed.

"How much longer?" he yelled to Johansen.

"Five minutes."

Too long. Five minutes was much too long.

"Make it three," Dern yelled over the wind, his worried eyes trained on the darkness ahead. "And radio the cops. We're going to need backup."

"For what?" Johansen asked.

"I wish I knew."

Hang on, Ava, just hang the hell on!

As Johansen reached for the radio microphone, Dern saw the few winking lights of Monroe far in the distance. Maybe they would make it. There was a chance! God he hoped so. Never had he felt so impotent. His back teeth ground together in frustration.

Khloe Prescott? She was behind it all? The murderer? Not Wyatt? Dern would have bet his life that Ava's dick of a husband had been behind the plot to gaslight her, had been partnered with the dead cousin. But now *Garrison* was injured? Maybe dead? At Khloe's hand?

His anxiety ratcheted up several notches. He only hoped Ava wouldn't do anything stupid as he stared ahead and tried to make out the huge mansion or dock of Neptune's Gate. But there was nothing but darkness.

Not a good sign.

The minutes stretched on forever.

Hurry, damn it!

He had to get to her.

Before it was too late.

Ice-cold water enveloped Ava, shocking her body, causing nerve synapses to spark for an instant, waking up her damned brain as she sank into the inky depths. Unfortunately, that skin-bracing moment of clarity lasted only a few seconds. She'd hoped the grogginess that had been overtaking her would be jolted out of her. But she'd been wrong. As soon as her body adjusted to the cold, her eyelids were heavy again. Adrenaline and icy water were no match for the drugs pumping through her veins, and deep in the salty water, she kicked without her usual strength. *Fight, Ava, fight,* the rational side of her brain silently screamed while the other, sadder part of her considered giving up. Letting go . . .

Slowly she rose to the surface, strings of air bubbles from her lungs spiraling upward with her.

There was a peacefulness under the water, a serenity, even though she heard the distant rumble of boat engines churning through the water, moving ever nearer.

She broke the surface and tossed her hair from her eyes, gulping air.

In the thin, bluish light from a boathouse security lamp, Khloe stood guard, as if she wouldn't allow Ava out of the water. Pale and thin, a little unsteady, she still brandished her knife, still had fight in her, as if she were unaware of the blood dripping down her arm or discoloring her sweater.

"Go ahead. Stay there," Khloe snarled, spying Ava and obviously satisfied to have her drown. "It's perfect. You'll die looking like the lunatic you are!" she yelled, but her voice was hoarse.

You die first, Ava thought, struggling to stay afloat and swimming closer to the dock.

"Just try it, bitch!"

The fight was leaving her, slowly seeping into the frigid, salty depths. Once a strong swimmer, she was now weak, losing blood, her will to live eroding.

She started to sink and flailed upward again, fighting the sedative. Cold water swirled around her, and she felt herself slipping ever deeper. Images of Dern and Noah filled her brain as she surfaced, coughed, her strength failing. Looking at the dock one last time, she saw Khloe, and this time someone was running through the shadows toward her.

Thank God!

Finally someone would help!

Tall, running fast, seeming familiar, he strode onto the dock and Khloe looked over her shoulder.

Watch out! Ava wanted to yell, to shout a warning. *She's got a knife!* But as she tried to force the words over her lips, she started to recognize her savior. Her eyes rounded in disbelief. No, no, no! It couldn't be.

But as the runner reached the glow of the lamplight, Ava saw the impossible unfold before her eyes as Wyatt reached his lover.

She couldn't believe her eyes; she had to be hallucinating.

He was dead from a knife wound he'd received from Khloe. Even she'd admitted to killing him to . . . to leaving him for dead.

Ava stared, transfixed, as she floated, her mind spinning in crazy circles. Was he real? Or a figment of her tortured mind?

Like Noah.

You really are crazy!

In disbelief, she watched as he wrapped his arms around Khloe, holding her close, and turned to look at the bay and his drowning wife. He smiled then . . . as if this were all part of his, or hers, no *their* plan.

Her splintered mind told her that Wyatt was a figment of her imagination. He had to be . . . Nothing made sense. *If Wyatt were truly alive, why would he and Khloe go to so much trouble to make you think he was dead, that Khloe had killed him?*

To ensure her descent into madness, or better yet, to make her look even less stable, more paranoid when she talked to the police?

She didn't understand, couldn't begin to fathom the depths of their depravity.

She felt the water dragging her down, pulling her under, and she stared through a watery field of vision to watch as he kissed Khloe hard, with more passion than she'd thought him capable of. To make a point. The injured woman tried to return his fire, but she was swooning, blood dripping from her arm, and she finally dropped her knife and flashlight.

Ava, in one of her last conscious thoughts, realized his murder was all an act, one to get Ava to react, to force her outside, onto the dock and into the water. Stupidly, she'd fallen for it. No wonder the knife Khloe had brought downstairs had glinted clean, without any trace of blood. He'd obviously been wearing a protective vest.

But Khloe had not. A killer to her very soul, so certain she would overpower Ava, she'd let down her guard, left herself vulnerable.

Through the watery haze, Ava watched them kissing, ignoring her, knowing that they'd finally won. She would die looking like the paranoid mental case they'd always claimed her to be. And even Khloe's wounds, which were visible, could be cast off as the result of a fight with Ava, who would be painted as the psychotic, knife-wielding assailant.

It was perfect . . .

Except Khloe seemed to be staggering, slipping out of Wyatt's arms.

Not that it was of any consequence.

Not anymore.

Slowly Ava sank, the water crashing over her, in the very position where she'd always seen her son. *God help me.* Her head was pounding and the steady *thump, thump, thump* she heard was out of time with her heart, a bright light as luminous as the moon.

It didn't matter.

So cold, she was so damned cold.

The bright light was beckoning her.

It was time to let go. . . .

"You got a gun on board?" Dern yelled over the roar of the boat's engine as the *Holy Terror* approached the island. The prow of the boat was cutting through the water, angling toward Neptune's Gate, close enough that the dock and boathouse were starting to emerge in the fog. There were other boats closing in on them, probably the sheriff's department vessels, but the *Holy Terror* was still in the lead. Still, Dern feared they were too late. His guts twisted at the thought, and he nearly jumped out of his skin to get to the island.

Johansen, standing at the helm, squinted into the murky darkness. "I got a spear gun. Why?"

"That all?"

"Fuck, yeah, it's all I got. All I ever needed. I'm a boat captain, not an assassin!"

"Get it! Wait, don't you have a flare gun?"

"Well . . . yeah."

"Get that, too!"

Johansen threw him a look. "Why? What the hell's going on?"

"Don't know, but it's not good."

Staring into the darkness, he saw the security lamp mounted on the side of the boathouse come into view. Its bluish, thin light illuminated the dock, and he made out the images of two people. They were clinging to each other. Embracing. Almost holding each other up.

"What the fuck?" Johansen saw them too.

So involved were they in each other that they didn't look up as the boat neared. And then he saw the third person, in the water, lying facedown.

His heart stopped.

Ava! Oh, for the love of Christ . . . "Over there!" He pointed at the lifeless body, but Johansen was already turning the prow so that they could get closer to the unmoving form.

"Son of a bitch," Johansen muttered.

Jesus, oh, Jesus! It couldn't be Ava.

On the dock, the man was waving them off.

As if he were afraid they'd hit the drowning woman.

"What the hell's going on here?" Johansen said. "Isn't that—"

"Wyatt Garrison." *The prick himself. Involved with another woman . . . Khloe? The woman who was supposed to have stabbed him? Now they were embracing.*

The whole scenario was bizarre, didn't match with Ava's panicked text, and yet there were dark stains on Garrison's shirt, visible from the boat. Had he been attacked in a lovers' quarrel and they made up?

He didn't know what the hell had gone down out here on this miserable island, but he didn't have time to figure it out. Johansen had pulled out the spear gun and the flare. Feeling time slipping away, Dern grabbed the smaller weapon, confirmed it was loaded. Ripping off his jacket and kicking off his shoes, he flung himself onto the deck rail and jabbed the gun into the waistband of his jeans.

"Holy Mother Mary," Johansen said, slowing the *Holy Terror* as close to the body as he dared. "What the fuck are you doing?"

"What does it look like?" As he heard shouts from the dock, Dern dived. Deep. Into the salty, frigid sea. He didn't give a damn about the rest of them; he just had to get to Ava. She couldn't be dead. Couldn't! There had to be time!

"What the fuck?" Snyder stared at the dock as they closed in on the island. The *Holy Terror* was already idling in the water not far from the boathouse, where two people, a man and a woman, were standing, huddled together. Another guy was swimming, and it looked as if there was a DB floating face-down.

"Looks like some major crap just went down," Lyons said as she snapped her pistol from its holster. "Get in close," she ordered the pilot. "It's party time!"

Snyder, too, had pulled out his sidearm while he observed the scene on the dock. The man—Garrison?—seemed to wake up and notice the police cutter for the first time. His face changed expression from curiosity to sheer horror, as if in that instant he woke up to the enormity of what was happening.

As the boat moved in closer, he started backing up, dragging the woman with him. But she seemed a dead weight. A scarlet stain was visible on her sweater, a similar one on the front of Garrison's shirt.

What the hell had gone on here?

"This isn't good," he said, but Lyons was keyed up. "We've got stragglers." Two people in the water, another at the helm of the *Holy Terror.* Too many people who could get in the way. One seeming already dead.

Lyons said, "Maybe now we'll finally get some answers."

Overhead, in the thin fog, the loud *whomp, whomp* of rotors announcing its arrival, a police helicopter roared, its searchlight bearing down on the scene.

Garrison, suddenly appearing like a caged animal—no more hotshot lawyer attitude—glanced up at the chopper, then at the police boat. He seemed to panic and tried to haul the dead weight of Khloe Prescott with him.

"Nowhere to run. He's on an effin' island, for Christ's sake," Lyons said, then picked up the bullhorn. "This is the police!" she said, her voice magnified over the water. "Wyatt Garrison, put your hands over your head!"

Ignoring the command, he changed direction and dragged Khloe toward the boathouse.

"No way, Jose! Move in," Snyder said to the pilot, reaching for his sidearm. "Block the exit. Don't let that boat get to the open water." He hooked his finger at the other boat. "And radio the bozo piloting that goddamned boat, the *Holy Terror.* Tell him to get the hell out of our way!"

Dern swam like hell toward Ava's motionless body.

Thwump! Thwump! Thwump! The sound of a helicopter's rotors tore through the night, and with it came an intense beam of light, illuminating the churning waters and the grounds of the estate.

God, how had this happened? How had he saved her once, only to lose her again? Rage fired his blood; adrenaline spurred him toward her.

Hang on, Ava. For the love of God, just hang on!

The sound of another boat's engine cut through the night, but Dern focused on the body, limp and floating. He reached her in seconds, flipped her body, and as he'd been trained, he swam with her to the shore and the dock where Wyatt stared in disbelief.

"This is the police!" a woman yelled through a bullhorn, the sound echoing over the open water. "Wyatt Garrison, put your hands over your head!"

Wyatt glanced up at the helicopter, then back at Dern. "Fuck this!" He dragged Khloe toward the boathouse, but she was a dead weight, her heels scraping the boards. As Dern reached the shore and the helicopter roared, the police ordered him to stop again, and this time he let go of Khloe and, as if seeing the futility of trying to save her, seemed to decide to save his own damned skin. While Khloe slid to the planks of the dock, he made a run for the boathouse.

"Stop!" the police ordered as they maneuvered their boat to cut off Garrison's escape. He slid to a stop and turned, ignoring orders to "Halt!" while Dern dragged a limp Ava onto the shore, carrying her over the rocks near the dock, watching as blood poured from a wound on her arm.

"Hang in there, Ava," he whispered, afraid she was already gone. At that thought, something deep inside of him twisted painfully. He had no idea how long she'd been in the water, but she wasn't breathing as he laid her on a strip of sand and checked her pulse. He felt nothing beneath his fingertips. He was too late! She was already gone, her body cold, her skin tinged blue.

"Come on, Ava," he said, "Come on," and he started CPR. He forced breaths into her lungs, did chest compressions, and he talked to her. "You can do this. Don't give up, damn it!" More air into her lungs. "Ava, please! Come back to me. Oh, God . . . don't die. Do you hear me? You. Can. Not. Die! I love you, damn it. Do you hear me? I love you." His voice cracked, and though he willed her to live, he felt nothing beneath his hands. No response to the breath he forced into her lungs.

Not a damned thing.

"He's getting away!" Lyons said, swearing under her breath as Garrison reached the boathouse and saw that he was blocked from making his escape. "Son of a bitch! Oh, shit, he's got a gun!"

Snyder focused on the lawyer, saw him reach into his pocket and withdraw a pistol. "Son of a bitch!" This wasn't going well. Not well at all. Already Dern had dragged the floater to the shore and was attempting CPR, but it looked too late for the woman. Though Snyder couldn't see her face, he'd bet his badge that the drowned woman was Ava Garrison.

Lyons clicked on the bullhorn again. "Wyatt Garrison, drop your weapon. Slowly! Then—Oh, crap!"

Blam! Blam! Blam!

Garrison was firing wildly. One bullet struck the hull and

another cracked the windshield of the department's boat. Then he spun and took aim at Dern and the lifeless body lying near him.

"No effin' way!" Snyder said, drawing a bead on him. He fired one warning shot as Lyons screamed into the megaphone, "Drop your weapon!"

"Oh, hell, he's going to do it!"

Ava gasped, her lungs gurgling, water spouting from her nose and mouth. Her lungs were on fire and she coughed, dragging in lungful after lungful of air. It was dark, the world swimming, and she saw Dern's face. Hovering over him was a bright light, and the noise was deafening, the air rushing wildly around them.

Where am I? She felt the sand beneath her, knew she was outside.

What's happening?

"Ava!" Dern grinned down at her as the world spun. Quickly she turned over and retched, salt water pouring out of her nose and mouth, her stomach and lungs expelling all the water invading her body.

She was sick again as everything righted itself.

Blam! Blam! Blam!

Gunshots?

In an instant, it all came back to her, and as Dern fell against her, instinctively protecting her body with his, she looked over his wet shoulder and saw Wyatt, crouching on the dock, his pistol aimed straight at Dern's back.

"No!" she screamed, terror rising in her eyes.

Dern turned, one hand going automatically to the waistband of his sodden jeans.

"Watch out!" she screamed, though her voice was raw.

Blam!

Another blast of Wyatt's gun.

The sand near her head exploded as the bullet hit.

Springing to a crouch, his body between hers and the barrel of Wyatt's pistol, Dern fired. Other guns blasted and she cringed. A hail of bullets hit the dock. Splintered wood went flying. Ava watched in horror as a massive explosion of color sparked from Wyatt's face. Flesh and skin ripped, his eyes went wild, and he shrieked in agony. Sparks caught his hair on fire, bright flames shooting upward from his head. Screaming, his body jerking like a macabre marionette as other bullets hit him, he spun, still on fire, blood spurting from his body, and fell into the black waters.

She was sick all over again.

And then Dern held her close to his body, his heart pounding as the chaos of the police descended.

"You're going to be all right," he whispered against her hair.

In the shelter of his arms, she believed him. "I love you," she whispered, and then with the loss of blood and near drowning, she let go, closing her eyes and letting the safety of unconsciousness drag her under. She thought she heard his voice crack as he said, "I love you, too," but then there was nothing. . . .

Chapter 47

Ava was going to be all right.

Dern had been told by the doctors attending her that she was fine, just recovering, that the coma she'd slipped into was the result of her wound and all the mental trauma she'd witnessed. He'd thought it all a crock, but he'd spent the next eight hours at her bedside, then gone home to shower, change, and take care of the animals. Despite all the chaos, the horses and his dog needed attention.

Once he'd finished his chores, he'd checked with the hospital, compliments of the prepaid cell he'd used when he called Reba, found out that Ava was still sleeping soundly, and decided to do a little investigating on his own.

The house was cleared out of all the residents, of course, all of Ava's employees and family having split. It was eerie to walk through the foyer and know that Wyatt and Khloe, both having died, would never set foot in the house again. Nor would Dr. McPherson or Jewel-Anne. Even Demetria had vacated the premises.

A ghost house, he thought, his boots ringing against the tiled foyer. Today, at least at this time, even the damned grandfather clock was silent.

He wasn't certain what he was looking for; he probably wouldn't find anything, but he walked through all of the rooms one by one and eventually made his way to the attic—the place where Jewel-Anne had started her gaslighting. It was eerie up here, with all the furniture draped and broken, the lights dim. In what had been the servants' quarters in a grander era, he made his way from the tiny kitchen to the living area and bedrooms, finding nothing of interest.

He'd walked back to the stairs and was about to leave when a glint caught his eye. Bending down, he spied an old Elvis CD in its case tucked behind the shade on a windowsill. Possibly of no consequence. But out of place. He picked it up. The plastic casing was cracked and opened easily, and the CD was obviously scratched. No wonder it had been left. About to set it back on the sill, he noticed the tiny booklet inside, a pamphlet with pictures of Elvis as a young man and the lyrics of the songs on the album. Kept all this time. He rifled through the thin pages and a small square of paper fell out, fluttering to the dusty floor.

It was probably nothing, maybe even the original receipt for the purchase, but when he bent down and picked it up, flipping it over, he saw that it wasn't a receipt but a picture of a boy of about four, a timid shot where he was looking up at the camera, only the hint of a smile visible. On the back, in writing Dern had seen before, was a simple note:

Noah. Age four.

He nearly dropped through the floorboards. Son of a bitch! The kid was alive! Ava's son was freakin' alive! That manipulative Jewel-Anne had known all the time and tortured Ava with the knowledge, tormenting her.

But where was he?

This was obviously Jewel-Anne's picture, so who would

know where . . . and then he realized the note wasn't written in Ava's cousin's hand. No, he'd seen the writing before—on notes left for the partially paralyzed woman.

From her nurse.

Damn it all to hell, Demetria knew where the boy was.

He was already flying down the stairs, ready to contact Snyder and find the damned nurse. One way or another, come hell or high water, Dern was going to locate Ava's son.

"Mrs. Garrison?" A woman's soft voice. "Can you hear me? Ava?"

The sounds were far away. Distant. A hand touched her shoulder.

Ava cracked an eye and the harsh light made her close it again quickly.

"She's coming around." Another voice, male.

"Mrs. Garrison, how're you feeling?" The woman again.

Like hell.

"Can you hear me? I'm your nurse, Karen. Ava, can you wake up for me? You're in the hospital."

"Whaaat?" she croaked.

"Ava? Thank God!"

She opened an eye and found Austin Dern near the bed where she was lying. Her throat felt like sandpaper, her eyes even worse. "What happened? Where . . . ?" But pieces of the horrid night were coming back to her.

"Shhh." He kissed her forehead and then tried to straighten, but she grabbed his forearm tightly, pulling at the IV in her arm.

"Tell me." When he looked at the nurse, a tall, lanky woman with frizzy red hair, Ava clenched her fingers. "Now."

"Go ahead," the nurse said. "But the police are going to want to talk to her."

"In a minute." Dern, looking like he'd been to hell and back, took her hand. "I have something to show you . . ." He reached into his pocket and took out a picture of a boy, about four, looking timidly at the camera.

"What?" she whispered, but knew in an instant that the boy was Noah. She blinked, biting her lip, fighting tears.

"I found him. He's fine. Healthy."

"*You found him?*" Ava's eyes filled with tears. She was certain she'd misheard, that this was another hallucination brought on by drugs. . . . "Don't lie to me, Dern . . . I'm serious."

"So am I."

She could hardly let her heart trust this. After all these years! Her fingers clutched his. "Where? How?"

"Demetria was in on it. Wyatt, too. They kept him in Canada. Vancouver."

"What?"

She blinked rapidly and threw back the bedsheets. "I need to get out of here. Noah . . . I don't . . ."

"He's coming home to you," Dern assured her. "Snyder's on it."

"Oh my God!" Was it possible? This was real, not the figment of her oh-so-willing imagination, not a dream.

"You're getting him back."

"Oh . . . oh God, finally. Her heart ached with the thought of seeing him again, holding him. Tears rolled down her cheeks, though her heart lifted. She could hardly let herself believe the news, but the picture . . . the picture was of Noah! "Is he all right?" she asked, trying to not panic. "Is he?"

"He's fine," Dern assured her.

The nurse said, "I think that's enough."

"No! I have to go to him!" she said, and tried to get up.

"No . . . wait," the nurse said. "I'll get a doctor to release you ASAP. I promise." She smiled and blinked, as if fighting tears. "Believe me, I understand. I'm a mother, too."

* * *

The next few days went by as slowly as sludge, and when Ava was released to her home, she found herself forever looking out to sea or taking a phone call only to find it was a reporter to whom she said, "No comment." Fortunately, Dern, the one person who had stayed on, was with her.

He and she were getting closer, though she was still tender, hadn't even yet buried Wyatt. Everything her scumbag of a husband and his lover had planned had been executed perfectly, until the ending, when it had all fallen apart for them and they were both killed. The police believed that Khloe had actually been the murderess, and Wyatt's role in that part of the scheme was murky. However, he had definitely been in on trying to make Ava go out of her mind, his intent to make her kill herself, though Jewel-Anne had probably just started the gaslighting out of envy and guilt for having given up her son.

Ava felt weird about all of that. Satisfied that Khloe and Wyatt were dead and had gotten what they deserved, yet sad as well . . . it was still all so messed up. And she couldn't help but wonder if others on the island had suspected what was going on. Trent and Ian? Jacob? Though they all claimed their shock and innocence.

Virginia and Simon had been conveniently off the island the night that Khloe had staged her lover's death and tried to kill Ava. Now they were swearing their innocence and had moved out. Ava's cousins, too, showing their true colors, were in the process of finding other living arrangements. Trent had flown home, and Ian had quit whining long enough to clean out his room. Even Jacob was in transition, insisting he wanted to leave this "sick house of horrors" ASAP. He had been home the night that Ava was nearly killed, probably stoned out of his mind, the volume on his television cranked into the eardrum-breaking decibel range. He swore he heard nothing outside the walls of his room that night and had somehow, despite the ear-splitting roar from his TV, slept through all of the hubbub.

Sure.

However, Ava didn't care about any of them. The staff could be replaced and her family wasn't close to her. Those who wanted to eventually connect again, maybe Zinnia or Aunt Piper, would try. Or maybe not. For now, everyone seemed to be giving her the space and time she needed.

That left her with Dern, a man she was getting to know day by day, the layers of his past unraveling.

So far, so good. At least she had hope for them—once the dust had settled on the shambles of her life.

Of course, the most important thing was Noah.

Finally on the third day, just when Ava thought she would truly go out of her mind, the call came through. With Detective Snyder's help, her son was coming home! He was four now and had been ripped away from the family who had stolen him, so it was going to be tricky. But she would be patient.

As clouds rolled in from the Pacific and the tide lapped at the shore, she waited for him at the end of the dock, ignoring the splintered bullet holes and bloodstains that couldn't quite be washed away.

Dern was at her side. In the two days she'd been out of it in the hospital, he'd been the one who had figured out what had happened. "It had to be Demetria," he'd told her when she'd been released from the hospital. "No one else could keep a secret and she was Jewel-Anne's biggest supporter; her confidante. Jewel-Anne convinced Demetria to steal her boy that night at the party. Wyatt knew all about it. They worked it out, to take him after you put him down. They had a boat ready. They stole into his room and had a friend who desperately wanted a baby boat him across the bay. They drove to a private airstrip and flew him by private plane to Canada. Vancouver.

Where with fake papers, Noah got lost in the crowd. But it's all being straightened out now." Dern hugged her and added, "Demetria felt horrible about losing Jewel-Anne. And she's undone about the murders. When I confronted her and showed her the picture I'd found, she broke down completely, told me everything, and now is dealing with the police and the FBI and the Canadian authorities. It's a legal and criminal mess, but one thing is certain: you're getting your boy back."

"Thank God."

"It'll be tough at first. He still thinks his 'mom' is in Vancouver. She'll be prosecuted of course."

"He'll miss her."

"The dad took off a year ago, so . . ."

"So those shoes won't be as hard to fill." She glanced up at him and he grinned, that sexy grin she found so damned endearing. "Are you volunteering?"

"You know where I stand." That she did. He'd professed to love her and, so far, intended on staying with her here, though he did own some property in Texas.

With Dern, anything could happen, but she had a good feeling about their relationship. A very good feeling.

Now, though, it was all about Noah; then again, it always had been.

The boat was drawing closer, knifing through the gray water, casting a thick wake. Every muscle in Ava's body was tense. The wind was up, blowing her hair in front of her face, and the smell of the sea was heavy today. From aloft, seagulls let out their plaintive calls, teasing the dog, who, feeling the tension in the air, hadn't left Dern's side, even as a sea lion cruised by the shore.

Ava barely noticed. All of her concentration was on the cutter from the sheriff's office and its precious cargo.

Heart trip-hammering, nerves strung as tight as bowstrings, she waited on the dock as the cutter docked, tying up.

Detective Snyder, in uniform, helped a lanky young boy onto the deck.

Her heart cracked. Noah! Though taller, no longer any baby fat visible, his hair a thick, curly brown, his eyes round, she recognized him as he walked along the dock, holding Snyder's hand.

Her throat was hot. Tight. Her eyes burning with tears. Did he remember her? That was probably too much to ask.

Dern squeezed her shoulder and she took a step forward.

"Noah?" she said, and the boy scowled, distrusting.

"My name is Peter."

"Of course it is. And I'm . . . Ava," she said, telling herself to take it slowly. God, oh, God, she wished that he would remember her, and there was a flicker of something in his gaze as he looked at the house, the grounds, and into Ava's face. But if she'd expected him to suddenly recall her and come running into her arms, she'd been wrong. Instead he looked from her to Dern and back again, then at Rover. "Is that your dog?" he asked.

"Yes." She nodded, fighting tears.

He smiled shyly. "I always wanted a dog."

"He's yours," Dern said.

"Really?" Noah's mouth rounded in surprise, and his little face brightened.

"Really."

Noah walked forward to pet Rover and was rewarded with a wet tongue to his face. "Eeewww!" he cried in delight, but kept petting the dog. Fighting tears, Ava squeezed Dern's hand, then let go as she walked up to her son, bent down, and gave him a hug. "Welcome, home," she said, her voice cracking. "Oh, Noah, welcome home."

"I told you my name's Peter," he said again.

"That's right." She laughed. "Well, Peter, I'm glad you're here!"

The dog, spying a squirrel, gave a sharp bark and took off,

and Peter didn't hesitate but gave chase. He was so much taller than he had been the last time she'd seen him two years earlier.

"I think he's gonna be all right," Snyder observed as he watched the kid run after the dog. He cleared his throat. Turning his gaze back to Ava, he offered a quick nod, as if satisfied. "You know, I think you're *all* gonna be all right."

Ava grinned. Basked in the thought. "Count on it," she said, and then, unburdened, she took off running, chasing after the boy she'd thought she'd lost forever, the son who was finally home for good.

In the book that fans of #1 *New York Times* bestselling author Lisa Jackson have been waiting for, New Orleans homicide detectives Rick Bentz and Reuben Montoya, who've seen some of the worst that evil can do, return to face a lethal ghost from the past . . .

There are killers so savage, so twisted, that they leave a mark not just on their victims, but on everyone who crosses their path. For Detectives Bentz and Montoya, Father John, a fake priest who used the sharpened beads of a rosary to strangle prostitutes, is one such monster.

Bentz thought he'd ended that horror years ago when he killed Father John deep in the swamp. But now there are chilling signs he may have been wrong. A new victim has surfaced, her ruined body staged in deliberate, unmistakable detail. Either it's a terrifying copycat, or Father John, the detective's own recurring nightmare, has come back to haunt New Orleans.

Another death, and another. Bentz is growing convinced that Father John isn't just back. He's circling closer, targeting those Bentz loves most.

And this time, he won't be stopped until the last sinner has paid the ultimate price . . .

Please turn the page for an exciting sneak peek of

Lisa Jackson's

newest Rick Bentz/Reuben Montoya thriller

THE LAST SINNER,

coming soon wherever print and ebooks are sold!

Chapter 1

New Orleans, Louisiana
October 2015

Faster!

I run, moving quickly.

Through the sheeting rain.

Crossing city streets.

Hidden by the shadows of the night.

Faster!

My heart's pounding, blood pumping through my veins as I splash through puddles and blink against the slashing rain.

I smell the earthy, ever-present odor of the Mississippi River. Familiar and dank.

With my poncho flapping, my boots slapping through puddles, I run along the alleys and streets of the French Quarter.

Faster!

Streetlights are glowing, their illumination fuzzy in the rainfall, soft light reflecting off the hoods of a few scattered cars parked near Jackson Square, rain water gurgling in the gutters, washing onto the street and pooling in the potholes.

This city is, and always has been, my home.

And I loved it.

Until I didn't.

Because of *her.*

My stomach clenches at that thought of what I've gone through, what I've had to endure. But now, after all this time, it's about to be over.

Faster!

With St. Louis Cathedral as my beacon, down the nearly deserted streets I fly. The cathedral rises high into the night, white-washed walls bathed in light, its three familiar spires knifing upward to the dark, roiling heavens. From habit, I cross myself as I hazard a glance to the highest spire with its cross aloft, but all the while, I keep moving, the wrought iron pickets of the fence surrounding Jackson Square in my peripheral vision.

On the far side of the cathedral, I slip into narrow Pirate Alley where a few lights in the windows of the shops are glowing, but the street itself deserted, all pedestrians indoors, waiting out the storm.

It's fine, I tell myself. No, no, it's good, because in spite of the inclement weather, she will be coming.

I know her routine by heart. And, I've double-checked to make certain that tonight she didn't vary from it, that her car is parked where it normally is three nights a week, so, tonight is the night. With the rain concealing so much, a wet shroud, I'll have more time and less chance of being observed, or worse yet, interrupted.

My heart is pounding, my chest tight in anticipation as I reach the end of the alley, near the Place d'Henriette DeLille. Here I wait, crouching low, catching my breath near the park. Swiping drops of rain from my forehead, I squint and stare across Royal Street, usually so busy with pedestrians, but tonight, thankfully, only spotted with a few brave souls dashing through the storm, all seeming too intent to get out of the downpour to notice me or even glance in my direction. It's too wet for most, a deluge, the wind-blown rain sheeting in the vaporous glow of the streetlamps, the pavement shimmering eerily, the night thick.

I check my watch, making certain I'm on time while water runs down my poncho to stream onto the cobblestones. My ski mask is tight over my nose and chin, but my hood is cinched tight around my face and no one should notice in the rain, though shaded glasses during the night might be considered odd. But this is New Orleans. Nothing here is really out of the ordinary. Anything goes.

Again I make the sign of the cross and let out my breath to count my slowing heartbeats.

And beneath my poncho, my right hand finds the hilt of my hunting knife, a sharp weapon with a thin blade that could whisk off the hide of an alligator and easily slice through muscle and sinew.

I've waited for this night for so damned long.

Now that the time has come, I'll savor it, that sweet, sweet taste of revenge. Licking my lips, my eyes trained on the building with the red door cut into a dimly lit alcove, a striped awning flapping with the stiff breeze, I wait. Then, I'm forced to move quickly, stepping deeper into the shadows as a man with a briefcase, head ducked against the wind, passes nearby. He's in a hurry to get out of the storm and doesn't so much as throw a glance in my direction.

I hear a siren in the distance and freeze, but the shrieks fade as the emergency vehicle speeds even farther away, unimpeded by much traffic on this stormy night.

Anxiously I stare at the red door.

"Come on, come on," I whisper.

But she doesn't appear.

Nervous now, I check my watch again.

She's late.

Five minutes late.

Damn!

Come on. Come on.

Heart beat pounding in my ears, I begin to sweat.

I'm breathing too fast.

Calm down!

Be patient.

But my nerves are strung tight, the muscles in my neck and shoulders bunched so tight they ache, my hand grasping the hilt of the knife strapped to my waist.

I know she's inside.

I passed her car, a little Subaru parked where she usually found a space when she visited the gym.

Noise!

Movement!

Out of the corner of my eye, I spy a couple dashing wildly through the storm. I turn quickly away to face the park just in case they glance in my direction and somehow see through my disguise. Sharing a shivering umbrella, they rush past, their coats billowing, the woman's laughter barely audible through the storm. Splashing by, they don't notice me.

Barely holding on to my sanity, I check my watch. Again.

Seven minutes.

Seven minutes late!

My pulse skyrockets. All my plans shrivel. Why would anything change tonight? She's always been prompt. I've timed her. On several different occasions. Like clockwork, she's always walked out the door within a minute or two of the hour.

I'm suddenly frantic. Unsure. Could she have left by another doorway? Because of the downpour? Did someone call her? *Warn* her? But no. No one knows what I'm planning. *No* one.

For a different view of the building, I cross the alley but, staring through the downpour, I see nothing out of the ordinary as I stare at the building with its recessed red door. Squint ing, I look upward to the second floor where the yoga class is held. The lights are still on.

And then the red door opens.

She steps out and into the storm.

My pulse ticks up. My blood pounds in my ears and drowns out the sounds of the city, the rush of tires on nearby streets, the gurgle of water in downspouts, the incessant pounding of the rain. All I hear is my own thudding heart.

Eyeing the black heavens from beneath the flapping awning, she clicks up her umbrella and begins jogging, hurrying across Royal Street, her boots splashing through puddles, the umbrella's canopy shuddering with the wind.

She's running straight at me!

My heartbeat is in the stratosphere.

Saying a quick prayer, I withdraw the knife, my thighs tight, ready to pounce.

Suddenly her stride breaks and she veers sideways!

What!?! No!

Did she see me? Anticipate my plans?

No. A skinny, drenched cat, caught in the storm, gallops across her path before diving under the protection of a parked car.

Muttering a curse, she hurries forward again, her umbrella her shield.

Not a good enough weapon, I think. No. Not nearly good enough. She's barely ten feet away when I notice a shadow behind her, a figure running through the curtain of the rain.

What? No!

She's nearly to me.

I coil, ready to spring.

"Kristi!" a voice yells and she half-turns.

Startled, I lose my concentration.

Who is that? Someone who knows her? A witness?

No, no, no!

I flatten against the wall of the cathedral.

In a blink, she steps deeper into the alley, sweeps past me.

What?! NO!

I take off after her.

This can't be happening!

Tonight is the night!

I sprint. Faster. Faster.

Splashing through the puddles.

I've waited far too long for this to go wrong.

I won't be denied!

I'm only a step behind.

Suddenly, in a flash, she whirls.

Faces me.

My heart stops.

She peers from beneath the umbrella's flapping edge, her face hidden in the darkness, her words hard.

"Who are you?" she demands. "Are you following me?"

Damn!

No time to answer.

The element of surprise is gone.

I leap forward, small knife clenched in tight fingers. As I do, I slash wildly, slicing the umbrella's canopy.

Just as she shoves the ferrule, the umbrella's sharp tip, straight at my eyes!

I duck.

The ferrule glances across my cheek and I stumble. Blood sprays, some onto the white walls of the cathedral as I land hard on wet cobblestones.

She jabs again! Throwing her weight into her makeshift weapon.

I feint, dodging the blow.

Spinning, I'm on my feet again.

I strike.

Hit her shoulder.

She yowls in pain and scrambles backward, flailing with the

useless, maimed umbrella. But I hold on. Drive deep. As far as my blade allows. Twist the knife as she screams.

"Kristi!" A deep male voice yells. "Kris!"

What? Oh, shit! I'd waited too long!

The man who was following is approaching fast, his footsteps clattering, splashing.

"Kristi! Run!" the man orders at the top of his lungs. "Run!"

I have to finish this!

I yank the knife's blade from her shoulder, hear the sucking sound, cut myself in the process.

Still she flails wildly with that damned umbrella, its canopy flapping, its steel spokes exposed and glinting in the barest of light from a streetlamp, its deadly tip menacing, slicing through the air too near my face.

This is *not* how it was supposed to happen, how with one swift blow to her jugular or her heart she would die in my arms, how I would exact my revenge as she looked into my eyes and realized in her dying moments who had taken her life and why.

"Ruuuuun!" the man yells and he's closer now. Too close.

I knock her umbrella away and raising my blade I pin her against the wall of the church with my weight. Blood streaks the white stucco. Her blood.

"You sick piece of—" She kicks upward, hard, the heel of her boot hitting me square in the solar plexus. The air rushes from my lungs. Still gripping my knife, I slice crazily, the blade whooshing through air as I land. Hard. Stunned. Pain radiating through me.

Hold on to the knife. Don't lose the damned knife!

But it slips from my fingers.

She's starting to come at me again, staggering upward.

I don't give her the chance to attack.

I ram her hard. Force her back against the church wall.

Craaack! Her head smashes into the wall behind her and she crumples, slithering to the street, leaving a red stain sliding down the stucco.

"No!" The man yells, springing forward, dropping the bundle he'd been carrying, flowers and paper scattering in the wind.

Scrambling on the street, I find my blade just as Kristi's would-be savior grabs me, strong fingers circling my neck.

I thrust upward.

The blade cuts into his chest, through flesh, marrow, and bone.

"Aaahhh."

Gasping for air, I rotate the blade. Hard. Force it upward.

His breath sprays me—air, spittle, and a few flecks of blood.

The hands at my throat fall away.

Blood from the cut on my attacker's chest rains on me, and I tear the knife from his torso to strike again.

He blinks. Horror giving way to rage. In a split second his fist slams into my face.

Pain cracks through my jaw, rattling down my spine. My legs buckle and I stagger to my knees.

He rounds on me again. Unsteadily. His legs wobbling.

I duck the wild swing. Thrust upward with my knife. Hit my assailant's thigh. Drive as deep as possible, all my weight into the jab.

He sways.

With all my strength, I force the blade to cut sideways, across the thick muscle.

Blood spurts.

More agonized screams.

And in the distance, sirens shriek.

Footsteps. Running. Hard. Fast. Splashing through puddles.

I fling the gasping man off and roll to my feet. From the corner of my eye I see that Kristi is rousing, blinking, her face ashen as she attempts to focus. "Oh, God!" she cries in agony as I stagger away. I see her stumbling forward, crawling to the dying man, cradling his head in her lap. "Jay!" she screams, her face in the dim light wrenched in pain as she holds him. "No. No. Oh, God. Oh, God. No, no, no!"

There isn't time to finish her. Already red and blue lights are flashing, washing the cathedral's walls in eerie strobing lights, lighting up the scene with its blood-stained cathedral walls, injured lovers, and scattered roses.

Without thinking, I pick up one of the long-stemmed buds. Then my mind clears. And I run. On unsteady legs, I sprint in the opposite direction of the police cars.

My face throbbing I head to the route I've planned for months, fleeing down the alleys and streets, avoiding as many cameras as possible, head down, the raging storm my cover.

"Jay!" Kristi's anguished screams follow me.

But I keep running, slipping twice, righting myself and catching a glimpse of the luminous eyes of the same shadowy cat I saw before. This time it is peering from beneath a scrawny bush.

Bad luck, I think.

Kristi Bentz is still alive.

I've failed.

This time.

But only for a while.

Keep moving. Just keep moving.

Don't panic. Do not panic.

Next time . . . the next time you won't be so lucky, Kristi Bentz. Stumbling, I hurry through the shadows and rain, dodging the few people I come across.

Still grasping my knife in one hand, I reach into a pocket with my other and rub the stones of a well-worn rosary. Praying, I cut down alleys and side streets, moving steadily forward. My heart is thudding, my jaw painful, but the glorious rush of adrenaline keeps me racing forward, putting much-needed distance between the cathedral and me.